LANA KORTCHIK grew up in two opposite corners of the Soviet Union – a snow-white Siberian town and the golden-domed Ukrainian capital. At the age of sixteen, she moved to Australia with her mother. Lana and her family live on the Central Coast of New South Wales, where it never snows and is always summer-warm, even in winter. She loves books, martial arts, the ocean and Napoleonic history. Her short stories have appeared in many magazines and anthologies. She was the winner of the Historical Novel Society Autumn 2012 Short Fiction competition and the runner-up of the 2013 Defenestrationism Short Story Contest. This is her first novel.

The Story of Us

LANA KORTCHIK

ONE PLACE. MANY STORIES

HQ
An imprint of HarperCollins*Publishers* Ltd
1 London Bridge Street
London SE1 9GF

This paperback edition 2019

1
First published in Great Britain by
HQ, an imprint of HarperCollins*Publishers* Ltd 2018

ISBN: 978-0-00-832306-6

Typeset by Palimpsest Book Production Ltd, Falkirk, Stirlingshire
Printed and bound in Great Britain by
CPI Group (UK) Ltd, Melksham, SN12 6TR

For my mum.
Thank you for always believing in me.

Part I – In Iron Shackles

Chapter 1 – Black Cloud Descending

September 1941

It was a warm September afternoon and the streets of Kiev were crowded. Just like always, a stream of pedestrians engulfed the cobbled Kreshchatyk, effortlessly flowing in and out of the famous Besarabsky Market. But something felt different. No one smiled, no one called out greetings or paused for a leisurely conversation in the shade of chestnut trees that lined the renowned street. On every grim face, in every mute mouth, in the way they moved – a touch faster than usual – were anxiety and unease, as if nothing made sense to the Kievans anymore, not the bombings, nor the fires, nor living in constant fear.

Most stores were padlocked shut and abandoned, and only one remained open on the corner of Taras Shevchenko Boulevard and Vladimirovskaya Street. A queue gradually swelled with people, until they spilled over into the road, blocking the way of the oncoming cars that screeched to a stop, horns blaring and harsh words emanating from their windows. Soon, as is often the case in a line for groceries, a heated argument broke out near the entrance to the store.

'I've been standing here since four this morning, I'm not letting you ahead!' screamed a red-faced man with dull eyes. He looked angry enough to strike the intruder, a small woman holding an infant.

'I have a baby. She hasn't eaten since yesterday,' the woman pleaded, lifting her little girl for everyone in the queue to see.

'So what? You are not the only one with a mouth to feed,' said the angry man.

The woman moved towards the end of the line, while her baby screamed at the top of her lungs.

'Do we have to listen to this?' were the parting words from the man.

'Come over here, my dear,' said an old woman dressed in a winter coat with a kerchief over her head, despite the mild weather. 'You can go in front of me if you like.'

'Why are you letting her ahead? We've been waiting for hours,' complained a matronly lady behind the old woman.

'And another two minutes won't make a difference,' replied the old woman in an *I-won't-hear-any-argument* voice. And apart from a few belligerent looks, she didn't get any.

As the mother thanked the old woman with tears in her eyes, two young girls and a boy approached the store from the direction of the Natural Sciences Museum. They didn't try to jump the queue but stood quietly at the back, unsmiling and serious, as if they were attending a lecture at a prestigious university.

'What are we queuing for?' asked Natasha Smirnova, a tall, dark-haired waif of a girl.

'Sausage,' said the old woman.

'Flour,' said the woman with the baby.

'Tomatoes,' said the matronly lady. But no one seemed to know for a fact, and the line didn't move, nor did anyone leave the store with bags of sausages, flour or tomatoes.

'That's good. Tomatoes will keep,' said Natasha.

'They won't keep,' replied her companion, a petite redhead

with a ponytail and a sulky expression on her face. 'We'll have to eat them in a week.'

'If we pickle them, we can have them all winter.'

'Winter? This war won't last till winter,' said the young mother confidently.

'You mean, *we* won't last till winter,' murmured the old woman. 'Not if the Nazis come here.'

'Haven't you heard?' said the old man directly in front of the woman with the baby. 'Chernigov fell last week.' The old man puffed his chest out, seemingly proud to be the bearer of such important news.

'What are you talking about?' exclaimed the old woman. 'If Chernigov fell, we would have known about it. We would have heard on the radio.' Others in line had interrupted their conversations and were now listening in, their faces aghast.

'Believe me, comrades, Chernigov is in German hands,' said the man, enjoying the attention. 'I heard it from my cousin, a captain in the Red Army.'

'My daughter is in Chernigov,' cried the old woman, wrenching her arms.

The queue fell quiet. Chernigov was only a hundred kilometres from Kiev. If Chernigov fell, was Kiev next?

'Let's go home,' said Natasha dejectedly. 'We won't get anything here. The queue is not even moving. Let's just go home.' She regretted stopping at the store and overhearing the conversation. Dread like liquid mercury spread inside her, heavy and paralysing.

The three of them made their way through the crowds towards Taras Shevchenko Park, wide-eyed at the commotion around them. Those who weren't busy queuing for food occupied themselves by looting and robbing. The Red Army had retreated in July, and the government evacuated in August. In the absence of any form of authority, no shop, library, museum or warehouse was safe. Men, women, even children, moved from store to store, laden with sacks and boxes, searching for something valuable,

5

preferably edible, to steal. Outside the entrance to the park, two men carried a piano and a woman struggled with a potted plant and a typewriter. Eventually, she placed the typewriter on the ground and took off with the plant. 'It's a palm tree,' said Natasha, watching the woman with a bemused expression on her face. 'I wonder what she's going to do with it. I'd take the typewriter if I were her.' When she didn't receive an acknowledgement from the redhead, she added, 'Lisa, will you look at that?'

'Who knows what she'll do?' replied Lisa, shrugging. 'Grow bananas? Barricade the door from the invading Germans?' She chuckled but her eyes remained serious.

When the woman disappeared around the corner, Natasha turned to Lisa. 'We should get going. If Papa realises we've left, we'll be in so much trouble.'

'Don't worry,' said Lisa. 'He's too busy searching his newspapers for news from the front to think about us. He won't even notice we're not there.'

Pulling Lisa by the arm, Natasha replied, 'He'll notice all right, especially if you don't get a move on.' At nineteen, she was only a year older than her sister but she was always the serious one, the more responsible one. Sometimes she admired Lisa's impulsive character, but not today. Not on the day when the Nazis were perilously close and their father was going to kill them.

Lisa turned her back on her sister, her long red hair swinging out to whip Natasha across the face. 'Alexei, are you coming?' Her voice was too loud for the muted street, and several passers-by glared in her direction.

Alexei Antonov, a blond, broad-shouldered boy, had stopped at what seemed like the only market stall in Kiev that was still standing. The stall boasted a great selection of combat knives, and Alexei was in deep conversation with the owner.

'Alexei!' Lisa called again. Her voice quivered.

Alexei handed the stall owner some money and pocketed a knife. 'Wait up!' he cried, breaking into a run.

'Dillydallying as always,' said Lisa, her plump lips pursed together in a pout. 'Keep this up, and we'll leave you here.'

'Nagging already? And we're not even married yet.' Pecking Lisa on the cheek, Alexei adjusted his glasses, his face a picture of mock suffering and distress.

'Get used to it,' said Lisa, pinching the soft skin above his elbow. He attempted a frown but failed, smiling into Lisa's freckled face.

They paused in the middle of the road and kissed deeply. A van swerved around them. The two lovers didn't move. They barely looked up.

'And this is why I walk five metres behind you. It's too embarrassing.' Natasha stared at the ground, her face flaming. Wishing she could run home but not wanting to abandon Lisa and Alexei in the middle of the street, she was practically jogging on the spot. 'You heard Papa this morning. Under no circumstances were we to leave the house.'

'We had to leave the house,' said Lisa. 'You know we did. It was a question of life and death.'

Natasha raised her eyebrows. 'A wedding dress fitting is a question of life and death?'

Lisa nodded. 'Not just any fitting. The final fitting.'

'The final fitting,' mimicked Alexei, rolling his eyes. 'I had to wait for you for an hour! An hour in the dark corridor.'

Lisa pulled away from him. 'You know you can't see me in my wedding dress before the wedding. It's bad luck.' She whispered the last two words as if the mere mention of bad luck was enough somehow to summon it.

'It's bad luck to be outside at a time like this,' murmured Natasha.

Lisa said, 'Don't worry. The streets are perfectly safe. And Papa will understand.'

'I doubt it. Just yesterday he said you were too young to marry.'

Lisa laughed as if it was the most preposterous thing she had ever heard. 'And I reminded him that Mama was younger than me when they got married. And Grandma was only sixteen when she married Grandpa. When Mama was pregnant with Stanislav, she was the same age as you.'

Exasperated, Natasha shook her head.

Lisa continued, 'Did you hear the dressmaker? Apparently, I have the perfect figure. Mind you, I still have time to lose a few pounds before the big day.'

Alexei ran his hands over her tiny frame. 'Don't lose a few pounds, Lisa. There won't be any of you left to marry.'

His words were interrupted by a distant rumble. Half a city away, the horizon lit up in red and yellow.

An explosion followed.

And another.

And another.

For a few breathtaking seconds, the ground vibrated. Somewhere in the distance, machine guns barked and people shouted. And then, as if nothing had happened, all was quiet again. On the outskirts of town, fires smouldered and smoke rose in a gloomy mist.

'Don't be scared,' said Alexei, pulling Lisa tightly to his side. 'There won't be much bombing today.'

'How do you know?' demanded Natasha.

'Just something I've heard. The Nazis don't want to destroy our city. They're saving it.'

'Saving it for what?' Lisa wanted to know.

'For themselves, silly,' said Natasha.

Lisa gasped and didn't reply. Natasha could tell her sister was scared because she no longer dawdled. Racing one another, they turned onto Taras Shevchenko Boulevard. It was sunny and warm, as if summer had decided to stay a little bit longer and wait – for what? The Nazis in the Soviet Union? The daily bombing? The sheer joy of nature in late bloom and its unrestrained abundance seemed out of place in the face of the German invasion. The blue skies, the whites and reds of the flowers, contrasted sharply with distant gunfire and burning buildings.

Posters adorned every wall, most of them depicting a comical figure of Hitler, his body twisted into a shape of a swastika. *We will kick Hitler back all the way to Germany*, the posters declared. On every corner, loudspeakers yelled out Soviet propaganda and occasional news from the front. Natasha wished the news were as optimistic as the posters, but it was rarely the case.

As she tried to keep up with her sister and Alexei, Natasha thought of the first time the bombs had fallen on Kiev, on Sunday 22nd June. She thought of the shock and the fear and the disbelief. Nearly three months on, they had become accustomed to the shelling, to the regular din of machine-gun fire, like a soundtrack to their daily lives. With dismay, she realised it had almost become normal. The realisation scared her more than the Nazi planes drifting overhead. She didn't want to accept the unacceptable, to get used to the unthinkable. But she knew she wasn't the only one feeling this way because there were more and more people on the streets during the bombings. Yes, they made an effort to walk closer to the buildings to avoid being hit, but they no longer slowed down, or sought shelter, or interrupted their quest for food. Even now, as explosions sounded, the queue outside the shop didn't disperse. As if nothing was happening, people continued to wait for their bread and their sausages and their flour, for all the things they needed to survive and stave off the war. What was happening to their city now, what had happened three months ago when Hitler attacked the Soviet Union, seemed like a nightmare that would never end. Natasha felt as if at any moment she would wake up only to find the streets of Kiev peaceful and quiet.

Since the day her city was first bombed in June, Natasha had waited impatiently to wake up.

In Taras Shevchenko Park, the ground was littered with shells that had once carried death but now lay peacefully at their feet.

Natasha could feel their sharp edges through the soles of her boots. One of her favourite places in Kiev, the park was unrecognisable. Anywhere not covered by pavement was excavated. In the last three months, it had transformed into what seemed like the habitat of a giant mole, full of holes and burrows. All the trenches that the Kievans had dug, all the barricades they had built, enthusiastically at the end of June, habitually in July and sporadically in August, now stood empty and abandoned. How meaningless it all seemed, how futile.

Uncertainly Lisa muttered, 'The Germans aren't coming here. Haven't you heard the radio?' Like clockwork every few hours, the radio and the loudspeakers outside screeched, 'Kiev was, is and will be Soviet.'

How ironic, thought Natasha. As if anyone believed it now.

'The Red Army will soon push Hitler back,' added Lisa.

'What Red Army?' muttered Natasha.

Suddenly, on the corner of Lva Tolstogo and Vladimirovskaya, Lisa came to an abrupt halt. Natasha, who was only a couple of steps behind, bumped straight into her sister. 'What—' she started saying and then stopped. Her mouth assumed the shape of an astonished 'O' but no sound escaped. All she could do was stare. From the direction of the river, hundreds of soldiers in grey were marching towards them.

Wide-eyed, the sisters and Alexei backed into the park and hid behind its tall fence, watching in fear.

The wait was finally over. The enemy were no longer at the gates. Surrounded by crowds of confused men, women and children and accompanied by barking dogs, the enemy were right there, inside their city, their grey uniforms a perfect fit, their green helmets sparkling, their motorbikes roaring, their footsteps echoing in the tranquil autumn air.

*

When they thought it was safe, the girls and Alexei ventured cautiously from behind the fence. The streets that were busy only moments earlier were now deserted. The silence was tense, expectant. And only occasionally, as they walked down Tarasovskaya Street, did Natasha hear loud voices coming from Lva Tolstogo Boulevard. Natasha felt a chill run through her body because they were not Russian voices but German. The unfamiliar sounds spoken so assertively on the streets of Kiev seemed to defy the natural order of things.

At the entrance to their building, Alexei tried to say goodbye but Lisa grabbed his hand. 'Where do you think you're going?'

'Home,' he said, making a half-hearted attempt to break free.

'It's too far. And too dangerous.' Alexei lived three short tram stops away. Since the tram was no longer running, it was a twenty-minute walk.

'I'd rather face the Nazis than your father.'

But Lisa was adamant. 'Don't go back to an empty house. Come home with us.'

Together the three of them climbed eight flights of stairs to the sisters' apartment. Natasha dawdled on the stairs, taking forever to find her key. She realised she didn't want to be the one to give the terrifying news to her family.

'Girls, is that you? We're in the kitchen.' Mother's voice sounded unusually shrill. Natasha took her time removing her shoes, hesitating before walking down the long corridor. Would Mother cry when she heard? And what would Father say when he realised that, despite his specific instructions, they were out when the Germans entered Kiev? A captain in the militia, he ruled the household just like he did his subordinates at work. He was strict, brusque, devoid of emotion, and everyone who came into contact with him was in awe of him. Everyone, that was, except her mother, who with a couple of well-chosen words could defuse even the biggest storm.

It was dim in the kitchen. The radio was playing Tchaikovsky's

Swan Lake, Natasha's favourite. The familiar chords never failed to make her smile, but today the music was accompanied by German shouts coming from the window, as platoon after platoon of soldiers in grey marched through the city. Lisa hid behind Natasha, all her earlier bravado forgotten. But Father barely glanced in their direction. His face ashen, he was bent over the table, every now and then barking short sentences into the telephone receiver that he cradled with his shoulder. 'Heavy losses? Southwestern Front destroyed?'

Natasha shivered.

'We saw—' Lisa started saying, her eyes wide.

'Have something to eat,' said Mother. She looked as if she had just stepped out of bed. Her hands, her long musician's fingers were fidgeting, picking up cups, wiping the table that was already clean. 'Alexei, please, come in. Would you like some soup?'

'We're not hungry, Mama,' said Lisa. 'We saw German soldiers outside.'

Father rose to his feet and, still holding the telephone, started pacing from one wall to the other. It took him three strides to cover the distance between the two walls. His steps resonated ominously in the quietened kitchen. Finally, he reached for a cigarette, even though he already had one in his mouth, and put the phone down.

'Bad news?' asked Mother.

Father didn't seem to hear. 'They're finally here. There are thousands of them in the city.'

Lisa nodded. Mother gasped. Alexei collapsed into a chair and said, 'Thousands?'

'I hope Stanislav is okay, wherever he is,' exclaimed Mother. Natasha's older brother Stanislav had been drafted into the Red Army in June. The family hadn't heard from him since.

Natasha whispered, 'What's going to happen to us? Papa, what are we going to do?'

Father startled as if her words woke him from an unpleasant

dream. He narrowed his eyes on Natasha and said, 'It won't be for long. We just need to sit tight and wait for the Red Army to come back.' As usual, his stern voice allowed for no arguments. And only his hands were shaking.

Natasha didn't know what to think. She didn't know what to expect. German occupation, what did it mean? She turned to her mother, who was fidgeting in her chair and not looking at Natasha. She turned to her father, who was smoking grimly and not looking at Natasha. She turned to Lisa and Alexei, who were staring out the window in stunned disbelief. Natasha suspected that her sister, who thought she knew everything but knew nothing, and her mother, too afraid to think straight, and even her father, who ruled their family with an iron fist, didn't have any answers.

The only thing Natasha Smirnova knew for a fact on 19th September 1941, when Hitler entered Kiev, was that life as she knew it was over.

*

All was quiet in the city at night, and Natasha, who had become accustomed to the distant sound of war, couldn't sleep. For three months she had dreamt of being able to go to bed and not hear the buzz of the cannonade, and not hear the explosions and the mortars that were getting closer and closer, as if seeking her out. But now, as she lay in bed with her eyes wide open, she didn't rejoice at the peace in Kiev. She didn't rejoice because of what this peace signified. The silence meant there was no Red Army, no planes with red stars on their wings and no chance of a Soviet victory. Instead, the enemy troops were finally here. Like an oppressive shadow, Natasha could sense their presence, even here in the safety of her bed. How would they treat the local population? What if right now, while Natasha was asleep, someone marched through the door and – and what? She didn't know what exactly she was afraid of, but she was afraid all the same.

It was an abstract fear of things to come, a fear that pulled on her chest and made her heart ache. From this moment on, Kiev was a city oppressed, occupied and enslaved. And no one she knew and loved was safe.

The clock in the corridor chimed midnight. Natasha, who was sleeping on a small folding bed in her grandparents' room, could hear Lisa tossing and turning in her bed in the room next door. Natasha got up and crossed the small space that separated the two rooms, peering in. Her eyes were used to the dark and she could make out Lisa's shape as she curled up in bed. Instantly she felt less lonely, and her heart felt lighter. The weight she was carrying wasn't hers alone. She had her sister to share it with.

'Lisa, are you awake?' she whispered, and her voice came out eerie and unfamiliar. She perched on the edge of her sister's bed.

'I am now.' Lisa didn't sound scared or uncertain. Just annoyed at being disturbed. 'What is it, Natasha? It's late.'

'What do you think is going to happen to us?'

'I guess the same thing that's been happening to us since June.'

'But now they're here.'

'There's nothing we can do about it. We'll just have to learn to live with it.'

'How do we do that, Lisa? How do we learn to live with it?'

'You heard Papa. It won't be for long,' said Lisa. 'Before we know it, our army will come back and boot the Nazis out.'

'Yes, but what if they don't? What if it takes months or even years?' Natasha shuddered. Years under German occupation? She couldn't imagine living like this for another day. Although she didn't know what to expect, her whole being rejected the idea.

'Let's take it one day at a time. Don't think about it now. Think about it tomorrow. Try to get some sleep. Goodnight, Natasha.'

'Goodnight, Scarlett O'Hara.'

It had always been like this. Natasha would be upset about something, and Lisa would tell her not to worry. Although a year younger, she never showed weakness, never opened up. But this wasn't another teenage drama. It wasn't a fight with her best friend Olga or a failed geometry test. It was the end of their life as they knew it.

Back in her own bed, Natasha dozed off, a troubled sleep with dreams of being pursued and lost. When she woke up, it was still dark. She wondered what time it was. What was it that had woken her? Footsteps! There they were again, soft and careful. Petrified, Natasha curled into a ball, trying to make herself smaller, less noticeable. She wished she was invisible, so that no one could find her and nothing could hurt her. And then she thought, *Is this it? Is this what my life has become? Is this what I have become, afraid of my own shadow?*

Through the paper-thin wall, she heard an urgent whisper. 'Lisa, wake up!'

'Alexei! What are you doing here?' Lisa seemed happier to be woken up by Alexei than she was by Natasha. She sounded honey-sweet. Natasha wondered if their voices would wake their grandparents but no, they continued sleeping, their breathing regular.

'I can't sleep,' said Alexei.

'I can't sleep, either.'

'That folding bed is so uncomfortable. And it's cold in the kitchen. The window is open.'

'Have you tried closing it?'

'No, I thought I'd come here instead.'

'So sleep here with me. I'll keep you warm.'

'Are you sure? What if your father finds out? He'll kill us both.' Lisa's bed creaked once, and then again, as Alexei climbed in.

'Who's going to tell him?' asked Lisa.

'He'll come into the kitchen in the morning and find my bed empty. What is he going to think?'

'You'll just have to wake up before him, won't you?'

'What about Natasha?'

'She's a sound sleeper. Besides, she'd never tell on me. She's my sister.'

There was a moment of silence that lasted far too long. Were they kissing? Natasha felt her cheeks flush in embarrassment. Maybe she could go and sleep in the kitchen on Alexei's folding bed. But that would mean admitting she had been awake all this time, listening in. And what would Father say if he found Natasha in the kitchen? Alexei and Lisa wouldn't be the only ones he would kill.

A pitiful sound reached her, like a kitten meowing. Lisa was whimpering softly and blowing her nose. It had been years since Natasha had heard her sister cry.

'Are you okay?' asked Alexei. 'Why are you crying? Do you want anything? What's wrong?'

'Everything,' said Lisa. 'Everything is wrong. What are we going to do?'

Natasha felt a wave of affection for her sister, who tried to comfort her and give her strength, even though she herself felt weak. Lisa was being so brave, and only now, in front of Alexei, did she show how she really felt. Natasha wanted to hug her sister, hold her in her arms and tell her everything was going to be alright. But Alexei was already doing that.

'Please, don't cry,' he was whispering. 'The most important thing is that we have each other.'

'That's all that matters to me, you know. That we are together. Nothing bad can happen to me while I'm with you. You'll protect me, won't you? From everything?'

'Of course I will.'

His voice cracked, and Natasha knew instantly something was wrong. But Lisa didn't seem to notice. 'We'll get married,' she was saying, 'and we'll start a family. We'll be so happy.'

'I have to tell you something,' said Alexei. All of a sudden, he sounded short of breath, as if he were walking fast up a steep mountain.

16

'What?' she prodded.

'I've been thinking and thinking about it.' He paused.

'Tell me.'

'I might have to go away for a little while.'

He waited for Lisa to reply but she was silent. The clock chimed three in the morning.

'I can't stay here and do nothing, Lisa. It's war. I need to do my bit for our country. I keep hearing rumours about the partisans. I'm going to find them, make my way east, join the Red Army. Before you and I can be together, we need to beat the Nazis. You do understand, don't you?'

'No, I don't understand,' Lisa sobbed. 'I don't understand why you'd want to leave me.'

'I don't want to leave you. It's the last thing I want. But how can we be happy while Hitler is in the Soviet Union? First we fight and then we build a life together. A happy, married life with children and grandchildren.'

'Grandchildren? Really?'

'I'm just thinking ahead. I love you, Lisa. I want to grow old with you. I want everything with you. But first, we fight. We can't take this lying down. We can't turn the other cheek.' Alexei's voice grew louder in the dark. 'Before we can start our lives together, we fight and we beat this,' he repeated.

'If you leave, you'll never come back. I can feel it! I'll never see you again.'

'Of course I'll come back. How could I stay away?' said Alexei. 'How could I stay away *from you*?' he added.

'Don't go!' Lisa pleaded. 'I don't want you to go. I can't imagine living without you.'

'It's only for a little while.'

'I can't imagine living without you even for a little while.'

'And I couldn't live with myself if I stayed here and did nothing. Even you wouldn't respect me if I did.'

'I just want you here with me. I want you safe. I love you.'

'And I want to be with you. It's all I've ever wanted. But we can't be selfish, Lisa. Boys as young as fourteen are running away to enlist. To fight, to make a difference. How will it look if I do nothing? Please, try to understand.'

'You would walk away from me, say goodbye and leave me in Kiev?'

'What choice do I have?'

Lisa sobbed and said nothing.

'Will you wait for me?' asked Alexei.

'What choice do I have?' she replied, and Natasha heard heartbreak in her voice.

'You could forget about me and marry someone else.'

'Not if you marry me first.'

'I'd marry you tomorrow if I could.'

They were silent for a while. Then Lisa said, 'Do you remember the day we first met?'

'When you refused to dance with me and pretended you already had a sweetheart? How could I forget?'

'When you told me I was the most beautiful girl you'd ever seen. And I did dance with you eventually.'

'Not before you made me beg for it.'

'See, that's why I could never marry anyone else. Who would put up with me?'

For a few minutes all Natasha could hear was Lisa's sobbing and Alexei's 'sh-sh-sh', like he was comforting a child. Then the sheets rustled, and suddenly Lisa was no longer crying. Alexei whispered, 'Lisa, what are you doing?'

'What does it look like I'm doing?'

'Are you sure about this?'

'Positive.'

'I thought you wanted to wait till our wedding night?'

'That was before.'

'Before what?'

'Germans in Kiev.'

A minute passed, then another. 'Are you sure?' repeated Alexei.

'We don't know what will happen to us tomorrow. We don't know if we have a tomorrow. I'm sure.'

Natasha squeezed her eyes shut and put a pillow over her head. Where was sleep when she needed it? If only she could summon it at will, then she wouldn't have to think about the grey uniforms flooding the streets of her childhood and she wouldn't have to hear her sister's bed creaking-creaking-creaking.

Chapter 2 – The Barbaric Hordes

September 1941

Early the next morning, Natasha opened the bedroom window. Four storeys below, Kiev looked like it always had, with its lush chestnut trees embracing the nearly empty streets and the autumn sky an unblemished blue. Nothing indicated that something out of the ordinary had happened. She could almost believe that she had imagined the devastating event of the day before if it wasn't for the occasional German soldier making his way down the street, if it wasn't for the fear on the faces of the handful of Soviet citizens who dared venture outside.

Their fear was contagious. Natasha closed the window.

Lisa burst into the room, grabbing Natasha in a bear hug and attempting to dance with her around the room. 'You're never going to believe it!'

'Let go of me,' exclaimed Natasha, extricating herself from Lisa. 'What's gotten into you?'

Lisa brought her face as close to Natasha's ear as she could and said in a theatrical whisper, 'Alexei and I. Last night we finally did it.'

Natasha couldn't help but smile. 'Did what?'

'Did what?' Lisa mimicked. 'Are you serious?'

Their younger brother Nikolai poked his head through the doorway, looked around to make sure their parents were nowhere to be seen and said, 'They had sex, silly.'

'Hey!' Lisa shouted indignantly.

'You're fifteen. What do you know?' exclaimed Natasha.

'Clearly more than you.' He poked his tongue out.

Lisa grabbed Nikolai's collar with both hands. 'Are you spying on us, you pest?'

Although shorter than his sister, Nikolai was stocky and well built. It didn't take him long to break free from Lisa's clutches and escape down the corridor. 'Come back here right now!' screamed Lisa.

Father's stern voice was heard from the kitchen. 'Quiet, girls. What's all this nonsense? This is not the time for silly games.'

'You can't tell anyone,' Lisa whispered to Natasha. 'Not even Mama. She'll just tell Papa and he'll kill me.'

Natasha had to pretend Lisa's revelation was news to her, otherwise she would never be able to look at her sister without blushing again. At the memory of the night before, of Lisa's tears and Alexei's heartbreak as he told her he was leaving, Natasha felt an emptiness inside her that even her sister's smile couldn't fill. But for Lisa's sake, she faked enthusiasm and said, 'Wait a second. I didn't hear anything last night. Where did you and Alexei…'

'You were probably out like a light as always. We could have done it in your bed next to you and you wouldn't even have blinked.'

'You didn't, did you?'

'Of course not. Alexei snuck into my room at night.'

Natasha laughed. 'You're crazy, you know that? Anyone could've heard you.'

'Well, it didn't last very long. He was back in his bed in no time.' There was a dreamy expression on Lisa's face. 'This is the most exciting thing that's ever happened to me.'

21

'I'm so excited for you,' said Natasha, tickling Lisa. 'Can I tell Olga?'

'Argh, no tickling!' cried Lisa, shoving Natasha's hands away. 'What did I just say? No one, not even Olga.'

'Oh, come on. She's my best friend. I can't keep this from her.'

'Okay. You can tell Olga and no one else. Promise.' When Natasha half shrugged, half nodded, her sister continued, 'I'm so in love, Natasha. I just can't believe it. I think this is it, you know. I feel it.'

'I should hope so. You are getting married, after all.'

'Don't worry. One day you'll meet someone, too. Then you'll know what I mean.'

Nikolai reappeared in the doorway. There was a mischievous grin on his face. 'So how was it? Your first time? Did you enjoy it?' Lisa roared and hit out at her brother, while he ran in the direction of the kitchen, shouting for help. Laughing, Natasha followed her siblings.

The whole family huddled around the kitchen table, talking, eating, drinking, and pretending their lives hadn't come to a halt when Hitler's Army Group South entered Kiev.

Natasha's grandparents – her mother's parents – were sitting pensively with their elbows on the table, meatballs and soup untouched in front of them. Only a year and a half ago, they had moved to Lvov, a beautiful old town west of Kiev, on the outskirts of Ukraine, just seventy kilometres from the Polish border. To Natasha, who had never been overseas, Lvov seemed exotic and almost European. On the first day of war, it had been bombed just like Kiev, but it was much closer to the front line and no longer safe. To Natasha's delight, her grandparents had returned shortly after and were staying with them once more.

In July, to the disbelief of the Smirnovs, Lvov had fallen. And now, despite Stalin's assurances to hold the Ukrainian capital at all costs, Kiev had followed suit.

Father was hidden behind a newspaper, but Natasha knew he

wasn't reading. He'd been staring at the same page for what seemed like forever. Finally, he folded the paper, took his glasses off and wiped them, as if doing so would enable him to see more clearly. 'Who would have thought?' he said. 'Such a shock. Such an absolute shock.'

'It was to be expected.' Grandfather shrugged, downing his vodka and spooning mashed potatoes onto his and grandmother's plates. 'Hitler's actions were predictable. I only wish Stalin saw that before it was too late.' Before he retired, grandfather was a history professor at Taras Shevchenko University. He still approached every problem in life with the logic and precision that his profession required. It was thanks to his respected position at the university that the family had their large apartment on Tarasovskaya Street in central Kiev.

'Deda, why were the Germans able to advance so quickly?' asked Nikolai, his gaze not leaving his beloved grandfather's face.

'We believed in the non-aggression pact with Germany so much that we ignored countless warnings. As a result, we were completely unprepared for the attack.'

'But the Red Army will come back. Comrade Stalin won't let the enemy deep into the country,' said Mother.

Grandfather shrugged. 'After all the Soviet atrocities in Ukraine, no one wants to fight this war for the Bolsheviks. The rate of desertion is almost unheard of. Men are mutilating themselves to avoid mobilisation.'

Natasha nodded. She saw them on the streets of Kiev every day. Men with fake beards that made them look older. Limping men, men with broken arms. 'Olga told me their neighbour tried to shoot himself in the foot. He missed and ended up killing himself.'

'Germans in one of Russia's most ancient cities! The idea is preposterous. No wonder Stalin's been telling us until the end that Kiev will remain in Soviet hands,' said Natasha's grandmother, an older, miniature version of Natasha's mother. She sighed and crossed herself, her face white with fear. Grandmother was deeply religious, something that even two and a half decades of Communist regime couldn't change. During the Great War she had been a nurse, and sincerely believed God had protected her from the horrors she had witnessed on the front line. After the war she had worked in hospitals, first at Central Military in Kiev and then at the Children's Hospital on Tereshchenkovskaya Street. When Natasha was a little girl, Grandmother often told her about the war and the horror it brought in its wake. The little Natasha had listened to the stories as if they were fairy tales that had no place in reality. Never had she imagined she would experience the horror first-hand.

'They are here now. Stalin will have to accept it. There's nothing he can do,' said Grandfather.

'Do *we* have to accept it?' demanded Mother.

'There's nothing we can do,' repeated Grandfather.

'Stalin should have protected us better,' whispered Natasha.

'All these fires in Kiev,' said Mother. 'A friend of mine lives in a village nearby. She told me the Soviets confiscated all her crops, and then one day the tractors came to destroy the fields. Her neighbour threw herself in front of a tractor and was arrested by the NKVD. No one's heard from her since.'

'Scorched earth policy,' said Grandfather. 'Just like at the time of Napoleon's invasion, the Soviet government destroyed everything that could be used by the enemy. Train stations, bridges, factories, power stations.' Softly, as if hoping no one would hear, he added, 'Food.'

'But, Deda, we are still here. We need food.' Natasha's hands shook as she scooped potatoes with her spoon.

'Speaking of food,' said Grandmother, 'I went to the water pump this morning and saw a notice glued to the wall of our building. The Nazis want us to hand in our food supplies. And our radio.'

Putting her spoon down, Mother said, 'We can't give our food away. It's a death sentence. We need to hide it.'

Father looked up from his plate. 'Hide what?'

'The food.' Mother looked around, as if making sure there were no German officers around to overhear. 'Not inside the apartment. In the garden maybe.' Breathing heavily as if fighting back tears, she turned to her husband. 'Where's your shovel, Vasili?'

'It's in the corridor, Mama,' said Nikolai. 'I just saw it behind—'

But Father interrupted. 'Are you serious? You want to hide the food?'

Mother fidgeted under his glare but nodded.

Father snapped, 'Hide it from the Nazis? Are you out of your mind?'

Natasha winced. Father's voice was too loud for the crowded kitchen. She looked at her brother just in time to see a piece of chocolate disappear into his mouth. 'Hey,' she hissed. 'Where did you get that? It's mine.'

'It's mine now. Finders, keepers.'

'Not fair. You ate your share yesterday.' But Nikolai only smiled and swallowed the remainder of the chocolate.

Mother mumbled, 'I just thought—'

'Well, think again. They will shoot you for hiding food.' The cup Father was holding in his hand quivered and some of his tea spilled on his shirt.

'Yes, and if we don't hide it, we'll starve. What do you prefer?'

'You're seriously asking me if I would prefer...' Father waved his hands dismissively.

Grandmother glared at Father and said, 'You're right, daughter. We need to hide the food.'

Father shoved his chair back and stormed out of the kitchen. For the rest of the morning, he remained on the couch, searching through his newspaper for news from the front.

*

25

After breakfast, Nikolai and Alexei joined the sisters in their room.

'Germans in Kiev,' said Alexei. 'Can you believe it?'

'I can't believe it,' said Natasha, looking up from her book. 'What's it going to be like?'

'Not much fun, I guess,' said Nikolai.

'I guess,' whispered Natasha.

'Soviet Union should have attacked first. Then we would have had a strategic advantage,' said Nikolai, as if he knew about such things. 'Have you heard what they've been doing in Poland? Burning, looting, killing, and...' He glanced at the girls and, to Natasha's relief, didn't finish his sentence.

Lisa, who was rummaging through her drawers, looked up and asked, 'Has anyone seen my blue notepad?'

'You mean your diary?' There was a teasing note in Nikolai's voice that he attempted to hide.

'Yes. My diary. I've been looking everywhere for it.'

'Haven't seen it,' said Natasha.

Lisa proceeded to search the bookshelves, peering behind every book.

Natasha turned to Alexei. 'Are you staying here with us?'

Alexei nodded. 'Your mama said I could stay for a bit.'

Lisa said, 'I'm so happy to have you here. It's like we're already married.'

Alexei laughed. 'Don't let your papa hear you say that.'

Coming close to Lisa, he attempted to draw her into a hug but Lisa pushed his hands away, muttering, 'I don't understand. I had it yesterday. What did I do with it?'

Watching the sly expression on Nikolai's face, Natasha whispered, 'Have you seen it?'

Nikolai whispered back, 'I hid it.'

'You hid it?' Natasha suppressed a giggle. 'Where?'

Nikolai reached under the mattress and extracted a blue notepad, opening it on a random page. 'I love him, I love him, I love him,' he read in a high-pitched voice. 'Yesterday we talked about—' A book expertly thrown by Lisa hit him, making him jump.

'Ouch,' complained Nikolai, rubbing his shoulder. 'You think violence is the answer to everything?'

'What's the matter with you two?' exclaimed Lisa, ripping the diary from her brother's hands. She left the room, dragging Alexei behind her and slamming the door.

'You've done it now,' said Natasha. 'You've really upset her.'

'You think she'll tell Mama?' For a moment Nikolai looked worried.

Seconds later, Mother entered.

'I guess yes is the answer to your question,' whispered Natasha.

Mother's hair was hidden under a kerchief. Dark circles under her eyes were clearly visible despite a thick layer of make-up. Her face was thunder. 'You two! Stop behaving like children. You heard your father. This is not the time for jokes.'

'But we are children, Mama,' muttered Natasha.

'And it's always time for jokes,' added Nikolai.

'I don't have the patience for this. You will both apologise to Lisa. Nikolai, you can clean the kitchen and help your grandfather hide the food in the garden.'

'Mama, Lisa torments us all the time,' said Nikolai. 'Just because we never tell doesn't mean—'

'Go to the kitchen.'

'But, Mama, we didn't mean any—'

'Now.' There was no arguing with Mother's no-nonsense voice.

'Don't send him to the kitchen, Mama. He'll only eat all the food,' said Natasha.

Nikolai left the room. Mother watched him until he disappeared around the corner. There was no anger in her eyes, only fear.

'Natasha, go with your grandmother.'

'Where is Babushka going?'

27

'She's taking our radio to the gendarmerie.'

The thought of seeing the Nazis up close didn't appeal to Natasha one bit. 'Can I help Nikolai in the kitchen instead? Someone has to make sure he doesn't eat everything.'

Mother glared at Natasha but didn't say anything.

'Why can't Papa go with Babushka?' demanded Natasha.

'Suggest it to your father if you feel like it.'

Natasha didn't feel like it.

*

It was after midday when Natasha and her grandmother set out in the direction of the gendarmerie that had just been established on the corner of Proreznaya and Kreshchatyk. Natasha moved slowly, reluctantly. She didn't want to leave the house because the streets, just like the people, had become alien and unfamiliar. In a small bag over her shoulder, she carried their radio receiver wrapped in an old newspaper. The day was too beautiful, the sun too bright, and the autumn leaves had just started to turn a dark shade of brown. Grandmother said, 'What a wonderful fall it could've been.'

On Pushkinskaya Street they ran into one of their neighbours. Bird-like, yellow-haired, bordering on skeletal, Zina Kuzenko looked extremely pleased with herself.

'Are you going to the gendarmerie, Zina Andreevna?' asked Natasha.

'Oh, no,' answered Zina. 'I'm Ukrainian, remember?'

'So?'

'So, I can keep my radio. And my food.'

'I don't understand,' said Grandmother. 'Why are you allowed to keep them?'

'Germans treat us as a privileged nationality. After all, they are here to liberate us from the Bolsheviks.' She rubbed her hands, looked around, lowered her voice and added, 'As far as I'm concerned, they're welcome here. We've had enough of the Soviet oppression.'

'How can you say that, Comrade Kuzenko?' Grandmother looked horrified.

'I am telling you, this might be a blessing in disguise. Germans are a civilised nation. They will bring the order and prosperity that the Bolsheviks never have. They will restore electricity and running water. There will be more food and we'll be able to buy European clothes. We won't have to queue for hours to get a loaf of bread.'

Grandmother said, 'Hitler will destroy us like he's been destroying the Poles, like he's been destroying the Czechs.'

'Honestly, Larisa Antonovna.' Zina always addressed Natasha's grandparents by their first and patronymic names, even though they had been friends for many years. Natasha suspected she was a little intimidated by them, especially since Grandfather had taught all of her children. 'Hitler could never be as bad as Stalin.'

Natasha had heard hushed rumours that Zina's brother had been shot by the NKVD, Stalin's secret police, and that her parents-in-law had died from hunger during the famine of 1932. There were whispers about Ukrainian farmers surviving on bark and roots, while their fields produced abundant harvests that were promptly seized by Stalin's henchmen, harvests that the farmers were forbidden to touch at the risk of a firing squad. But just like Hitler's army on the streets of Kiev, Stalin's atrocities were hard for Natasha to fathom. It was like something out of her grandfather's history books, gruesome events that belonged in the Reign of Terror of the French Revolution, and not in their quiet and familiar Ukrainian reality. It was definitely never mentioned on the Soviet radio.

'The Bolsheviks starved us and shot us, and now they want us to die for them in their war,' said Zina. 'I personally see nothing worth risking my life for.'

29

'What a tragedy,' said Grandmother. 'What a tragedy for a citizen to wish for the defeat in war of her own country.'

'Blame the Bolsheviks. We would rather live under Hitler than under Stalin. How much longer can we live in constant fear?' said Zina. 'You are a member of the Communist Party. How can you justify Stalin's actions?'

'The end justifies the means, Comrade. The state clothes us, feeds us, protects us from the enemy. All it asks for in return is loyalty and commitment. Is it too much of a sacrifice for you to make?'

'No, Larisa Antonovna. The state demands our lives and in return drags us down to slavery. It's serfdom, that's what it is.'

'You shouldn't talk like that, Zina. God forbid anybody hears you,' said Grandmother, shuddering.

'Things have changed. The Bolsheviks are gone. We have nothing to fear now.'

Natasha wished she could cover her ears and not hear their conversation. How could Zina, whom Natasha had known since she was a child, welcome the enemy to Ukraine as if they were the long-awaited liberators? How could she rejoice, when the rest of the country was mourning? Natasha hoped Zina was the only one who felt this way, but then she saw a woman across the road welcoming German officers with flowers and a loaf of bread. Natasha wanted to run to the woman and tell her she should be ashamed of herself, but she didn't. What difference would it make?

Natasha closed her eyes and tried to remember what her life had been like before 22nd June. She longed for the time when all she had to worry about was an argument with her sister and her university entrance exams. How trivial it all seemed now. Although it was only a few short months ago, it felt like a distant dream.

Shaking her head, Grandmother walked off. With an awkward wave to their neighbour, Natasha followed.

All the Soviet posters – in particular those depicting Hitler as a comical swastika-shaped figure – had evaporated as if by magic, replaced with placards that proclaimed, 'Hitler is a hero and a saviour!' Above the red university building, there was a white flag with a black swastika. When Natasha saw it swaying in the wind, she stopped dead in her tracks, her heart pounding. The flag screamed to Natasha that Kiev no longer belonged to her.

No glass was left in the university windows. It was nothing more than a ghost building, and Kiev was nothing more than a ghost town. Hardly any Kievans ventured out, but those who did looked uncertain and afraid. Nor, it seemed, did the invaders know what to do when faced with the local population. The Soviets and the Germans simply watched each other cautiously without saying a word.

And the Red Army was retreating further and further east, retreating irrevocably and irretrievably, away from Kiev and its inhabitants, away from the Smirnovs.

Occasionally, Natasha would notice German soldiers with cameras. They photographed the civilians, the burnt-out streets, the bombed-out buildings. She had never seen cameras such as the Nazis possessed. In fact, everything they had, their machinery, their equipment, their weaponry, was unlike anything she had ever encountered in her Soviet life.

'Look at that truck, Babushka,' whispered Natasha. 'Could you imagine anything more sleek and shiny?'

'That might be so but they won't get to Moscow in their sleek and shiny truck. We'll push them back where they came from before you even know it. Remember, we have what the Nazis don't.'

'What's that?'

'We have the heart. And soon they'll learn that. They'll learn the hard way.'

'Not soon enough,' whispered Natasha.

At the gendarmerie, the queue spilled all the way down

Kreshchatyk. People were clenching their food and their radio receivers. One man brought a machine gun, one woman a live goat on a rope. Grandmother and Natasha joined the hushed group of people at the back of the queue.

A few hours later, a grim Natasha passed her radio to a grim German officer who barely glanced in her direction. Without the radio, there would be no more news from the front, no more connection to the outside world that still remained free from Hitler's clutches, no more hope. Natasha felt more isolated than ever as they made their way home, down the streets that were teeming with grey uniforms.

'I can't bear the sight of them,' said Grandmother, glaring at the German soldiers. 'Let's walk through the park.'

'I'm not sure it's such a good idea, Babushka,' said Natasha. It was getting dark and the park looked deserted.

'It's quicker that way. The sooner we get home, the better.'

'But…' Natasha stopped. She had never seen that look on her grandmother's face before. It was as if all her strength had suddenly left her.

They walked through the park.

Chestnut trees that were so festive and jolly in summer now stretched their skinny branches in their direction, silently swaying in the wind. Electricity hadn't been restored yet, and the sky was ominously black with heavy cloud. Natasha felt the hairs at the back of her neck rise in fear. She sped up, pulling her grandmother by the hand.

They'd almost reached the other side of the park when a German officer approached them. He was wide and stout, and his face was round like that of an owl. He seemed unsteady on his feet. When he spoke, his breath reeked of alcohol.

'Hold it right there,' he barked in his guttural voice.

Natasha's knees shook under her, and she avoided looking at the Nazi officer. There was not a living soul in the park, no one but Natasha and her grandmother, who were glancing at each other in fear, and the German, who was smirking in the dark.

'Where are you headed?' he demanded. Natasha's German was good enough to comprehend the gist of what he was saying.

She struggled for breath. No matter how hard she tried, she failed to fill her lungs with air. Finally, she pointed in the direction of the gendarmerie and muttered, 'Radio.'

He said something fast, motioning at his watch.

Grandmother took Natasha's hand. 'What? What's he saying?'

'I'm not sure. Something about a curfew.' All the while, Natasha's eyes darted around the park for a way out, for someone to help them. *Please, God*, she thought. *Don't let us face him alone.* But the park remained empty.

A lecherous smile spread over the officer's face, and his eyes focused on Natasha's lips, slowly travelling downwards, as if drinking her in. She could sense his gaze, and it made her queasy. She recoiled, covering her chest. The soldier slurred his words, leering suggestively. His arm went around Natasha's waist and he pulled her closer, stroking her hip. Natasha felt his putrid breath on her cheek. She was unable to struggle, unable to speak, unable to scream.

Grandmother yanked the officer's arm away from Natasha. 'Get your filthy paws away from her, you Nazi pig. Go back to wherever it is you came from and leave us alone, you hear? You disgust me, all of you.' Natasha was grateful that the German couldn't understand Grandmother's words. Unfortunately, the expression on her face, her gestures, her tone of voice left little doubt as to her meaning.

The officer pushed Natasha aside and turned towards Grandmother, who wailed, 'There's a curse on all of you. You'll pay for everything you've done. You hear me? Everything!'

Grandmother stepped in front of Natasha, shielding her from his eyes. The soldier swore under his breath, roughly pushing her aside. Grandmother stumbled and fell. 'Babushka!' cried Natasha.

But before she had a chance to help, Grandmother was up, shaking her fist at the officer.

'Babushka, no!' cried Natasha, but it was too late. Enraged, Grandmother raised her hand and slapped the officer hard across the face. He was too intoxicated to stop her, and for a second he just stared, blinking uncertainly. Screaming obscenities, Grandmother spat in his face. The soldier swore and reached for his gun.

'No!' shouted Natasha but her voice was weak, and it was lost in the gunshot. As if in slow motion she watched her grandmother fall. She screamed louder. Then she was no longer screaming, she was howling. Everything went dark and she barely knew where she was. She kicked and shrieked, and through the haze of her tears she saw the Nazi raise his gun and point it at her. She shut her eyes, wishing she knew a prayer. When the second shot sounded, Natasha was still for a moment, anticipating a sharp pain. But she felt nothing.

Slowly she opened her eyes.

The German officer was lying motionless in a pile of leaves, his unblinking eyes staring, the drunken smirk frozen on his face. Without looking around, Natasha hurried to her grandmother's side. 'Babushka! Wake up,' she whispered, nudging her. 'Please, wake up.' Silently she cried.

'Are you okay?' she heard in Russian. A second later, she felt a gentle hand touch her shoulder. She raised her head.

A dark-haired soldier was looking down at her.

In the light of the torch he was holding, Natasha noticed he was wearing a uniform, but it wasn't the grey German uniform that she had come to loathe so much, nor was it light green like the ones she had seen on Red Army soldiers. His trousers and tunic were khaki brown, his helmet a murky green.

Natasha opened her mouth to speak, but she couldn't get the words out. It was as if something was obstructing her throat, making it hard to breathe. Mutely she pointed at her grandmother.

34

The soldier kneeled and searched for Grandmother's pulse. Then he touched her forehead. 'I'm no doctor but she's still alive. She's breathing, faintly. I can help you carry her home. Do you live far?'

Natasha hesitated. Although he had just saved their lives and although she desperately needed to get her grandmother home, how could she accept help from a soldier wearing a uniform she didn't recognise? But then she thought she could hear German voices and the sound of boots steadily approaching. She looked around but couldn't see anyone yet. It was just her, Grandmother and the stranger in the park. But what if the sound of gunshots had attracted the attention of the German patrol? 'Not too far,' she said, glancing at him.

He lifted Grandmother gently, supporting her head as if she was a baby. 'Show me the way.'

'Thank you,' Natasha thought she said. She could feel her lips move but couldn't tell if any sound came out.

She touched his sleeve and he smiled. 'You're welcome.'

As they walked side by side in silence, the soldier in long measured strides, Natasha in short hurried ones, she stroked Grandmother's hand, begging her to hold on. Her face, her hands, her jacket were covered in Grandmother's blood. Tears were blinding her, and twice she tripped and almost fell. The soldier towered over Natasha. To see his face, she would have to lift her head. Lowering her eyes, she watched her grandmother instead, straining to hear if she was still breathing.

There was about half a kilometre separating the park's gate from her building. Six hundred long strides for him, a thousand shorter ones for her. And on every stride, on every breath, she prayed to God to keep her grandmother alive. 'Please, God,' she whispered to herself. 'Please, God.' A thousand strides, a thousand please-Gods.

It was the longest walk of Natasha's life.

But when they finally reached her building, Natasha found

herself reciting a different prayer. *Please God*, she thought, *let the yard be deserted*. She didn't want to be seen walking side by side with an enemy soldier. The thought left her feeling uncomfortable and guilty – he was only trying to help. To her relief, there was no one in the yard. The soldier carried Grandmother up the stairs, and Natasha followed, her heart beating fast. The landing was dark.

'Reach into my pocket and get a torch,' said the soldier. Natasha blushed but did as he said. The torch gave a flickering circle of light, bright enough to illuminate the drab walls of the communal corridor.

Before she knocked on the door, Natasha said, 'My family should be home by now. They'll help me with Grandmother.'

She imagined her father's reaction if she turned up with an enemy soldier by her side. It didn't bear thinking about. But she didn't know how to tell him she didn't want him to come in with her. She didn't have to say anything. The soldier seemed to understand. Gently he placed Grandmother in her arms and said, 'Be careful walking outside after dark. The curfew is at eight. And the streets aren't safe.' He spoke Russian fluently, and yet, Natasha could swear that he wasn't Russian. His voice carried a hint of something foreign.

'Thank you,' whispered Natasha. She noticed that his eyes twinkled in the dim light of his torch. They were kind and deep, the colour of chocolate. His hair was dark and his smile was wide on his face. It was a smile that inspired trust. She couldn't help it, she smiled back – and felt her cheeks burning. She thought he was the most handsome young man she had ever seen. 'Thank you so much.'

'You are welcome. Shall I send a doctor to look at your grandmother?'

Natasha shook her head. 'Our family doctor lives nearby.'

The soldier saluted Natasha.

She watched him go, her eyes wide, her mouth open, as if she was about to say something. When he disappeared down the stairs, she realised she hadn't even asked his name.

*

Petr Nikolaev, the Smirnovs' family doctor, lived in a six-storey building across the road. After she told the family what had happened, Natasha and Mother set out in search of the doctor, leaving Grandmother in Grandfather's loving care. The two of them crossed the road, walked through the front door of the doctor's building and up the stairs, finally stopping outside Petr's apartment.

The smell of roast chicken permeated the communal corridor. Natasha could hear the high-pitched chords of a guitar and a rowdy song. '*Ein, zwei, drei,*' came slurred words from behind the solid oak door. Natasha hesitated, but Mother shrugged and knocked on the door, a determined expression on her face. A German soldier, bare-chested and inebriated, opened the door. He stretched his hand out as if for a handshake, but before he had a chance to touch them, the two women turned on their heels and flew down the stairs, taking two steps at a time.

Natasha and her mother walked all the way to Podol, searching for another doctor they knew, but they were as unsuccessful there as they were on Tarasovskaya. Exhausted, they hurried back. Natasha prayed that her grandmother hadn't taken a turn for the worse.

Lisa was by Grandmother's side, crying softly into her hands, while a bedraggled looking Olga Kolenova was stroking her back and telling her everything would be alright.

Natasha sat next to her sister, her face wet from tears, her eyes sore. The Germans had only been here one day, and already someone she loved dearly was hurt. Was it a sign of things to come? A chilling thought ran through her mind, paralysing her. It was the same thought she hadn't been able to shake ever since the incident in the park. What if something happened to her grandmother? What if she didn't get better? What would it do to Grandfather, to all of them? Natasha couldn't imagine a life without her beloved Babushka, who had always been there, taking her to kindergarten and to school, cooking for her and teaching her how to cook, reading to her and teaching her how to read. One day, when a four-year-old Natasha had begged her to read more – one more paragraph, one more page, one more chapter – Grandmother had said, 'Why don't I just show you how to do it yourself?' And then she had shared her favourite books with Natasha, and they'd become Natasha's favourite books. Everything she was, Natasha realised, was thanks to the people she loved. How did she go on with her life and not feel her grandmother's soft hand on her forehead, and not see her reassuring smile? Natasha's heart was heavy with fear. And something else, too. A blinding, scorching anger. How dare that despicable Nazi try to take her grandmother away from her, in a split second, with a careless movement of his hand, as if her life meant nothing, when to Natasha it meant everything?

'How is Babushka?' asked Natasha, placing her hand on Grandmother's forehead. It felt warm and clammy.

'Your Babushka is not too good. She's burning up. Don't worry, a doctor is on his way,' said Olga.

Olga was Natasha's best friend in the whole world. They had met at kindergarten when they were three and had been inseparable ever since. They had read the same books, passionately discussing the love life of Tolstoy's Anna Karenina and the incredible adventures of Dumas' musketeers. They had learned to play piano together and joined the chess club together. And because Natasha and her sister were so close in age, Olga was Lisa's friend, too, even though Lisa couldn't play the piano, had no interest in chess and was incessantly bored by Tolstoy.

'You found a doctor? Oh, thank God.' Natasha looked her

friend up and down. Olga was wearing what looked like an old sack, her head was covered with a tattered kerchief, and there were smudges of something dark all over her face. Soot, decided Natasha. Soot or dirt. 'Olga, why are you dressed like that?'

'I'm just trying to make myself less noticeable,' said Olga. 'The Germans won't leave me alone. Can't walk down the street without getting harassed.'

'Good thinking,' said Lisa, wiping her face and sniffling. 'No one in their right mind would approach you looking like this. You scared me when I first saw you.'

'You'd be surprised,' said Olga. 'Every time there's a knock on the door, Mama makes me hide in the wardrobe. This morning I was in the wardrobe for an hour.'

'That's your own fault for being gorgeous,' said Natasha, hugging her friend. Olga was strikingly beautiful with her heart-shaped face, dark hair that ran all the way down her back and large brown eyes. 'I'm glad you came.'

For a few moments the girls were silent. Finally, Olga said, 'I'm sorry about your babushka. She'll feel better soon, you'll see.'

'I hope so,' said Natasha quietly.

Lisa interrupted, pulling her sister by the sleeve. 'Natasha, I haven't told her yet! I was waiting for you.'

'Told her what?'

'About me and Alexei!'

Natasha pushed her sister's hands away and said, 'Lisa, honestly. I have other things on my mind right now.' Lisa's eyes filled with tears, and Natasha felt bad. 'Tell her now,' she said softly.

'Tell me what?' Olga demanded.

But before Lisa had a chance to say anything, the girls heard voices in the corridor. The loud sounds were unmistakably German.

'Oh no,' whispered Lisa. 'What do they want now?'

'Don't worry,' said Olga. 'It's probably the doctor.'

'Olga! Is he German?' asked Natasha, horrified.

'Yes, but he's not so bad. He moved in with us yesterday, took my cousin's room. He's quiet and polite. Keeps giving me biscuits.'

A short, chubby German doctor soon appeared in the doorway, trailed by Mother, who hopped around him, trying to push him out of the way. 'You can't just march in here. Leave us alone. You aren't welcome here.' The doctor swatted her hands away and muttered something in German.

Olga looked flustered at the commotion in the room. She waved her hands at Mother. 'Don't worry, Zoya Alexeevna. This is Hans. He's the doctor for the German regiment who is living with us.'

'Let the man look at Larisa,' demanded Grandfather, gently pulling Mother away.

Mother left the room but came back two minutes later, carrying a thick candle. 'Borrowed it from Zina,' she explained.

All eyes on him, the doctor examined his patient in the flickering light of the candle. He said something in German, and Olga translated. 'Your grandmother is very lucky. The bullet got lodged in her shoulder. She's lost a lot of blood and has a fever. She needs plenty of fluids and rest.'

The doctor removed the bullet, administered something for the pain and bandaged Grandmother's shoulder, covering her with a blanket. Grandmother looked whiter than the pillow she was resting on.

'I'll come back to check on her tomorrow,' said the doctor.

Mother embraced him and shook his hand, tears streaming down her face. 'Thank you, thank you so much,' she repeated.

Later that evening, after everyone had gone to bed, Natasha curled up on a small folding bed in her grandparents' room, watching the candle that was living out its last seconds on Grandmother's bedside table. 'Dedushka,' she whispered to her grandfather. 'Why did the German doctor help our babushka? He doesn't seem like the rest of them.'

'There are Nazis and there are Germans. Big difference,' replied

Grandfather, his voice nothing but a hushed murmur in the shady room. 'Just like us, most of them don't want any part of this war.'

'Dedushka, what is going to happen to Kiev?'

'Nothing. Kiev has survived its fair share of invasions in the past. It's not going anywhere.'

'Kiev, maybe. But what about us?'

Grandfather didn't reply.

'Oh Dedushka,' she whispered, squinting in the dark and noticing how frail he suddenly looked. She squeezed in on the couch next to him, putting her arms around him. 'We'll be fine. You're right as always. Kiev is not going anywhere, and neither are we. Not without a fight.'

Chapter 3 – The Soldier

September 1941

In the morning, Grandmother's forehead felt even warmer than the day before.

'Are you okay, Babushka? How are you feeling?' Natasha whispered when Grandmother opened her eyes.

'I'm fine, child. I'll be good as new tomorrow. Don't you fret,' said Grandmother, but her voice was so weak, Natasha could barely hear her.

Trying not to cry, Natasha rushed downstairs to fetch a bucket of water from the pump, in her haste spilling at least half by the time she made it back upstairs. She boiled the kettle, soaked some barley in hot water and cooked a porridge, without milk and without butter but with some salt she retrieved from their hiding place in the garden. Grandmother's eyes were dull and her lips moved listlessly as she ate. She only nodded when Natasha said, 'I'll go to Olga's and get the doctor, Babushka. He's staying with them, remember?' Kissing her grandmother, Natasha threw on her mother's favourite jacket and left.

Olga wasn't at home and neither were her mother or grandfather. But the doctor was. Natasha begged him to check on her grandmother, and he promised to be there in an hour.

On the way home Natasha couldn't help but notice that the streets were much busier than the day before. Not only ubiquitous grey uniforms but Soviet citizens, too. A number of houses on Kreshchatyk sported yellow and blue flags. Natasha presumed they had been placed there by the Ukrainian nationalists. In all of her Soviet life she had never seen a Ukrainian flag being flown, and now not just one but a dozen sprang up on the tall buildings of central Kiev as if they belonged there. Next door to the former Children's World, the largest toy store in Kiev, which now housed the gendarmerie, a large crowd gathered around what looked like a newspaper glued to the wall. People pointed, shouted and gesticulated. Intrigued, Natasha approached. It was the first edition of *Ukrainian Word*. Hoping for some news from the front, she skimmed through the first page and turned away in disgust. The nationalists were using the German invasion as an opportunity to advance their cause now that the Bolsheviks were gone. They were lauding the German aggressors as heroes of the new Ukraine, blond knights who had arrived just in time to save their Motherland.

Wait till I tell Grandfather about this, thought Natasha. And then her gaze fell on a piece of paper next to the newspaper. In Russian and German, it read:

'People of Kiev! A terrible crime has been committed. Anyone with information about the murder of an Oberleutnant in Taras Shevhenko Park on 20th September is required to come forward immediately. If you have seen or heard anything that leads to capture of the traitors responsible, you will receive a bag of flour and a bag of sugar. If the traitors are not apprehended, all of the Kievan population will be severely punished.'

Natasha remained rooted to the spot, her face aghast. But then she noticed a man with a grey moustache stare at her for a second too long. What if he could see in her eyes that she was the one responsible? She forced her face into an indifferent smile, tried to stop her hands from trembling, and then turned around and walked away as fast as she could.

When she reached Taras Shevchenko Boulevard, her hands shaking again and her forehead creased in worry, she thought she spotted a familiar face in the crowd. She paused in the middle of the street. Paused not consciously, not out of deliberate choice, but because her knees turned to jelly, making it impossible to walk. She could almost swear that the tall man she'd caught a glimpse of was the soldier from the park. She squinted, blinked, blocked the sun with the palm of her hand, and rose to her tiptoes to see better. A group of German officers walked by, shielding the man from view, and Natasha jumped up and down, trying to see behind them. She would have pushed them out of the way if she could. Praying that he was still there, she hurried around the German officers.

Clearly, he'd had the same idea because as soon as she rounded the officers, Natasha bumped straight into him and almost fell. He caught her by the arm. Flustered, she looked up into his smiling face.

Her heart racing, she wanted to apologise for knocking into him like that but for a moment couldn't speak. She had forgotten how tall he was and how handsome. He was dressed in civilian clothes today. *Of course*, thought Natasha, *it's Sunday*. If only she had known she would run into him! She would have worn her smartest dress and left her hair down, so that it framed her face attractively. She wished she had worn her mother's high-heeled shoes instead of her drab, comfortable ones. She wished she had some lipstick on her pale, trembling lips. Anything to make her feel less shy around him.

'I thought it was you,' he said, and his eyes twinkled. They were the colour of chocolate, just like she remembered from their brief encounter the night before. They looked even darker now in the sun than they had in the light of his torch in her shady apartment. His hair was raven black and there was a tiny scar above his left eyebrow.

His dark-eyed, dark-haired confidence made her even more nervous. Blinking, she looked down into her hands. 'What are you doing here?' she asked.

'I was just…' He hesitated. 'Actually, I was coming to see you. I wanted to see how your grandmother was.' He watched Natasha intently. She adjusted her hair, cursing her plain ponytail, and raised her face to him. 'So how is she?' he asked.

'She's weak. Burning up. We are hoping she'll get better but…' She sighed.

They were standing in the middle of the street, facing each other, while all around them pedestrians, cars and motorcycles whizzed past, and a bizarre cacophony of Russian and German mingled with honking horns and barking dogs. Natasha barely noticed any of it.

'Can I walk you home?' he asked, smiling into her timid face. Natasha felt her heart and lungs melt, and a warmth trickled down her body all the way to the soles of her feet.

They walked down Taras Shevchenko Boulevard and along Tarasovskaya in silence. Every now and then, their arms touched. And every now and then, Natasha would raise her head and look up at him, hoping he wouldn't notice. The silence between them felt tense but it didn't feel awkward. Natasha knew she had to say something. Preferably something witty and humorous but at that point anything would do. Trouble was, Natasha couldn't think of anything, witty or otherwise.

Finally, she muttered, 'I'm glad I bumped into you. I wanted to thank you…' She paused. 'For saving us.'

'No thanks necessary,' he replied. 'I'm Mark, by the way. What's your name?'

'Natasha,' she said quietly.

'Natasha,' he repeated.

She liked the way he pronounced her name, drawing out every syllable and making them sound soft, melodious. Again, she wondered about his accent.

He stretched his hand out and she shook it, her own hand barely half the size of his. She didn't want him to let go and for a few seconds, he didn't.

'Mark. Are you...' She paused. 'Are you German?' Holding her breath, she waited for his answer.

'God, no. Hungarian. From Vacratot.' Seeing the confused expression on her face, he added, 'It's a small village near Budapest.'

'I don't know anything about Hungary. Is it far?'

'Not that far.' He was looking straight at her, and Natasha felt her cheeks burn. She stared at the ground. Mark continued, 'We share a border with Ukraine, as well as Romania, Croatia, Slovakia and Serbia.'

'Sounds far,' said Natasha. Other than her trip to Lvov last year, she had never been outside of Kiev. 'Where did you learn to speak Russian so well?'

'My parents are from Moscow. They left Russia during the Great War. Two of my brothers were born there.'

'Two brothers? How many do you have?'

'Six.'

'Any sisters?'

Mark shook his head. 'I'm the middle child, and I think by the time she'd had me, Mum was desperate for a little girl. She kept trying and trying. And now she's stuck with seven boys. She calls us her football team.'

'I have two brothers and a sister. We're close, but Lisa can be very annoying. We're fighting constantly.'

'I know what you mean,' he said. 'I used to fight with my brothers all the time. I really miss it now. Strange, isn't it?' Suddenly his smile was gone, only to come back a few seconds later wider than before.

46

'Not that strange. You must miss home so much. Are your brothers soldiers like you?'

'Four of them, yes. It was quite a tragedy for my mother, watching us leave one after another.'

'Hungary, huh,' said Natasha. 'Aren't you German allies?' She remembered reading about it in the papers. Hungary had joined Hitler's side in June, shortly after his attack on the Soviet Union. The country had a pro-German government but was reluctant to take part in the war. When the Hungarian town of Kassa was bombed, they blamed the Soviets for the bombing, finally allying with the Germans. Natasha's grandfather was adamant that it was Hitler himself who had orchestrated the bombing to push Hungary into the war.

'Reluctant allies,' replied Mark, raising his head and appearing even taller. Something flashed through his eyes and for a second he looked sad. Transfixed, Natasha watched him.

'And yet, here you are, in Ukraine, on Germany's side. Fighting for Hitler.'

'None of us had much choice. That's another reason why this war is such a tragedy for my parents. They're still very Russian at heart, despite the decades they have spent in Hungary.'

'I can imagine,' said Natasha. 'My older brother Stanislav is fighting somewhere. Mama cries almost every day.'

Mark said, 'Hungary had no enthusiasm for the war. Yes, our political leaders made the decision to join the German side but no one felt any sympathy for this decision. Most of us were horrified by it. We thought it was a big mistake. No one I knew volunteered for this war.'

'What happened when the war started?'

'I was a member of the anti-fascist society at university, and we protested on the streets, encouraging soldiers to desert. In the end, it became too dangerous and we had to stop. And then my brothers and I were drafted. At first, my parents hid us in a barn on our farm. But we were discovered, my father was arrested, and before I knew it, I was on a jam-packed train headed for Lvov. And here I am, a sergeant in the Hungarian regiment, fighting against my beliefs.'

How terrible, thought Natasha, touching his hand softly – wanting to touch his unsmiling face.

'The country wasn't prepared for war. We have no equipment, no machinery. Our mobile units are made up of bicycles. Our tanks are so fragile, they get stopped by pumpkin vines before they even make it to battle. But that's not the issue. The issue is that we are unwilling participants in a capitalist war none of us can identify with. That we are dying for a principle we don't believe in.'

Natasha was so engrossed in what he was saying, she didn't notice when they arrived at her door. They paused in the middle of the yard. Thankfully, it was deserted – she didn't want the conversation to end.

'We're stationed at the library on Institutskaya Street,' said Mark. 'Do you know where that is?'

Natasha nodded. 'It's a good library. With a great collection of the Russian classics.'

'Which I've already discovered. When I'm not on duty, I read. I just started Lermontov's *Hero of Our Time*.'

'I love Lermontov. Even his prose reads like poetry. I've been rereading Tolstoy's *War and Peace*.' She glanced at a passing Nazi patrol. 'Kind of ironic, really,' she whispered. 'My grandfather doesn't approve of that book. He's too pro-Napoleon to enjoy Tolstoy's writing.'

'Pro-Napoleon?'

'Oh yes.' She smiled, imagining her grandfather in the fervour of one of his Napoleonic lectures. 'He calls Napoleon a giant among pygmies. He says that…' She tried to mimic her grandfather's voice but failed, giggling. 'If I remember correctly, his exact words were…' She paused. 'Ah yes, bigoted and corrupt Europe drowning in vices of the ancient regime was not ready

48

for Napoleon's progressive vision and far-sighted reforms. According to my grandfather, Napoleon was a genius who was at least a hundred years ahead of his times.' Seeing the bemused expression on Mark's face, she explained, 'My grandfather is a history professor. One of the most respected in all of Ukraine.' The familiar pride turned her voice a pitch higher. 'I want to teach at university one day, too.'

'What are you going to teach?'

'Well, I was supposed to start my literature degree at the Taras Shevchenko University this month. If the Germans hadn't...' Suddenly she was too sad to continue. She changed the subject. 'So what's your favourite book?'

He took her hand and smiled. Her heart beat faster and she no longer wanted to cry. 'I can't decide between *The Count of Monte Cristo* and *The Three Musketeers.*'

'Dumas, really? I read the whole collection of his works when I helped out at the university library before the war.'

Mark watched her, and she watched the ground under her feet. He asked, 'Would it have been your first year at university? How old are you, Natasha?'

Her face red, she whispered, 'Nineteen.' Raising her eyes to him, she tried to guess how old he was. He looked young, like Alexei, but unlike Alexei's, his eyes seemed older, more serious, almost grown up. 'What about you?'

'Twenty-two.' He smiled. 'I have something for you.' He rummaged in his rucksack and handed her an object made of glass and metal.

She examined it. 'Is— is it...' she stammered. 'You brought me a kerosene lamp?' She blinked.

'Now you'll have enough light to read and look after your grandmother in the evenings.'

'Thank you so much,' she whispered, touched. There was a sudden tension between them, a tension she didn't know how to break. The door to their building opened and a neighbour marched outside, glaring in their direction. Natasha was grateful that Mark wasn't wearing his Hungarian uniform. She said, 'Well, I'd better go. It's getting late.'

But she was reluctant to leave. She stepped from foot to foot and finally said, 'Mark, I saw a notice near the gendarmerie. They are looking for those responsible for the murder in the park.'

'Of course they are. That's to be expected.'

She looked around, making sure no one was there to overhear. 'What if they find out it was us? I'm so afraid.'

'Don't be. No one saw us. There was no one around.'

'Are you sure?' She tried to think of what happened that evening but couldn't remember anything beyond her terror and Grandmother's motionless body on the ground.

'Positive.'

'But what do they mean, the whole population of Kiev will pay for the murder?'

'Threat and intimidation are their favourite techniques. That's how they operate. Don't worry. You are safe, as long as you don't tell anyone you were in the park that day.'

'I won't tell anyone,' she murmured. But she didn't feel safe.

He smiled nervously, clenching his rucksack. 'If it's okay, I'd like to see you again.'

Her face brightened. 'I'd like that.'

'How about if we meet at the same spot on Kreshchatyk tomorrow? Around eleven?'

Natasha nodded, grinning despite her best efforts not to. She waved and walked towards her building. When she reached the front door, she turned around and found him still in the same spot, looking at her. 'Mark,' she called out. 'Thanks again for helping us last night.' Then she disappeared inside, running up one flight of stairs and pausing at the grimy communal window, so she could watch him cross the yard and disappear around the corner.

*

When Natasha returned home, she found the whole family gathered in the living room and Mother cooking in the kitchen. 'Where have you been?' asked Mother, and Natasha avoided her eyes when she told her about her visit to Olga and her conversation with the doctor.

'I'm glad you're back. Lunch is almost ready,' said Mother, opening a can of fish and stirring something on the stove.

'This looks like potato peel,' said Natasha. 'Fried potato peel.' She picked one up, examined it, placed it in her mouth. It was crunchy and a little bitter. It would have been better with some butter but they didn't have any.

'I got half a kilo of potato peel at work,' said Mother. Every day she had to report to school, even though there were no classes and no pupils. Mother and five other teachers spent their mornings reading, talking and playing cards at the empty school cafeteria. 'I was lucky to get any. There wasn't enough for everyone.'

'They taste nice, Mama,' Natasha said uncertainly.

'We hardly have any food left. Almost no food left at all.'

It was true. They didn't have much to begin with, and now with seven mouths to feed, their supplies were dwindling. There were only a few cans of fish, a jar of pickled tomatoes, some flour, barley and carrots. 'Don't worry, Mama. We have enough for another week. We'll figure something out.'

'Maybe the Germans will start feeding us soon,' said Mother.

'I'll believe it when I see it,' Grandfather muttered from behind his book.

'You never know, they might,' said Mother. 'After all, they don't want us to starve. They want us to work.'

Father marched into the kitchen, followed by Lisa. In his hands he was holding an old book, which he placed on the kitchen table with a loud bang. He narrowed his eyes on Natasha and demanded, 'What is this?'

Natasha picked up the book. It was Tolstoy's *War and Peace*, but not a copy she recognised. 'I've never seen it before in my life. Where did it come from?'

'That's what I want to know,' bellowed Father.

'It's *War and Peace*, Papa, can't you see that?' piped in Lisa, hiding behind Natasha.

'Not just any *War and Peace*. The first edition. Do you know how much it costs? And I found it under the table in the living room, collecting dust. Now you need to tell me where it came from and don't pretend that you don't know.'

Lisa lowered her gaze. 'It's from the library, Papa. Before the Germans got here, everyone was taking books, so I thought Natasha would be pleased because it's her favourite—'

'You stole this? From our library?' he asked, sounding incredulous. When Lisa didn't answer, Father raised his voice a touch louder. 'No daughter of mine is going to act like a thief, war or no war.'

'You got it for me?' Natasha was touched and thrilled to be in possession of the first edition. 'Thank you.' Reverently she examined the book. She wanted to hug her sister, but Father was glaring at her with anger, and she quickly returned the book to the table.

Mother said, 'Don't be upset, Vasili. It's socialist property. The Nazis could never appreciate it. We can keep it safe until the war is over. Besides, it's only a book. Last week I saw one of the neighbours return home with three sacks of sugar and a sack of potatoes.'

'That's disgraceful.'

'I thought so too but now I wish we took some food when we had the chance. It's better that our people have it than the enemy.' She straightened her back and looked at Father, as if daring him to argue. He didn't.

The potato peel didn't go down well with the family. Lisa refused to eat them. Father complained through every mouthful. Only Nikolai finished his share and eagerly asked for more.

Lisa said, 'Natasha, are you okay? You haven't said a word all evening.'

'I'm fine,' Natasha muttered, balancing a potato peel on the tip of her fork.

'What are you thinking about?'

'The Germans,' she lied, when all she could see was Mark's face, all she could hear was his voice as he told her about his life. She couldn't believe she was seeing him again tomorrow! Only twenty hours and thirty-five minutes to go. 'Stanislav. You think he's out there somewhere, giving the Nazis a hard time?'

Mother sniffled. 'At work people were talking... about the Battle of Kiev.'

'What about it, Mama?' asked Nikolai.

'They said it was devastating for our army. Today we went to the hospital and looked through the lists of wounded soldiers but I didn't find...' She fell quiet. On the table in front of her was an old photo of Stanislav and Natasha, taken when they were still at school.

Nikolai mumbled, his mouth full. 'Letters can't get through now that the Germans are here. That's why we haven't heard from Stanislav. I'm sure he's fine, Mama.'

'I bet when the Red Army kicks the Germans out, we'll receive a hundred letters from Stanislav, all at once. You know how much he loves to write,' said Lisa.

Mother coughed and changed the subject. 'Timofei Kuzenko is drinking obscenely. Yesterday he threatened Zina with an axe.'

'Not with an axe?' exclaimed Lisa, her eyes wide.

'Can you imagine? She was so scared; she knocked on our door and asked me to hide five bottles of vodka in our apartment. And the axe.'

Father, who didn't approve of drinking, said, 'I heard vodka's a valuable commodity on the black market. We could get some fresh bread for it. Maybe even some meat.'

53

'We can't take Zina's vodka, Vasili,' said Mother, wiping her face. Her eyes were swimming in tears.

Natasha looked at the photograph on the table, at her eight-year-old self, at her older brother. She squeezed her eyes shut, squeezed her fists, squeezed everything to stop herself from crying. Where was their brother, their grandson, their son? She had to know. How could she go on, not knowing? 'Let's go, Mama,' she whispered. 'Let's go to Zina. She still has her radio. She might have some news from the front.' Mother nodded, staring at the young Natasha in the picture, at the older Natasha in front of her.

Together they crossed the narrow hall and knocked on Zina's door. From the corridor they heard her husband Timofei. He was snoring raucously. When they walked in, they saw him sprawled on the couch, motionless and stiff.

'Zina Andreevna,' pleaded Natasha. 'Do you still have your radio? Any news from the front? My Mama is desperate.' *I* am desperate, she wanted to add.

'What radio?' screeched Zina, raising her head.

'Don't you have your radio anymore?'

'Hungarian soldiers barged in earlier and took it. They took everything. Our food, our clothes, our cutlery, all of our money.'

'Hungarian soldiers?' exclaimed Natasha, stumbling.

'They told us to move out of our apartment by tomorrow.' Zina cried. 'What are we going to do? Where are we going to go?' All her earlier bravado, her hope for a better life, it was all gone.

'Filthy pigs,' muttered Timofei, trying to sit up in bed and failing.

Natasha hugged Zina affectionately. 'Come and stay with us. Is it okay, Mama?'

'Thank you, dear,' whispered Zina. 'You have a kind heart.'

That night, Natasha lay on her folding bed, holding her grandmother's hand and listening to her laboured breathing. She wanted to cry but couldn't. Only twelve more hours until she saw Mark's breathtaking face. Would she be able to sleep? Her heart was threatening to break out of her rib cage. This unfamiliar feeling that had her in a vice ever since she'd set her eyes on him filled her with joy and excitement, but her joy was mixed with fear. He was a Hungarian soldier sent to Ukraine to support Hitler's troops. And she was a Soviet girl, who was completely and irrevocably under his spell. What was she going to do?

She tried not to think of Zina's words about the Hungarian soldiers. Mark wasn't like that. He was different.

To take her mind off Mark — as if it was possible — she thought of her brother.

*

June 1941

Mobilisation orders arrived at the end of June, the day after the Germans bombed Kiev for the first time. Men aged nineteen to twenty-two were already in the Red Army, and now that the war had started, men aged twenty-three to thirty-six were being drafted. The family walked Stanislav to the crowded train station. Everywhere, it seemed, there were young men in uniform; alone and surrounded by families, some of them were laughing and chatting, while others smoked solemnly, sipped cheap kvass, and chewed their hastily made sandwiches.

'Seems like yesterday you walked me to school every day down this road,' Natasha said to Stanislav. She had always thought she was the luckiest girl in the world to have an older brother. Her best friend Olga wasn't so lucky. She was an only child.

'I know,' said Stanislav, smiling. 'You always had a mob of young boys following you around. Remember when one of them left a love letter in our mailbox, and I read it aloud at dinner? You didn't speak to me for a month. You were eight.'

'A love letter and a chocolate that you ate. I'm still upset about

that. You can be so annoying.' She looked into her brother's face, fighting her tears. She wasn't going to cry in front of him. She was going to wait till later.

'Annoying and protective.'

'No, just annoying.'

Natasha took Stanislav's hand in hers. She didn't want the walk to the station to end just yet, but it wasn't far, and soon they were there.

In the sea of weeping women and sombre men, Natasha hugged her brother and said, 'Promise to write. And please, please, please, come back soon. I still need you to protect me.'

Lisa hugged her brother and said, 'I'm glad Alexei is only eighteen. He's not enlisting yet.'

Nikolai couldn't say anything because he was struggling to hold back tears, so he hugged his brother in silence.

Mother wiped her eyes with her handkerchief. 'It's so unexpected. I wish we had some warning, more time to prepare.'

'It's okay, Mama,' said Stanislav, putting his rucksack down on the pavement and embracing his mother. 'It's easier this way.'

'On the train, eat the boiled eggs and bread I packed for you. Wear your jumper if it gets cold.'

'A fine soldier I would make, wearing a jumper at the end of June.' Seeing his mother's stricken face, Stanislav added, 'I love you, Mama. Please, don't cry.'

'When are we going to see you again? What are we going to do?' Mother sobbed.

'Soon, Mama, I promise. I'll be back soon. This war won't last long. A couple of months at most.'

'Look after yourself, son,' said Father. 'We'll see you when it's all over.'

In silence they watched Stanislav as he climbed into the carriage and turned around, a sad smile on his face. 'Girls, look after your mother,' he said, saluting them once more, and then the train was moving and the Smirnovs were running along the platform to catch one final glimpse of their firstborn son and older brother. Soon he was gone but still they stood, watching the train that carried Stanislav to the front, until the train, too, had disappeared. Then they went home, where they had dinner without their son and without their brother. As they chewed their meatballs and vegetable salad, the girls and their mother and even Nikolai cried quietly into their plates.

Chapter 4 – The Bleak Despair

September 1941

After breakfast the next morning, Natasha read to her grand-mother, a little bit from *The Three Musketeers* and a little bit from *The Count of Monte Cristo*. And as she read Mark's favourite books, she imagined his smile. Only two hours to go till she saw him again. Finally, when Grandmother nodded off to sleep, Natasha closed the door to her bedroom, got dressed and brushed her hair.

She wished she had some make-up, some perfume, anything to make her more attractive to him. She peered at her reflection in the mirror. Peered at her light-green eyes, at her pale skin, pale eyelashes, pale everything. She longed for some colour in her face, a shade of red for her lips, some pink for her cheeks. She rummaged in her sister's drawer and found some lipstick and mascara.

When she was ready, she locked the door behind her and practically ran downstairs. She was afraid that the sound of her beating heart would wake her grandmother and alert her father to the fact that something remarkable was happening on this unremarkable Monday morning.

She was almost at the bottom of the stairs when she bumped into her sister. Lisa sang tonelessly as she walked through the front door of their building. If Natasha wasn't in such a hurry, she would have recognised Lisa's voice in time to hide behind a pillar. But as it was, she was moving with such a speed, she almost knocked her sister off her feet.

Lisa stopped singing. 'Ouch,' she said. 'What's the matter with you?'

'Sorry, I was just leaving.'

Lisa peered at Natasha suspiciously. 'Going somewhere special?'

'Not really. Just to see Olga.'

Natasha made a move to get past her sister, but Lisa grabbed her by the arm, blinking and staring.

'What's wrong?' asked Natasha.

Lisa said, 'Come here for a moment. Under this window.' After a second or two of incredulous observation, she exclaimed, 'I knew it.'

'What?' Natasha wondered how long it would take to get around Lisa and to the front door, but her sister was clutching her arm so tightly, it was impossible to move. 'Let go, you're hurting me.'

'What is going on?' demanded Lisa.

'What do you mean?'

'Tell me right now where you're going.'

'I told you. To see Olga.' What time was it? Natasha didn't want Mark to wait for her. What if he thought she didn't want to see him?

'And what's that on your face?'

'Don't know what you mean.'

'Do you wear make-up for Olga now? Natasha, I've known you all my life and never, not once, did I see you with mascara on. Just look at your eyelashes!' Lisa examined Natasha's face as if she had never seen it before.

'I wear make-up sometimes. You just never noticed.'

'Never noticed? You don't even own make-up. You say mascara makes your eyes water. Hang on a second, is that my make-up you're wearing? Did you take it out of my drawer without even asking?' Lisa put her hands on her hips, letting go of Natasha.

Once again Natasha tried to get past Lisa, but her sister was too fast. She blocked the way. 'So what? Like you didn't take that scarf without asking? It's Mama's favourite,' said Natasha, pulling at the silky shawl that was skilfully arranged around Lisa's neck.

Lisa ignored her, sniffing the air around her. 'And what's that smell? Is it Mama's perfume?'

'Lisa, what do you want?' Natasha wished she had left a minute earlier. Had she done that, she would have been halfway to Kreshchatyk by now.

A neighbour walked past, glaring at the girls. The sisters fell quiet, waiting for him to pass. When he was gone, Lisa said, 'Are you going to tell me what's going on or do I have to follow you?'

'You're going to have to follow me,' said Natasha, shaking with impatience.

'Fine. Keep your secret. Won't be the first time,' said Lisa, moving sideways and letting her sister go.

Natasha breathed out in relief and opened the door. Only when she was outside did she realise that Lisa was close behind her. 'What are you doing?' asked Natasha.

'What does it look like I'm doing? Going to see Olga, of course,' said Lisa, sniggering.

Natasha watched Lisa for a mute moment and then said, 'You know what, Lisa? I don't feel so good. Why don't you go to Olga without me? Tell her I said hi.'

Not waiting for her sister to reply, Natasha turned on her heels and disappeared through the front door of their building. She ran up one flight of stairs to the window, just in time to see Lisa vanish around the corner.

*

60

When Natasha thought it was safe, she emerged from her hiding place. Looking around cautiously, half expecting her sister to jump out from behind the next tree, she set off in the direction of Kreshchatyk. Her hands trembled in fear, in excitement. What if he wasn't there? Or worse – what if he had given up on her and left? Although she didn't own a watch, she knew she must be quite late.

Natasha almost sprinted down the street, despite the shoes that were half a size too small and pinched her feet mercilessly. And there, on a bench under a golden-brown chestnut tree basking in timid autumn sunlight, was Mark.

Her heart skipped a beat at the sight of him. And then it struck her: *He's not wearing civilian clothes today, he's wearing his uniform.* What would people think when they saw her strolling hand in hand with a Hungarian soldier? What if someone she knew recognised her? Would they tell her parents? Would they call her names and spread awful rumours? Would they think she was betraying her country, just like the women she'd seen welcoming the Nazis to Kiev? She shuddered.

But he was here, waiting for her, and at that moment in time, it was the only thing that mattered.

He stood up to greet her, and suddenly she didn't know what to do. Did she hug him? Did she shake his hand? What was the acceptable protocol for a Soviet girl meeting a Hungarian soldier on the streets of occupied Kiev? He was so tall, she couldn't raise her eyes high enough to see his face. She stared at the buttons of his tunic instead. 'I'm so sorry I'm late,' she blurted out. 'My sister… She wouldn't let me out of her sight. Have you been waiting long?'

'Not too long. Do you want to walk to Taras Shevchenko Park?' Natasha happily agreed. She knew there were only a handful of warm days left before winter arrived, bringing with it the icy cold and the gloomy skies. It was a beautiful sunny day and the park was bathed in autumn colours. The ground hid under a thick carpet of leaves, and Natasha enjoyed the soft feeling under her feet.

The trenches stood empty, their mocking mouths agape.

They ambled side by side, not looking at each other. 'I come here all the time when I'm off duty,' said Mark. 'I love the park.'

Natasha wanted to tell him that she loved the park, too, but then she glanced at the spot where three days ago a German officer shot her grandmother. And she didn't say anything.

'I'm sorry about your grandmother,' said Mark, as if he could read her mind. 'Is she feeling any better?'

'Not better. Not worse. Just... the same.'

They walked in silence past the trenches, past the chestnuts clad in shades of red and brown, past the gigantic Taras Shevchenko monument, whose bronze eyes seemed to follow them in motionless curiosity. When they were level with the monument, Natasha took Mark's hand. But then a Soviet couple strolled by, and the woman narrowed her disdainful eyes at Natasha. 'You should be ashamed of yourself,' she exclaimed. And Natasha let go of Mark's hand. To hide how much the confrontation had upset her, she bent down and picked up a leaf of a particularly bright tint of gold.

'Don't worry about her,' said Mark.

'I'm not worried.'

'She's only saying that because she's scared and upset. And who can blame her?' When Natasha didn't reply, he added, 'Taras Shevchenko is my mother's favourite poet. "*And with my heart I rush forth to a dark tiny orchard – to Ukraine.*"' He recited the famous poem in Ukrainian with his eyes closed, as if in his thoughts he was far from Ukraine, from the occupied Kiev and from Natasha, in a small Hungarian village called Vacratot.

'I know this one. We learnt it at school.' Natasha was quiet for a moment, trying to remember. '"*I think a thought, I ponder it, and it's as though my heart is resting.*"' When she looked up, she saw he was staring at her with such intensity, she blushed and let go of the leaf she was still holding. In silence she watched as it hovered for a fraction of a second in the breeze, before slowly drifting downwards. 'Your mother speaks Ukrainian?' she asked at last.

'She understands it. When she was a child, she spent every summer in Ukraine with her grandparents.'

'What is she like, your mother?'

'She's very kind. I've never heard her raise her voice. We are very close.'

'I'm close to my mama, too. My papa, not so much. Lisa is his favourite.'

'My dad and I always fight. He's authoritative, strict, doesn't talk much. Except when we're arguing. Then he seems to have a lot to say.'

'I know what you mean,' said Natasha, thinking of her own strict, authoritative father. 'What do you argue about?'

He frowned. 'Pretty much everything. The farm. My choice of friends. What I should study at university.'

'What did you study?'

'Physics.'

Natasha looked at him with admiration. 'Physics! You must be a genius. It made absolutely no sense to me at school.'

He laughed. 'Hardly a genius. Just curious about how things work.'

'What did your father want you to study?'

'Agriculture. He wants me to take over the family business. And I can't imagine anything worse. Hence the arguments.'

'You know what my grandfather says?'

'What does your grandfather say?'

He looked like he was making a conscious effort to remain serious. His lips trembled as if he was on the verge of laughter. Was he teasing her? She blushed and for a moment forgot what she was about to say. 'Oh, yes. My grandfather says arguments are good. It's when people stop talking that something's wrong. Not that he's ever argued with a living soul.'

'He's very wise, your grandfather.'

'Are your grandparents still alive?'

'No, they died before I was born. They lived in a village not far from here. Would you believe it, we passed it in a truck on the way from Lvov. I always wanted to see where my family came from. Just not like this.' A cloud passed through his face.

Turning away from him and towards the lush greenery of the park, she said, 'You should see this place in April. Beautiful red tulips everywhere. We used to come here all the time. My brothers and sister, my friend Olga.'

They ambled full circle around the park and sat on a bench, only a small space between them. He was so close, if she reached out, she could touch him. She didn't. Her hands remained firmly in her lap. She couldn't watch his face, so she watched the Germans strolling leisurely past and the Soviets walking in hurried strides.

'I brought you something,' said Mark. He opened his rucksack. There were four cans of meat, two cans of pickled tomatoes, a loaf of bread, a dozen apples and a kilo of potatoes. Whole potatoes and not just peels. *That'll make a pleasant change*, thought Natasha.

'Oh, that's wonderful. Thank you so much.' She clasped her hands together at the thought of the feast they were going to have later.

'You're welcome. They don't feed us as well as the Germans, but we still get some food.' Looking straight at her, he smiled. And looking down at the ground, she smiled back.

'So let me get this straight,' she said. 'In Hungary, you have a king and a regent. I find it hard to believe. It's like something out of a Dumas novel.'

'I guess it is. I've never given it much thought.'

'It sounds too much like a fairy tale to be true. All we have is Comrade Stalin.'

'And don't forget the Bolsheviks.'

'Well, no. Not anymore,' she whispered. In the distance, an aircraft roared past. She could just make out the swastika on its fuselage. 'What do you do now you're in Ukraine?'

'Guard strategic objects. Bridges, railway stations. Occasionally do some translating. Speaking Russian helps. But mostly, I'm on city patrol. I walk around, making sure nothing untoward is going on.'

'Such as what?'

'Well, last night, for example, I came across an old man who was detained for not handing in his food supplies. Two privates were interrogating him. He hardly had any food left, but they looked like they were ready to shoot him.'

Natasha shook her head. 'If Germans take our food, how do they expect us to live? So what did you do?'

'I sent them away and walked him home. He said I looked just like his grandson. Kept shaking my hand. Gave me an onion and a hammer. I gave him some bread and returned the onion. Figured he needed it more than I did.'

Natasha was unable to take her eyes off him. She no longer cared who saw them. She took his hand. 'So that's what you do. You help people.'

'I try my best but there's only so much I can do. Ever since we entered Ukraine... What can I say... The things we've seen here. Not just me but everyone else at the regiment is disgruntled. Men are wondering what we're doing here. Certainly not protecting Hungary from the Bolsheviks like our government keeps telling us.'

They sat on the bench in silence. He didn't say anything, and she couldn't think of anything to say. Finally, she murmured, 'You ever think of home?'

'All the time. Hungary is stunning in autumn.'

'As stunning as here?' She gazed at the carpet of red leaves.

'Different.'

'I love Kiev. I love how green it is. They say you can walk across the whole city without leaving the shade of its trees. It's beautiful, don't you think?'

'It is, very.'

What was that expression on his face? Natasha suspected that he wasn't thinking about Kiev at all. They moved closer to each other, and she told him about her summers in the village with Olga and their one trip to Lvov. He told her about his parents' farm and what it had been like growing up in Hungary. Natasha watched his face, watched his lips move. She was transfixed, mesmerised by him. Having been born in Ukraine, she couldn't imagine a life different from her Soviet reality. She had never met anyone who had visited another country, let alone lived in one.

When he told her it was two in the afternoon and time for him to report to his regiment for duty, she couldn't believe it. They had walked and sat on the bench and talked for almost three hours. It didn't feel like three hours. It felt like three breathless minutes. Natasha didn't want to say goodbye.

'Can I walk you home?' asked Mark.

Eagerly she nodded. It was only a five-minute walk, but it meant she could have him all to herself for another five minutes. But then she remembered all her fears about being seen with him. She remembered the woman in the park and her angry words. She tried to come up with an excuse, tell him that she was meeting Olga or catching up with her sister, but her lips were not used to lying. Looking away, she shook her head.

'It's okay. I understand,' he said.

'You do?' She brightened. 'How about I walk you to your barracks instead?'

On the way to Institutskaya Street Natasha put her arm through his. She could feel his fingers gently stroking the palm of her hand. In front of a thick wooden door that led to the barracks, she hugged him goodbye, taking the bag of food. He held her close and for a few seconds didn't let go. His fingers were touching her hair. 'I love your hair braided. You look very Russian.'

'I am Russian,' she whispered. She could swear her heart stopped for one whole minute. She wondered what it would feel like to feel his lips on hers. He kissed her forehead, opened the door and waved.

If it wasn't for her mother's shoes pinching her toes, Natasha would have skipped all the way home.

*

Olga had heard from a neighbour that one of the stores on Proreznaya Street had sugar and butter. She told Natasha, and the two girls, who hadn't seen butter since June, rushed to the store and joined the line, shivering in the rain. The girls were the only ones talking in the sea of gloomy and mute faces.

Natasha desperately needed to confide in someone. If she didn't share her feelings with another living soul, she wasn't going to make it through her day. How could she, when she couldn't breathe for the burning inside her chest and all she could hear in her head was his name? Never having been in love before, she wanted to climb to the top of the tallest building in Kiev and shout his name for everyone to hear. 'It's so good to see you, Olga,' she said. 'I have so much to tell you.'

'That's lucky because this could take a while.' Olga pointed at the queue stretching for what seemed like a mile in front of them. 'What do you want to tell me? Something good?'

'Something wonderful.'

'Tell me, quick. I need good news to take my mind off things.'

Natasha peered into her friend's face. Olga had lost weight and when she moved, it was in slow motion, as if every step drained what little energy she had. 'Is everything okay? You don't look so good.'

'I'm just worried, Natasha. I keep hearing rumours—'

'Rumours of what?'

'Just the things the Nazis are doing to the Jewish people in Europe. Haven't you heard?'

'I haven't heard, no,' said Natasha, instantly feeling guilty for thinking only of herself. And of Mark.

'Ever since they've come here, I haven't been able to sleep. What are they going to do to me and my mama once they find out we are Jewish?'

Natasha squeezed Olga's hand, trying to reassure her. 'There are hundreds of thousands of Jewish people in Kiev. What can they possibly do to all of you?'

'I've heard of ghettos in Poland and… I don't know if it's true, but someone told me they've shot thousands in Kovno in July.'

'That's impossible! It's just a rumour, Olga, nothing else. Why would they kill so many people? They need someone to work for them, to man their factories, to bake bread and make munitions.'

Olga's face looked lighter, not as grim. 'You think so? I hope you're right.'

'Of course I am. They want us to see them as liberators. How will they keep up the pretence if they do something so terrible?'

'Like they care what we think.' Olga shrugged.

'We'll be okay. We'll get through this.' More than anything Natasha wanted to believe her own words but how could she, when all she saw around her was misery and despair? And judging by Olga's face, she didn't believe her either.

'Tell me your wonderful news. It will cheer me up.'

Natasha took a deep breath and told Olga everything. In a tiny whisper, so no one else would hear, she told her what happened in the park and about her secret meeting with Mark. 'Wait till you see him. You are going to love him. He's kind and attentive and handsome.'

Olga watched her intently, her own predicament seemingly forgotten. 'You sound so happy,' she said, but her face remained dull, as if anyone sounding happy in the face of the Nazi occupation was something to worry about.

'He does make me happy. When I see him, nothing else matters. Not the Germans in Kiev, not the war, nothing.'

'You said he's Hungarian. Natasha, they're allied with the Nazis.'

'Don't you think I know that? But he had no choice. He was forced to enlist and fight for Hitler.'

'I'm not saying this to upset you. And I *am* happy for you. I just don't want you to get hurt, that's all. You only have one heart. Don't give it away too freely. What future could you possibly have together?'

The queue wasn't moving. There were no arguments and no confrontations to distract Natasha from Olga's words. The same words that echoed in her head ever since she met Mark. 'It's war, Olga. What future do any of us have?'

'You say Mark is here against his will. But he's still here. He's still our enemy.'

'It's not like that,' protested Natasha. 'He helps people. He saved me and my babushka. He can do more good here than anywhere else.'

'He's still on Hitler's side. He didn't jump off the truck bound for Ukraine and join a partisan battalion fighting against the Nazis. He didn't risk his life and his family's lives to avoid mobilisation.' Natasha felt tears perilously close. She clasped her fists to stave them off. Olga added, 'All I'm saying is, people all over the world are risking their lives to fight Hitler. If Mark didn't want to be here, he wouldn't be here. How long have you known him? What makes you think you can trust him?'

Telling Olga had been a mistake. Underneath her friendly concern, Natasha could sense something she didn't like. A current of disapproval and incomprehension. 'He's a good person,' she said. 'Kind, caring, supportive. He saved my life. He's good person,' she repeated softly, as if it wasn't Olga she was trying to convince but herself.

After they queued for an hour, the store manager came out and said there was no sugar or butter left in the store. Nothing left in the store at all. A hundred hungry and disgruntled Kievans left empty-handed. Olga seemed preoccupied, and Natasha didn't want to talk about her fears anymore because talking about them made them seem real. The girls walked five blocks to Tarasovskaya Street in silence.

*

When Natasha returned home, she saw two Gestapo officers smoking outside her building. Autumn sun reflected off the silver buttons of their uniforms, and their left sleeves were adorned with swastikas. Natasha couldn't bear the sight of the frightening symbol. She lowered her gaze. The two of them scared her so much that she forgot all about Mark for the few seconds it took her to cross the yard. She sped up, wishing she had dressed down like Olga.

In the kitchen, she opened Mark's bag and placed everything on the table. In their hiding place in the garden they still had a few cans of fish and some barley. There was plenty of tea in the cupboard but no more salt or sugar.

'Natasha! Where did you get all this?' exclaimed Mother. Startled, Natasha turned around. A look of confused disbelief was on Mother's face.

'Aren't you supposed to be at work?' asked Natasha. She fidgeted under her mother's glare.

'There was no one there, so I came home.'

Natasha wished she had a plausible explanation for what seemed like a feast set out on the kitchen table. She couldn't think straight, and blurted out the first thing that came to her mind, vaguely aware that it would be all too easy for Mother to check her story. 'Olga's mama sent the food. She went to the village this morning.' She felt her face burn.

'How odd,' said Lisa, who had just appeared in the kitchen, trailed by Alexei. 'We just ran into Oksana Nikolaevna. She didn't mention anything about the village.' She fixed her eyes on Natasha. 'Did she, Alexei?'

'No, she didn't,' confirmed Alexei.

'Must have forgotten,' mumbled Natasha.

Mother picked up a can of meat and, adjusting her glasses, turned it this way and that. 'What strange writing. What language is it?'

Natasha panicked. Because she didn't know what to say, she nearly opened her mouth and told her mother everything. But Lisa's mistrustful eyes stopped her. 'Hungarian,' she muttered. 'They have a Hungarian officer living next door.'

'He shared his food with Oksana? That's nice of him,' said Mother, examining a tin of tomatoes.

'I thought the food came from the village?' demanded Lisa.

'The potatoes did,' mumbled Natasha, suddenly feeling like a wild animal caught in the headlights.

'I think Natasha's got a secret admirer and she doesn't want to tell us,' said Lisa, tickling her.

Natasha pulled away. Trouble was, in their small kitchen she couldn't step back far enough to get away from her sister. 'Don't be silly, Lisa.'

'Is that who you were wearing make-up for? Look at her face, Mama. And she's wearing your shoes.'

'I can wear what I want.'

'Don't get so defensive, I'm only joking.'

'Why are you wearing my shoes?' asked Mother distractedly.

'Couldn't find mine.'

'Oh, really?' Lisa pointed at Natasha's old boots that were in their usual spot in the corridor. 'Who are you trying to impress? The Germans?'

Alexei chuckled. Natasha frowned. Mother groaned. 'Girls, stop bickering and help me make lunch.'

They were busy cutting potatoes – whole potatoes and not just peels, thanks to Mark – when there was a loud knock outside that was immediately followed by another one, even more demanding. The Smirnovs fell quiet, exchanging a worried look. Mother went to answer the door, while the sisters poked their heads around the corner cautiously, ready to disappear back to the safety of their kitchen if the situation called for it.

The two Gestapo officers whom Natasha had seen downstairs pushed their way into the small corridor, followed by a young Ukrainian girl. Natasha guessed she was their interpreter. Lisa glared at the girl and muttered, 'What a disgrace,' to which Natasha squeezed her elbow and whispered, 'Be quiet!'

The taller of the two Nazis barked something in German and the girl translated, 'Any men here aged sixteen to thirty-five?'

Mother shook her head. 'No, there aren't. No men here at all.' She glanced at Lisa, who turned around to warn Alexei. But it was too late. He had just appeared in the crowded corridor, wondering what all the commotion was about.

Lisa tried to protect Alexei, to shield him from view, to push him back in the direction of the kitchen. But she wasn't fast enough. The men saw him. '*Kommen Sie mit*,' said the shorter of the two. His words didn't require translating because the gesture that accompanied them made it very clear what the officer wanted. When Alexei didn't move, one of the officers wrestled him away from Lisa's desperate embrace. As they were exiting the apartment, Lisa threw herself between the Germans and Alexei, but the officers pushed her away and ushered him out the door. Lisa stood as if rooted to the spot, watching Alexei until he disappeared down the stairs. When she could no longer see him, she slid down the wall onto the floor, whimpering. Glancing at her distraught sister, Natasha ran down one flight of stairs, catching up to the Ukrainian girl and pulling her by the sleeve. 'Where are they taking him?' she asked quietly.

'I can't tell you that,' cried the girl. 'They'll shoot me.' Her eyes were two dancing pools of silent fear.

'They won't shoot you. Listen… What's your name?'

'Tanya.'

'Tanya, did you see my sister? She's devastated. They're getting married next month. Just tell us. It won't do any harm.'

Tanya hesitated.

Natasha continued, 'You aren't German. You're one of us. Help your own people. Please.' She wanted to squeeze the girl's hands until she cried out, wanted to shake her scrawny body until the truth came out. She resisted.

Tanya looked around cautiously. 'It's to do with the murder of the officer in the park a few days ago. They arrested a hundred people so far. That's all I know.'

'They arrested a hundred innocent people? Why?'

'To make an example out of them? To make sure it doesn't happen again? How the hell do I know?' Tanya shrugged as if to say, *What is it to me*?

'What do you mean, make an example?' cried Natasha but Tanya was already running after the officers, her high heels click-clacking sharply on the sandstone of the stairs.

Slowly Natasha walked up the stairs. She didn't know how to face her sister. If she could, she would have run after Tanya and onto the sunlit street, where she wouldn't have to endure Lisa's tears. Lisa was still on the floor, sobbing loudly and wiping her face with her fists. Natasha's hands shook when she told her sister what she had discovered.

'What do they want with him?' wailed Lisa.

Natasha shrugged, her heart heavy, her eyelids heavy, everything of hers heavy, even the palms of her hands that were stroking Lisa's quivering back.

'Mama, what do they want with him?' repeated Lisa, almost hysterical.

'They'll probably question him and let him go. He had nothing to do with the officer's murder. They'll see he's innocent.' Mother put her arms around Lisa. 'They will, darling, don't you worry. It will be okay.' She tried to make her voice steady but failed.

Lisa sat up straight as if struck with a sudden idea. Her moist eyes glistened. She turned to Natasha. 'You saw who killed the officer in the park, didn't you?' When Natasha didn't reply, Lisa raised her voice. 'Didn't you?' She shook her sister the way Natasha wanted to shake Tanya a few minutes ago. 'Natasha, you have to tell them.'

'Tell them? Tell them what?'

'Tell them who it was.'

For a few seconds Natasha couldn't speak. The words died under Lisa's indignant stare.

'Natasha, did you hear me?' Lisa shook her one more time.

'I heard you.'

'You have to tell them.'

'I wish I could Lisa. But I didn't see who it was. It all happened so quickly.' When she heard the lie slip effortlessly off her tongue, Natasha was horrified at herself. She realised she had told more lies in the past few hours than she had in her entire life. The effort of it all made her lips tremble.

'I'm your sister,' said Lisa. 'Where is your loyalty?'

Natasha extricated herself from Lisa's grip. 'Lisa, I can't tell them something I don't know. I have no idea who it was. I was in such a shock, I hardly looked at him. I wouldn't recognise him if I ever saw him again.' Natasha lowered her eyes.

'In that case you must go and tell them it wasn't Alexei.'

Mother said, 'They mustn't know Natasha had anything to do with it. Or they'll arrest her, too.'

'Mama's right. They'll realise Alexei's innocent and let him go. He's got nothing to hide. Let's wait and see what happens.'

'Wait for what? For Alexei to die?'

'He won't die. Trust me. They have no proof. Nothing to link him with the murder.'

Natasha stroked Lisa's head, trying to convince her sister that everything was going to be alright. Trying to convince herself that everything was going to be alright.

*

Natasha barely slept at all that night. As she listened to her sister sob on her bed hour after heart-wrenching hour, she couldn't see straight through her guilt and her remorse. Should she have told Lisa the truth? Should she have done more to help Alexei? She thought of meeting him for the first time, over a year ago, thought of Lisa's smile as she introduced them. Of Alexei playing pranks on them on their family trip to Lvov, when he had placed a live frog under Natasha's pillow. Lisa had found it hopping around their tent, and her screams could be heard all the way to Kiev. Alexei was like another mischievous younger brother, and Natasha loved him dearly. How could she not help him?

But to betray Mark after he had saved her life? She couldn't do that, either. Besides, Alexei was innocent, while Mark wasn't. Why would the Gestapo punish Alexei for something he didn't do? It didn't make sense. Mark was an entirely different story, however. Natasha shuddered as she imagined what the Gestapo would do to him if they knew it was him who had shot the officer in the park. As Natasha tossed and turned and wished she was deaf so she wouldn't hear her sister cry, she whispered like a mantra to herself, 'He doesn't need my help. He'll be fine. He hasn't done anything wrong.' If only she kept repeating it long enough, she could make herself believe it.

Early in the morning, the girls thought they heard a soft knock, but when they rushed to the door, there was no one outside. It was still dark outside, but instead of going back to bed, they got dressed and hurried to Alexei's apartment, even though Natasha suspected he wouldn't go back there. No one was waiting for him at home.

Lisa had a key to Alexei's flat, but her hands shook so badly she couldn't fit it in the lock. Natasha took the key, patted Lisa's hand, and opened the door.

The apartment was empty.

Lisa went from room to room, searching for him. When she realised he wasn't there, she slid into a chair and hid her head in her hands. Suddenly she looked spent, like a deflated balloon, without air and without hope. Nothing was left, not even the strength to walk. Helplessly, she cried.

'Come on, Lisa,' said Natasha. 'Let's go to the gendarmerie. We'll tell them it wasn't Alexei.'

'Will they believe us?'

'I don't know. But we have to try. You were with Alexei when Babushka and I… When the officer was killed in the park. We'll tell them that. Mama can confirm our story. Papa, too. He's a respectable man, a captain in the militia. If they don't believe us, surely they'll believe him?'

Lisa didn't reply, but her eyes sparkled with hope and determination. No longer crying, she walked so fast, Natasha could barely keep up. It took them three quarters of an hour to reach the corner of Proreznaya and Kreshchatyk. It was still early, and the streets were deserted. The heavy metal door of what until recently had been the Children's World store was closed and padlocked. The sisters waited.

After about an hour a young woman walked up the stairs, fiddled with the lock, and pulled the door with both hands. Natasha thought the woman looked familiar. 'Katya, is that you? What are you doing here?' Katya was the older sister of one of Natasha's friends.

There was something different about Katya. It wasn't her face, made up to perfection as always, or the way she wore her hair, straight down her back, or the way she dressed, in strict, under-stated clothes. No, it was something in her eyes. She said, 'I work as a receptionist. What are you doing here?'

Lisa emitted a scornful snort. 'Working for the Germans?' she demanded and was about to say something else when Natasha pinched her forearm with all the strength she could muster. 'Ouch,' muttered Lisa. Natasha looked around. The street was still empty. She leaned closer and in a loud whisper related everything she knew about Alexei. Even before Katya had a chance to reply, Natasha could tell by the way her chubby face contorted that the news wasn't good.

'You're too late,' said Katya. 'They hanged them at dawn. Hanged them all.'

Natasha gasped. She felt her sister's hand go limp in hers. Lisa moaned and sank to the pavement.

'Their bodies are still in the park for everyone to see.'

Natasha covered her ears. She didn't want to hear. Her chest was burning as if a sharp object was lodged there.

Katya continued, 'Go home, girls. There's nothing you can do.' Not looking at the sisters' faces, she quickly disappeared inside, shutting the door behind her.

'No,' Lisa howled. 'No.'

'I'm sorry, Lisa. I'm so sorry,' repeated Natasha, clutching Lisa's shaking body tightly to herself, while inside her head, a voice repeated, *It's all my fault, it's all my fault.*

Lisa sobbed and didn't reply.

'Come on, Lisa,' said Natasha, in vain trying to lift her sister off the pavement. 'Let's go home.'

Lisa shook her head, staring into distance.

'Let's go, Lisa, get up.' *It's all my fault, it's all my fault,* like a broken record in her head.

'Leave me alone,' whispered Lisa, shivering.

Natasha pulled and shoved but failed to move her sister. She sat next to her, hugging her close. 'I'm so sorry, Lisa,' she repeated, almost choking on her tears.

Silently they sat.

'I wish the person who did this would die,' said Lisa finally, her voice hollow.

'They'll pay for everything they've done. You'll see. They have to.'

'No, I don't mean the Nazis. The person who killed the officer in the park. Alexei died because of him.'

'Lisa, not because of him!' Natasha inhaled sharply. She found it difficult to speak. Her throat was too dry. 'It wasn't his fault. He did it to help us. He saved our lives. Me, Babushka, we wouldn't be here if it wasn't for him.'

'If he came forward, Alexei would still be alive.'

'I'm sure he didn't know about... about this.' If Mark had known about this, he would have confessed. Wouldn't he? 'If you want to blame someone, blame the Germans.'

'I blame you. It's your fault.'

'You don't mean that. You're upset. Let me take you home,' said Natasha, putting her arm around Lisa. Lisa pulled away and got up, slowly walking down Kreshchatyk. Natasha followed her. Lisa didn't speak when they reached Taras Shevchenko Boulevard. When they were walking past the park, she pulled away from Natasha and towards the gate.

'Lisa, no. You don't want to see,' begged Natasha, horrified. She grabbed Lisa's hand.

'Leave me alone,' screamed Lisa, pulling away so hard that Natasha lost her balance and fell. A number of people, most of them German, turned around and looked at the two girls. There was so much hatred in her sister's eyes, Natasha almost expected Lisa to hit her. But she didn't. When she spoke again, looking down at Natasha, her voice was no longer loud. 'You should've told them what happened. For once in your life you should've thought of someone other than yourself. But you didn't, and I'll never forgive you.'

Lisa stormed off, leaving Natasha frozen in shock in the middle of the street.

*

On the stairs of her building Natasha bumped into the Kuzenkos, who were resting on what looked like a sheet filled with clothes. Timofei muttered something under his breath. Zina slept noiselessly. Natasha shook her awake. 'What are you doing here, Zina Andreevna? Come and stay with us.' But Zina only lowered her head and pointed at the Smirnovs' front door, her eyes wide and staring. Natasha wondered what Zina was trying to say. She didn't have to wonder long. At home, she found everyone jammed into their small kitchen, even Grandmother, who was lying on the folding bed someone had brought from the bedroom. The table was gone, but still there was no room in the crowded kitchen. Loud voices were coming from the living room.

Loud German voices.

'They told us we could have the kitchen. They are going to force us from our home soon. Just like they did the Kuzenkos. Filthy animals! They can't do this to us!' exclaimed Mother, shaking her fist.

'They are the conquerors, Zoya. They can do anything they want,' said Grandfather.

The Nazis in their house! For the last few days, Natasha had felt her heart sink every time she was about to leave her apartment and step onto the streets that were swarming with grey uniforms. But at home, she had almost felt safe. Now this safety, illusionary though it had been, was gone. There was nowhere for her to hide. Nowhere to turn.

Natasha cried as she told her family about Alexei.

'I'll go and find Lisa,' said Mother, tears in her eyes. 'She needs to come home.'

After she left, Natasha sat with her grandmother, cradling her head in her lap. 'How are you feeling, Babushka?' Grandmother groaned. 'She's not getting any better,' Natasha whispered to her grandfather.

'No, she isn't.' Grandfather's face looked grey, as if all life had been sucked out of it.

Mother returned, dragging a hysterical Lisa with her. Natasha wanted to hug her sister, but something in Lisa's eyes stopped her. She watched helplessly as Lisa curled up in the corner and didn't move. She seemed oblivious to the Germans in their home and didn't participate in conversation, nor did she have any of Mark's potatoes that Mother fried together with the Hungarian canned meat. Her eyes remained vacant and staring.

What if Lisa meant what she had said in the park? What if she never talked to Natasha again? Could Natasha live with that? Could she live with her closest confidant, the one person she had always counted on, not being there for her? She didn't think so.

And what if, despite what Natasha had been telling herself, it was all her fault? Was there anything she could have done differently? She wished she had told Lisa the truth and lived with the consequences. And yet, to betray Mark, to condemn him to a certain death, was impossible. But what about Alexei? Had she condemned him to a certain death? Was she condemning her sister to a life of heartbreak? She had never thought of herself as selfish before, but now she wasn't so sure.

Natasha felt an unfamiliar despair pull at her chest, a bleak hopelessness she had never experienced before. A thousand lies she had spun, the truths she hid, the falsities she left out in the open, the deaths of so many innocent people, her sister's heartbreak… it was all too much. If Mark was fighting on the German side, wasn't he a part of the horror that was happening on the streets of Kiev? If she continued seeing him, would a little bit of that gruesome responsibility be hers, too?

She turned towards her family's distraught faces, towards their grief and anxiety, towards a small plate of potatoes on the table. There was no comfort in the kitchen and no comfort inside Natasha, because at that moment she decided to tell Mark she couldn't see him anymore. She owed that to Lisa. And to Alexei.

*

After breakfast the next morning, Natasha hurried out in search of Mark. Over and over she rehearsed the words she was going to say to him, but the points that seemed so solid the day before sounded like poor excuses now that she was about to face him.

She imagined his beautiful face, his dark eyes as they lit up with joy at the sight of her. She whispered his name to herself and her heart beat faster. If she told him she didn't want to see him again, it would be the biggest lie of all. But she had to do it. If she continued seeing him after everything that happened, she would be turning her back on her sister and her family. She would be betraying everything she believed in.

Natasha reached the barracks at eleven and asked a sentry to find Mark. A part of her hoped he wouldn't be there. But a few minutes later, Mark appeared. When he smiled, she felt her heart melt a little. Before she had a chance to change her mind, she muttered, 'I need to speak with you.'

'Let's go around the corner,' he said. 'We can talk there.'

They found a bench and sat next to each other, their arms touching. He gave her a piece of bread and a bar of chocolate. She pushed them away but he insisted. She tasted a little bit of the bread. White on the inside and golden on the outside, it was so delicious; it melted in her mouth, just like the bread of her childhood.

He watched her eat in silence, and when she finished, he asked, 'What did you want to talk to me about?'

She hesitated. How could she explain all her fears and all her doubts without hurting his feelings? Then again, she was determined to stop seeing him. His feelings were going to get hurt no matter what. Just like hers. 'I can't do this anymore. Meeting you like this. We need to stop…' She couldn't face him. Turning away from him, she watched half a dozen Nazi officers as they strolled briskly past.

'You don't want to see me anymore?' he repeated as if he

81

couldn't believe what she was saying. She could hardly believe it herself.

'What future can we possibly have together?'

'I don't know but I want to find out.' He put his arms around her and turned her towards him, forcing her to look at him. 'Natasha, I don't think I could stop seeing you. I'm not that strong.'

He wasn't making it any easier for her. She stared at him mutely, pleadingly.

'If you are done with me, I'll understand,' he continued. 'It will break my heart but I'll respect it. But if you want to stop seeing me because of the circumstances we are in… I don't know why, but I think it was meant to happen this way.'

'What do you mean?'

'I was meant to walk through the park at the precise moment you needed help. It wasn't just a coincidence.'

It was true, she owed him her life. But it didn't change anything. 'What about the war? The Germans? Everything is against us.'

'The war won't last forever. At this rate there will soon be no men left to fight it.' He smiled gravely. 'As long as we have each other, we'll figure it all out. We'll make it work.'

A couple of days ago she had believed it, too. But now everything was different. 'Alexei is dead,' she whispered. She moved away from him on the bench, wiping her face.

'Alexei?'

'My sister's fiancé. She is heartbroken. They were going to get married…' She couldn't continue.

His face fell. 'What happened?'

'The Nazis killed two hundred Soviets for the murder of the officer in the park. Alexei was one of them. They died because of us, Mark. It's all our fault.'

'They killed two hundred innocent people? Why?' On his face she saw disbelief, incomprehension and, finally, horror.

'You tell me. You are one of them.'

'I am not one of them.' His shoulders stooped, as if her words were a weight pulling him down. 'I'm so sorry, Natasha. I had no idea.'

'What would you do if you knew? Would you come forward and tell them it was you?'

'To save two hundred innocent lives? Yes, I would.'

'I don't believe you.' She was shivering and couldn't get warm. He shrugged and turned away from her. She added, 'What we are doing is wrong and you know it.'

'What are you talking about? Can't you see? It's the only thing that's right.'

'I know it's wrong because I have to keep you a secret from everyone I love. I have to lie to everyone I know. When I walk down the street with you, I pray we don't run into anyone who could recognise me.'

'When the war is over, we won't have to hide. This day will come, we just have to be patient.'

Natasha prayed for the day when she could tell the whole world about her feelings for Mark, when she could bring him home and introduce him to her family. When she imagined this day, she felt the cold despair inside her melt a little. But then she remembered Olga's words. 'You are on their side, Mark. On Hitler's side. You are a part of this horror. Don't you feel responsible for what is happening?'

'Every day of my life. But what choice do I have?'

'There's always a choice. They sent you here, to the Soviet Union, to fight against us. Yes, it wasn't what you wanted for yourself. But you made a choice to go along with it. Because it was easier, because it was safer. I understand.' She looked up into his face and her lips trembled. 'But everywhere in the world, people risk their lives to defy Hitler. How can I be with someone who chose to support him?'

He staggered away from her as if she had slapped him. So much hurt was in his face, so much shame, she regretted her words instantly. She wanted to hold him close and tell him how sorry she was. But instead, before her resolve weakened, she got up and walked away, her tears blinding her.

*

Despite all their prayers, Grandmother didn't get better. Natasha ran to fetch the doctor, but all she found was a terrified Olga who hid in the wardrobe and didn't come out until she heard Natasha's voice. The German doctor was no longer staying with them. He had disappeared the day before, and no one knew what had become of him.

On the way home, Natasha knocked on Petr Nikolaev's door, her heart skipping in fear as she recalled the drunken Germans in his apartment. She didn't expect to find the doctor and wasn't surprised when there was no answer.

As she cooked lunch, she tried not to think of Mark because thinking of him filled her with agony. She tried not to look at her sister, who hadn't moved from her corner. Lisa's eyes were closed and her body rocked to some sad, monotonous melody that only she could hear.

'Babushka, I made some barley. Please, have some. You need your strength,' Natasha begged, holding the small plate in her lap with hardly a handful of gluey flakes boiled in water, with no milk, no salt and no butter. 'If you don't eat, you won't get better.'

'Maybe it's for the best.' Grandmother's voice was faint. It was barely a whisper.

'Don't say that, Babushka. You'll be okay. Once the fever goes, you'll be good as new.' Natasha adjusted her pillows.

'It's better not to see what's happening to Kiev. What's happening to all of us.'

'Please, Babushka! Don't talk like that. We are all still here and we need you.'

Grandmother groaned and lifted her head, swallowing a

spoonful of barley. Chewing seemed to take the last energy out of her. She collapsed on the bed, breathing heavily.

Now that summer was truly over, it got dark early. It was barely seven in the evening when the family gathered in the shadowy kitchen, Mark's kerosene lamp illuminating the room, the walls, and their pallid faces. No one spoke. Grandfather held Grandmother's hand, watching as she shuddered in her sleep.

Gradually, one after another, they drifted off to sleep. Mother and Father stretched out on the floor, Lisa was in the corner, Nikolai and Grandfather slept in the two armchairs that the Germans let them take from her parents' bedroom. Only Natasha remained by the little folding bed, afraid to close her eyes, afraid to miss what could be the last moments with her grandmother.

In the eerie light, Grandmother's face was still, her skin grey. 'Babushka?' Natasha whispered, shaking her grandmother's hand that was cold and motionless. 'Babushka!'

'Yes, dear?' said Grandmother softly.

Relieved, Natasha asked, 'Were you asleep? Does your shoulder hurt?'

'Doesn't hurt as bad as before.'

'That's good!' cried Natasha. 'It's good, isn't it?' She moved a strand of grey hair that was covering Grandmother's eyes.

'Yes, dear, it's good.' Grandmother coughed heavily.

Natasha watched the kerosene flame that was quivering on the shelf. 'Remember the soldier who helped us?' Grandmother shook her head. Natasha looked around to make sure everyone was sleeping. 'He's Hungarian. His name is Mark.' Her voice was barely audible. She didn't want Grandmother to notice her heartbreak. 'I saw him again and thanked him for saving our lives.'

'Bless you, child.' Grandmother's trembling hand touched Natasha's face. 'May God protect you and guide you for as long as you live. May He bring you all the happiness you deserve.'

Natasha cried, silent tears that no one could see in the dark.

'Babushka, remember when I was five and we went to pick raspberries in the forest? And I ran after a squirrel and got lost?'

'I remember.'

'On the way home I cried so much, you let me eat all the raspberries we picked. There was nothing left for the pie.'

'Your papa wasn't pleased.' Grandmother's wrinkled face relaxed into a sad smile.

'I love you, Babushka.'

'I love you too, child.'

Natasha blinked her tears away. Her heart hurt.

She struggled to stay awake but couldn't. When the first rays of sun woke her up, she was still holding her grandmother's still hand. She shook her grandmother, slightly at first and then more and more desperately. Grandmother didn't stir. Her unblinking eyes stared through Natasha. Her body was stiff.

'Babushka,' Natasha whispered, no longer crying. She kissed her grandmother's forehead, kissed her eyes closed, then woke the rest of the family. Tears rolled down Grandfather's wizened face. Nikolai was sniffling in his armchair, and even Lisa got up and embraced Mother, who was sobbing uncontrollably. Father was mutely staring into space, his eyes red.

'Alexei is dead, and now Babushka,' whispered Nikolai. 'Who will be next?'

Chapter 5 – A City Ablaze

September 1941

The small house on the outskirts of Kiev smelled of incense and garlic. Natasha inhaled, trying not to sneeze. The curtains were tightly drawn, and a yellow candle was the only source of light, illuminating old books and parchments on the shelves, and dried herbs tied together with twine. Outside, there was a chicken coop without the chickens and a doghouse without the dog. Natasha suspected the pigsty she had noticed in the far corner of the garden was empty, too. The Nazis had requisitioned the birds and the animals, just like they had requisitioned all their food supplies.

Natasha and her mother watched as a withered old woman in front of them chanted under her breath. Natasha didn't believe in clairvoyants, but Mother had insisted they visit Marfa, who had accurately predicted Zina's marriage. According to Zina, everything Marfa foretold had come to pass. And now here the two of them were, looking for answers no one else could give them.

Natasha suspected Marfa wasn't the one with the answers either.

'What do you want to know?' squawked Marfa, reaching for a rusty pot filled with green liquid.

'Yes, yes.' Mother shuffled from foot to foot. 'Just about my son… Stanislav. He left for the front in June. We want to know if he's okay.'

The woman hummed and mumbled, mumbled and hummed. Her voice was unexpectedly deep for someone so frail. She sprinkled some powder of an unknown origin in the pot and waited, her mouth moving in incantation. Natasha glanced at the door, pondering how long it would take to make her escape. Soon, the candle flickered and died, and Natasha could no longer see anything other than the woman's creased face and crooked smile.

Suddenly Marfa fell quiet. She whispered, 'He was wounded.' Natasha felt her mother's hand grab hers tightly. 'He's better now. He is fighting. Pray, and he'll come back to you. There's great strength in prayer. When the Red Army comes back, so will your son.' Mother's grip relaxed.

Feeling slightly braver, Natasha muttered, 'I have a question.' Both Marfa and her mother turned around. It took Natasha a few seconds to find the courage to say, 'Will I ever get married?'

The clairvoyant took Natasha's hand, turning it over. Natasha wondered how Marfa could see in the dark. Clearly she couldn't, because she grunted, released Natasha, and stumbled towards the table in search of matches. The candle burning bright once more, Marfa scrutinised Natasha's hand. 'Yes,' Marfa murmured. 'Your husband will be tall.'

Tall! Natasha held her breath, while her heart pumped sadness through her veins. Over and over she replayed her last conversation with Mark. Why did she have to say such hurtful things to him when all he'd ever done was help and support her? She wished she could take every hurtful word back.

'He'll have blond hair and green eyes,' continued Marfa.

'Dark hair, you mean?' exclaimed Natasha. Her mother raised an eyebrow. Natasha stared at the floor.

Mother interrupted, 'One more thing. Will we win the war over Germany?'

'That, Comrade, even I can't tell you.'

Mother paid Marfa with their last can of meat. On the way home, she was almost cheerful. 'Marfa's never been wrong. If she says Stanislav is okay, he must be okay.'

Natasha didn't want to share her opinion of Marfa and her credibility with Mother. She couldn't remember the last time she'd seen Mother smile like this. Besides, she too wanted to believe her brother was safe.

Mother practically ran home, eager to give the good news to the rest of the family. Natasha could barely keep up.

It took them two hours to reach the centre of Kiev, and when they did, they found it more crowded than usual. It seemed to Natasha that people were not so much walking to get somewhere as walking *away* from something. The streets were swarming with Nazi uniforms, and in place of the usual confident smirks, there was panic on their faces. 'What's going on?' asked Mother. Natasha didn't know, so she didn't reply. And that was when they heard the first explosion. People were shouting, German and Russian voices sounding equally desperate, equally afraid, but the shouts were soon lost in more explosions.

Mother and daughter paused for a second, glancing at one another, and then increased their pace. The smell of fire – putrid, acrid, heavy – intensified as they got closer to the town centre. Finally, opposite the university they saw flames. The blaze coloured the sky red, rising above the buildings, embracing them like fiery snakes. The smoke made Natasha's eyes sting. She coughed and gasped for breath. Mother directed her towards Taras Shevchenko Park, where Natasha was able to breathe freely again. But then she looked up and saw the spot where the Nazis had executed Alexei. Once again, her chest constricted as if the smoke was still filling her lungs.

When they finally returned home, Natasha hesitated before

89

walking through the door. She was no longer thinking about the fires, or Marfa and her predictions, so afraid was she of facing the Nazi officers who were living with them. The Nazis behaved as if the Smirnovs didn't exist, like they were pieces of furniture that had come with the house. Only occasionally would they order one of them to fetch water from the pump or boil the kettle. Every time she heard German spoken in her home, every time she caught a glimpse of a Nazi officer coming out of the bathroom, Natasha would hold her breath in silent fear. This fear sat like an ice block inside her, thawing away a little when the Nazis went out during the day, but never truly going away.

All was quiet in the apartment. The Germans were nowhere to be seen. Thank God.

In the kitchen, Mother opened the curtains. Natasha could see a cloud of dark smoke rising above Kreshchatyk.

'It's the Nazis. They're burning our Kiev. They are going to destroy the city and all of us with it,' said Father at dinner that evening. Natasha didn't think it qualified as dinner. All they had left was a handful of potato peel, three wilted carrots, and one tin of tomatoes. Divided among six people, it was nothing. Grandfather had had to pierce an extra hole in Natasha's belt because her clothes were hanging on her like a tent. Father had no cigarettes left, and he was even more morose than ever. Being around her father at the best of times was like walking on thin ice. A careless word, a hasty gesture, a mere look and the ice could break. But these days things felt even more volatile.

'Can't be the Germans,' said Nikolai. 'I heard them earlier. Apparently something happened at the gendarmerie.'

'What happened?' Natasha wanted to know.

'A bomb went off or something. Many Nazis died, some of them high-ranking officers.'

'You heard them? I didn't know you spoke German.'

Nikolai shook his head. 'I don't. Lisa translated.'

'Oh.' Natasha looked at her sister, who was mutely staring out the window.

'Could it be the partisans?' asked Mother, pouring herself a cup of strong tea. They still had plenty of tea.

'I hope so, Mama,' said Natasha. There were no definite reports of any organised partisan activity, but the city was abuzz with hopeful rumours.

'It's the Bolsheviks. They mined all the important buildings in Kiev before they left. Just like 1812 when Moscow burnt in front of Napoleon and his troops,' mumbled Grandfather. Ever since they had buried their grandmother, he almost never spoke, never moved from his chair and no longer read his books. He had always been slim but now he looked transparent. His clothes hung loosely on his withered frame and his eyes were dull.

'Dedushka, you need to eat,' whispered Natasha, placing her own potato peel on his plate and doing her best to ignore her rumbling stomach.

Natasha suspected Grandfather was right. The fires were the parting gift for the Nazis from the Bolsheviks. Explosions continued through the night. The deafening sound would reach them first, and then the ground would shake. Night no longer existed. It was as bright as day outside, but the light was frightening and had an orange tinge to it. Curled up in bed, Natasha listened to Lisa's breathing. It sounded heavy and laborious, as if Lisa was crying. Natasha hadn't seen her sister cry since Grandmother died. All Lisa did was stare mutely into space, as if she no longer cared what was happening around her. Surely the tears were a good sign?

'Lisa, are you awake?' asked Natasha.

Nothing from her sister.

'How are we going to live without our babushka?'

Still nothing.

'Remember when we were six and seven, and Babushka took us to buy a puppy? She said every family needs one because a dog means unconditional love. And then she fought with Papa, who didn't want a dog. I don't know what she'd said to him, but he agreed to keep Mishka. And she was right. He was our best friend. Remember?'

Lisa didn't reply but lay still like a mouse, not moving and no longer crying.

'I love you, Lisa. And I'm sorry,' said Natasha.

As Natasha looked out the window, it seemed to her as if all of Kiev, from Podol to Lavra, was in flames. She knew that for as long as she lived she would not forget the inferno that was destroying her beloved city. And for as long as she lived, she would not forget the helplessness she felt as she watched building after building collapse, as if they were made not from brick and mortar but paper.

*

Since she was a little girl, Natasha had loved sewing, loved the satisfaction of creating something new, the feeling of being just like her mother, so grown up as she pressed on the little pedal and watched the needle go clunk-clunk-clunk through the cotton of a half-finished dress or a shirt or a pair of trousers. The whirring noise of her mother's sewing machine had never failed to bring her comfort, and even now, it drowned all the other noises in her head, except for Mark's name and the insistent din of *It wasn't my fault*.

'Lisa, look what I've made for you,' she said to her sister one afternoon. 'A new dress.'

Lisa didn't look up. What was it she was reading? Natasha peered closer and recognised Lisa's diary. The same diary her brother had hidden as a prank on the first day of the occupation. Why did it feel like a lifetime ago?

'Oh Lisa, what are you doing? Why are you reading that? You'll only upset yourself.'

'Today is six months since Alexei asked me to marry him,' said Lisa. She narrowed her accusing eyes on Natasha.

'Why don't you try this on?' Natasha held out the dress she'd spent the last few nights making for Lisa.

'I don't want a new dress, Natasha.'

'When have you ever said no to a new dress? Look at this fabric. It's pure silk. I found it at the market. They wanted my golden earrings for it. The ones Mama gave me for my sixteenth birthday. But it was worth it. Just look at it.'

'I don't want a dress. I want Alexei back.'

Natasha sat down on the floor next to Lisa, fighting an urge to hold her close. 'Remember when Mama made us identical dresses? You refused to wear yours because you didn't want people to think we were twins. Even at five you wanted to stand out. But all I wanted was for everyone to know we were sisters.'

Nothing from Lisa, not even a shrug.

'It wasn't my fault, Lisa,' said Natasha, unable to take the heartbreak in Lisa's eyes.

'Wasn't it?'

'Of course it wasn't. I'm sorry I couldn't save Alexei. I wish I knew who killed the officer.' As the lie slipped off her tongue, Natasha looked away, so afraid was she that Lisa would read the truth in her eyes. 'You can't punish me forever.' When Lisa didn't reply, she added, 'Look what else I have for you. Some chocolate.' It was the chocolate Mark had given her the last time she saw him. The dull ache inside her chest intensified.

'Where did you get that?' Lisa asked suspiciously.

'From Olga,' replied Natasha, without thinking twice. She was becoming more and more accustomed to lying.

'Where did Olga get it?'

'I don't know. I didn't ask.'

'I'm not hungry. I just want to be alone.'

Natasha placed the dress and the chocolate on the chair next to Lisa and went to clear the dishes. When she returned, Lisa was gone, but the dress and the chocolate remained. Natasha picked up the dress and threw it inside the wardrobe. Like any sisters, Lisa and Natasha had often argued in the past. Sometimes, they had arguments that resulted in the two of them not talking to each other for a few days. But this empty chasm between them was new, and Natasha didn't know how to breach it.

*

That evening, Mother came home from work with a handful of ration cards. 'At last. They've decided to feed us.'

The family gathered in the kitchen. 'Two hundred grams of bread a week? Five hundred chestnuts? Are they serious?' grumbled Father.

'What are they trying to do, starve us?' exclaimed Natasha.

'I guess it's easier than just shooting everybody,' said Mother, who since their visit to the clairvoyant no longer spent her evenings crying over the picture of Stanislav.

'I'd pay to see the Nazis live on two hundred grams of bread a week,' said Nikolai.

'They just want to force us to Germany for work,' muttered Natasha. She kept hearing rumours about forced mobilisation to the Reich, but as yet there was no sign of it.

At five the next morning, a bleary-eyed Natasha and her disgruntled father queued up for their food. 'The earlier the better,' said Father. 'Who knows how much bread is available.'

They waited in line for five hours. Just like in Soviet times, the queue spilled out of the shop and all the way down the street. But the people in this queue were different. There were no shouts, no raised voices, no fighting. Scared and subdued, the Soviets waited in silence for the tiny morsel of bread that the Nazis had decided to spare them.

Natasha wished her mother had accompanied them to the store. Father barely uttered a word until, finally, at ten o'clock they received their bread. Father was right to go to the store early. There were no chestnuts left and as soon as they were served, the store closed. Everyone in the queue behind them left empty-handed. And yet, no one dared to argue. Father hurried Natasha home, hugging the bread close to his chest, as if afraid someone would jump out from behind a tree and wrestle it from him.

When Natasha was a child, she had loved going to the store, choosing her bread and then carrying it back, still warm and smelling like nothing else in this world. Nikolai, Lisa and Natasha would take turns biting the chunks off the golden crust as they walked home until, to the fury of their father, nothing remained but the white insides. She missed that bread. What she now saw in front of her was nothing like that. Clay-like, odourless and heavy, it crumbled and fell apart under the knife.

'What's the matter with this bread?' asked Nikolai, poking it with a fork.

'It must be made from reserve flour,' said Mother.

'What's reserve flour?'

'Millet, barley, lupine and chestnut.'

'That's why it tastes so bitter,' said Natasha.

'It's not bread, it's brick. I'm not eating brick,' said Mother, putting her portion back on the plate.

'Speak for yourself,' said Lisa, swallowing her own bread and reaching for Mother's.

'Here, Lisa, have some of mine,' said Natasha. Lisa ignored her.

The family were having their tea when a thin German soldier appeared in the kitchen. His face was freckled, his hair red, his feet outsized and his eyes downcast. His cap was in his hands. He couldn't have been older than eighteen. Natasha recognised him as one of the soldiers staying with them. Mother, Natasha and Grandfather stared at him in silence. Lisa was taking slow and thoughtful sips of her tea. It was so quiet, Natasha could hear a mosquito buzzing.

At first, the soldier said nothing but looked around the room, examining each of the Smirnovs with great attention. Finally, his gaze stopped on Lisa and he smiled. Then he took one giant step towards an empty chair and sat down, placing his cap on the table but not letting go of it. He continued to twist it, as if battling with nerves.

Mother stood tall in front of the soldier. 'What are you doing here? What do you want from us?' He shook his head to indicate he didn't speak any Russian. It didn't seem to deter Mother, however. 'You can't just waltz in here. This is our home. You're not welcome. Don't they teach you manners at school?' She turned to the rest of the family. 'Why do I even bother? All they know is how to kill innocent people.'

'It's their house now, Zoya,' said Grandfather.

'It will never be their house. They can stay here but soon—' Mother didn't finish her sentence but shook a fist in the German's direction. Fortunately, he didn't seem to notice. He was looking at Lisa, who, having finished her tea, was staring at a spot on the wall.

'What are you waiting for? Go back where you've come from,' Mother demanded.

This time the soldier looked straight at Mother and, to everyone's surprise, started crying. His shoulders shook as he buried his face in the palms of his hands and muttered something incoherent in German.

Mother was taken aback but only for a minute. Invigorated by the effect her words produced on the young boy wearing a German uniform, she continued, her voice even louder, 'Yes, cry, you filthy Nazi. Soon all of you will be crying. Who invited you to this country? Look at the misery you've brought, look how many people you've killed. Where is my eldest son? Where is my mother?'

The soldier stopped crying. He smiled at Mother and said something.

'He says his name is Kurt,' explained Natasha. 'That's the only thing I understood.'

The German reached into his pocket and showed them a picture that was turning yellow around the edges. In the photograph, a young couple held hands and smiled at one another. 'It must be his parents,' said Natasha. 'This photo looks quite old.'

'He must miss them. Look how sad he is,' said Grandfather.

'*He* is sad? No one's invited him here.' Mother threw a look of disdain in the soldier's direction.

'Come on, Mama. Be reasonable.'

'Natasha, ask him what he wants from us,' said Mother.

The soldier kissed the photograph before putting it away. Through it all he never stopped talking.

Grandfather said, 'Gosh, he can talk. Just listen to him. And I thought Nikolai talked a lot.'

Another photograph appeared in Kurt's hands, this time of a young and beautiful girl in a wedding dress.

'I think he's saying that he has a wife back home,' said Natasha.

'How long is he planning to sit here? It's late, I must go to work.' Mother's eyes remained on the soldier, and her face was still guarded, but her voice was no longer angry. 'No manners,' she muttered under her breath.

'I don't know, Mama. He looks lonely.' Even though the soldier was German, Natasha wasn't afraid of him. There was something helpless in the way he looked at them with his big, sad eyes, the way he talked in his boyish voice. Natasha handed him a piece of German-issue bread. 'Here, try some.'

Kurt brought the bread close to his face and inhaled, then tore off a tiny piece and placed it in his mouth. A few seconds later he said in broken Russian, 'Bad bread. Terrible bread.' To the amusement of the family, he handed the remainder of the bread to Natasha and shook his head. Then he said something to her, sensing she was the only one who could understand him.

'What's he saying?' demanded Mother.

'I don't know, Mama. He speaks too fast.'

The German repeated his speech, slowly this time, drawing out every word, pointing first at himself and then at the Smirnovs. This time Natasha was able to grasp the gist of what he was saying. 'He thinks we're a wonderful family. We remind him of his family back in Germany, whom he misses very much. Being here makes him feel like home. He thinks he's lucky to be staying with us.'

Kurt looked like a little boy, happy and excited. Even Mother seemed touched. Her face relaxed into something resembling a smile. The soldier saluted the family and left, but returned a moment later, handing Natasha a jar of jam.

When he was finally gone, Natasha said, 'Mama, look! Strawberry jam.'

Mother said with a sigh, 'He's a mere boy, younger than our Stanislav.'

Grandfather nodded. 'What a waste this war is, what a shame, for our people as well as most Germans.'

When Nikolai returned from the library and heard about the encounter, he demanded his share of jam from Natasha.

'You're too late, we ate it already,' said Natasha, hiding the jar behind her back.

'No, you didn't. I know you too well. You wouldn't leave your poor brother to die from hunger.' He pulled Natasha's hair with one hand, while with the other reached for the jam.

In the evening, everyone had a small piece of bread with some jam. Everyone, that is, except Mother, who refused to touch anything that had come from the Nazis, and Lisa, who didn't seem interested. Natasha waited for the delicious sweetness to fill her mouth and relished it on her tongue. She didn't want the taste to end.

Chapter 6 – The River of Death

September 1941

The next evening, Natasha hurried to Kreshchatyk. Every day, she would try to exchange her books for something to eat, but she hadn't been successful. The villagers asked for gold and valuables, sometimes warm clothes and furniture, but they were not interested in books. A couple of days ago Olga had received a dozen potatoes for her brand new fur coat. 'What will you wear in winter?' Natasha had asked.

Olga had shrugged. 'Who knows where we'll be in winter. But we need to eat now.'

Kreshchatyk was cordoned off, and no one was allowed to pass. A strong wind was blowing, and the fire that had been consuming Kiev for the last few days was spreading fast, its golden glare reflected in every window. Proreznaya and the corner of Pushkinskaya were ablaze. An explosion startled Natasha, and she backed away, turning her back to the fire. But even with her back turned, she could still see a dark cloud hanging over Kiev. A dark cloud that seemed to swallow the entire city whole. There was nothing left, not even a glimmer of hope.

Every bench was occupied, and the Soviets huddled together

in small groups, their possessions by their feet. Some of them still wore their pyjamas, as if the fire had surprised them in the middle of the night. Natasha suspected these poor people had slept right here, on the benches. Curfew was no longer observed now that the Kievans had nowhere to go.

On Lva Tolstogo a large procession ambled past Natasha in the direction of the river, reciting prayers and hymns in monotone voices with dull faces, icons and crosses raised high above their heads. It was as if two decades of Communism with its enforced atheism and a ban on religion had never existed. Faced with a crisis, people turned their eyes to God as if He was their only hope.

Unable to get through to the centre of town, Natasha turned back. When she was around the corner from home, she noticed a blue piece of paper glued to a wall of a tall building. She didn't think much of it at first, so many notices appeared from the Nazis almost every day, but when she read it, a chill ran through her. The Jewish population of Kiev was ordered to appear on the corner of Melnykova and Dokterivska Streets, at a place called Babi Yar near the Lukyanovskoe cemetery, bringing their valuables and a change of clothes. They had three days. Failure to do so was punishable by death. Natasha wished she could run to Podol and warn Olga, but it was after curfew and not safe out.

*

Natasha was still in bed when she heard a soft knock on the door. *It couldn't be the Germans*, she thought. The Nazis didn't bother knocking but walked straight in. When they did knock, they did it loudly and persistently. The sound outside was more like a mouse scratching. Natasha opened the door to a flustered Olga.

'Olga, I'm so glad to see you. I was just about to come and find you.' She didn't know how to bring up the notice on the door, but then she saw a blue piece of paper in Olga's hand. She motioned her friend inside and closed the door behind her.

'Can't stay long. My mama's waiting for me at home.' Olga's face was no longer covered in grey smudges, but her hair was messy, and so were her clothes. Her eyes were round, panic-filled.

Natasha hugged her friend. 'Is your mama making anything nice for dinner?' Olga's mother was the best cook Natasha knew. 'Maybe some of her signature blinis or pelmeni? If she is, I'm coming with you.'

'Blinis, I wish,' said Olga, and the two of them smiled sadly. 'How is Lisa? Still upset?'

Natasha nodded. 'Heartbroken.'

'I can imagine. Not talking?'

'Oh, she's talking all right. Just not to me.'

'Not to me, either. I tried to speak to her yesterday.'

'I didn't know you came by yesterday.'

'You were out. Where were you, by the way? Your mother said you're hardly ever home.'

'Oh, here and there. Nowhere. Keep your shoes on,' said Natasha as Olga tried to take her boots off. 'It's cold. Come and try some of our German-issue bread.'

'It's alright. You can keep it. I already had mine.'

'What? All two hundred grams? It was supposed to last you two weeks.'

The girls chuckled, and then Olga sighed. 'How I wish we'd evacuated in summer. We'd be safe now and...' She looked away without finishing her sentence.

'God knows we tried.'

'Yes,' whispered Olga. 'We did try. When we couldn't get on the train, you know what I thought?'

'What?'

'That maybe we're meant to stay here. Maybe it's a good thing. Leaving seemed so final. Like we were willingly giving up our Kiev to the Nazis. I almost felt relieved. But I'm not so sure anymore.'

Natasha peered into her friend's face. 'Olga, are you alright? Is it the order from the Nazis? I saw it yesterday.'

Without a word Olga handed the piece of paper to Natasha. It was crumbled as if a nervous, trembling hand had clutched it too tight. Natasha unfolded it. 'Too dark to read. Let's go to the kitchen.'

In the kitchen, behind the wooden door that separated the Smirnovs from the Nazis, Natasha looked at the same notice she'd seen the day before. 'Olga, you can't go,' she said. 'It's too dangerous.'

'What choice do we have? Mama thinks they'll send us to Germany for work. That's why they ordered everyone to bring a change of clothes. But I don't know what to believe.'

'Lukyanovskoe is near a train station. Maybe they will send you to Germany,' said Natasha. It was in line with the rumours she had heard. Yet, something was bothering her. Something wasn't quite right, like a book that was out of place on her otherwise perfect bookshelf.

Grandfather said, 'You mustn't go, young lady. We are talking about at least a hundred thousand people. There aren't enough trains to transport you all. You'll be going to your death.'

Natasha shuddered.

Father said, 'Why would they kill so many people? It's not in their best interest.' He turned to Olga, who looked sick with fear. 'They'll probably exchange you for German POWs.'

'The Nazis have been building concentration camps and segregating Jewish people for years,' said Grandfather.

'Concentration camps?' exclaimed Olga, her face pale.

'What goes on inside them, no one knows. And it's best not to find out, don't you think?'

'We'll find a way to hide you...' Natasha gazed at the door that was too thin to block the loud German songs seeping in from the living room. She trembled. There was only one person who could help them. Mark. If only she hadn't pushed him away.

'If we don't go, they'll shoot us. And it's not just me, it's Mama. She would never disobey an official order.'

'What about your grandfather?'

'My grandfather isn't Jewish. He wanted to come with us but we convinced him not to. He's sick and too old to travel. He can stay home and wait for us to come back.' Olga contemplated Natasha's pale face. 'Don't worry. It will be alright. Whatever happens, it can't be as bad as this life. Worst-case scenario, they'll send us to Germany. So what if they do? There, at least, they'll feed us and we'll have jobs.' She tried to sound cheerful, but her voice cracked.

'That's not the worst-case scenario,' muttered Natasha.

Olga went home to help her mother pack, leaving the blue piece of paper crushed on the kitchen floor. It rolled into a corner and remained there, drawing Natasha's gaze. As hard as she tried, she could think of nothing else.

*

As fast as she could, Natasha ran to Institutskaya Street. She didn't know how long she sat on the bench opposite the building that had once been a library but now served as barracks for the Hungarian garrison. Soldiers walked in and out, none of them Mark. Finally, when she was almost ready to give up and go home, she thought she saw the familiar tall silhouette. Calling his name, her heart in her throat, she hurried across the road.

He heard her and stopped abruptly. In the middle of the street flooded with German uniforms, the two of them stared at each other in silence. He looked like he hadn't slept well the night before. His eyes were dark, his face thinner than she remembered. Finally, he said, 'Natasha, what are you doing here?'

'I need to talk to you.'

'What's there to say? You made your feelings clear.' His voice was cold but his eyes didn't leave her face, as if he was trying to commit it to memory like a poem.

'I'm sorry for all the terrible things I said. I didn't mean any of them. I was upset—' She fell quiet, suddenly overwhelmed and light-headed at the sight of him.

'It's alright. I deserved them.'

'I shouldn't have said... It's not my place to tell you...'

'Don't worry. I understand.'

'You do?'

'Of course.' He spoke to her as if she was a stranger. And who could blame him? 'What are you doing here?' he repeated.

'I need your help. We're in trouble, Mark.' He waited for her to continue. She took a deep breath and said, 'Here I am, asking for your help after all the things I said. I'll understand if you want nothing to do with me.'

His face softened. 'I'll be happy to help. Just tell me what you need.'

'My best friend Olga is Jewish,' she blurted out, looking around first to make sure no one could overhear.

'Ah,' he said quietly. And in his eyes she saw the reflection of her own fear.

'What are the Nazis going to do to them?'

'I don't know their exact plans. But I know Hitler swore to rid Europe of all the Jewish people. He's talking of exterminating them wherever he goes.'

'Exterminating them?' she whispered in horror. 'But why?'

He didn't reply. She suspected he didn't have the answer.

'Can you help Olga, Mark? Take her away somewhere, hide her and her mother from the Nazis? If you do this, you will save their lives. I'll be forever grateful to you.' She felt tears running down her face and turned away from him, hoping he wouldn't notice.

He pressed her hand reassuringly and smiled warmly. 'I'll do my best.'

*

Natasha practically flew up the four flights of stairs leading to Olga's apartment, falling and hurting her leg. Ignoring the sharp pain in her left knee, she hopped up the remaining steps and knocked on the Kolenovs' door, her face red with exertion, with fear. There was no answer, and for one dreadful minute she thought she was too late. Her hands trembled as she knocked and knocked, calling Olga's name. When Olga's mother finally opened the door, Natasha was so relieved, she was ready to kiss her.

'Good timing,' said Olga's mother, smiling at Natasha. 'We're just about to leave.'

'Please, don't go, Oksana Nikolaevna. It's too dangerous.'

Oksana didn't reply but motioned Natasha in, closing the door behind her. Olga appeared in the corridor. Her hair was tied in a ponytail, her dress looked new, and not her usual grey but bright red. There was lipstick on her lips. 'Good, you're here. You can walk us there.'

Their bags were packed. They were ready. Natasha hesitated. To convince them to stay, she had to tell Olga's mother about Mark. To save their lives, she had to trust them with hers. She watched Olga, her best friend in the whole world, whom she had known since kindergarten and had never been apart from for longer than two weeks. Olga's face was grey from fear. The shadows under her eyes gave her a ghostly appearance. Natasha was prepared to reveal her secret if it meant her friend could live. It was worth it.

'Oksana Nikolaevna, I know a Hungarian soldier who can help. His name is Mark. He saved my life, and now he can save yours.' She fell quiet for a moment, her hands trembling.

'What makes you think our lives are in danger?' asked Oksana. 'Why would they kill us? We haven't done anything wrong. They need people to work in their factories, that's all. We'll have jobs and places to live. We'll have food.'

'Mark told me Hitler swore to exterminate all the Jewish people

105

in Europe. I don't think you'll be transported to Germany. They are going to kill you. Grandfather thinks so too. You shouldn't go.'

Oksana's face darkened. 'What choice do we have, child? The first Nazi patrol that checks our papers is going to take us away.'

Natasha lowered her voice, speaking very fast. 'Mark and I have a plan. As soon as it gets dark, he'll take you away from Kiev. He'll be waiting for us at seven with a car.'

'I'm too old to hide, child,' said Oksana, shaking her head.

'I would rather hide than walk straight into a Nazi trap, Mama,' cried Olga, looking out the window at the procession of people moving towards the cemetery. Natasha followed her gaze. Most people dragged so many boxes and sheets filled with clothes behind them, they were bending under the weight. One woman brought a gramophone. One man held a Russian samovar. Natasha hoped Mark and her grandfather were wrong, and that wherever these people were going, they would need a gramophone and a samovar. Unfortunately, she couldn't remember a single occasion when her grandfather had been wrong.

A crowd of spectators gathered, and some people followed the procession, eyeing it with curiosity. It was quiet in the room, and through the open window Natasha could hear the voices outside. A large, dishevelled-looking man shouted, 'Where are you going, people? They are going to shoot you.'

An old woman replied, her voice trembling, 'Shoot us? Look at us. Why would they waste their bullets?' Men had been drafted into the army, and it was mostly women, children and old people marching to their unknown destiny.

Someone cried, 'What are we going to do? What's going to happen to us?'

And another voice replied, 'I told you we shouldn't go. You old fool, you never listen.'

Everywhere Natasha looked, she saw grief, tears and terror.

Olga said, 'What if these people are right? What if they are

106

going to kill us? Mama, I just turned nineteen. I don't want to die.' She blinked, her eyes glistening. 'Whenever I thought about my future, I always assumed I had many long years ahead of me. I've never been anywhere, never done anything. There's so much I want to do. So much to see.'

'Let Mark help you,' Natasha pleaded, pulling Oksana by the sleeve.

'Disobey the official order?' exclaimed Oksana. 'Punishment for that is death.'

'You can trust Mark. He will save you.'

'And he's prepared to risk his life for us?'

'He's prepared to help.'

'This could be our only chance, Mama,' said Olga. Uncertainly Oksana nodded. Olga turned to Natasha. 'Tell Mark we'll be waiting for you both at seven.'

Relieved, Natasha hugged her friend close and whispered, 'Thank God. I don't know what I would do if I lost you, too.'

*

At home, Natasha sat next to her grandfather, watching the clock, wondering what Mark was doing, wondering what Olga and her mother were doing. A German officer barged in and demanded to see their passports. After he left, Grandfather said, 'They're searching for Jewish people. It's the second inspection today.'

'What will they do to them?' Natasha whispered. Grandfather didn't reply.

In the afternoon, a dishevelled Zina, who had been staying with a neighbour, knocked on the door. 'You are not going to believe it,' she said, her eyes wide. 'My cousin lives not far from Babi Yar. They've been hearing gunshots all day. The Nazis are killing all those poor people. No one is leaving there alive, no one at all.' She trembled, her earlier hope for a better life nothing but a distant memory.

Something exploded inside Natasha when she heard Zina's story. She slid into her grandmother's rocking chair, her legs no longer able to support her. Hugging her stomach, she rocked back and forth. *Zina is mistaken*, she repeated to herself. *Her cousin is mistaken. He didn't see anything.* What Zina had just told them was impossible. No human society was capable of such pointless, unwarranted destruction. It was just a rumour, nothing else. Zina loved to gossip. It was in her nature to exaggerate.

Rumour or not, the condemned kept walking. The doomed procession was a terrifying sight. Poor lost souls ambled past Natasha's window, heads bent, eyes dull, feet dragging, with Nazi guns pointed at them. As she watched the horrific human river trickle towards Babi Yar – the human river that, far from diminishing, had grown to almost twice its original size – her every bone, her every vein was chilled.

'Animals! What are you going to do to them?' screamed Mother at the Nazis, who were having breakfast in the living room. Kurt wasn't among them, or Natasha would have asked him what was happening. To Natasha's surprise, the soldiers ignored them. Was it her imagination, or were the Germans themselves more subdued, as if shocked by what was happening? When Natasha met them in the corridor, they didn't raise their eyes to her.

'Poor Kiev. Our poor people. What cursed times we live in. What black times,' repeated Grandfather, weeping softly.

'Beasts!' Mother wriggled her arms. 'Can you believe that some Soviet women are sleeping with them? I see them all the time. Walking hand in hand, selling their souls and bodies for a piece of bread. What a disgrace!'

Natasha's tea cup trembled and fell. Blinking fast, Natasha stared at the brown blotches, at the shreds of glass on the kitchen floor. What would her mother say if she knew about Mark? Would she turn away from her? Would her whole family turn away from her? Natasha didn't care. She closed her eyes and thanked God for Mark, who had saved her life and was now about to save her best friend from a horror she couldn't even begin to fathom, an evil the likes of which she couldn't imagine.

*

As Natasha waited for Mark to pick her up in his truck, she heard loudspeakers come alive with music and speeches, just like they did before the German occupation. The only difference was that they were now broadcasting in German. Kiev had become a German city living on German time, an hour behind the Soviet Union.

Natasha wished she had a clock, so she would know what time it was. Every time she saw the headlights of a car approaching, she prayed it was him.

Finally, a truck pulled up and she saw Mark in the driver's seat. She ran to him as fast as her legs would carry her, and when she got in, she asked, 'Are we running late? They'll wonder where we are.'

'We are right on time.'

They set off. Faster-faster-faster, she repeated to herself, watching the familiar streets zooming past. But Mark was already driving as fast as he could without attracting the attention of a Nazi patrol.

Other than to ask for directions, he didn't say a word to her. Natasha wasn't used to his silence. She shuffled uncomfortably in her seat. 'Are you alright? You seem...' She searched for the right word. 'Tired.'

'One of my friends at the regiment, Greg, was shot today.' She could see his hands gripping the wheel tightly. 'He was sent to Babi Yar to supervise...' His voice broke. Taking a deep breath, he continued, 'He tried to help a young girl escape. Her grandmother and parents were killed in front of her. She was hysterical. He hid her in his truck but they were caught.'

Her heart pounding in terror in her chest, she reached for his

109

face, touched his unshaven cheek. 'I'm so sorry,' she muttered. 'Do you hear me, Mark? I'm so sorry.'

'Greg was shot as a traitor for helping a child. And I need to write to his mother. I need to write to the woman who's already lost her husband in this war and tell her what happened to her son. How will I find the right words?'

'Tell her the truth. Tell her that her son died a hero.'

'I wish I could. But our letters are monitored.'

Natasha looked into his tormented face. 'I'm so sorry,' she repeated.

He didn't reply, his eyes on the road.

When they turned onto Olga's street, she asked, 'Where will you take them?'

'East. They'll be safe in unoccupied territories.'

'How can I ever thank you?'

'No thanks necessary.'

When they finally arrived, Natasha looked up at her friend's windows. They were dark like every other window in the building. Natasha imagined Olga and her mother in a rush of last-minute preparations, glancing at the clock, waiting for the knock on the door.

In silence they walked up the stairs. The door opened before they even reached Olga's apartment. Natasha expected to see her friend, but it was Olga's grandfather Mikhail who met them. Natasha hadn't seen him for a few weeks, and he looked older by years, stooped and grey in the light of Mark's torch.

'Are they ready?' asked Natasha after she greeted Mikhail and introduced Mark. She looked past Mikhail into the dark corridor. It was deserted. 'It's past seven. We need to hurry.'

Mikhail didn't reply at first. His eyes were swimming in tears. Natasha knew instantly something was wrong. 'Where are they?' she whispered, her voice that of a stranger, hoarse and breaking.

'They came for them twenty minutes ago. The patrol. They took them away. I couldn't stop them.' The old man broke down

110

in sobs in front of them. 'I couldn't stop them,' he repeated over and over again.

Natasha, who was sobbing herself, held Mikhail in her arms as if he was a baby, stroking his back and telling him that his daughter and granddaughter were going to be just fine, that they would be sent to Germany for work, that they would be fed and clothed and safe. Another lie she wanted so desperately to believe.

*

When they were outside, Mark said, 'I'm so sorry about your friend.' His face was anguished.

Natasha couldn't reply without breaking down. She clasped her fists, trying to stave off the pain, to delay it, to not let it anywhere near her. Blindly she followed Mark, barely knowing where they were going. He was taking her to the river, she realised. When they reached the parapet, he put his arms around her. It felt so good, to be touching him again, to be touched by him. In a tiny voice she said, 'We missed them by twenty minutes.' And whimpered like a wounded animal in his arms.

He kissed her lips, kissed the tears off her face. 'I'm so sorry,' he repeated. 'Do you hear me? I'm so sorry.'

Natasha felt something exploding inside her, in grief, in heart-break. She hid her face in his uniformed shoulder.

Mark said, his gaze on her face, 'I've been thinking about what you said to me. Remember you told me there's always a choice? Well, I'm ready to make mine. Faced with the horror of it all, I can't continue to do nothing. I can't continue to turn a blind eye and pretend I am not responsible...' He fell quiet.

'It's not your fault. You're not responsible for what's happening at Babi Yar.'

'I keep telling myself that but...' A German truck drove past. A German plane floated by, the noise of its engine reverberating long after it was gone. 'Many Hungarian soldiers are deserting. The Ukrainians encourage us to do so all the time. They offer us clothes and places to hide. That's all I can think about. If I deserted, I could look at myself in the mirror. I could live with a clear conscience.'

'Yes, but for how long? What happens to the deserters who are caught? What happens to Hungarian soldiers who turn their back on Hitler?'

Mark shrugged. 'One of the soldiers from our regiment was found in a cellar on the other side of Kiev. He was shot.'

'You can't risk your life like that. You can do more good if you stay alive. In your own small way, you can help people. Like you helped me and my babushka. Like you tried to help Olga.' She trembled. 'First Alexei, then Babushka, and now Olga,' she said. 'Please, don't do anything reckless. I couldn't bear it if anything happened to you.'

'Your babushka?'

She nodded. He pulled her closer, whispering how sorry he was.

'Is there any chance Olga could be alright? Any chance at all, Mark?'

She needed him to lie, so she could hope. But he shook his head and said, 'Oh Natasha.'

His face looked grim in the dusk. She wanted to touch him, wanted the comfort of his lips on hers. 'Once, when we were twelve, Olga and I had an argument. Over something silly, I don't even remember what. We didn't speak for a whole week. It was the only time we ever fought but, Mark, it was the longest week of my life.'

His arms around her hunched shoulders, his face in her hair. For a long time they were quiet. At last, he said, 'I love you, Natasha.'

She thought she misheard, thought she imagined the words she had longed to hear. 'What? What did you say?'

'You heard me. I said…' His lips were a mere millimetre away from her ear. 'I love you.'

'You do?' She hid her face in his tunic.

'I do'. He smiled expectantly, as if waiting for something.

She knew what he was waiting for. And she wanted to say it back. She had imagined saying it a thousand times through anxious days and sleepless nights. But now that she was actually facing him, she couldn't do it. So much fear in her heart, so much doubt, and yet he was right. What she felt for him, what he felt for her, it was the only thing that was right.

'Come on, say it,' he murmured. 'Natasha, I've never felt this way before.'

She raised her eyes to him. 'I love you, too,' she whispered. Saying it made her heart a little lighter. She repeated, 'I love you, Mark.'

Chapter 7 – The New Beginnings

October 1941

The first snow fell in Kiev, and its virginal quilt covered everything in sight. It hid the ground and the leafless trees, the withered grass and the empty trenches. But it couldn't hide the skeletons of burnt-out buildings. And it couldn't hide the procession of people walking to their deaths down Kreshchatyk, past Natasha, past their old lives, and past the city that they had called home.

As a child, Natasha had loved the first snow and would hurry outside, trailed by her brothers and sister, to touch the snowflakes, to taste them, to feel them melt on her fingers. Even now, in the midst of occupied Kiev, there was something festive about the snow settling on tired earth.

It was cold and a thousand daggers pierced Natasha's skin despite three layers of clothes. She could see her breath, like a ghostly vapour leaving her lips, only to melt away in the icy air. The snow that fell earlier was now completely gone. Nothing covered the damaged streets. Natasha wished for fresh snow. She wished for summer. She wished it wasn't war. But most of all, she wished she and Mark could be together, without having to hide their feelings for each other, without the lies and the deception. Out in the open for everyone to see.

On the corner of Tarasovskaya and Zhilyanskaya, Natasha noticed a few corpses neatly laid out on the ground. She turned away, not wanting to see. She was becoming accustomed to the sight of death on the streets of Kiev. Death had become so commonplace that it no longer scared her. What it did was leave her cold inside, frozen and empty and confused, as if the first snowflakes were settling in her stomach and not on lifeless streets.

As Natasha walked past a library, she thought she caught a glimpse of something, a swatch of colour on the white snow. Slowing down, she realised the Nazis had discarded a whole collection of classics. Abandoned on the frozen ground, the books looked so pitiful, she couldn't resist picking one up. It was Dumas' *The Count of Monte Cristo*. Wiping the cover with her mitten, she placed the heavy-bound book in her bag.

She saw Mark around the corner from her building and, making sure no one was watching, she wrapped her arms around him and squeezed as hard as she could.

'Ouch,' he exclaimed. 'I think you cracked my ribs.'

'Your ribs are just fine. Is it my fault that I can't get enough of you?' Lately she hadn't been able to take her eyes off him. Was it her imagination, or did he get more handsome every time she saw him? 'Here, I brought you something.' She reached into her bag and showed him the book.

'*The Count of Monte Cristo!*' he exclaimed.

'I know it's your favourite novel.'

'Thank you. Since we moved out of the library, I haven't had a chance to read.' Mark's barracks had moved to Podol and were now located on Frunze Street in what before the war was a large clothes store.

'Do you have any news from the front? What's happening in the rest of the Soviet Union?'

'They don't tell us much. I know the Nazis are a hundred

kilometres from Moscow. Leningrad is in its death's throes. The Germans talk about the war as if they've already won it. They think victory is only a few weeks away.'

'It's not, is it? It can't be.'

'I hope not. But Hitler is aiming to take Moscow before the 7th of November. He's already planned the celebratory parade.'

She shivered and pulled her hat down. She didn't want to talk about the war anymore. 'Have you heard from your parents?'

'Not since September. Letters take weeks, sometimes months.'

'We haven't had any letters since—'

'Natasha!' came a voice from behind them.

Her heart beating fast, she slowed down. She thought she recognised the voice. Letting go of Mark's hand, she turned around and found herself face to face with a dumbfounded Nikolai. 'What…' he started saying and stopped. A thousand questions were in his eyes as he gazed from Natasha to the soldier in Hungarian uniform.

Natasha didn't know what to say. She didn't know what to do. 'Nikolai, this is Mark.'

Mark stretched his hand out for a handshake, but Nikolai didn't respond. Gaping at them, he turned on his heel and marched off.

After a short silence, Natasha said, 'I'd better go.' Kissing Mark goodbye, she hurried after her brother.

She caught up to him on the stairs of their building. 'Nikolai, wait! I need to talk to you.'

'Nothing to talk about.' His voice was cold.

'Please, don't tell anyone you've seen us,' she pleaded. 'They won't understand.'

'Of course they won't. Why would they?'

He walked up a few steps. She followed. 'Nikolai, stop. Slow down for a minute.'

She caught his coat sleeve. He shook her off and spun around, glaring down at her from the step above. 'What are you thinking?' he snarled. 'You're the last person I expected this from.'

'Expected what? It's not what it looks like. We love each other.' Nikolai stared at Natasha as if she was speaking Hungarian. She wanted to tell him Mark had saved her life. That he tried to save Babushka's life. But to reveal this secret was to put Mark at risk. Natasha couldn't do it, even if she knew she could trust Nikolai with her life. 'He helps us. He brings us food. Without him we would starve.'

'He fights for Hitler.'

There they were, like a sharp slap across the face, the words she tried not to tell herself every night before she fell asleep. Natasha recoiled as if Nikolai had physically hit her. 'It's not like he had a choice. You think he's happy to be here? His parents are Russian, just like us.'

'If what you're doing is right, why hide it? Why keep it a secret? I know why. Because it's not right, and you know it.'

Natasha had to raise her head to look into his face. She had never seen him like this before. Suddenly he reminded her of their father.

'Don't worry,' he said. 'I won't tell anyone. But not because I want to protect you. Because I'm ashamed.'

Speechless, breathless, unable to move, Natasha watched as her brother turned his back to her. Up the stairs he ran, taking two steps at a time.

'Nikolai,' she cried, her heart racing. He didn't acknowledge her, didn't even pause. When Natasha heard the door slam, she leant on the wall and stared into the darkness of the stairwell. She didn't want to go home.

*

When Natasha finally mustered enough strength to climb the two remaining flights of stairs, she heard loud voices coming

117

from the top floor. She paused, wondering what was going on. The two apartments upstairs had been vacant since August when their neighbours had evacuated. *The Nazis must have moved in there too*, thought Natasha, and she was about to unlock the door when she recognised her sister's voice. 'Stop touching me! I don't want you to touch me,' Lisa shrieked like a woman possessed.

Natasha dropped her keys and ran upstairs as fast as she could. Outside apartment number twelve, she found Lisa struggling against a red-faced Kurt, who had his arms around her and his face in her neck.

'Let go of me! Leave me alone!' cried Lisa. 'Who do you think you are?' She pushed and shoved, but wasn't strong enough to extricate herself from Kurt's embrace. And he looked like he had no intention of letting her go.

'What the hell are you doing?' exclaimed Natasha, pulling Kurt by the arm. Instantly he released Lisa, muttered an embarrassed apology and disappeared down the stairs.

Lisa was out of breath, and her hands shook too much as she tried to button up her blouse.

'Are you okay?' asked Natasha, helping Lisa with the buttons and collecting her gloves off the floor.

'Does it look like I'm okay?'

'What were you doing up here with him?'

'He said he had presents for me. A bar of chocolate. A pair of stockings.'

'And you didn't think he'd want something in return?' Lisa's innocence surprised Natasha. It was so unlike her sister.

'I wasn't thinking, okay? I thought he was nice. Not like the rest of them.'

'He *is* nice. And crazy about you by the looks of it.'

'He's married, for God's sake. I thought I could trust him.' Suddenly Lisa looked like a little girl, lost and afraid. Natasha couldn't help it, she hugged her sister tight, expecting Lisa to push her away. But Lisa didn't push her away. Instead, she hid her face in Natasha's hair and cried softly. Natasha inhaled, finding comfort in her sister's familiar scent. She realised how much she'd missed being able to speak to her sister without seeing hatred in her eyes. How much she'd missed the closeness the two of them had once shared.

'He was offering you a pair of stockings. What did you think was going to happen?' asked Natasha when Lisa stopped sobbing.

Lisa smoothed her coat, placing her gloves in her pocket. She looked more composed but her voice trembled when she said, 'What am I going to do, Natasha? He won't take no for an answer.'

'Next time he wants to give you a pair of stockings, don't fall for it.'

'I think it's too late for that. He won't leave me alone. Thank God you came by when you did or who knows what would have happened.' Lisa leaned into Natasha. 'Everything is such a terrible mess. I miss Olga so much. Remember when you would sneak out and catch a train to visit her in the village? She was your best friend. You two were so close, always whispering, swapping secrets, sharing adventures. I was so jealous. I didn't think I would ever miss her. Oh Natasha, what are we going to do?'

Natasha hugged Lisa. 'You are my best friend, Lisa. You are my sister and I love you. And we are going to be just fine. We still have each other.'

'I wish Stanislav was here,' said Lisa. 'Everything would be alright if only Stanislav was here.'

'We all wish he was here.'

'We are not safe anymore, not even in our own home. I can't relax for a moment. When I go to sleep, I wonder if I will wake up with Kurt in my bed, holding me down. He's the conqueror. He thinks everything in our house belongs to him. Including me. He'll keep trying till he gets his way. As long as he's here, he'll just keep trying.' Lisa sniffled and leaned on Natasha's shoulder, quivering like a frightened kitten. 'What am I going to do? I'll have to give in because he'll never leave me alone.'

'You don't have to do anything you don't want to do,' said Natasha, stroking Lisa's dishevelled head. 'We'll just have to hide you from him, somewhere he wouldn't think of looking. I went to visit Olga's grandfather this morning to see if he was okay. He's lonely and sad, and asked us to stay with him for a while. That would be nice, wouldn't it? He has a big apartment all to himself.'

'There are no Germans living with him?' Lisa's eyes lit up with hope.

'No Germans. And he could do with the company now that—' Natasha's voice cracked. She cleared her throat and continued. 'Now that Olga and her mama are gone.'

'It would be so nice to get away, to not have Kurt breathing down my neck. Thank you, sister. You saved my life. Let's talk to Mama about it.'

'Yes, let's talk to Mama right away,' said Natasha, smiling at the thought of no longer living with the Nazis only a thin plank of wood away.

'I don't think I can live without Alexei, Natasha. I tried. I wake up every morning and think, this is it, this will be the day I'm going to feel better. But then every evening I lie awake thinking, I can't do this anymore.'

And Natasha stopped smiling.

*

Before they even had a chance to take their coats off, they heard Mother calling them. *What's happened now?* wondered Natasha as she hurried to the kitchen with Lisa. They found Mother pointing at the kitchen table, her eyes wide. 'Where did that come from?' So much contempt was in her voice, so much disapproval, Natasha expected to see a gun or a Nazi uniform or at the very

120

least the latest edition of the *Ukrainian Word*. What she did see, however, was a loaf of bread. It wasn't anything at all like the bread they picked up from the store. It didn't look like it was made of reserve flour, tasteless and clay-like. This bread was white, with a golden crust, and smelt delicious.

'Kurt must have left it for us,' said Nikolai. Even though he had never met Kurt, he had a lot of respect for the German soldier because of the two bars of chocolate he had given them over the past few days.

'He must be feeling guilty for what he did,' said Natasha, glancing at Lisa, who was cowering in the door, as if expecting Kurt to suddenly jump out at her and drag her away.

'What did he do?' asked Mother absentmindedly.

Lisa remained silent, so it was Natasha who said, 'He won't leave poor Lisa alone. I found him practically assaulting her on the stairs.'

'He did what?' exclaimed Mother. Anger flashed through her eyes. 'That Nazi snake assaulted my daughter? I knew he was no good, just like the rest of them.' She made a move as if to go after Kurt immediately and bring him to justice.

Natasha put her hand on Mother's shoulder, stopping her. 'I'm sure he doesn't mean any harm. He seems to be head over heels in love with Lisa, that's all.'

'He won't take no for an answer,' mumbled Lisa, not meeting their eyes. 'I'm afraid of him, Mama. I don't know what he might do. It's not safe for me here. Please, can't we go somewhere else?'

'Go where? Wait till I get hold of him. I'll tell him what I think of him—'

'Stop it, Mama. You don't want to get in trouble with the Germans,' said Natasha. 'Mikhail wants us to stay with him. Now that Olga and Oksana are gone, he's lonely and sad.'

'I'm not leaving our apartment to the Nazis,' said Mother adamantly. 'This is our home.'

'It is our home. But look at us. All we have left is this kitchen. Soon they'll force us onto the streets like they did the Kuzenkos. Mikhail doesn't have any Germans staying with him,' said Natasha.

'And I'm not safe here,' reminded Lisa.

'Come on, Mama,' said Nikolai. 'We'd all be better off without the Nazis in the same house.'

'Mikhail needs us,' added Natasha.

'I'll think about it,' said Mother. 'But we can't accept this bread. It's Nazi bread and I won't take anything from them.' She shook her head, her eyes on the loaf. 'We must give it back.'

'Give the bread back, Mama?' Natasha's mouth slid open. 'Are you serious?'

In silence they looked at the bread that was sitting in the middle of the otherwise empty table.

'We can't eat it,' insisted Mother.

'We have to, Mama,' said Natasha. 'We have nothing else.'

'Look at this bread. It's just like our Soviet bread. It smells exactly the same.' Nikolai inhaled. Suddenly he looked light-headed. 'It's made from Soviet flour in Soviet factories by Soviet workers. It's our bread. Not German.'

'He has a point, Mama. It *is* our bread. Just because Germans occupied our Kiev, it doesn't make it theirs,' said Natasha. She would have said anything if it meant having a slice of bread. Her stomach rumbled. When was the last time she'd had a proper meal? She couldn't even remember. 'If we eat it, it's one less loaf for the Germans. And Nikolai is right. We do need it.'

Mother brought the bread to her face. 'It does smell just like our bread.' For dinner, they had a large piece of bread each, and it tasted as delicious as it looked.

*

The next day, a miracle happened. Cold running water and electricity were restored. No more reading by the kerosene lamp. No more going downstairs to fetch a bucket of water. It was as if some degree of normality, however small, was gradually returning to their lives. Even though Natasha would never see her grandmother, Alexei or Olga again. Even though their city was ablaze. Even though the river of blood was still flowing through Babi Yar.

The whole family was gathered in the kitchen. Lisa was drinking tea, Grandfather was reading, Nikolai was gazing out of the window, and his face was as grim as the darkened sky. Father was sleeping, and Mother was comforting their neighbour Masha Enotova, who was sobbing and wiping her face with the back of her hand. Masha and her husband had a two-bedroom apartment downstairs. They had eight children, seven of whom slept on the floor stacked next to each other like sardines. Their last child had been born only four months ago and had a crib all to himself in his parents' bedroom.

'Oh, Zoya, what was I to do? I felt so helpless. My poor baby! He melted away in front of my eyes, and there was nothing I could do.'

'Shhh, shhh,' repeated Mother.

'I had no milk for him. When I finally got some on the black market, it was too late. I wish it was me and not him. Why couldn't I have died instead?'

'Don't say that.' Mother rocked Masha in her arms as if she was an infant. 'Don't talk like that. Your children need you.'

Masha looked up, and her eyes sparkled. 'I swear I won't let anything happen to the rest of my children. I'll do whatever it takes to keep them alive. Whatever it takes, Zoya!'

After Masha left, for a long time no one spoke.

'There are no stray cats or dogs left in Kiev. Did you notice that?' asked Lisa. 'I haven't seen one in weeks. Have they all been eaten?'

'Pigeons are gone, too,' said Natasha.

'Where did the pigeons go? They aren't cats. They are much harder to catch.'

'Apparently the Germans got rid of them.'

'Got rid of them? Why?'

'Who knows. In case we use them to send notes to unoccupied territories?' Natasha looked at her brother, but Nikolai wasn't looking at her. Mother moved around the jam-packed kitchen like a ghost, slowly packing what little belongings they had.

Natasha made sure she packed her favourite book, Tolstoy's *War and Peace*. She packed Mark's kerosene lamp and an old black-and-white photograph of her grandmother. She looked around. Where was the thing she was searching for? There it was, on the fridge, next to Grandfather's glasses.

She caught up to her brother in the corridor. The Germans were out. Thank God for this small mercy.

'Here, Nikolai. You might want to take this.'

Nikolai still seemed upset, but Natasha could tell he wasn't upset *at her*. If anything, he seemed relieved they were talking again. 'The scarf Babushka was knitting,' he exclaimed, touching the soft wool. 'Still smells of her. Jasmine and valerian.'

'I finished the scarf for you last night. It'll keep you warm.'

Nikolai unfolded the scarf. It was long, almost as long as him. He looked as if he was about to cry.

Making sure there was no one else around, Natasha whispered, 'Nikolai, I don't expect you to understand but please trust my judgement. I didn't ask for any of this. It happened. It was meant to happen.'

'You're my sister and I worry about you. You know what I saw yesterday?'

'What?'

'Three women beaten by the Soviets because they were seen walking with the German officers. They left them bleeding in the middle of the road.'

'Don't worry, it won't happen to me. People don't hate Hungarians like they hate the Germans.'

'I hope you're right. But please, be careful.'

'Don't worry. I am.'

'Oh yeah? That's why I stumbled on the two of you kissing practically outside our windows? Lucky it was me and not Papa.'

Natasha knew Nikolai was right. Her father's anger was like the burning Ukrainian capital. All the waters of the Dnieper would have been insufficient to put it out. 'Thank you for being so understanding,' she whispered.

'So what are you planning to do?' asked Nikolai. The scarf was wrapped around his neck like a purple python.

'About what?'

'About Mark.'

'Why do I have to do anything?'

'You don't think about the future?'

'What future, Nikolai? We are taking it one day at a time.'

Natasha wandered from room to room, whispering her good-byes, making her peace with the place where she'd grown up, the place filled with so many happy memories. It wasn't just a house, it was an old friend whom she had loved and cherished. Her heart was heavy. Would she ever come back here again? She felt as if she was leaving her old life behind forever.

What would the new life bring them?

She paused in her brothers' room. Her grandmother's jumper was still draped on the back of a chair. Natasha buried her face in its reassuring softness, envisioning her beloved grandmother's face. What did Nikolai say? Jasmine and valerian. Through her tears Natasha smiled.

Dozens of trophies lined the shelves next to Stanislav's bed. He was a keen boxer, and Natasha would often watch him, clenching her own fists as he clenched his in the ring, fighting a nervous sensation in the pit of her stomach that would transform into triumph or despair, depending on the outcome of that particular round. She wished she could take at least one of the trophies with her, but there was no space in her little bag.

There were two unoccupied rooms at the Kolenovas' apartment. Lisa, Natasha and Nikolai took Olga's bedroom, while Mother, Father and Grandfather shared the living room. After being confined to the small kitchen for so long, Natasha felt as if they were royalty living in a palace. Before going to bed, Lisa and Natasha went through Olga's old photo albums. They looked at photos of Olga and Natasha riding bicycles, chasing each other in the park, rowing and swimming in the river. Natasha rubbed the pictures with her finger, stroking Olga's smiling face. How could she live without her best friend for the rest of her life, when she couldn't imagine living without her for a week?

'Do you think she's still alive?' asked Lisa.

Natasha thought of Mark's friend, killed for trying to protect an innocent girl. She thought of the two of them rushing to Olga's apartment only to find her gone. *I don't think so*, she almost said. But then she saw the heartbreak in her sister's eyes and whispered, 'Of course she is. As soon as the war is over, she'll come back. Her mama, too.' Lisa smiled, visibly relieved, and Natasha thought, *Here it is, another lie on my conscience.* But even though she hated deceiving her sister, she knew it was what Lisa needed to hear. To face everything the future had in store for her, she needed Natasha's lie, so she could have hope.

'Lisa, look. It's you as Cinderella,' Natasha exclaimed, pointing at one of the photographs.

Lisa peered at the picture in the light of a candle. 'When was it? Second, third year of school?'

'I think so. We were eight and nine.'

Lisa grinned. 'Just look at my gown. Have you ever seen anything so beautiful? I remember having to fight every other girl at school for the role.'

'They didn't stand a chance. You were the most beautiful Cinderella. Everybody said so.'

Natasha closed the old album, putting it back in the drawer. She blew out the candle.

Lisa whispered, 'I still feel like my heart's been ripped out. Will it ever get better?'

Natasha suspected Lisa wasn't talking about Olga anymore. 'It will. With time, it will.'

'You're always in and out of the house. Where do you go?'

'Nowhere. To the market, mostly.'

'You are being careful, aren't you?'

'What do you mean?'

'You know what I saw out of the window this morning? A young girl, still a teenager, heavily pregnant. Germans were leading her somewhere. She couldn't walk very fast, so they pushed her. They pushed her and pushed her until she fell. They got angry and hit her in the face with a rifle. Then just left her bleeding in the snow. No one dared help her up.'

The sisters fell quiet. Natasha could hear the wind howl outside. It sounded like a frightened animal. She shivered and pulled the blanket over herself. Finally, Lisa whispered, 'I'm scared, Natasha.'

Natasha was struggling to stay awake. Her eyelids were heavy, her eyes hurt. She kissed Lisa's cheek. 'What are you scared of?'

'Dying. Would you believe it? I never really thought about it before. But now it's all I can think about.'

'I know what you mean.' It was another lie. It had never even occurred to Natasha. She was scared, too, but not for herself. 'I'm sorry about Alexei. You know that, don't you?'

'I know,' whispered Lisa.

From her sister's regular breathing, Natasha knew Lisa was asleep. She covered Lisa with a blanket, brushing a loose strand of hair away. She wished she could sleep as easily. But how could she, when only a few days ago her friend Olga was in this bed, unaware that her time was almost up. She'd had hopes and dreams, and an image in her head of what she wanted her future to be, and now none of it mattered anymore, because Olga was gone. One minute she was here, laughing and hugging Natasha, sharing confidences and telling her to hope. The next, she was gone.

Natasha closed her eyes and felt for Olga. Was she still out there, waiting for a better time so she could see Natasha again? Trembling, Natasha called out to her in the dark. *Olga, can you hear me? Are you still here? Since we were three years old, hardly a day went by when I didn't speak to you. And here I am, still speaking to you, still telling you about my fears and my heartache, but in reply I hear nothing but silence. Please, come back, so I don't feel so alone.* In her best friend's bed, clasping Olga's favourite teddy bear, Natasha cried for her best friend and prayed for a miracle that would change their lives for the better, because she didn't think they could possibly get any worse.

Chapter 8 – The Snow and the Illusions

November 1941

November came in a flurry of last autumn leaves and wet snow. Natasha thought of balmy summer evenings with longing as she put on layer upon layer of clothes and battled the wind, and endured the snow. She covered her face with a scarf and pulled her hat over her ears but still, the wind seeped through and the snow singed her skin.

And winter hadn't even started.

Ilinskaya Street, where the family had moved, was situated in Podol, one of the oldest suburbs of Kiev that lay on the right bank of the mighty Dnieper. Podol was the very spot where Kiev had begun, many centuries ago. In ancient times it was home to merchants and traders. Hundreds of years later, not much had changed: Podol had retained its rowdy beauty and exuberance. Until now.

'Did you know Podol burnt down in 1811? Most of it was destroyed,' Grandfather told Natasha one grim November afternoon.

'I didn't know that.' Natasha was looking out the window at the empty square where, as a child, she had often played with Olga and her dog Mishka.

'Yes, before Kreshchatyk as we know it today even existed. Back in those days, Podol was the administrative and cultural centre of Kiev. It *was* Kiev.'

'Why did it burn, Dedushka?'

Grandfather's shoulders stooped. 'I guess for the same reason Kiev is burning now.'

The Smirnovs had been lucky to find a place to live. After a month of relentless fires, many people were homeless. Having her own bed to sleep in and a room to share with her siblings, being able to walk from room to room without fear – what a relief! Natasha would have rejoiced if it wasn't for the bleak news from the front. According to the *Ukrainian Word*, Simferopol and Kerch had been taken by the Germans. Orel, Belgorod, and Kharkov were in Hitler's hands. Although bombed every day, Moscow and Leningrad were still fighting for survival. Kiev was still burning, and executions at Babi Yar continued, even though the river of condemned had gradually dwindled to a creek. Not because the Germans relented, no. Because there was hardly anyone left to execute.

Olga's grandfather Mikhail was a retired railroad engineer. In his spare time, he was a keen historian and ancient coin collector. The Germans had confiscated his extensive collection on the first day of the occupation, but Mikhail kept photographs of every coin and entertained the Smirnov children for hours, telling them the history and funny anecdotes behind each item.

Natasha was pleased to see an occasional smile on Grandfather's face as he engaged in lively historical debates with Mikhail. Their favourite topic was Napoleon. Tirelessly the two of them dissected the Napoleonic period under the microscope of their historical knowledge, examined it from the vantage point of hindsight and drew their – often conflicting – conclusions. Natasha held her breath, listening eagerly, unlike Lisa, who would roll her eyes and stick her tongue out, whispering 'Boring' to Natasha.

'Napoleon was nothing like Hitler,' Grandfather would argue.

'Did you know that in fifteen years in power he didn't initiate a single war? He was always fighting defensively. He is judged for having been militarily superior to his opponents, that's all.'

To which Mikhail would reply, 'What about his Egyptian campaign? Did he fight defensively then?'

'Napoleon was not in command then. The Directory was. In 1798 he was a mere general.'

On and on it went. Did Napoleon have the right to proclaim himself Emperor? What was he thinking when he embarked on his disastrous Russian campaign? Was his return from Elba an unprecedented triumph or a dire mistake? And was he a despicable dictator or a progressive force in history? No detail was spared, no stone unturned. Every reform, campaign and move was analysed. Although Grandfather was a professor with many decades of experience, he had found a worthy opponent in Mikhail.

Mikhail was what Natasha's grandfather called a perpetual optimist. But occasionally, when he thought no one was looking, Natasha would find him hunched over the kitchen table, an old photo of Olga as a five-year-old in front of him.

And he wasn't the only one. One morning, Natasha found Nikolai at Olga's desk, absentmindedly going through her bookshelves. Her textbooks, her school notepads, her music sheets. Her favourite books, toys, records. When he looked up and saw Natasha watching him, he said, 'She taught me how to ride a bicycle, you know.'

'She did?'

He nodded. 'Right here, in the park outside. I was six and kept falling off and grazing my knees. I'd cry, and she'd tell me not to be a baby. Get up and try again, she'd say. And I would.'

'That sounds just like her.'

'And when I finally got the hang of it, she told me I could have her old bike because every boy needs one growing up.'

'I remember that bike. It was rusty and old.'

'But it was all mine.' He looked out the window with a faraway expression on his face, as if he could see his six-year-old self racing a rusty old bike through the park. 'Do you think we'll see her again?'

It was the same question Natasha had been asking herself since Olga left, the question that filled her heart with pain and longing. 'Of course,' she whispered. But by the expression on Nikolai's face, she knew he wasn't convinced.

The apartment on Ilinskaya was filled with ghosts. Everywhere she turned, Natasha saw Olga's heartbreaking face. There she was, on her bed, reading aloud from a tome of Pushkin's poems to Natasha and Lisa. And if Natasha looked out the window, Olga was there, building a snowman. In the kitchen, she would ask Natasha if she wanted a cup of tea, and Natasha would shake her head, but Olga would pour her one anyway. And every time Natasha would reach out to touch her, Olga would be gone like an early morning dream. But Natasha would still be there, lost and alone, with her soul in pieces.

There was a piano in the living room, and every day Natasha would beg her mother to play. At first Mother refused, saying she was too exhausted. On the first day of November her school had finally reopened to pupils. Hardly anyone had sent their children to school, however. Parents didn't want to take the risk. They preferred to have their little ones nearby where they could keep an eye on them. The school had no heat and no water. There were no textbooks, no teaching plans and no class journals, only Mother's experience and heart.

And yet, Natasha didn't think exhaustion was the reason Mother didn't want to play the piano. The spark was gone from her eyes, and her shoulders were stooped with worry. She was an old woman at fifty. Natasha thought music would cheer her up, would cheer all of them up. And so she didn't give up – every evening she would ask her mother to play, until one day Mother finally relented, and the apartment filled with familiar chords of

Tchaikovsky and Mozart, Beethoven and Bach. The whole family gathered around the piano, their heads moving in time to music, hands clapping and feet tapping. Tears were in Grandfather's eyes, and Natasha couldn't help but cry herself, so many happy childhood memories were conjured by the sounds that escaped from under her mother's skilful fingers. Even Father was smiling, and Natasha hadn't seen him smile since before the war had started.

It was 5th November and Father's birthday. The family gathered in the kitchen, but no one was in the mood to celebrate, least of all Father himself. Mother's piano fell quiet for the evening, and Father perched on a chair, drinking tea and reading his newspaper. Every few minutes he would swear quietly, cursing the paper's pro-Hitler tone and anti-Bolshevik propaganda. 'Kerch and Sevastopol are bombed,' he muttered.

'By the Nazis?' asked Mother.

'Who do you think?'

Waltzing into the kitchen, Lisa said, 'Natasha, can you make me a cup of tea?'

'But they said two days ago that Kerch and Sevastopol were in German hands. You read it to me yourself. Remember?' said Mother.

Nikolai said, 'Lisa, don't you know how the teapot works?'

'Yes, Lisa, why can't you pour your own tea?' muttered Natasha. Lisa frowned. Sighing, Natasha reached for a cup. 'Okay, I'll do it.' Pouring the tea, she added, 'Papa, if they already took these cities, why are they still bombing them? It doesn't make sense.'

Lisa took the tea from Natasha, and without thanking her sister, sat down next to Mother. 'I heard the Germans no longer take prisoners but shoot everyone on sight. Does the paper mention anything about that?'

Father said, 'They don't know what they're saying. Every word is a lie. Just look at this. It says here the Red Army is destroyed. And yet here they say Moscow is resisting. How can

Moscow resist if the Red Army is destroyed?' He pushed the newspaper away with disgust. It slid off the table and landed on the floor. Natasha picked it up. Every day she read the paper with trepidation, her heart stopping every time another Russian city was ceded to the Germans, another piece of Russian land was lost, possibly forever. But she still read every word, hoping for a titbit of good news, something to lift her spirits. To find good tidings, she had to read between the lines of extensive Nazi propaganda. The newspaper said that Leningrad was starving and was about to give in to Hitler. It was good news. Leningrad still held.

'This tea is cold,' grumbled Lisa. Everyone ignored her.

'Feodosiya was taken,' whispered Natasha.

Nikolai said, 'Don't worry. They won't hold it for long. The Red Army will retake it soon enough.'

'I thought the Red Army was destroyed?'

'Only in the papers,' said Nikolai, winking.

Natasha wished she shared her brother's confidence. The truth was that with every newspaper, with every bleak report from the front, with every lost town and every burnt village, her faith dwindled.

*

Early the next morning, Natasha hurried to Kreshchatyk to meet Mark, who was on city patrol. Trams were running again, but it was mostly the Germans who used them. They rode the trams for free and occupied the front of the rusty carriages. The Soviets were allowed to ride at the back but had to pay for their tickets. Natasha heard rumours about shootings on carriages and dead bodies thrown out of the doors. Dead Soviet bodies.

She didn't want any trouble. She walked.

The Soviet statues of Lenin and Stalin had been pulled down only to be replaced by German monuments of military figures, people with moustaches whom Natasha didn't recognise. Only the statue of Vladimir the Great, the city's protector, the oldest monument in Kiev, still stood on the Vladimirovskii Hill, the very spot where Prince Vladimir baptised Kievan Rus one sweltering July ten centuries ago. The sight of Saint Vladimir holding his shiny cross in blessing made Natasha feel less afraid as she made her way down the deserted riverbank.

Now that the city was occupied, Kreshchatyk had been given a German name: Eichhornstrasse, in honour of the German general who had entered Kiev during the Great War in 1918. Many buildings sported yellow-and-blue Ukrainian flags, as if the Nazis would ever allow an independent Ukraine. The streets were empty. The majority of the Germans had moved to Kharkov, and Kiev stood ghost-like and shrouded in eerie silence.

Natasha didn't recognise the streets of her childhood. She didn't recognise the burnt-out buildings, the blackened trees or the scorched earth. Occasional explosions were still heard, and fire was still a problem. Every day new notices appeared on the walls, threatening mass executions if the fires didn't abate. *You will pay for every burnt-down building*, these notices seemed to shout from every street corner. As if Kiev hadn't already paid with thousands of lives lost in the ravines of Babi Yar.

Uspensky Sobor, one of the most beautiful cathedrals in Ukraine, had been destroyed. Built in the eleventh century, it had withstood the Mongol invasion, countless earthquakes and floods, only to collapse in flames when Hitler's troops marched through Kiev. Many people saw it as a bad sign. It was as if the very soul of Kiev had died that day. But Natasha knew that the soul of Kiev had died in September, the moment the first German boot touched its soil. And it continued dying with every new atrocity, every blue notice on the wall, every dead body swollen and disfigured by hunger.

The ice had already etched elaborate patterns on the windows, as if winter had decided to lay its claim on Kiev early. Natasha was exhausted after her brisk walk. The sheer weight of her winter clothes was dragging her down. She stopped to catch her breath and saw Mark turn the corner.

Her weakness, her fatigue, her heavy heart were all forgotten. She ran to him just as he ran to her. They embraced on the empty frozen street. Mark's uniform felt so thin under Natasha's fingers. It was the same threadbare uniform he had worn in September. She wriggled out of his arms. 'Don't you have a coat? A hat? Something warm?'

'They ordered winter uniforms but they haven't arrived yet. This is all we have.' He smiled at the horrified look on Natasha's face. 'Don't worry. It's not that cold.'

'Not that cold? It's minus fifteen. And going to get even colder. I'm cold just looking at you.'

'Come closer. I'll warm you up.'

She came closer. 'Here, have this.' Taking off her scarf, she wrapped it around him. Immediately the skin of her neck felt numb.

'You can't give it to me. You'll freeze. Besides, how would I look patrolling the streets in a pink scarf?'

She protested but he ignored her. Kissing her, he enveloped her in her scarf. His neck and ears were bright red.

'I wish you'd listen to me and take the scarf. You'll get frostbite,' she said. 'Why don't you walk me home and I'll find you something warm to wear? We still have Stanislav's winter clothes.'

His arm around her, they meandered back to Podol. On every building, Natasha saw placards depicting German soldiers, German planes and German tanks. 'Wait. What does it say?' asked Natasha, pointing at one of them. They slowed down to read. *The place of every Ukrainian is by the side of the German army as it fights against the Bolsheviks for the new European order.*

The placard was pasted to a wall of a restaurant that sported a 'Germans only' notice on the door. There were many such establishments springing up all over the city; restaurants, cafes and shops where the Soviets were not allowed, filled with food and luxury goods and warm clothes, where smiling German officers drank beer, ate fresh meat and bought delicious bread, looking out the windows at passers-by who were dying from hunger and cold. Everything in the city was for the Nazis, and it seemed that the ghost town of Kiev itself had become German, too.

'Do you ever go to these places?' asked Natasha.

Shaking his head, Mark said, 'Never. A couple of soldiers from our regiment went to a Germans-only café a couple of days ago. They got thrown out and beaten badly.'

'Promise me you'll stay away.'

'Don't worry. We don't mix with them unless we absolutely have to. We have nothing in common.'

'I know you don't,' said Natasha. She took off her mittens and entwined her fingers with his. 'You know, now that we have a piano at home, everyone's feeling much more cheerful, even Papa. Yesterday I actually heard him attempt a joke.'

'I'm so glad you're settling in okay.'

'And Mikhail is so happy to have us there. I just wish Papa had a proper job. He was forced into rebuilding roads and bridges twice this week. Under German machine guns. It brings him down. If he was working, they would leave him alone.'

'I don't know about your father but I could get *you* a job.'

'Really?' She was surprised. In occupied Kiev, jobs were almost as hard to come by as bread.

'There's a new cafeteria opening in Podol. They're looking for a cook and a cleaner.'

'A cook? You've obviously never tried my cooking. I burn eggs when I boil them.'

He chuckled. 'One day you'll have to cook for me. I'm a big fan of burnt eggs.'

'One day I will. But you might regret it.' She smiled and felt her cheeks burn when he smiled back. 'No, I wouldn't make a good cook. No one other than you would eat my food. A cleaner, on the other hand... that would be alright.'

'I know it's not much but it's better than nothing. It's safer to be working. And you'll have food.'

'It would be better to feel like I'm doing something.'

'And I could visit you at the cafeteria and walk you home after work. Would you like that?'

'You'd walk me home every night?'

'Every single night.'

Mark kissed her fingers. 'Put your gloves back on. Your hands are icy.'

As they strolled through the empty streets, Natasha was counting Ukrainian flags until she came across a white flag with a black swastika. She shuddered and lowered her head. She didn't want to see the unthinkable but there was no avoiding it. The unthinkable was everywhere. It was swaying in the breeze on top of the university building, sauntering past her in a grey uniform, cruising leisurely through grim November skies. The unthinkable had become her life.

Mark interrupted her thoughts. 'I received a letter from my parents today.'

Natasha looked up into his beaming face. *He must be missing his family so much*, she thought. 'How are they?'

'My sister-in-law had a baby boy. I'm now an uncle.'

'That's wonderful news! Your brother must be so happy.'

'Unfortunately he's in a Ukrainian village somewhere and they don't know how to reach him. They haven't had news of him in a very long time.' He frowned, but only for a second. 'I wrote to my mother and told her about you.'

'You did?' Natasha was pleased. 'I wish I could tell my family.' In a different life, she would have brought Mark home for dinner with her and introduced him to everyone. Mother would feed him her signature pelmeni, and Father would offer him a cigarette, which Mark would politely decline. Grandfather would find out his views on Napoleon, and Nikolai would challenge him to a game of chess. Natasha had always assumed that, when she fell in love, she would share every little detail with her sister, just like Lisa had once shared every little detail about Alexei. Not being able to tell Lisa about her feelings made Natasha feel like something was wrong with the world.

They walked hand in hand past the Smirnovs' old building on Tarasovskaya. 'I miss our old building,' she whispered. After a month of fires, she was pleasantly surprised it was still standing.

'There's no place like home,' said Mark.

'If you could live anywhere in the world, where would it be?'

'I wouldn't mind, as long as my family were nearby.' They walked slowly, pausing every few minutes to kiss. Thankfully, the streets were deserted. 'Somewhere by the sea. Maybe France. I love the water. We spent a month in Marseille once when I was a child. It was the best holiday of my life.'

'You've been to France? Are you allowed to go overseas?'

'Of course we are. Only in the Soviet Union are citizens prisoners in their own country.'

'I never thought about it like that. We don't feel like prisoners.'

'Why would you if you never knew any different?'

'We definitely never questioned it.' She looked up at him. 'What was it like, Marseille?'

'Loud, rowdy but infinitely beautiful. It's got so much history. And the Chateau d'If—'

'You saw the Chateau d'If from *The Count of Monte Cristo*? Now I know you're making it up.'

He looked at her, laughed, shook his head, then kissed her on her icy cold nose. 'One day I'll take you to all the places you read about in your favourite Dumas novels. We'll see Paris, Marseille, La Rochelle, Corsica. We'll go anywhere you want.'

'Wouldn't that be great? To go anywhere we want. It's my grandfather's dream to see Corsica. His hero Napoleon was born there.'

'Corsica is incredible.'

'You've been there, too?' Her mouth slid open in amazement.

'Yes, a few years ago. The whole island is a shrine to the Emperor Napoleon. Streets, hotels, restaurants, cafes, everything is named after him and his family. There are monuments to him on every corner. And do you know what the Corsicans do for Napoleon's birthday?'

'What do they do?'

'Every year on the 15th of August, they celebrate with music and military parades. For a week they march and they fire their cannon and they salute their emperor.'

'Grandfather would love that. That's the problem with being a history professor in the Soviet Union. You can never visit the places you teach about. He's been to Borodino, though. You know where that is?'

'My mother told me about it. It's near Moscow, isn't it?'

Natasha nodded. 'Lisa and I were so jealous when our dedushka went to Moscow. We've never been anywhere. But you know, I would rather go to Marseille. I would simply faint if I saw the Chateau d'If.'

A group of German soldiers ambled past. Natasha fell quiet. When they disappeared around the corner, Mark said, 'Okay, it's your turn now. If you could live anywhere in the world, where would it be?'

She thought about it. 'I always wanted to live in Leningrad.' Leningrad, which was fighting for its life at that very moment. 'No, not Leningrad. Anywhere in the world? Maybe Australia.'

'Why Australia?'

'Why not? Australia is an enchanted fairy-tale place full of magical creatures.' She stared at the ground. 'And I could do with a little bit of a fairy tale in my life right now.'

'Australia is so far. You have to cross the ocean.'

She smiled into his sceptical face. 'I always wanted to see the ocean. And it is far. Far from the war and Hitler. It's safe.'

He had nothing to say to that.

When they neared Natasha's building, she let go of Mark's hand. 'Wait here,' she said, disappearing behind the front door. Upstairs, she searched for the bag of Stanislav's clothes, finally finding it in the corridor. Nearby was a fur hat she hadn't seen before. Assuming it had belonged to Stanislav, she placed it in the bag, too. From one of the cupboards she fetched a spare blanket, the warmest she could find. It occurred to her that maybe she should ask before taking something that didn't belong to her. But the questions, the explanations! She shook her head and walked outside, soundlessly closing the door behind her.

'Thank you,' said Mark, taking the bag and the blanket.

In his face there was everything she was hoping to see – joy, gratitude, love. Her heart soared. 'You are welcome,' she said. 'Now you'll be warm. And you'll think of me whenever you wear the clothes.'

'I don't need a coat to remind me of you. I think about you all the time.'

'All the time?' Her breathing quickened.

'Yes,' he whispered, catching her in his arms, pulling her close.

'Me, too,' she said. Her chest was burning despite the bitter wind.

*

A few days later, Natasha was in the kitchen, preparing a meagre breakfast. Three eggs divided among seven people, barely a spoonful each. Now that winter was on their doorstep, they had no more potato peel, let alone whole potatoes. They had no more carrots. For many weeks now they hadn't received any bread from the store. The family subsisted solely on Mark's food. Every time Natasha cut the bread he had given her and every time she cooked the barley he had brought, she raised her eyes to heaven in silent thanks. She was thankful for the little they had because other people had nothing. She often thought of Masha Enotova's distorted face as she cried helplessly for her baby. Just like hunger, helplessness had become the one constant in their lives.

Hunger was a powerful motivator. Many Soviets, who until recently were adamantly anti-German, chose to work for the Nazis rather than die from starvation. More and more people signed up for the militia or worked as interpreters in German organisations. Who was Natasha to judge them? Now that November was here with its piercing wind and debilitating food shortages, working for the Germans was no longer a question of morals but survival.

'You won't believe what I found in Olga's drawer,' said Lisa.

'What?' asked Natasha.

'Antonina.'

'Antonina? Who's Antonina?' She stirred the eggs, wanting nothing more than to devour the whole thing herself.

'Your favourite doll. You never went anywhere without it.' Lisa shook the old doll in front of her sister. 'Don't you recognise her?'

Natasha swatted Lisa's hands away. 'Stop going through Olga's drawers and help me with lunch.'

Lisa didn't move. 'So tell me about this job. How did you find it?'

'I was walking past this new cafeteria—'

'You just happened to walk past?'

'Yes, Lisa. They hired me as a cleaner but they need a cook, too. Why don't you apply?'

Lisa's eyebrows shot up. 'Me, work? Like I don't have enough problems.'

'It's safer to have a job,' said Natasha.

'It's okay, I never leave the house. Unlike you.'

'A job might do you good. Distract you.'

Lisa sniggered. 'You think a job would distract me? Seriously? Cooking for other people? You know I hate cooking.'

'I know you do. You only enjoy eating.'

Just as Natasha was taking the eggs off the gas, she heard Mother's voice. 'Has anyone seen Stanislav's old clothes? I can't find them anywhere.' Natasha's hand trembled and the pan went flying, trickling eggs all over the kitchen floor.

'Are you crazy? You almost hit me with that pan,' exclaimed Lisa, pouting.

'Stop complaining and help me, Lisa.'

'Is everything alright?' asked Mother.

'Yes, everything's fine. I just dropped the pan.' Natasha crouched on the floor, spooning the eggs onto the plate that Lisa held for her. Once, in her happier, pre-war life, Natasha would never think of eating anything off the floor, even if it was her favourite chocolate, even if it was her grandmother's delicious blinis. Not anymore.

Mother looked under the table and behind the door. 'Where could they be? I was sure I packed them. Vasili, have you seen Stanislav's old things?'

'No, I haven't, Zoya,' said Father, striding into the kitchen. 'And I can't find my winter hat, either. It was minus twelve today, with the wind. I was outside in minus twelve without a hat.'

Natasha remembered the fur hat she had given Mark, thinking it was Stanislav's. She pretended to busy herself with breakfast, keeping her eyes down, sensing the impending storm and doing her best to ignore it.

After a few more minutes of futile search, Mother said, 'Did we leave them on Tarasovskaya? I'll go there later today and check.' With a dejected sigh she perched on a chair.

'Don't go to Tarasovskaya, Mama. It's too dangerous,' muttered Natasha, placing the plate of eggs on the table.

'We need the clothes,' said Mother. 'I wanted to take them to the market. Now that it's cold, we can get some nice cheese for them and maybe even some milk.'

Natasha took a deep breath. 'The clothes aren't on Tarasovskaya, Mama.'

'They aren't?'

Father narrowed his eyes on Natasha. Unfortunately, Natasha was all too familiar with the look in his eyes. She knew it didn't bode well. She cleared her throat. 'I gave the clothes away.'

'You what?' bellowed Father, stepping closer.

His enraged face was only inches away from hers. She squeezed her eyes tight, thinking of a plausible lie to tell her parents. Praying for a lightning bolt, a thunderstorm, an explosion, anything that would stop her father from looming over her as if he was about to wrestle the frying pan from her shaking hands and use it to beat her to the ground. Her mind was blank. She said, 'There was this boy. He was... He was homeless and had nowhere to go. With Stanislav away, I thought we could spare the clothes; he hasn't worn them in years anyway. Without them the boy would freeze to death.' She stared at the stains that the eggs had left on the kitchen floor. They were barely visible. She wished she was barely visible, too.

'That's good of you, daughter,' said Mother. 'What a kind heart you have. I'm so proud of you.'

'You're proud of her?' shouted Father. 'We could've exchanged these clothes for food. She took the food from our mouths and gave it to a complete stranger. What are we supposed to eat?'

'It's war, Papa. We must help people. If only in a small way.'

'Help people? And who will help us? Everyone's looking out for themselves. It's the only way to survive!' shrieked Father, leaning over Natasha. Lisa took one look at her father's angry face and withdrew to the safety of the bedroom. She left the door open, however, so she wouldn't miss a word. Father shook Natasha, whose body had gone limp in his arms. 'What were you thinking? Now thanks to you we're going to starve. Because, guess what, there's no food left.'

Natasha tried to push her father's hands away, but he was much stronger than her and wouldn't let go. 'Leave me alone,' she cried. 'It's only thanks to me that we haven't starved yet. I'm

144

the only one who brings food home. When was the last time you got us anything to eat?' Natasha couldn't believe the words coming out of her mouth. And judging by the expression on her mother's face, neither could she. Father let go of Natasha. His face was red, and he looked as if he was having trouble breathing. 'Papa, I'm sorry...' she muttered.

But it was too late.

'How dare you?' he roared. His voice quivered. 'How dare you talk to me like that? I'm your father.' He raised his hand as if to strike Natasha but seemed to change his mind at the last moment. 'And where is this food you bring coming from? You think we are stupid? Or blind?' Natasha blinked and averted her eyes. Father went for her once more, shaking her like a kitten.

'Vasili, please, don't,' exclaimed Mother, touching his hand. Natasha squinted, waiting for the storm to pass. It wasn't the first time her father had hurt her. She knew it wouldn't be the last. He cursed under his breath and pushed her so hard that she careered onto the floor, knocking into a chair.

Natasha cried out. Rubbing her throbbing ankle, she looked up at her enraged father, then crawled away from him to the nearest wall. She felt sad, ashamed and angry. But angry most of all. She couldn't control herself as she shouted, 'Maybe if you were the father you were supposed to be, Babushka would still be alive. It should have been you. You should have gone to the gendarmerie that day and not us. But you refused to go. You refuse to lift a finger for your family.' She saw the colour drain from her father's face. He made a move in her direction, but Mother restrained him.

Natasha dashed out of the kitchen, slamming the door behind her. She expected her father to follow, but he didn't. When she reached her room, she collapsed on the bed, sobbing. Lisa held her, stroking her hair, 'Don't cry. It'll be okay. Everything will be okay.'

'How?' cried Natasha. 'How will it be okay? Babushka is gone, and Olga too. Alexei—' Natasha felt her sister's body flinch as if

145

in terrible pain. Lisa continued stroking her head without saying a word.

Soon Lisa left, but Natasha stayed in the room, listening to her parents' raised voices. She had never heard them argue before, but now they were screaming at each other, and it was all her fault. Natasha had always hated confrontations. In most situations, even when she was upset, she'd preferred to say nothing, because once something was said, it couldn't be unsaid. What had come over her? Standing up to her father didn't make her feel better, quite the opposite. All the hurtful things she had said to him ran through her mind, and she wished she could take every single one of them back, even if most of them were true.

*

Natasha didn't know how long she stayed in bed, hidden away from the world under Olga's blanket. Soon her parents' voices faded away and all she could hear was the old clock on the wall counting down the seconds, the minutes, the hours. Natasha tried to find peace in the measured pulse of the clock and failed. There was no peace inside her. She didn't want to stay at home any longer and, luckily, she didn't have to. It was her first day at the cafeteria. A little nervous, a little upset, Natasha dressed quietly and stood outside her parents' door for a few thoughtful moments. She knocked. The door remained firmly shut. She knocked once more and, when there was no answer, she left the apartment.

It was overcast, not a ray of sun penetrated the heavy cloud. Snow mixed with rain settled on the ground. It didn't take her long to walk to the other side of Podol, where the cafeteria was located in a side street. The cafeteria served mashed potato with no milk and no butter, and chicken broth with hardly any chicken. The food was expensive and unappealing, but Natasha estimated at least two hundred people in the queue. Men, women and even children were fighting and shoving each other. Only the strongest and the pushiest made it to the front of the line. How they managed to eat, Natasha didn't know. The piercing glances of hungry onlookers were enough to put anyone off their food. Those few lucky ones that managed to get their food gulped everything down in seconds, looking around as if afraid that they would be beaten to death for their meatless broth and their butter-less mashed potato.

Everything in the cafeteria was dull. The room looked as if the colours had run out, pale wallpaper with flowers barely visible, beige tables, old chairs that were once bright yellow but were now the colour of grey sand, muddy brown floors, people's dim eyes. And only a large portrait on the wall was bright and new. From this portrait, a square-shouldered and moustached Hitler glared at Natasha in triumph, as if everything in the cafeteria belonged to him.

Natasha received a mop, a bucket, and a kerchief to tie around her head. Her job was to clean the floors and wash the dishes with water she was to fetch from the pump. She ambled through the large hall, trying not to drop the dirty dishes that she piled on top of each other, half a dozen at a time. Trying not to look at the wall from which Hitler's beady eyes followed her every move.

Around lunchtime she thought she spotted a familiar face. She put her mop down, watching an old man in a threadbare coat. With his matted beard and unkempt hair, he looked like a home-less man, the likes of whom Natasha saw every day. She was about to go back to work when the man turned around and faced her. To her dismay, Natasha recognised Professor Nikitin, Grandfather's colleague from university and one of his closest friends. Professor Nikitin taught astronomy and was highly regarded in academic circles. Now he was dragging his emaciated body from table to table, picking up plates that had already been licked clean and desperately searching for leftovers.

Her mop forgotten on the floor, Natasha approached her grandfather's friend. 'Stepan Ivanovich, come with me, I'll find you something to eat,' she said, pulling his sleeve. He glanced at her in his usual absentminded manner, and Natasha could tell he didn't know who she was. There was no recognition in his face, nothing in his face at all except confusion and hungry impatience. Still, he followed her to the kitchen. She made him sit in a chair and asked one of the cooks, a large woman called Sonya, if she could have her lunch. Sonya poured her a plateful of broth that looked like nothing more than warm water. Natasha carried it to the professor. She watched as he devoured the food, trying to forget that she herself hadn't eaten anything that day. She rummaged in her bag and gave him a stale piece of bread she had packed that morning.

There was something in his eyes that scared her. 'Stepan Ivanovich, where is your daughter? Your grandson? Are they well?'

He looked at her as if she spoke a language he didn't understand. Stuffing the bread in his mouth, he sauntered back towards one of the tables, picking up an empty plate. Natasha looked away. Even the sight of Hitler watching her sombrely from his wall was infinitely preferable to the sight of her grandfather's old friend, a respected professor at the university, as he searched other people's plates for scraps to eat.

In the evening, Natasha asked her supervisor if he wanted her to lock up. The middle-aged balding man looked at her with disdain and said in Ukrainian, 'Don't speak Russian to me again. You're not in Moscow. This is Ukraine. From now on, address me in Ukrainian.' Natasha didn't want to be the one to tell him that there was no Ukraine, there were only Soviet territories occupied by Hitler. She didn't know how to say it in Ukrainian, so she said nothing. 'Yes, lock up after you're done,' he barked.

When Natasha thought her spirits couldn't sink any lower, Mark came to see her, and she felt her heart soar and her long day melt away. She had a wet mop in her hands and when she saw him, she let it fall to the floor and rushed into his arms. He pulled her close, kissing her on the lips. 'Wait,' she giggled. 'Let me wash my hands. I'm all dirty.'

He didn't let go. 'I don't mind,' he said, laughing. The cafeteria was empty, but for the flustered Natasha, whose heart was racing all the way from Kiev to Lvov and back, and Mark, who was holding her so tight, it hurt her to breathe. Her hair was hidden under a kerchief, and she wore an unbecoming pair of dark trousers. They belonged to her mother and were slightly too big for Natasha. But Mark was looking at her as if she had never looked more beautiful. 'I just stopped by to see how your first day was going,' he said. 'And bring you these.' In his rucksack, there was a bag of flour and a bag of barley.

'Thank you,' said Natasha. 'I'll tell Mama I got them at the cafeteria.'

'And look,' said Mark, handing her something wrapped in a piece of paper.

She removed the paper and looked up in surprise. 'Cake! I can't believe it. Where did you get it?' It suddenly occurred to her that she had had nothing at all to eat that day.

'Some factories resumed work,' he replied. 'As well as weapons and bread for the Germans, they're making cakes.'

'It's as if life is returning to normal,' she said. Except there was nothing normal about a life in which Natasha mopped the floors in a cafeteria filled with starving Soviets, most of them women and children, under the watchful eye of Hitler's portrait on the wall. Even though it was getting dark, out of the corner of her eye she could still see him. Was it her imagination, or did the Führer smirk at her from the confines of his wooden frame?

'How was work?' asked Mark.

Why was he looking at her like that? 'What?' exclaimed Natasha, blinking fast. 'Do I have cake on my face? What is it?'

He shook his head, but she wiped her face anyway. 'Work was…' What to tell him? Did he need to know about the incessant stream of the hungry and the destitute, of frantic children pleading with tears in their eyes for just one spoonful of potato, of broth, of something, anything to soothe their aching stomachs, of frantic Natasha begging the cook for a spoonful of something, anything to give to the crying children and of the cook telling her that not only could she lose her job but she could be shot for stealing food? 'It was okay.' When she said that, she didn't meet his eyes. 'I'm exhausted but it's better than sitting at home doing nothing. How was your day?'

'Quiet, thankfully. I was translating some documents.' She peered at him closely, at his tired eyes, his weary but smiling mouth. Was there something he was hiding from her, too? He pointed at the mop and asked, 'Can I help you with anything?'

She nodded. 'Yes, thank you. I'm almost done.'

Mark fetched some water from the pump and mopped the floor while she cleared the dishes. She wiped and washed and scrubbed until her hands were blister red. When Mark was done with the floor, he came up close behind her and put his hands around her. She dropped the dishrag she was holding. Slowly he stroked her arms. Without a word, she turned around and looked into his face. He kissed her then, running his hands through her hair. She felt light-headed and giddy, the way she would feel riding a bicycle at a high speed down a steep slope when she was a child. She felt childish now, being close to him and not knowing what to do. He put his hands under her blouse and touched the bare skin of her back. He stroked her hips and the nape of her neck.

She stood in front of him in silence, her hands raw, her heart raw. His fingers under her blouse stroked the soft skin of her stomach, moving higher and higher, finally circling her nipples. Big circles, smaller circles, faster and faster, while his lips on hers never stopped, kissing her with such force, such abandon that she couldn't help it, she groaned. She felt something unfold inside her, unfold and engulf and spiral out of control.

'You've never done this before, have you?' he whispered.

Her cheeks burnt. She didn't reply.

'Look at you. You are so unbelievably beautiful.' His voice was hoarse. 'We can go as slow as you want. We won't do anything until you are ready, okay?'

'Okay,' she whispered faintly.

'You want me to stop?'

'I don't know,' she said.

He kissed her neck, kissed the base of her breasts, pulling her blouse off. Loud voices were heard outside. She held onto her blouse, pushing him away. 'Stop,' she whispered.

Somehow, he took his hands and his lips away. A part of her felt relieved but another, bigger part craved his touch. She breathed softly, shallowly. He sat down on the cold floor and rested against the wall, motioning for her to join him.

Their bodies intertwined, her head on his chest, his heart beating into her cheek, his fingers stroking the palm of her hand, he smiled and reached into his backpack. 'What's that?' asked Natasha when he showed her a book.

'You don't recognise it?'

It was too dark to see. He found his torch. In the circle of light, she looked at the cover.

'Is it *The Count of Monte Cristo*?' She faintly remembered the day she had found the book in the snow.

He nodded. His arm around her, he flipped through the book, not stopping until the last page. 'Listen to this. I love this part.' His face serious and his eyes sad, he read, '"Until the day when God shall design to reveal the future to man, all human wisdom is summed up in these two words – wait and hope."'

'Wait and hope,' she repeated. 'Isn't that what our life is all about? Especially now.' He didn't reply. He was watching her with a smile on his face. Remembering his fervent hands on her bare breasts, she blushed. 'Do you carry this book with you everywhere you go?'

Without saying a word he nodded and moved closer, his lips on hers, his hands on her back, burning her.

She groaned. He stopped. But she couldn't stop blushing.

Blinking fast, she said, 'I love *The Count of Monte Cristo* but I don't know if I agree with Dumas' concept of revenge, of taking justice into your own hands, deciding the destinies of others. Shouldn't it be up to God?'

'I don't think Dumas approves of revenge, either. Not revenge that knows no boundaries, no limits, the kind that takes over your life until there's nothing left. Which is why his book ends on a note of forgiveness, on the importance of letting go.'

'It makes you wonder whether absolute evil exists. Or whether darkness has redeeming qualities, just like everything else. Dumas certainly thought so.'

'What do you think? Does Nazism have redeeming qualities?'

'No, not Nazism.' She touched the cover of *The Count of Monte Cristo*. It was stained with mud, with snow. 'Such a beautiful novel and so tragic. Such love and such betrayal,' she whispered.

'All great love stories are tragic. The classics knew it well. Dumas, Pushkin, Tolstoy.'

Kissing his unshaven chin, she said, 'Did you know that, just like in *The Count of Monte Cristo*, there's a treasure hidden right here, in Kiev? Centuries ago, there was a group of outlaws living in the caves of Pechersk Lavra. They'd buried all the money they had stolen and no one's found it yet.'

'How do you know this?'

'My mama told me when I was a child.'

'Does your mama know where the treasure is?'

'Hmm. We went looking for it when we were children. Stanislav, Lisa, me.' She held her breath. 'And Olga,' she added in a tiny whisper.

'What about Nikolai?'

'He was too young for treasure hunts.'

'Did you find anything?'

'We didn't get very far. But we did come back with a bucketful of apples. It was the season for them.'

The torch and the book back in his rucksack, they clung to each other in the dark, whispering unconnected words into each other's mouths. It was long past curfew when Mark walked Natasha home, but she wasn't scared. She knew that nothing bad could happen to her while he was by her side. When they said goodbye at the entrance to her building, she stood in the doorway and watched him walk away until she could no longer see him.

*

Home was just as dim, just as colourless as the cafeteria. The colour faded from Mother's face as she sat at the kitchen table, sobbing into her hands, surrounded by sombre faces. Everyone was in the kitchen. Everyone except Father.

'Mama, what happened? Where is Papa?' demanded Natasha.

Mother cried and didn't answer. Lisa cried and didn't raise her eyes. It was Grandfather who said, 'Your papa was arrested an hour ago.'

Natasha sank into a chair. It was her father's favourite chair and normally she wouldn't dream of sitting in it, but her legs refused to support her. It was the chair or the floor. 'Arrested? Arrested for what?' No one replied. 'Arrested why?' she repeated, louder.

'He confronted the Nazi supervisors for not letting the men take a break for food and water. Timofei, who was with him at the time, said he was magnificent, talking to them as if they were his subordinates in the militia,' explained Grandfather sadly.

Natasha could imagine her father's face as he squared up to the Nazis, demanding fair treatment for his fellow workers. It was so typical of him, to succumb to his anger without a thought for his safety. He was never one to accept injustice. Never one for caution, either, raising his voice first and thinking of consequences second.

In bed that night, Natasha prayed for sleep the way she had once prayed for the war to end. Sleep was oblivion, albeit temporary. She prayed and thought of her father. Although they had their disagreements, she knew in her heart that he loved her very much. In his own distant way, he had always been there for her. It was her father who had taken Natasha and Lisa ice skating in winter and rowing on the river in summer. It was her father who had helped her and Lisa with their maths homework. When she was seven, he'd taught her and Lisa how to play chess, even though Mother said they were too young. When she turned eight, he gave her a bicycle and taught her and Lisa how to ride. What she said to him that morning was unforgivable. If only she could see him one more time and tell him how sorry she was.

Chapter 9 – The Icy Fortress

November 1941

Natasha heard from a neighbour that most of the prisoners arrested that week had been taken to Brovary, a prison camp across the river. 'It's one of the biggest camps in Kiev. Our Papa must be there,' Natasha said to her mother, who hadn't moved from Father's favourite couch, his pillow under her head. She looked like she hadn't slept since Father had been arrested. Natasha wanted to put her arms around her mother, to comfort her, to inject some life into her dull face. But nothing she could say would make her feel better. Having met Father when they were both fourteen, she had never been apart from him. Now that he was gone, she looked lost and confused, as if without him by her side she didn't know how to go on.

At five on Saturday morning, Natasha packed what little bread they had, and the four of them set out for the prison camp, leaving Grandfather and Mikhail at home.

As they made their way towards the river, covering their faces with scarfs to protect them from the blizzard, Natasha noticed a group of German soldiers, who were pulling their cannon with oxen. She paused, transfixed. She had never seen an ox on the streets of Kiev before.

'What, German trucks don't start in this weather?' muttered Lisa.

'Serves them right,' exclaimed Natasha. 'If our army doesn't finish them off, maybe the cold will.'

'Not much chance of that,' said Nikolai, pointing at the fur hats and sheepskin coats the Germans were wearing. 'They're warmer than we are.'

Mother remained quiet but shook her fist in the direction of the soldiers. Fortunately, they were too busy with the cannon to notice.

Brovary was on the opposite bank of the Dnieper. Although snow hadn't settled yet, the river was frozen in places. It was unprecedented for the ice to form on the Dnieper before February. But the mighty river, so beautiful and full of life as it flowed steadily towards the Black Sea, had stopped dead, just like Kiev had stopped dead the day Hitler's troops marched through its petrified streets.

Natasha pulled Nikolai by the sleeve of his oversized jacket. 'Remember, we built a swing on that tree over there?'

'I remember. We used it to catapult ourselves into the river. It was such fun.'

'It was. You loved it so much, you wouldn't let anyone else have a go.'

'I was a child then.'

'It was only a year ago.'

'Exactly.' He was no longer smiling. 'Remember, Lisa got so scared, she refused to let go of the rope? She never did jump in the river. Alexei had to help her down.'

Natasha nodded and glanced at her sister. At the mention of Alexei, Lisa paled and looked at the spot where what seemed like a lifetime ago five carefree teenagers were enjoying what was to be their last carefree summer. Something in Lisa's eyes looked broken.

Natasha thought with longing of summers past, of scorching afternoons filled with laughter and childish abandon. She glanced at the dead cattle scattered along the riverbank, at the sombre faces of everyone around her. So far removed was this reality from her childhood memories, so alien was this landscape she knew so well, Natasha wondered whether it was real or a terrible dream from which they would soon wake up.

Half a dozen boats made their slow way through patches of river untouched by the ice. It seemed to Natasha that the whole female population of Kiev was gathered on the bank, waiting to cross. The Smirnovs joined the queue. Mother put her arm around Natasha, and together they stared at the dull river. Natasha didn't cry. It was too cold to cry. She whispered, 'Oh Mama. I feel awful. Why did I have to say such terrible things to Papa? I don't want the last words we ever exchanged to be bitter.'

Mother shuddered. 'Don't say that. Your father will be back. One way or another.'

'You think so?

'I know so.' And a bit quieter, 'I have to believe it.' On the icy riverbank Mother held Natasha. 'You know, when you were two and sick with pneumonia, your father stayed in hospital with you for a week. He read to you and fed you and didn't sleep for many nights. And when one of the nurses told him to go home, you know what he said?'

'What did he say?'

'That they would have to drug him to force him to leave you.' Through her tears Mother smiled. 'No matter what you said to each other, no matter how upset you were at one another, he knows that you love him very much. And he loves you.'

It took the family three hours to get a boat. And when they did, so many people piled in, the boat almost sank. They made it across safely, but the cabin flooded, and Natasha's boots filled with water.

In Brovary, hundreds of women and children were searching

for those they loved, just like Natasha and her family were searching for the one they loved. A few hundred men crouched behind barbed wire, huddled close to stay warm. The prisoners were a sorry sight. Barefoot, their feet red and swollen, they raised their eyes to women and begged for food. They drank from puddles on the ground and threw themselves at the food offered by women and children as if it was the last thing standing between them and death. They ate the potatoes raw before the German rifles came down on their backs. The Nazis grabbed the women, hit them and pushed them out of the way. And still it wasn't enough to deter them from coming close to the men. The noise was deafening. Transfixed, Natasha watched the commotion, watched as one of Dante's nine circles of hell came to life right in front of her.

'The trick is to wait for the sentry to look away and then pass the food to the prisoners,' whispered Nikolai.

'Why are you whispering?' demanded Lisa.

'Can you see Papa?' asked Mother.

They looked and looked. Natasha stood on her tiptoes, eyes watering in the wind, but she was too small to see behind the prisoners. Hunched and destitute, they were still taller than her. The Smirnovs walked up and down the camp, expecting any minute to catch a glimpse of the familiar face, of a disdainful mouth, a headful of brown hair. There was no sign of him. Soon more boats arrived and more women came, pushing them away. The curfew was now five o'clock. They couldn't stay in Brovary any longer. Dejected, they meandered back. Natasha closed her eyes to not see the dead cattle on the bank, to not see her mother's tears. She wondered how her father was going to survive the prison camp, because no one could live with what they had just witnessed for long.

*

The Smirnovs were not going to give up so easily. Their father needed them, wherever he was, and they were going to find him, if only to see his face one more time and to tell him to hold on. As they were getting ready to leave for Brovary the next morning, the doorbell rang. Natasha opened the door to one of their neighbours, a shrivelled old lady who lived on the third floor. 'I heard you were going to the prison camp,' she croaked. 'My son is there. Would you be kind enough to take a note for him? And here are some eggs. If you could take them for him, too, I would be very grateful. I would go myself but...' She pointed at her left leg that was a few inches shorter than her right.

Lisa pushed Natasha out of the way and glared at the old woman. 'Leave my sister alone,' she said. 'It's too dangerous. The guards beat you for passing notes to prisoners.' She slammed the door in the woman's face.

'Lisa, don't be cruel. I'd be willing to help her.'

Lisa shrugged as if to say, *suit yourself*.

Natasha ran after the woman, who had barely made it down one flight of stairs. 'Wait! I'll take the note. And the eggs.'

'Thank you, my dear,' said the old woman. 'Thank you for your trouble.'

'It's no trouble at all.'

'God bless you for your kind heart.' She made a sign of cross on Natasha. 'My name is Claudia. If you ever need anything, anything at all...'

'How are we going to find your son?'

'His name's on the envelope. Just give the letter to the first prisoners you see and ask them to pass it on.'

Natasha spent the next twenty minutes writing her own letter to her father, ripping up one draft after another. Nothing she said seemed adequate. In the end, she wrote, 'Dear Papa, I'm sorry for what I said. I didn't mean it. Please come back soon. Love you and miss you, Natasha.'

The word soon spread, and by the time the Smirnovs were

ready to leave, Mother had collected a large bag of food from the neighbours, and Natasha had two dozen notes for prisoners. It seemed every family in the building had a son, a husband or a father in the camp.

Even before they crossed the river, they knew something was wrong. Instead of going to the camp, people were walking away from it, carrying their provisions, their meatless soup, their frost-bitten potatoes, their butter-less porridge. The camp had moved, everybody said. Natasha and her family refused to believe it. They crossed the river just like they had done the day before. Unlike the previous day, however, the boat was almost empty. On the other side of the river, the Smirnovs walked in silence next to half a dozen women.

'Where are you going?' asked an old man, who was returning to the city. 'There are no prisoners left in Brovary. No one there at all.'

'Where did they take them?' Mother wanted to know.

But the man only shrugged.

'I'm not giving up,' said an old woman wearing a string of onions around her neck. 'My grandson is there. He's got pneumonia after sleeping out in the open for too long. If I don't bring him food, he'll die.' She looked as if she was near death's door herself. She could barely walk, and yet she kept going. The Smirnovs walked next to her.

Where only a day ago there was hell on earth, was now nothing but silence. Nothing but barren land. Only barbed wire and half a dozen dead bodies remained. Natasha couldn't look at the bodies but she couldn't look at her mother's face either. She looked away, back at the river, gloomy and grey, and her tears stung her cheeks in the cold. She folded and unfolded the envelope meant for her father.

Lisa hugged her close. 'Don't worry,' she whispered. 'Whatever you said in your letter, deep in his heart he already knows it.'

Silently they made their way back.

When they reached Podol, Mother joined a queue at one of the stores, hoping for some bread. Natasha suspected she wanted to be alone, so she could cry for her husband unobserved.

The brother and sisters continued home. On Spasskaya Street, they saw a large crowd gathered around a group of prisoners. They approached the prisoners, and Natasha looked into every gaunt face, hoping and praying that her father was among them.

He wasn't.

A woman in the crowd next to Natasha said, 'They're Red Army soldiers. Germans left them here to convince us our army's been defeated.'

'They'll need more than a handful of starved men to convince us of that,' mumbled Natasha.

The prisoner closest to them was unconscious. He was flat on the ground and his head, only a few centimetres from Natasha's foot, rested in a puddle of water. No one had dared to help him up. A Nazi officer stepped over the soldier, pushing him with his boot. Natasha waited for the German to disappear before she whispered, 'Let's drag him to safety.'

Lisa glared at her. 'Drag him where? Are you out of your mind?'

'If we don't and the Germans return, he won't be able to walk and they'll shoot him. He'll die.'

'And what about our safety?' demanded Lisa.

Nikolai interrupted, 'Natasha is right. We can't leave him here.'

'You think I'm going to risk my life for a complete stranger?' Lisa sneered.

'A complete stranger who almost lost his life fighting to protect you from the Germans.' Nikolai glared at Lisa the same way Lisa had been glaring at Natasha a few seconds earlier. Lisa turned away.

Natasha said, 'Just imagine if it was Stanislav or Papa. Imagine if they were in trouble and no one volunteered to help them.'

Lisa mumbled, 'Do what you want. I'm going home.'

Nikolai and Natasha watched Lisa until she disappeared behind a building. 'What's the matter with Lisa?' asked Nikolai. 'She's never been like this before.'

'Alexei is the matter with Lisa,' said Natasha.

The two of them pulled the soldier towards a nearby yard, concealing his unconscious body behind a wooden shed. Nikolai said, 'We should wait till it's dark to get him home.'

'And get detained for breaking the curfew? Why don't we just carry him through the back streets?'

'And if we are stopped?'

'We can say he's our brother who's been wounded. He's not wearing a uniform. No one will know he's a soldier in the Red Army. But we'll need help. We can't carry him ourselves. He's too heavy.'

'I'll find someone,' said Nikolai, turning on his heel and disappearing in the direction of home.

At first, Natasha watched the road, praying that Nikolai would come back before a Nazi patrol did. Then she examined the soldier. He was tall and broad-shouldered. Through his tattered clothes she could see the wiry muscles of his arms. It was impossible to say what colour hair he had. His face and body were covered in dirt. His forehead was bleeding as if he had been struck with a blunt weapon, possibly a rifle.

While Natasha was studying him, the soldier groaned and opened his eyes. They were the eyes of an old man on a young man's face. The colour of his eyes, green like the grass, looked especially striking on his grimy face. Natasha wondered what he'd been through to be able look at her with *that* expression. She took his hand and said, 'Don't worry, you're safe. I'm just waiting for my brother, and then we'll carry you home.'

'Who are you?' His voice was that of an old man too, hoarse and dull and without hope.

'My name is Natasha. We'll look after you. I wish I had some food or water but I don't. Can you wait till we get home? You can stay with us till you feel better.'

'Thank you,' he croaked and closed his eyes again.

'What's your name?' Natasha wanted to keep the soldier talking. She didn't want him to fall asleep, leaving her alone in the deserted yard.

'Yuri. Yuri Korovin.'

'Are you a soldier in the Red Army?'

He nodded. 'I was.'

Yuri was about to say something else when Nikolai returned with a neighbour, and together they carried the soldier to Ilinskaya Street. Mother, who had returned from the store empty-handed, moved her belongings into the room Natasha and Lisa shared with Nikolai, giving up her couch to the rescued prisoner.

Nikolai helped the soldier to the bathroom, where he washed and changed into some of Father's clothes. After he had a piece of bread, Yuri stretched out on the couch and pointed to a book on the table. '*War and Peace*. My favourite.'

'Mine too,' said Natasha.

'I like your name. Natasha Rostova is my favourite character.'

'Mine too,' she said quietly.

'Please, can you do me a favour?'

'Of course. Anything.'

'Read to me till I fall asleep. Unless you have something else to do.'

'It will be my pleasure.'

As she read late into the night, Natasha thought, *What a miracle to have a Red Army soldier asleep under our roof*. It was a good sign, she was sure of it. Every time she stopped reading, thinking Yuri had fallen asleep, he opened his eyes and said, 'Please, don't stop. I love this part. Read some more.' And she did.

*

Was it Natasha's imagination or had time slowed down, finally coming to a halt around four in the afternoon? From the moment

163

she stepped through the cafeteria doors, she watched the clock that counted down the seconds next to the portrait of Hitler on the wall. She counted down with it, and this was how she knew that the thin metal hand took twice as long as normal to make a full circle around the dial. Today her hands shook so badly – in impatience, in anticipation – she dropped two plates and a tea cup. Fortunately, only one of the plates broke. As she thought of Mark's hands on her breasts, she blushed and her stomach churned with nerves.

As soon as he walked in, he told her to put her coat on and follow him. 'Where are we going?' she demanded as they made their way through the dark streets. It was so cold, she could see her breath as she spoke.

'It's a surprise.'

He tightened his fingers around hers, and instantly she felt warmer. 'You have a surprise for me? What is it?'

'If I tell you, it will no longer be a surprise.'

'How far is it?'

'Not too far.'

'How long do we have to walk?'

'Ten minutes at most.'

'Tell me what it is!'

'I'm not telling you,' he said, smiling from ear to ear. 'You are going to have to wait.'

'But I want to know now.'

'You can't wait ten minutes?'

Increasing her pace, she tried to keep up with Mark. She felt a warm trickle of excitement spreading inside her, as if they were just a regular couple in love with not a care in the world. But then a Nazi patrol barged its way past, and a chill ran through her. 'Mark, do you know where the Brovary prison camp has moved to?' she asked.

'The Germans are taking the prisoners outside of Kiev. Where, I don't know.'

'They are taking them away? Why?'

'I guess they don't want anyone to witness the abysmal conditions of the camps.'

'It's too late. That camp was...' She paused, unable to find words gruesome enough to describe what she had seen.

'I know. Apparently the cries of starving, freezing prisoners were keeping Kievans awake at night. And every morning there were hundreds of corpses on the ground.'

'But why move the prisoners? Since when do they care about what we think?' She thought of the thousands of innocents that had been marched to the ravines of Babi Yar. Marched in broad daylight, in front of everyone.

'They don't. They're killing all the disabled and mentally ill people at Kirillov Hospital as we speak. But these are prisoners of war. It's different.'

She trembled. 'They are killing the disabled people?'

'Using deadly gas in specially designed vans.'

'Oh my God!' She squeezed her eyes shut in horror and almost tripped on the ice.

He held her up. 'I have more bad news. Donbas and Yalta are in Hitler's hands.'

Yalta was a resort town on the northern coast of the Black Sea. Natasha, who had never seen the sea before, had always dreamt of visiting it.

'That means all of Ukraine is now occupied.'

She couldn't believe it, didn't want to believe it. 'All of Ukraine? Are you sure?'

'Afraid so. But Leningrad and Moscow are still holding.'

'That's good news.' She sighed.

There must have been something in her voice, a sadness that had caught his attention. He looked at her closely. 'Why did you ask about the prison camp? What happened?'

Crying, she told him about the fight with her father and the arrest, and how they combed every inch of Brovary prisoner camp looking for him. He pressed her hand gently. 'I'm sorry about your father,' he whispered.

'I know,' she said, reaching for him. 'So am I.'

'Your mama is right, you know. No matter what you said to each other, he knows how much you love him.'

'I'm sure he does,' she said, barely audible, not at all sure. 'I have more news.' She told him about the Red Army soldier they had rescued on the way back from Brovary.

When she finished, Mark said, 'That's an amazing thing you've done for that man. Where did he fight?'

'I don't know. He was still asleep this morning when I left for work. Imagine if he knows Stanislav. Wouldn't that be wonderful?' Natasha could see the outline of his face in the light of a street lamp. She was no longer crying. How could she, when he was looking at her with such love, such tenderness, such wonder? 'What is it? Why are you looking at me like that?'

He pulled her closer. 'Natasha, I've never met anyone as caring and unselfish as you. Here you are, saying goodbye to your brother, losing your grandmother, your best friend, your father, starved, scared, with no means to survive, and yet, not once did I hear you complain. Instead, you help others. You have the kindest heart of anyone I know.'

'I don't have the kindest heart.' She blushed. 'You do.'

'Do you have any idea how much I love you?'

'And I love you,' she whispered.

He paused in a dark doorway. 'We are here,' he said, reaching into his pocket for a key and unlocking the door.

'What is this place?' she asked as they walked in. When Mark pulled the light switch, she found herself in a ghostly forest of flowers, old and dry, with petals wilted and limp. They seemed to reach for her, clinging to life even in death.

'An old florist shop. When I came across it, I thought you would like it.'

'It's so spooky in here!' She shivered.

'But in a beautiful way. Look at all these flowers. It's like they are frozen in time.'

'Yes, it looks like a graveyard of old flowers. I personally prefer them fresh.'

'You do? Wait here for me.'

He disappeared through the back door and she waited impatiently, pacing on the spot and rubbing her hands to warm up. Finally he invited her in, and when she walked through the door, she gasped in wonder. The room was cosy and warm, with a fire cracking in the fireplace. In its dancing light, Natasha could see flowers everywhere – fresh roses, carnations and daisies. The room was filled with them. On the floor and on the table, on the shelves and on the mantelpiece, there were vases and bouquets. Rose petals were strewn on the floor, forming a shape of a heart. On the table, in what little space remained between the flowers, someone had laid out a feast, with white bread, sausages and cheese, smoked fish, chocolate and sweets.

'You did all this for me?' she exclaimed.

He nodded. 'It's almost two months since we met. I wanted to do something special.'

'But I don't understand. Where did you find fresh flowers in November?'

'I can't tell you that.' He laughed.

'Why not?'

'Because then you'd know all my secrets.'

'I can't believe you would do this for me.'

'I wish I could do more. I wish I could bring you flowers every day.'

He made some tea on the portable stove in the corner of the room and they sat down to eat. Natasha devoured the food as if she hadn't eaten in days, while Mark hardly touched anything. 'Thank you so much,' she said to him, suddenly shy.

'You are welcome.' He pulled her closer and undid the rubber

167

band that held her hair in place. She wore a long skirt and her mother's blouse. She was glad she'd had time to scrub her hands clean and apply some lipstick. She kissed him. 'I missed you at the weekend.'

'I missed you, too.' He let go of her for a second, reaching into his rucksack. 'I have another surprise for you.'

'More surprises? You are spoiling me. What is it?'

'Guess.'

'Is it a book?'

'No.'

'Is it edible?'

'No.' He laughed and pinched her. She fell quiet, watching him. He said, 'Do you give up?'

'Never! Is it something I would like?'

'I hope so.'

'Is it... Let's see... Is it a puppy?'

His eyes widened. 'A puppy? No. I don't have a puppy here with me or you would have heard it barking by now.'

'What is it then? Tell me.'

'Do you give up?'

'Never! Is it a cake?'

'Cake is edible. Therefore, it's not cake. Do you give up?'

She nodded.

He nudged her. 'Come on, say it.'

She pushed him with her fists but said, 'I give up.'

'Good. Now close your eyes.'

She did as he said. A second later she felt a smooth, possibly wooden, object in her hands. This object rattled when she shook it. She opened her eyes and cried, 'A chessboard! Where did you get it?'

'Borrowed from my commanding officer. He never goes anywhere without his chess.'

She undid the metal strap and opened the box. 'I haven't played in ages. Years. Father taught us how to play when we were little.'

At the thought of her father, she felt tears swell up in her eyes. She blinked them away.

'Still remember how?'

'Hopefully I remember enough to beat you.'

He laughed. 'It might be easier than you think.'

'Why is that?'

'I've never played before.'

'Never played chess?'

'No.'

'What do they teach you in Hungary?'

'Not much.' He found his torch in his rucksack. 'You'll have to show me how the game works.'

'Under one condition.'

'What is it?'

'I'll teach you if you tell me where the flowers came from.'

'Do you really want to know?' He was teasing her. She could see it in his eyes.

'If you want to learn how to play chess, you'd better tell me.'

'An old woman who lives not far from our barracks grows flowers in a greenhouse. It's her passion. She says while there are flowers, there's life.'

'She's right,' said Natasha, touching the stem of a rose. 'They are so beautiful, so full of life. And she let you have some?'

'In exchange for food, yes. Now, why are you crying?'

'No one's ever given me flowers before.'

She couldn't take the intensity in his face. Shyly she turned away from him and towards the table. The chess set was unlike any she had ever seen before. The pieces were large, heavy and elaborately carved. She looked at them in wonder. Finally, she said, 'Pick a colour. Black or white? Which one do you want?'

'White.'

'Oh no you don't. Let's do it the proper way.' She took one white piece and one black piece and hid them behind her back. 'Which hand?'

'Left.'

She opened her left fist. 'Damn it. Okay, you get to be white.'

'What does that mean?'

'You go first.' She separated the pieces by colour and set up the board. 'You have eight pawns, one king, one queen, two rooks and two knights. Oh yes, and two bishops.'

'Sounds complicated.'

'Not really.' She laughed at the confounded expression on his face.

'What is the aim of the game?'

She chuckled. 'You really don't know anything about chess, do you?'

'I told you. So what do I do?'

'Protect your king at all times.'

'Which one is the king again?' His eyes twinkled. She couldn't tell if he was serious or if he was teasing her.

'The one wearing the crown,' she said.

'Okay, I understand.'

'Are you sure? You look confused... Ready to play? It's your go first.'

'What do I do?'

'Move your pawn two squares forward.'

'Which one? I have eight.'

'Start with this one.' She pointed at the pawn in the middle of the board.

'Why this one?'

'Just do it. Don't ask questions.'

He held her gaze as he moved the pawn forward. 'What kind of teacher are you? Alright, done.' Then he pulled her closer across the chessboard, squeezing her. She frowned. 'Be serious. Don't distract me. I need to decide on my strategy.' She moved her own pawn.

'Me again?' He moved the same pawn another two squares.

She grabbed his hand just as he was about to put the pawn

down. 'You can't do that. You can only move one square.' Taking the piece from him, she placed it back.

'Hold on, what are you doing? You told me the pawn moved two squares…'

'Only on the first move.'

'You're cheating. Making up the rules as you go along.' He pinched her.

She pinched him back. 'You think I need to make up rules to beat you in chess?'

They continued playing. In ten minutes Mark lost half his pieces. Natasha lost one rook. She looked at the board, considering her next move. 'Wait a second,' she exclaimed. 'Where did my knight go?'

'What's a knight? What does it look like?'

'Just because you lost both of yours…' She shoved him. 'It looks like this.' She pointed at his knight that was now lying defeated on the floor. 'Where is it?'

'Haven't seen it.' He struggled to keep a straight face.

'You're such a liar. I had it a minute ago. What did you do with it?' She looked around, checking under his rucksack and lifting the chessboard, careful not to disturb the pieces.

She could tell he was trying not to laugh. 'I don't know what you mean. Not my fault if you can't keep track of your own knight.'

'I won't play if you steal my pieces.' She pouted.

'But that's the only way I can win.' Finally, he looked like he couldn't stand it anymore. He burst out laughing.

'Come on, tell me. Where did you hide it?'

'Haven't seen it,' he repeated.

'And if I search you?'

'Go ahead.'

She climbed over the chessboard, knocking the pieces out of position. Finally settling on his lap, she tickled him under his shirt.

'Here it is. I knew it. You were sitting on it. Cheater!' She pushed him as hard as she could. 'That's it, you lose.'

He lifted her up, bringing her close. 'I lose, do I? I have a beautiful girl sitting in my lap. Does that sound like losing to you?'

'Loser,' whispered Natasha, no longer thinking of chess.

The chessboard was all but forgotten on the floor. She longed to feel his hands on her bare back. She longed for his touch but was too afraid to ask.

She didn't have to. His hands slipped under her blouse, caressing her with a perplexing familiarity, as if he had touched her like this, naked under his fingers, many times before.

This time she didn't hesitate, stroking him through his clothes. His body was strong and muscular. Feeling brave, she unbuttoned his shirt and pulled at it until he removed it. Natasha looked in wonder at his bare chest and his bare arms. She had never seen him naked before. Never seen any man naked other than her brothers when they were children. Giddy and disoriented, she could barely sit up straight.

Gently he lowered her on the floor. 'Ouch,' she whispered.

'What is it?'

'The knight.'

He removed the chess piece, and they kissed. He was on top of her, she was underneath him. Seconds, minutes passed. 'Are you sure about this?' he whispered.

She couldn't, wouldn't answer. Even though she had never been more sure of anything in her entire life. Even though she craved him like she had never craved anything before. He must have taken her silence as a yes. Undoing the buttons of her blouse, he slipped it off. As he did that, his hands trembled, just like hers. He removed her skirt. She was next to him in nothing but her stockings and underwear.

'I can't believe how beautiful you are. Are you nervous?' he whispered. She shook her head but it didn't fool him. 'Don't be. We don't have to do this if you don't want to.'

'I want to,' she said, and her voice quivered. Did he hear her? He was watching her and not moving, as if waiting for something. She nudged him and pulled him closer. She didn't want to wait any longer.

'We can go as slow as you want. Anytime you want me to stop, just tell me.' His hands were on her, probing, touching, stroking. His lips tickled her, light kisses like butterfly wings in her hair, on her cheeks and on her mouth. Before she knew it, she was naked on the cold floor. Bare in front of him. Even though she was burning inside, she shivered. 'Come here,' he said, helping her up and guiding her to the couch. Standing in front of her, he undressed quickly. When she saw him naked next to her, she gasped.

He whispered, 'Natasha, you are the best thing that's ever happened to me. Please, don't be scared. I'll never hurt you.'

'I'm not scared,' she replied, wanting him to touch her again, feeling cold where his warm hands had just been.

'Then why are you trembling?'

'I'm not.' She trembled.

His lips were on her neck. 'Why are you crying?'

'I'm just so happy. I love you.'

'Please, don't cry. Don't you know how much I love you?' he asked, leaning over her. She nodded and placed a hand on his chest. She could feel his heart beating fast.

When he brought himself on top of her, she squeezed her eyes in fear. And then she felt his lips on her eyelids and opened her eyes.

'Ready?' he whispered.

Everything else ceased to exist. The war, the hunger, the fear. All she could see, all she could feel was him. She was enthralled, captivated by him, forever. Her old life, her new life, she forgot it all right there as Mark made love to her for the first time.

'Put your legs around me,' he whispered. She tried to do as he said but couldn't, so she wrapped her arms around him instead.

She watched his face as his breathing became heavier, struggling for her own breath. When he stopped, still panting, still clasping her in his arms, she touched his lips with hers, not wanting it to be over just yet. Wanting the exquisite pain to last. They lay in each other's arms, kissing deeply. She was no longer scared or shy around him, and so she traced his skin with her fingertips.

'I love you,' she whispered.

'I love you too.'

Chapter 10 – At the Crossroads

December 1941

A thick blanket of snow covered the streets in December and all of a sudden, Kiev looked fairy-tale beautiful again, just like it did before the war. On the way home from work Natasha would pretend that once again their city was free. That she was free. But then a Nazi officer would stroll past and glare at Natasha. She would see a dead body in a snowdrift or a building so blackened by the fire that no amount of snow could disguise it. And Natasha would no longer be able to pretend.

One day, in the second week of December, she was brushing the snow off her coat, having just walked in, when Nikolai motioned her into the kitchen, his mouth twitching in excitement.

'What is it, Nikolai? Let me take my coat off.'

'I need to talk to you.'

'Wait, I'm covered in snow.'

Nikolai paid no attention to Natasha. He tap-danced on the spot, his feet moving to some rapid tune that he alone could hear. 'Did you know Yuri is a partisan?' His usually steady voice sounded high-pitched.

'I didn't know that.'

'Well, he is. He told me himself.'

'What else did Yuri tell you?'

'That he has managed to get a fake passport. He doesn't have to hide anymore.' Nikolai's face grew serious. 'I've been thinking about it for a while now. I'm going to ask Yuri if I can join.'

'Join what?' asked Natasha, absentmindedly undoing her shoe laces.

'The partisans, silly.'

That made her look up from her shoes into her brother's eager face. 'You are too young. It's dangerous.'

Nikolai jumped on the spot, pretend-sparring with an invisible opponent. 'You are never too young to stand up to the enemy.'

Natasha tweaked her brother's ear. 'Don't let Mama hear you talk like that.'

Natasha could understand Nikolai's exhilaration. Having Yuri living with them made her a little exhilarated herself. When he was around, she felt a little less despondent. In his late twenties, he always had a twinkle in his eyes and a smile on his face. Only occasionally would Natasha catch a glimpse of sadness on his face, the sole indication of the ordeal he'd been through. His height, broad shoulders, kind smile, everything was to his advantage. A sergeant in the Red Army, he was taken by the Nazis at the Battle of Kiev with the rest of his regiment. He was the only one of his comrades to survive the prison camp. During long evenings after work, Natasha would sit next to Yuri and Grandfather and Nikolai at the kitchen table, listening to Yuri's stories about the prison camp. He could never talk about it without lighting a cigarette; Natasha could understand why. 'Did anyone ever escape?' she'd asked one day at dinner.

'In the beginning, yes. But nine times out of ten, the Nazis would catch them and shoot them.'

'Did you ever think of running?'

'I did once, yes. Two of my friends and I were all set to go.'

'What happened?'

'They died of dysentery before we had a chance.'

'Oh,' whispered Natasha. Her face fell.

'I'm not complaining. I gave the Nazis a hard time before I was captured. And now thanks to you I can fight them again. What more can I wish for?'

Soon Natasha stopped asking about the prison camp. She didn't want to think of her father living a nightmare day after day, night after night.

Now, Natasha followed her brother to the living room, where Yuri was teaching an indifferent Lisa how to play the Russian Fool. Lisa had just lost a game and was shuffling the cards, muttering unhappily.

'Natasha, Nikolai, come and join us,' said Yuri.

Smiling shyly, Natasha shook her head. 'I don't know how to play.'

'I've never met anyone who didn't know how to play the Russian Fool.'

'Natasha doesn't need to play the Russian Fool. She is the Russian Fool,' said Nikolai, reaching out and pinching her. 'You'll just have to teach her.'

'What do you say, Natasha? Would you like to learn?' asked Yuri.

Nikolai giggled. 'Natasha's a chess player, not a card player. She's far too serious. I'll play, though.'

'I'll play, too.' Natasha sat next to Nikolai. 'If you show me how.'

Yuri explained the rules and they began. Lisa was no longer losing because Natasha was. 'What do I do now? Take another card?' she demanded, wondering why she had agreed to play in the first place.

'I don't think so. You already have a handful.'

'That's not a good thing, is it?'

'Well, no. In a game where the goal is to get rid of the cards, that's not a good thing.' Yuri grinned at Natasha.

'Is it my go?' she asked, dropping her cards, picking them up again, arranging them in ascending order.

'It's my go,' said Lisa, who seemed to be enjoying the game a lot more now.

She chose a card from her neat six-card hand and put it down on the table. 'Yuri, tell her.'

'It *is* her go. You miss a turn. And don't show us your cards. You're supposed to hide them.'

Natasha hid her cards. 'Why is it never my go?'

'Because you lose every hand.' Yuri chuckled. 'You have to win a hand to have a go.'

'It's too complicated.'

'Surely not as complicated as chess?'

Natasha blushed, thinking about the last game of chess she'd played with Mark.

'Let's play the next game open-handed. Then I can help,' said Yuri.

Natasha wasn't sure she wanted to play another game. 'Maybe tomorrow.'

'Dinner's ready,' called Mother from the kitchen. Natasha was relieved. Getting up, she threw her cards on the table.

In the doorway Nikolai pushed past her, whispering loudly, 'Loser!'

Yuri winked and said, 'You know what they say. Unlucky in cards, lucky in love.'

Nikolai chortled. Natasha blushed.

On the way to the kitchen, Lisa pulled Natasha into their bedroom. Closing the door behind them, she whispered conspiratorially, 'I think Yuri likes you!' She sounded surprised, as if Yuri liking her sister was the last thing she expected.

'Don't be silly, Lisa. Of course, he doesn't like me.'

'He does. He's been asking about you.' Lisa gave her a knowing look. It occurred to Natasha she hadn't seen Lisa smile mischievously like this in a very long time. It was as if the old Lisa was back, leaving the new sour-faced and apathetic Lisa behind.

'Really?'

'Yes, really. He asked about your job at the cafeteria.'

'That doesn't mean he likes me.'

'But then he asked whether you had a sweetheart.'

'I don't believe you.' Natasha knew her sister well. Lisa was prone to exaggeration.

'If you don't believe me, ask him.'

'I'm not asking him,' exclaimed Natasha, horrified.

'Why not? I dare you to.'

'Don't be silly, Lisa.'

'Don't you like him?'

'Sure I like him, but only as a friend.'

'He's very handsome.'

'Well, if you think he's handsome, why don't you ask him to take you out?'

Lisa's friendly smile vanished. She stared at Natasha with heartbreak in her eyes, as if her sister had physically assaulted her. 'Alexei has only been gone two months. How can you say that?' Before Natasha could apologise, Lisa added, 'I thought you'd be pleased. It's not like you are seeing anyone. Or are you?'

'Of course not,' mumbled Natasha, but Lisa continued to watch her in silence, as if waiting for something. What was that expression on her face? She looked like she was challenging Natasha, who wasn't up to a challenge, not even a small one.

*

The cafeteria was serving borscht. As Natasha meandered through the cafeteria hall with her eyes half open, she thought of long summer afternoons from her childhood, of Grandmother's borscht of a lifetime ago, meaty and thick with vegetables, generously laden with sour cream and olive oil. The soup Natasha saw in front of her today, however, was different. There was no sour cream, no potatoes, and hardly any meat. It was nothing but hot water, coloured pink by a few thin slices of beetroot.

And yet, Natasha spent all morning eyeing it and at lunch she devoured every spoonful. She couldn't remember the last time she'd had borscht. When she finished her lunch, she was still hungry. She had barely enough energy to put one foot in front of the other as she went about her daily tasks. As November turned into December, it had become harder and harder to get out of bed in the morning, to stay awake, to stay warm, to sustain an illusion of a meaningful existence.

It had become harder and harder to survive.

Natasha mopped and cleaned, when in the far corner of the cafeteria she noticed a man. She wasn't sure what attracted her attention. Was it the way he leaned to one side, his body stiff and lopsided, a half-empty plate in front of him, his hat covering his eyes? Or was it simply the fact that he had been sitting there for too long, not moving and not lifting his spoon? Natasha put her mop down and approached him.

She touched his shoulder. He didn't budge. She addressed him. He didn't reply.

She couldn't see his eyes under the hat. Her hand trembling, she moved the hat to one side. The man stared at her and through her, sorrow frozen on his face forever, his lips constricted in a terrible grimace of a smile. Natasha cried out, letting the hat fall to the floor. Then she crossed herself and called for help.

*

That evening, Mark said, 'I'm so glad I can see you in the evenings. This cafeteria job has been a godsend for us.'

Natasha couldn't bear the look on his affectionate face. She couldn't bear his joy. She turned away. She didn't want to say anything, but the man's chilling stare haunted her. She blinked. 'I saw a dead man today. He died right here at the cafeteria as he was eating his soup. No one noticed until I found him. It's like I'm used to it now. It's all become so normal.'

They sat next to each other on the floor. His arms were around her. 'War,' he said. 'There's nothing normal about it.'

'I remember when having a fight with my mama seemed like the end of the world. I miss those days.'

'I wish I could protect you from all of it. From the war, from the Germans, from the hunger. I wish I could take you away from all of this. One day this war will be over. And you'll be able to go outside and not be afraid. You'll be safe and I won't have to worry about you.'

For a few seconds she watched his face in silence. 'Do you worry about me?'

'Every day.'

'Don't. Nothing's going to happen to me.' She worried about him, too, but didn't want to tell him that.

Outside, the tram rolled past and someone shouted in German. Inside, there was nothing but the tick-tock sound of the clock on the wall. *How strange*, thought Natasha. The clock that was so slow in the mornings sped up in the evenings like a runaway train. The hours rushed by in a matter of minutes.

Mark said, 'I made some enquiries. It looks like most of the prisoners from Brovary were taken to Belaya Zerkov.'

Natasha had heard about the prison camp in Belaya Zerkov. Men didn't last long there at all. How could they, with the guards' bullets, the cold and the hunger, the typhus and dysentery to contend with? Every morning, the Germans removed truckloads of dead bodies, disposing of them in the nearby ravines. 'I don't think we'll ever see our father again,' she whispered. Hiding her face in his tunic, hiding her heartbreak and her fear, she wept.

'You've got to have faith.'

'Faith? To stop the Germans, what we need is a miracle.'

'Miracles can happen. At least now the Red Army soldiers know what's in store for them in the Nazi prison camps.'

'That's a good thing?'

'Definitely. Before, hundreds of thousands surrendered to the Germans. Now, they grit their teeth and fight.'

'They have no choice.'

'Exactly. Germany might still lose this war.'

'Will they, really? They seem undefeatable.' Natasha didn't want to talk about the war anymore. She was on the floor next to Mark, her hands in his, her head on his chest. It wasn't close enough. She climbed into his lap. 'Today is Stanislav's birthday. He's turning twenty-seven. Mama will be so sad. We haven't heard from him in months.'

'Stanislav is fine. Better than fine. He's fed, he's fighting. He's better off than you are.'

'I hope so. All Mama does is cry. Sometimes I dread going home.'

'Then don't. Stay with me.' Mark removed a loose strand of dark hair from her face and kissed her. She kissed him back, closing her eyes. She didn't want the kiss to end.

'I couldn't. I wouldn't want Mama to worry. She worries too much already. Besides, don't you have to get back to the barracks?'

'I do.' He whispered in her ear, 'I wish we didn't have to say goodbye.'

'I know. Sometimes I dream of running away together. Just you and me. Can you imagine?'

'I can imagine. Somewhere like Australia?'

Natasha watched him. His face was impassive. Only his eyes twinkled. She giggled and shoved him. 'Stop teasing me. I can never tell when you're serious and when you're joking.'

'If not Australia, then where?'

'It doesn't matter. Anywhere where there isn't a war on,' she said.

She nestled into his neck. She loved it when he was unshaven. His cheeks felt like sandpaper.

He tickled her through her blouse, and when she didn't react, he put his hands under the thin material and traced her skin with his fingers. Suddenly, she no longer wanted to cry.

*

Though it had been weeks since Mother had been to work, her colleague Ivan stopped by one morning with half a kilo of bread the school had received for the teachers. Natasha divided it into eight parts, thankful for Ivan's kindness. He looked like he could do with some extra bread himself.

In the kitchen, Yuri was slicing and stirring, whistling a war tune under his breath. Mother's apron fastened around his hips, he twirled around their portable gas cooker as if he belonged there. Natasha had never seen a man prepare food before. Her father only ever entered the kitchen to eat, smoke or read his paper, and her brothers didn't even know how the stove worked.

'Where did you learn how to cook?' asked Natasha.

Yuri looked up and winked. 'They teach us everything in the army.'

'Everything?' teased Nikolai, who was pretending to read a book but in reality was watching Yuri's every move.

'What are you making?' asked Natasha. 'Smells amazing.'

And it did. So much so that Lisa poked her head through the kitchen door, her hair messy, as if she had just woken up.

'Fried beetroot,' said Yuri. 'Courtesy of my mama. And guess what I got at the market today? A whole spoonful of butter.'

'I didn't know you had family here.' Natasha was instantly curious. Yuri rarely spoke about himself.

'Not anymore. I looked for Mama but... the house was empty. No one's been living there in months. I found a sack of old beetroot in the kitchen.'

'A whole sack of beetroot! That will last us a while,' exclaimed Lisa.

'You think your mama evacuated?' asked Natasha.

'I hope so. We have family in Kharkov but as you know…' He fell quiet.

'Kharkov is now in German hands, just like Kiev,' finished Natasha. Yuri nodded, turning to the stove.

'You can stay with us as long as you want,' said Nikolai.

'You will, won't you?' demanded Lisa.

Yuri smiled. He had a good smile, open and kind. 'If you'll have me,' he said.

Nikolai danced on the spot. 'Of course we'll have you. Natasha here has the biggest crush on you. Have you noticed the way she looks at you?'

'Nikolai, what's wrong with you?' Natasha's cheeks were burning. She knew her face must have gone bright red. To hide her embarrassment, she pinched her brother's arm.

'Ouch,' yelped Nikolai, pulling a face at Natasha.

'Will you grow up?' she said. 'What are you, five?'

'Better five than nineteen going on fifty. Look at your face. When was the last time you did anything fun?' When Natasha pinched him again, he squealed, poking his tongue out. 'Yuri, tell her.'

'I'm too old for Natasha. She can do a lot better. She probably has young men following her by the dozen.'

Lisa chuckled. Natasha blushed deeper. She desperately needed to change the subject. Pointing at a piece of paper on the kitchen table, she said, 'What's that?' It looked like a page from one of her school notebooks.

'Read it,' said Yuri.

Natasha struggled to decipher the hurried scribble. 'Soviet citizens! The Germans are deceiving you. Moscow was, is, and will be ours! When Hitler tells you that the war is over, he is lying! Soon the Red Army will be back. Ukraine will be Soviet once more. Until then, continue to resist and kill the occupants! Don't believe the German propaganda. It's better to die fighting than to live in slavery! Death to the Nazi pigs.'

184

Natasha blinked and read it again. 'You wrote this?'

Yuri nodded. 'I'm going to make copies and distribute them in crowded places.'

Glancing at Yuri's barely readable scrawl, Natasha said, 'You might need some help with that.'

Yuri laughed, 'I think you might be right.'

Nikolai performed a few excited pirouettes around the kitchen, the leaflet bopping up and down in his hand. 'Can we distribute them, too?'

'That is too dangerous,' said Yuri. 'Your mama would never forgive me.'

'The more dangerous, the better!' exclaimed Nikolai. 'We want to do our bit to help the Motherland.'

Natasha almost choked with laughter, and Yuri said, 'That's the spirit.'

Natasha took the piece of paper from Nikolai. 'Are you sure about this? I mean, what difference can it make?'

'It's a start. It will raise people's spirits, inspire them to resist. Besides, it's only a small part of what we do.'

'What else do you do?' Nikolai stopped dancing and stared at Yuri. He lowered his voice. 'How can we help?'

'First of all, remember Gregory?'

'The man with a moustache who came to see you yesterday?'

Yuri nodded. 'He's an interpreter, working for the Germans.'

'Are you serious?' cried Nikolai.

'And you brought him here?' gasped Natasha.

Yuri smiled. 'Not everything is what it seems. Appearances can be deceiving. Gregory is a partisan. He feeds false information to the Germans. Not every time but occasionally, when it's beneficial to us, he changes documents or misleads them in other ways. Thanks to his efforts, twenty Ukrainian administrators who were extremely loyal to the Nazis were shot this month alone.'

'Shouldn't you be fighting the Germans and not the Ukrainians?' asked Lisa.

185

'We fight the idea, Lisa, not the nationality. That's what this war is all about. Ideas. Anyone sympathetic to the Nazis is our enemy. Our aim is to create intolerable conditions for the Germans and destroy them by whatever means possible. Sabotage, misinformation, discrediting their propaganda, even killing them on the street when possible.' As three pairs of eyes watched him with fascination, Yuri turned off the gas and said, 'Dinner's ready.'

They had fried beetroot and a small piece of bread each for dinner. For once there was plenty for everyone, and it felt like they were having a feast. After dinner, the four of them copied the leaflets under the light of Mark's kerosene lamp. At midnight, when they ran out of paper, they went to bed, but Natasha was too excited to sleep. It was reassuring to know that there were people in Kiev who were still resisting. People like Yuri and Gregory.

*

Natasha watched Mark's face across the chessboard. He looked so sweet when he tried to concentrate. She couldn't resist, she reached out and stroked his cheek. 'Your move,' she said.

'Wait. I'm thinking.' She tickled him. He smiled. 'Don't distract me. I can do this. I know I can.' He looked at the board and frowned.

'I don't think you can. I think you're all out of options.' She rubbed her hands, anticipating her victory.

'If I do this…' He reached for his knight.

'If you do that, you lose. And if you move your rook, you lose.'

'You might be right. I *am* out of options. Come here!' He held her. 'Why do you always win?' Her hair was up in a ponytail. He undid it and kissed the tip of her nose.

She laughed. 'Why do you always lose?'

'You don't give me much choice, do you?'

'Another game?'

'Maybe later.' By the look on his face, Natasha knew he was no longer thinking of chess. 'I love your dress,' he whispered. 'Are you allowed to dress like that for work?'

'I'm allowed to wear a dress to work. Next week we might get real uniforms.' She let go of his hand and reached for the chess pieces, placing them inside the chessboard. 'I'm glad I taught you how to play. This is fun.'

'Yes. Now you have to teach me how to play well.'

'So you can beat me? I don't think so.' Through the broken window she could hear music. 'What's that song?' asked Natasha.

'It's called "O Tannenbaum".'

'What's a tannenbaum?'

'A Christmas tree. Germans are celebrating Christmas.'

'Today?' She was in his arms, and it felt so comforting, so relaxing. She let her eyes droop.

'Christmas Eve is tomorrow.'

She reached under his shirt. Pushing her away, he cried, 'Oh my God, your hands!'

'What about them?'

'They're freezing. Why are they so cold?' She took her hands away. 'Wait. Where are you going?' he asked.

'I thought you didn't like it.'

'I never said I didn't like it.' He put his own freezing hands on her.

'Oh no, this is torture,' she squealed. 'Stop it this instant!'

'Never!' He kissed her.

When he let go, she said, 'Christmas Eve! Is that why I saw a beautiful tree on Pochtovaya Street? It was so pretty, all baubles and lights and tinsel. Just like our New Year's tree, but instead of a red star there was a golden figure at the top.'

'An angel. It's a Christmas tradition.'

'We don't have anything like that here. No religion in the Soviet Union. It's a shame, really.' Carols were playing on the radio. Natasha paused to listen. 'Do you celebrate Christmas in Hungary?'

'We're lucky. We celebrate it twice. In December with everybody else and in January because my parents are Russian Orthodox. My mother is very religious.'

'Just like my babushka.' She hugged him tightly. 'Happy Christmas, Mark,' she whispered.

'Happy Christmas, Natasha! I love this time of year. The whole family gathers together, and Mother makes roasts, Russian salads and Russian cakes. Sometimes we go ice skating and sometimes we sit around the fireplace and play the guitar. My father is quite the singer.'

'Your Christmas sounds wonderful. A bit like our New Year's Eve. It's my favourite holiday. There is something magical about it. You say goodbye to the old year and welcome the new one. It's a fresh start, a new beginning. Last New Year's, Lisa was waiting for Alexei to propose. She interrogated me day and night. I don't know why she thought Alexei would confide in me.' Natasha sighed. 'I can't wait for this year to end. It's been the worst year of my life.'

'It wasn't all bad. It was the year I met you.'

Instantly she felt guilty. 'You're right,' she said. 'It wasn't all bad.' The street lights outside flickered. The music died away. 'Are you doing anything on New Year's Eve?'

'I don't think so. I'll write to my parents. I've never spent holidays apart from them before.'

Natasha nodded. 'It's our first New Year's without Papa and Stanislav. I wish I could invite you home. They say the way you welcome the New Year is the way you're going to spend it. And I want to spend it with you.'

'Just think about me at midnight and I'll think about you.'

'You think that will still work?'

'Of course it will.' She must have looked worried because he laughed and said, 'I had no idea you were so superstitious.'

'Every Russian is. Aren't you?'

'Not in the slightest. What will you do for the New Year?'

'Everyone is too sad about Papa to celebrate. Mama's not up for much these days. Yuri cheers everyone up a bit. He's so easygoing and funny. Nikolai absolutely adores him. He follows him around like a love-struck puppy. We all adore him.'

There was a frown on Mark's face. Pretend or real? Natasha couldn't tell. 'You're not jealous, are you?' she asked.

'Me? Never!' Effortlessly, as if she was a porcelain doll, he lifted her up and placed her on his lap.

'I only have eyes for you. You know that, don't you?'

He nodded and smiled. His frown was gone.

'Good,' she said. 'Did I tell you that Yuri managed to tune into Moscow on his radio? Kalinin is still Soviet. And there was something about Leningrad, too, but he lost the signal.'

'Be careful. You can get shot for having a radio. Where did Yuri get it?'

'I'm not sure. One day he showed up with a watch and a radio. He hides it on the roof. You know what else we heard? That there are 423,000 people living in Kiev at the moment.' His frown was back, and this time she could tell it was real. 'Mark, how can that be? There were over a million people before the war.' When he didn't reply, she asked, 'What happened to everyone?'

'Some evacuated before the Germans got here. Others...' He paused.

'Don't say it.'

She wished it was darker in the room, so she couldn't see the steely expression on his face. There was something despondent in the way he pursed his lips, in the way his jaw stiffened. 'The Germans are planning to reduce the population of Kiev to a hundred thousand. There just isn't enough food for everyone,' he said.

'What do you mean, reduce?' She could sense he didn't want to tell her. 'Mark, what are they going to do to us?'

'Soon mass transportations to Germany are going to start.'

'*Mass* transportations?' Natasha slid off his lap. She searched his face for hidden clues. There was something in his eyes that she didn't like. As if he knew too much and didn't want to tell her.

'To them the population is nothing but a source of slave labour. To make the most of it, they're going to transport workers to factories all over Germany.'

Natasha shivered. When she spoke, she tried to sound confident but failed. 'They can't send me to Germany. I have a job in the cafeteria.' She fell quiet. No one else in her family had a job, not even Mother, who had stopped going to school the day Father was taken.

'What I'm saying is, you might not be safe here for much longer. You need to think about leaving Kiev.'

She blinked. Did she hear him right? Did he just say, leave Kiev? 'What do you mean? The Germans will never let me go.'

'Natasha, there's something I need to tell you.' His voice was grave. Where was the light-hearted smile, the teasing banter? 'Our regiment is being recalled to Hungary. We're going back.'

'You're leaving?' Was it her voice that sounded so hoarse? She didn't recognise it.

'I have no choice.'

For a moment nothing could be heard but drunken German voices outside and Natasha's breathing, heavy and irregular. She longed for Christmas carols, for a voice on the loudspeaker, a German voice, a Soviet voice, anything to fill the empty darkness. Finally, she said, 'I'm so happy for you. You're going home. You'll see your family again. You can forget the Soviet Union like a horrible nightmare. You can forget all about the war.' Through her tears she smiled.

'Natasha, you don't understand. I want you to come with me.'

'Come with you?' She thought he was joking. But his eyes were serious.

'In Hungary you'll be safe. We can be together.'

'What about my family?' She struggled to get the words out.

'Didn't you say you wanted to run away with me? To Australia, France, anywhere as long as we were together? Well, now we can.'

'It was a fantasy, a dream, nothing more.' When he didn't reply, she added, 'We have to think about other people.'

'What about us?' he demanded. 'I know it's difficult but the most important thing is your safety. And you're not safe in Kiev.'

'No one is safe in Kiev. Yet no one is leaving.'

He raised his voice but only for a second. 'They don't have a choice. But you do. You can come with me.'

'How could I go without my family? How could I leave them here to die?'

What he was suggesting, it was impossible. Why couldn't he see that?

He said, 'I wish I could take all of you to Hungary. But I can't. Gestapo checkpoints are on every major road. Taking you across will be risky enough.'

'How will you hide me?'

'I won't. You'll be out in the open, next to me. One of our nurses was killed a week ago. I have her travel documents and her uniform.'

Natasha shuddered. Could she cross Europe pretending to be someone else? Could she travel in a truck full of Hungarian soldiers across war-torn countries wearing the uniform of a dead nurse? What if they were stopped, and she was expected to speak Hungarian? What if she was discovered? There were so many what ifs. She clenched her fists. 'When do you leave?'

'In two weeks.'

Two weeks! Silent tears filled her eyes. Thankfully, he was staring out the window. He didn't seem to notice.

'Natasha, the most important thing right now is your safety. When the war is over, we'll come back. We'll find your family again.'

Natasha imagined her beloved grandfather's smiling face. She imagined her mother's tears as she cried night after night, not only for Father and Stanislav but for Natasha, too. 'I could never leave them.'

'I don't understand. I thought it's what you wanted. To be with me.'

'It was.' Her eyes pleaded with him in the dark. Pleaded for a way out, for a solution. 'It is,' she repeated, quieter. 'I don't want to upset you, but my family needs me. They wouldn't want me to go.'

'It's not about what they want. It's about what you want.'

'I could never do anything to hurt them.'

'I know. You never think of yourself, only of others. That's one of the many reasons I love you.' He moved away from her and immediately she felt cold. She wanted his body next to her again. 'Promise you'll think about it,' he begged.

'I can't promise you that. Please, understand. I can't leave them here. I love my family.'

'And I love you. I can't leave you here, either.'

'When you leave, my heart will be broken,' she whispered softly. So softly that he couldn't have possibly heard. Her chest was hurting, her throat was parched. Shuddering, she pulled him close. His fingers on her bare skin felt like fire. It hurt to touch his face and it hurt to kiss him. It hurt to take deep, measured breaths, too, so she took tiny, shallow ones, all the while touching him, kissing him, soaking him up through her skin.

192

Chapter 11 – The Impossible Choices

December 1941

Lisa slipped into the room as Natasha was getting dressed. Natasha turned away. She didn't want her sister to notice her tears. But Lisa looked through Natasha as if she wasn't in the room. 'Going somewhere?' she demanded.

Talking, such a simple act, so why did it require all her strength, the strength she didn't have? 'Yes, we're going to distribute Yuri's leaflets. Why don't you come? We can use all the help we can get.'

Lisa looked at Natasha like she had just invited her to dig a trench in the Taras Shevchenko Park. 'Are you crazy? It's too dangerous.'

'I know it is. But it's worth it. It's a chance to help our people fight the Nazis.'

Lisa shook her head as if helping her people fight the Nazis was the last thing she wanted to do. Natasha didn't say another word. She was in no mood for arguments.

Yuri had told Natasha the market was the best place to distribute the leaflets. It was busy, and people were distracted. Therefore, it was to the market that Natasha and Nikolai headed, moving as fast as they could to keep themselves warm. Although the stores were closed, they still retained the old signs: meat, cheese, sausages, fish. Was there really a life when these items were not only readily available but taken for granted? Was there a life when Natasha could walk to the store and queue up for white, beautiful bread that didn't crumble under her fingers and didn't taste like cement? As she walked through eerie streets, passing ghost-like Soviets and self-satisfied Nazis, Natasha couldn't imagine that life.

She put one foot in front of the other silently and methodically. If only she focused on the task at hand, if only she thought of nothing but helping Yuri, she would have no space for other thoughts and other feelings. If only.

Natasha didn't know where to turn. On one side, there was Mark, the man she loved more than anything in the world. And on the other, her family, who *were* her world. She'd never spent a day without her parents and siblings before, how could she board a truck bound for Hungary and leave them behind? How could she turn her back on them? She had only known Mark for two months, but she'd been with her family for a lifetime.

But turning her back on Mark and continuing as if she'd never met him was equally impossible. She could hardly remember the person she'd been before she'd met him. Could she go on with her life and not see his smiling face and not feel his beating heart? She didn't think so.

Natasha slipped on the ice and waved her arms to regain her balance. Nikolai caught her mid-fall and said, pointing across the road, 'Look, pigeons! They're back.'

'Indeed they are. Can you believe it?' Such a small thing, and yet, it was enough to make her look up from the frozen ground and smile. It was a victory, however small. *Wait till I tell Mark*, she thought. And then she remembered he was leaving, and her smile vanished.

'The Nazis ordered them all destroyed but here they are. What did I tell you? It's not just us. Everything is resisting,' exclaimed Nikolai. 'You still think they're going to win?' Sliding on ice, he zoomed down the street.

'Wait, you're walking too fast!' Natasha caught up to her brother, hugging him. 'I love you, Nikolai. I wish I had your optimism. What's your secret?'

'No secret. But if we give up, we'll die. Staying positive is better than dying.'

Yuri was right, the market was crowded. Men, women, even children were shouting, arguing and shoving each other. The Kievans brought their best clothes, their jewellery, their furniture, hoping to exchange them for something, anything, to eat. Villagers arrived with their meagre produce, knowing that food was in high demand in these dire times and eager to obtain something valuable for their withered carrots, tiny potatoes, eggs and milk.

Natasha and Nikolai were grateful for the commotion. It made their job easier. They moved through the crowd swiftly, hiding Yuri's leaflets in people's pockets, placing them in their baskets and carts. It took them ten minutes to get rid of all the leaflets. Just as they were about to leave, content in the knowledge that they had accomplished their mission safely and in record time, Nikolai exclaimed, 'Look, it's Masha Enotova!' He waved and shouted, 'Masha!'

Natasha looked at the emaciated woman Nikolai was pointing at. Crouched on the ground, her hand outstretched, her lips perched, she was begging for loose change or a piece of bread.

'Nikolai, that's not Masha. Quick, let's go home. It's cold,' said Natasha.

Nikolai hesitated. 'I could swear it was her.'

Natasha was about to walk away when the woman raised her head. It *was* Masha.

'Masha,' cried Natasha. 'What are you doing here?'

With great difficulty Masha's eyes focused on Natasha. There was a long silence, and then she laughed. Her laughter scared Natasha so much that she recoiled from her mother's friend, taking a few steps back and almost falling on the snow. Masha looked drunk. Her movements were jerky and her eyes unclear. Natasha wondered where Masha managed to find any vodka. It was one of the most sought-after commodities at the market. But when Natasha came closer, she realised that Masha didn't smell of alcohol. She was sober, and yet, she looked deranged.

'Masha, what are you doing here?' asked Nikolai. Masha didn't reply. She stared at Natasha as if trying to remember who she was.

Natasha didn't know what to say. She regretted approaching the woman. 'Masha, where are your children? Your husband?'

'Gone. Every single one of them, gone.' Masha slurred her words. Her body swayed.

'Gone where? Are they in the village with your mother?' Natasha asked, even though she knew in her heart that the answer would be no.

Masha wailed, 'Dead. They're all dead.'

Nikolai stepped from one foot to another. Natasha gasped. 'What happened?'

'The Germans happened. The war happened.'

Natasha backed away from her.

'Tell your mama to come and find me,' said Masha, her body rocking. *So she did recognise me*, thought Natasha.

'Let's go, Nikolai.' She grabbed her brother's hand, and they walked back in silence.

At home, she wanted to tell her mother about Masha but couldn't. It wasn't the fact that Masha had lost her entire family that stunned Natasha. She had seen death before. And it wasn't the fact that Masha was begging for a living that shocked her. They were all doing their best to stay alive. Natasha was shaken because the woman she and Nikolai encountered at the market

196

had nothing in common with her mother's vibrant friend. Even though she had survived, somewhere along the way Masha Enotova had lost herself.

*

Natasha shuffled through the crowded cafeteria. From table to table she moved, her gaze fixed on the floor and her face blank. She didn't want to look at the misery and the hunger, the tears and the heartbreak. If she could, she would have done her work with her eyes closed. It occurred to her that the only thing that helped her through her day was her evening time with Mark. A few hours that showed her that she was still alive and not dead.

'Only ten days left,' she whispered to him in the evening.

'Don't do that. Don't count the days.'

'Ten days with you. I'm lucky. It's more happiness than most people have in their lifetimes. It's more than Olga ever had.'

'Natasha, I can't go without you. If you can't leave your family, I'll stay too. I'll stay here with you.'

Her heart beating fast, she touched his face. 'Can you even stay here if your regiment goes back?'

'I'll find a way. I could remain behind and join a partisan battalion in one of the villages. I'll fight the Germans. In my own way I'll help free the world of Hitler.'

Was that his big plan? She shuddered. 'You can't do that. You'll die.'

'No, I won't. I will live with a clear conscience and with you. We can be together. We'll wait out the war. We'll have a life together. A happy life.'

'I don't know what's going to happen after the war, but my grandfather says the Bolsheviks will be back as soon as Ukraine is back in Soviet hands.'

'And what have they got to do with us?'

197

'It could mean reprisals against those who collaborated with the Germans. What do you think Stalin will do to someone who fought on Hitler's side? Mark, whether we win the war or not, you and I will always be on different sides.'

'Then as soon as the war is over, as soon as it's safe, we'll go to Hungary and take your family with us.'

She saw it in his eyes – he was dreaming, clutching at straws. Neither of them had a plan. 'Can't you see?' she exclaimed. 'You won't last a day in the partisan battalion. Someone will denounce you to the Germans.'

'Natasha, you're my life. If I return to Hungary without you, I'll be leaving my heart here.'

He blinked, and in his eyes she saw his heart. His mind was made up. She knew that no matter what she said, she wouldn't be able to change it.

'If you stay, I stay,' he continued. 'I'd rather risk my life and have a chance here with you than be safe at home knowing I'd left you to die.'

'If you stay here you'll be condemning yourself to certain death.' She closed her eyes and prayed for strength. Finally, she forced the words out, 'You have to go home. After the war we'll find each other again.'

'Is that what you want?'

She nodded, teeth clenched.

'I don't believe you,' he whispered. 'I thought you said your heart would be broken if I left?'

So he did hear me, thought Natasha.

Mark lifted her chin, forcing her to look at him. 'I'm not going anywhere without you. It's as simple as that. Understood?'

She shook her head. 'I won't let you stay here.'

'You need me here to protect you.'

'And who will protect you?' She raised her voice. 'Who will comfort me when you're arrested, when you're taken to Babi Yar and put in front of the Nazi machine guns?' She was shaking.

'How will I live without you, knowing that you died because of me? I can't let you stay here.'

'If you stay, I stay,' he repeated, his voice low.

'What about my family? What if Papa and Stanislav come back?'

'Talk to your mother, Natasha. If she had a choice of having you with her or having you safe, I know what she'd choose. She'd carry you against your will and put you on that truck herself if she had to.'

Somehow, knowing her mother, knowing her selfless love for her family, Natasha knew Mark was right.

'You won't have to worry about hunger. You won't have to worry about the Germans. You won't have to drag yourself out of bed every morning to go to work through burnt-out streets to scrub floors and watch people die. You'll be looked after. You'll be with me.'

'Have you even mentioned this idea to your parents?'

His eyes lit up as if he could tell her resolve was weakening. 'I don't need to. They'll be happy to have you.'

She realised that there was only one thing she could say, only one thing she could do to save him from a certain death in the Soviet Union. Because in her heart she knew that he wasn't going anywhere without her. 'I'll talk to Mama,' she whispered.

*

Just like Natasha had predicted, there wasn't much celebration at the Smirnovs' that New Year's Eve. Yuri was away on partisan business. Everyone else was in bed. Only Natasha sat at the kitchen window, staring at the falling snow. It was half past eleven in the evening.

Would the next year bring victory or more humiliation? Natasha couldn't imagine living like this for much longer. Something had to bring them relief but what? She felt that only a miracle could help them. As the terrible year of 1941 slipped away, Natasha sat in the dark and prayed for a miracle. She was no longer thinking of Kiev and the streets of her childhood. She was thinking of Vacratot, a small village not far from Budapest.

Would she even be here this time next year? Or would she be in a foreign country, far from her family, alone and afraid? No, not alone, but with *him*. Wasn't that all that mattered?

She walked to the bedroom. 'Mama! Are you asleep?' she whispered, even though she knew Mother was awake by the tiny sobs that were coming from her bed. Natasha perched on the bed next to her. 'Are you okay? I want to talk to you about something.'

Natasha could just make out her mother's silhouette in the shady room. Mother's voice was barely audible. 'Do you think about them? Wonder if they are still alive?'

'All the time.'

'Natasha, I can't feel them out there anymore. I can't feel their presence. They just seem…' She fell quiet. After a few seconds, she added, 'Lost.'

'Don't say that, Mama. Papa has only been gone a few weeks. And Stanislav will come back. As soon as the war is over, they'll both come back.'

'What if they don't? What if they never come back? I don't think I could bear it.'

Natasha couldn't bear it either. She remembered Mark's words. 'We have to have faith. Without faith, there's nothing,' she said.

'I don't think we'll ever see them again.'

'Mama, please don't cry.'

'Sometimes I think they're the lucky ones. Death is better than living like this. Anything is better than living like this.'

'Don't talk about them like they're dead. They're still alive, and wherever they are, they're waiting to see us again, just like we're waiting to see them.'

'Do you really believe that? Do you believe Olga is still alive?'

'No, not Olga,' said Natasha in a tiny voice. She reached in her pocket and felt for her brother's picture. Stroking its smooth edges made her feel a little bit better. It was as if her brother was still with her. He wasn't lost, nor was he dead. Here he was, in her pocket, on a small black-and-white photograph.

'You know what the worst part is? The uncertainty. I wish we knew, one way or another. Then we could grieve and go on with our lives. But this wasting away waiting for the news that never comes, it's killing me.' Mother buried her face in the pillow. 'At least I still have the three of you. Masha doesn't have anyone.'

'Did Nikolai tell you?'

Mother nodded.

Kissing her, Natasha said, 'We're not going anywhere, Mama, I promise. We'll always be with you. Go to sleep. You'll feel better in the morning. It's a new year, a new beginning.'

'You wanted to talk to me about something?'

'It was nothing, Mama. Happy New Year.'

When Natasha returned to the kitchen, with only ten minutes remaining until midnight, she found Lisa sitting at the table. Natasha wondered what her sister was doing in the dark, but she didn't ask, so glad was she to have someone to talk to. In her superstitious mind, being by herself on New Year's meant she would be alone, without her family, all year. And she didn't want that.

'Tell me a secret, Lisa,' she whispered, perching on a chair next to her sister and reaching for her hand.

Natasha and Lisa had a tradition. Every New Year's Eve, just before the clock chimed twelve, they would exchange secrets. The person with the most outrageous secret won. The loser had to do anything the winner wanted for the next week. Natasha had never won, because no matter how good her secrets were, Lisa's had always been better. Even if Natasha suspected her sister made them all up. One year, when the girls were nine and ten, Lisa had claimed she'd surprised Zina kissing a man who wasn't her husband on the stairs of their building. The next year, she had told Natasha their history teacher fell over on the way to the cafeteria and split his pants. Now, as they waited out the last minutes of 1941, Natasha desperately needed one of her sister's made-up stories to transport her back to her childhood where she'd been safe.

'I don't have any secrets.' Lisa's voice was dull, sleepy. In the light of the street lamp outside, Natasha could make out her stooped shoulders and downcast eyes.

'I don't believe you. You always have secrets.'

'I can't do this anymore. I can't go on as if nothing is wrong. There are times when I'm numb inside. I go through my days like an apparition, and in the evenings I don't even remember what I've done. Does that sound normal to you?'

Mutely, Natasha shook her head.

'But then there are days when everything inside me is burning with pain, with heartache. On days like that I long for that numb feeling. It makes life so much easier.'

'You are hurting. It's understandable. We've all been through so much. Too much is broken. But it will get better, Lisa. The war will be over, and everything will get better.'

'Yes, but Alexei won't come back. Not after the war, not ever.'

Natasha had nothing to say to that.

Lisa continued, 'If you could see what's inside my head, you'd be horrified. Do you know how I know? Because when I look inside my head, I'm horrified at the darkness I see.'

'I wouldn't be horrified, Lisa. You are my sister. I'll always love you, no matter what.'

'Do *you* have a secret to tell me?' asked Lisa, her hand limp inside Natasha's.

After a long pause, Natasha said, 'No, Lisa. You know me. I don't have any secrets.'

'Are you absolutely sure?' asked Lisa, pulling her hand away.

Natasha nodded, even though Lisa couldn't see her in the dark.

The clock chimed midnight, ushering in 1942. Natasha turned away from her sister and thought of Mark, thought of his arms around her, his smiling face, his lips on hers. She didn't want to welcome the New Year without him, so she felt for him in her thoughts and imagined him holding her close, whispering how much he loved her.

Chapter 12 – A Beacon of Happiness

January 1942

Natasha was making her slow, drowsy way to the water pump, an empty bucket hooked on her arm, a scarf wrapped around her head. It was early, and the winter sun peeked timidly through the cloud, illuminating the city half hidden away by snow. It wasn't fresh snow anymore. It wasn't white or pure or soft like feathers. It was all grey ice and brown slush, muddy, dull and deflated. Natasha looked at the familiar streets of her childhood, damaged by bombs, blackened by fire, but so infinitely dear to her heart. If she followed Mark to Hungary, would she ever see Kiev or her family again?

Natasha was just about to fill her bucket with water when she heard mortar shots. The unexpected noise made her stop in her tracks, drop the bucket and, not pausing to catch it as it rolled down the hill, she ran back home. Mother, Nikolai and Lisa were already by the kitchen window. Natasha was just in time to see a tiny dot of a plane as it vanished into the distance, its machine guns popping and cracking long after the plane had disappeared.

It was at this plane that the mortars were firing.

'That was our plane. A Soviet plane!' exclaimed Nikolai, his voice raising a few octaves too high and then falling to almost a whisper.

'Are you sure?' asked Natasha. She had a sudden desire to hug her brother and twirl him in a mad tango around the kitchen.

'Positive. I saw a red star on the fuselage.'

'You imagined it, silly,' said Lisa. 'A Soviet plane! What nonsense.'

Nikolai glared at his sister. 'You think you know everything, smarty-pants? Then explain why the Germans were firing at their own plane.'

Lisa had no answer to that. Four pairs of excited eyes stared out of the window at the quiet street. For a minute, no one spoke.

Natasha said, 'We haven't seen a Soviet plane since—'

'Since September,' interrupted Mother. 'And the paper said yesterday that the Soviet Air Force was destroyed.'

'You still read the papers, Mama? It's all lies, every last word,' said Natasha.

'The Red Army must be closer than we think,' concluded Mother.

The plane was the first sign of life from the territories unoccupied by Hitler that they had seen in a long time. Once again, the electricity had been cut off a while ago. No electricity meant no radio, which meant that the Smirnovs had no way of knowing what was happening in the outside world. Yuri's radio remained hidden on the roof, under a pile of bricks, concealed by half a metre of snow. Mother finally noticed Natasha's boots, and her smile vanished. 'Shoes in the house? Take them off immediately and sit down. Breakfast is almost ready.'

'What's for breakfast?' Nikolai wanted to know.

Mother pointed at two large beetroots and a potato. The vegetables were wrinkled like an old man's face, as if they had spent not just three winter months but a number of years hidden away in the cellar. Mother proudly brought them home from the market earlier that morning and was slicing them into wafer-thin, almost

205

transparent portions. She looked around for something to cook them in. The shelves were empty. 'I don't understand. Where did all our pots go? We had at least half a dozen.' She looked under the table and in the compartment behind the long bench where Olga's mother had stored carrots, potatoes and aubergines in their other, pre-war life.

'Mama, stop,' said Lisa. 'It's just beetroot, we can eat it raw.'

'It's half frozen. You'll get a terrible stomach ache.'

'I like the crunchy noise it makes in my mouth,' said Nikolai, reaching across for a piece of beetroot.

'Either way, I would still like to know what happened to the pots. Not a single one left. How strange.'

Lisa coughed. 'I traded our pots and pans, Mama,' she said. 'And one of our knives.'

'You traded them?' asked Mother. She sat down, watching Lisa through narrowed eyes.

Lisa turned as red as the beetroot juice on Nikolai's fingers. She withered under Mother's probing gaze. Finally, she looked away and said, 'I gave them to the Germans.'

'You did what?'

Lisa muttered, 'Didn't you see the notices outside? They were offering bread for our metal.'

Mother's face deflated as if all the air had left it. 'What were you thinking?' she exclaimed. Nikolai, who was stretching for another piece of beetroot, thought better of it. Mutely he glanced from Mother to Lisa.

'It's not like we have anything to cook. We haven't used the pots in weeks. They gave me bread, Mama,' pleaded Lisa.

'Where is this bread?' asked Natasha eagerly. Her stomach was rumbling. Even the thought of tasteless German-issue bread made her mouth water.

'I ate it,' mumbled Lisa. 'I was so tired after the long walk, I didn't think I could make it back. I needed it.' She contemplated the unsmiling faces around her. 'I was so hungry.'

'Typical,' muttered Nikolai.

Natasha watched her sister for a second or two and then said, 'We're all hungry. You were tired? It's not like you even have a job. What do you do all day?'

Mother slumped in her chair as if Lisa's admission sapped her of all her strength. 'We all saw the notices, Lisa. Yet not one of us had even considered giving them anything. You should be ashamed of yourself.'

'But what harm can it really do?'

'What harm, did you say? What harm?' Mother repeated, blinking fast. 'Before you rushed to get a piece of stale bread, did you perhaps pause for one second to think why they were asking for our metal?' When Lisa shook her head, Mother continued, 'They are using pots and pans to make weapons.'

Lisa cowered in her chair, her face paling. 'I'm sorry, I didn't think.'

'You never think. I hope you enjoyed your bread because it paid for bullets that might kill your brother and father. What a bitter piece of bread that must have been.'

Lisa opened her mouth as if to say something but no sound came out. She closed her mouth and ran out of the door. 'Where is she off to?' asked Nikolai. Mother shrugged.

An hour later Lisa returned. She sat down at the kitchen table next to Mother, next to Natasha, all tears and tangled hair, twisted mouth and twisted arms. 'I tried to get our pots back. The collector didn't want to hear. I'm so sorry, Mama.' She sobbed hysterically, rubbing her face with her clenched fists until it looked bright red.

'No use crying over spilt milk,' said Mother. 'What's done is done. Here, we saved you some food. Next time I hope you think twice before doing something so stupid.'

'That's likely,' muttered Nikolai. Natasha pinched him and he poked his tongue out, which was still red from beetroot.

After Mother and Nikolai left, Natasha sat next to Lisa. 'Don't cry.'

'It's just all too much, you know? Everything is too much. Alexei and Babushka and Olga. This life, always scrambling for a piece of bread. I can't take it anymore.'

'Remember what you told me on the day the Germans got here? Let's take it one day at a time. Today we had food. Let's not worry about tomorrow just yet.'

'I didn't mean any harm, you know. And now everyone hates me.' Lisa's shoulders heaved.

Her arms around her sister, Natasha whispered, 'I don't hate you, Lisa. And they don't, either. They will get over it soon enough, you'll see.'

Sobbing, her head in her hands, Lisa muttered, 'I still miss him, you know.'

'Of course you do. But time will help.'

'It's got nothing to do with time,' said Lisa. Her voice was no longer quivering and her eyes were dry.

*

That afternoon at the cafeteria, Natasha was surprised to find a piece of real meat in the soup she was given for lunch. It was such a long time since she had seen meat, she had almost forgotten what it looked like. Yet, she could swear that this meat tasted like nothing she had ever had before. Its texture was rough and it was difficult to chew. She poked it uncertainly with her fork.

'What is that?' she asked Alina, one of the waitresses.

Alina replied through a mouthful of soup, 'Who cares? Eat and don't ask stupid questions.'

'Wouldn't want to eat a rat or a mouse. I heard they could poison you.'

'I think you're safe. There aren't any mice left. They've all been eaten already.'

'It's an old horse,' said the cook, a plump woman with milky-white skin and pale red hair, which she wore in a braid that reached all the way down her waist.

'Can I have some more, please?' asked Natasha, passing her plate.

As soon as the cafeteria closed, Mark walked in, shivering, shaking the snow off his boots. He took his hat off and said, 'Minus twenty-seven outside.'

Natasha unbuttoned his coat and pressed her body close to his. She buried her face in his chest and inhaled. He smelt of snow. 'It's unbelievably cold. I've never known it to be this cold in Kiev,' she said.

'I'm glad I have Stanislav's clothes. Our winter uniforms never showed up.'

'Grandfather believes nature itself is fighting the Germans. Just like in 1812 when Napoleon invaded Russia. It was a freezing winter then, too.'

'As always, your grandfather is right. Now that winter is here, the Germans are struggling. Many are in hospital with frostbite.'

'I saw something funny this morning. A dozen soldiers rubbing their faces with snow, while their commander shouted something in German. Can you believe it? They think they can warm themselves up by doing that.' Natasha chuckled but Mark wasn't laughing. He wasn't even smiling. 'What's wrong?' she asked, instantly worried.

'Listen, Natasha. Things here are only getting worse. This morning I watched as a hundred Soviet sailors were being marched to Babi Yar.'

The mere mention of Babi Yar was enough to make her tremble. Too many ghosts were conjured by these two words, too many horrific memories. She shook her head to stave off the ghosts.

Mark continued, 'They walked right past me. Singing and joking while their hands were tied behind their backs with barbed wire.'

Natasha looked away from him and out of the window at the fresh snow. She knew what he wanted her to say.

Afterwards, when he walked her home, she turned around and saw him wave. His face so handsome in the moonlight – his smile so bright, his eyes so kind – her heart felt a little warmer, a little less afraid. The timing was right. She had to talk to her mother.

*

As soon as Natasha let herself in, she knew that the timing wasn't right. While she was taking her boots off, brushing the mud and snow off them, German voices reached her from the living room. When she walked in, she saw three tall officers looming over Mother, talking impatiently. Mother's head shook, her voice trembled. 'What is it? What do you want?'

'They're looking for warm clothes, Mama,' said Lisa.

'Well done, you metal thief. You speak German now?' said Nikolai. Lisa recoiled away from him, tears in her eyes.

'Warm clothes? What warm clothes? We have nothing.' Mother turned to the Germans. 'Nothing! You have to go.' She pointed at the door, and her gesture was firm, even though her hand shook.

Natasha managed to get past the Germans and pull her mother back. 'Mama, what are you doing? Let them take whatever they want. It's not worth it.'

Pushing Lisa out of the way, the officers proceeded to search the house. Ignoring Grandfather and Nikolai, they threw everything off the shelves, unmade their beds and even rolled up the carpets. Finally, laden with the Smirnovs' winter coats and Mikhail's sled, the Nazis departed.

Mother cried as she cleared up the mess. 'They already took everything. What more do they want? When is enough going to be enough for these people?'

'I wouldn't call them people,' muttered Nikolai.

'What do you expect? They're cold. It's a harsh winter this year,' said Natasha.

'They're cold? What about our prisoners?' cried Mother. 'They keep them naked in minus twenty. And what about us? What are we going to wear?'

The Germans' visit left everyone shaken and confused. Only Grandfather, who never despaired, didn't lose his good humour. 'The Nazis are beginning to beg,' he said. 'First the metal, now the clothes. That's good to see. We might still win this war.'

*

It wasn't until the next morning that Natasha got a chance to speak to her mother alone. They were in the kitchen, peeling potatoes. They would have six potatoes for breakfast and six for lunch. Less than one potato each. 'Mama, we have no cookware left. How are we going to cook these?' asked Natasha. If she was completely honest, she didn't care about cooking the potatoes at all. She was so hungry, she would gladly devour them raw.

The knife moved swiftly in her mother's hand as she replied, 'Don't worry. Anna Andreevna, our chemistry teacher, lent me a pan. She was glad to help.' Mother sighed and put the knife down. 'You know, I didn't even recognise her this morning. She looks ten years older than the last time I saw her.'

'What happened to her?'

'Her daughter was killed.' She raised her eyes as if in prayer. 'I don't care what happens to me anymore. I'm beyond caring. All I care about is you. How do I keep all of you safe?'

Every night Natasha had heard her mother toss and turn. Grieving over the past, struggling to come to terms with the present, worrying about the future. Natasha hesitated. How could she not say anything now?

Before she had a chance, however, they heard Nikolai's agitated voice that was shortly followed by the agitated Nikolai himself. 'Mama, Natasha, look,' he said, waving a newspaper about.

'Wait, stop fidgeting. You're making me dizzy,' said Mother, taking the paper from Nikolai and spreading it on the table. Curious, Natasha glanced over her mother's shoulder. Across two pages, in three languages – German, Ukrainian and Russian – the paper invited the Soviets to travel to Germany for well-paid work, promising good working conditions, plenty of food and comfortable lodgings.

It didn't take long. Just like Mark had predicted.

As Nikolai skipped back to the living room with his newspaper, Mother said, 'Yesterday they grabbed people on the streets and put them on the train to Germany. Against their will.' She paused, picked up a cup, glanced at it absentmindedly, placed it back. 'I wish I could take you away from Kiev. Somewhere safe.'

Natasha took a deep breath. 'Nowhere in the Soviet Union is safe,' she said, high-pitched and edgy.

Mother watched Natasha in silence as if waiting for something. Then she blinked, looked away and said, 'Can your young man help?'

Natasha dropped the potato she was holding and watched it roll under the table. Numbly she stared at her mother, who continued, 'I know he's not free to come and go as he pleases but he's not watched like we are watched. Is there anything he could do?'

Natasha coughed nervously. 'How do you know about him?'

'Come on, I'm your mother and I'm not blind. He should be able to protect you...'

'Mama, wait. How did you know?'

'Nikolai saw you outside our building on Tarasovskaya, remember?'

Natasha remembered. She was going to have a serious conversation with her brother. But there was no disapproval on Mother's kind face as she watched her daughter with a smile. Natasha's anger vanished. How could her little brother keep a secret of such magnitude from their parents when she herself had struggled to do it? 'Did Papa know?' she asked.

'Of course.'

'Why didn't he say anything?'

'He was going to. He was quite furious. I had to be very firm with him.'

'Why did you stop him?' Natasha shivered and looked around, as if expecting her furious father to leap at her from behind the kitchen door.

'Because I've never seen your eyes sparkle like that before. You were glowing from the inside. I didn't want you to feel like you were doing something wrong before you had a chance to enjoy this feeling.' She took Natasha's hand. 'Meeting your father is one of the most precious memories of my life. I didn't want anything to ruin the memory of your first love.'

'He's wonderful, Mama. Just wait till you meet him. You'll love him, I know you will.'

'Couldn't he take you some place safe? Maybe a village some-where?'

'Ukrainian villages are not safe anymore, either. You know that. Most of them have been burnt.' It was now or never. Before her courage vanished completely, Natasha took a deep breath, clasped her hands tight behind her back and muttered, 'Mark's garrison is being recalled back to Hungary.'

'He's leaving?'

'Well, no. He refuses to go without me.'

Mother frowned. Almost inaudibly she said, 'You're lucky. He cares about you very much.'

'Mama, he wants me to go with him. He thinks it's too dangerous in Kiev.'

'He's right. It *is* too dangerous in Kiev.'

'He won't go back without me.' Natasha waited for Mother to say something, anything. But Mother remained quiet. 'Mama, tell me, what should I do?'

Mother took off her glasses, raising her unprotected eyes to her daughter. 'Is that what you want? To go with Mark?'

'I want to be with him but I don't want to leave all of you behind.'

Mother nodded sadly. 'But maybe the distance is a good thing. The further you are from Kiev, the better. The further you are from the Soviet Union, the better.' Thoughtfully she replaced the glasses on her face. 'I think you should go.'

'Go to Hungary?'

'Hungary is not occupied. You'll have food, you'll have a better life.' When she said it, she didn't look at Natasha.

'You think I should go and leave all of you here?' Natasha thought of the crowded railway station last June, her mother's tears and her brother's reluctance as he boarded the train headed for the front.

'We'll be fine. I'll feel much better knowing you're okay. Once the war is over, you'll come back.'

'Mama, why are you crying?'

'I'm not crying, child. The most important thing is your safety right now. Will the road be dangerous?'

'We live in an occupied city, Mama. Getting out of bed in the morning is dangerous.'

'I wish we could all go with you. I worry about Nikolai. He's getting too involved in Yuri's business. Five partisans were hanged on Kreshchatyk this morning.'

They clung to each other in silence. The mother, hiding her true feelings because she would never put herself first. And the daughter, searching for courage in her mother's arms. Finally, Mother said, 'Don't feel bad. People move away, build their own lives far from their families. Your father moved to Kiev from a Siberian village. And my parents came here from the Urals when they were younger, leaving their parents behind.'

Natasha was glad she had confided in her mother. Even though she was still afraid, she wasn't as afraid as before.

When she looked up, she saw her brother standing in the doorway. She knew only too well the expression on Nikolai's

214

face. It was the same expression he'd had when he was accosted by a school bully at seven. And when a dog had chased him at eight. And when he'd fallen off a tree at nine. Now, as he watched Natasha with tears in his eyes, he suddenly looked like a child again. And Natasha did what she had done all those other times— she put her arms around her younger brother to reassure him, to give him comfort, to take the pain away. But when Nikolai spoke, he didn't sound like a child at all. 'Mama is right. You'll be safer away from Kiev. We'll miss you so much, but we'll feel better knowing we don't have to worry about you anymore.'

'Mark will look after me. He always does. He saved me, you know. It was him who shot the officer in the park. If it wasn't for him—' She paused, unsure how to continue. If it wasn't for him, she wouldn't be here now. But Alexei would. 'He didn't know about the reprisals until afterwards,' she added in a tiny voice. 'He would never have let those innocent people be killed if he knew.'

'Of course he wouldn't have, darling,' said Mother. 'I can't wait to meet him, so I can thank him for saving your life.'

'I can't wait to meet him, so I can warn him to treat you well, or he'll have me to deal with,' said Nikolai.

Natasha held him close. *I only have two more days of hugging my brother*, she thought, and suddenly felt like someone had punctured her heart with a needle, letting all the air out. It felt hollow, even though it was full to the brim with love.

Outside, floorboards creaked. A sudden thought chilled Natasha. 'Where is Lisa, Nikolai?'

'I don't know. She was right behind me.'

But when Natasha went looking for her sister a few minutes later, Lisa was nowhere to be found.

*

215

When Natasha was younger, she had imagined going to university, meeting a young man, getting married and having a baby here in Kiev, close to her family. She had imagined becoming a teacher like her mother or even a professor like her grandfather. Then the war had intervened, and that imaginary life faded away like a dream that belonged to someone else. What would the future bring her, away from everyone she loved, away from Kiev?

As she listened to the tick-tock of the clock, Natasha wondered how many days she had spent thus, waiting out the war, counting the seconds and hoping for the best. But now everything was about to change. She was ready.

As soon as Mark walked through the door in the evening and enveloped her in a hug, she told him about her conversation with Mother and Nikolai. Such relief was on his face, such joy. As usual, he brought her something. As they sat on the floor next to each other, she unwrapped the package eagerly. There was some white bread, a piece of cheese and an apple. An apple in winter! She blinked in amazement.

'The truck will pick you up tomorrow at four. Don't be late. I'll be driving.'

For a second she stopped eating. 'Where will I be?'

'In the back with the other soldiers.' Her face must have changed because he added, 'Don't be scared. It will be alright.'

'I'm not scared.' She tried to sound brave, for him. 'Are we passing Lvov?' He nodded. She smiled. To see a town filled with so many memories, to catch even the slightest glimpse of the streets she knew, how wonderful. But then it occurred to her that Lvov was occupied just like Kiev was occupied. Had Lvov become scorched earth, too? Had it burnt like Kiev had burnt? Did Lvov, too, have its own Babi Yar? The smile vanished off her face.

'Pack as lightly as possible,' said Mark. 'When we get to Hungary, my mother will lend you some clothes until we can buy you something new. She's a size or two bigger but it doesn't matter.'

'Mark, when do you think I'll see my family again?'

His arms around her tightened. 'As soon as the war is over, we'll come back to Kiev together. You, me, a baby…'

'A baby?' She looked up into his face.

He picked her up off the floor and positioned her on his lap. 'Wouldn't your mama like a grandchild?'

'She would, so much. She loves children.' The thought of having a child far from home, away from her mother and the rest of her family, filled Natasha with dread.

Mark said, 'I hope you love children, too, because I want at least a dozen.'

'A dozen?'

'I come from a big family, remember? All boys, though, and I always wanted a sister. We'll have to keep trying till we have one of each.' He grinned.

Uncertainly, she grinned back. 'I want children so much. But I also want my family around when I have them.'

'I know it feels terrible to leave your family behind. I wish you didn't have to go through that. I wish there was another way.'

But they both knew there was no other way.

'In Hungary we can be alone together and not worry about being heard. We won't have to hide. Everyone will know you're mine.'

'I love you, Mark. Did you know that? I love you so much.'

'I love you, too. You're the best thing that's ever happened to me and I want to marry you.' There were tears in his eyes.

'You do?' she whispered. There were tears in her eyes, too.

'I do. What do you say? Will you marry me?'

She sat up, watching him in disbelief, kissing the top of his head. Then she brought his face to hers. She wanted to see his eyes. 'I will. Of course I will.' She blinked.

'As soon as we arrive, I'll give you my grandmother's ring. It can be your engagement ring. Then you'll never forget that we're getting married.'

'Like I need a ring to remind me I'm yours. How could I forget?' Feeling suddenly shy, she buried her face in his shoulder.

'I'm so glad you are coming with me. I could never leave Kiev without you.'

As they made love, they kept their clothes on because taking them off required too much effort, too much time. Over and over Mark whispered how much he loved her. Natasha wanted to say it back, wanted to tell him that she loved him more than life itself but she was too weak. She bit her lip to stop herself from moaning softly into his chest, right where his heart was.

Chapter 13 – Freedom's Elusive Glare

In the living room, under a pile of old newspapers, Natasha found Stanislav's old backpack and filled it with her clothes, a small piece of bread and a couple of books. She filled her pockets with family photographs and made sure she packed her passport, her birth certificate, and her high school certificate, just in case. Mark told her to bring her documents so that they could get married as soon as they arrived in Hungary.

Natasha didn't want anyone other than Mother and Nikolai to know about her departure. It was safer that way. But she couldn't leave without seeing her grandfather one last time. She needed to say goodbye to her dedushka, who had given her his love for history and interest in how things worked. Her dedushka, who had always told her she could do anything she put her mind to, who believed in her when no one else did. Her dedushka, whom she loved unconditionally and who loved her. She paused at his door, searching her heart for courage.

Grandfather was reading. For a minute she watched his kind face, wondering if she would ever see him again.

'Why are you crying, my dear?' Grandfather asked. 'What happened?'

'Nothing, Dedushka. Everything is fine. I just feel so lost sometimes, that's all.' She sat on the bed next to him. 'You know, when I was little, I wanted to be just like you when I grew up. You always seem to know what to do, no matter what. How do you do that?'

'The trick is to always follow your heart, even if it's the hardest choice you could possibly make. Only then will you have no regrets in life.'

'I wish I could do that. I wish I was strong like you.' Natasha studied her grandfather's face. She wanted to memorise every little detail. 'What are you reading, Dedushka?'

It was a textbook on military history from antiquity to modern times. 'Knowledge of the past will arm us in the present,' he said.

The textbook was at least eight hundred pages long. She looked at the table of contents. 'See, there were other horrible wars in the past and people survived them. We'll survive this one, too.' Suddenly she felt like crying. 'Napoleonic Wars. The Thirty Years' War. Imagine a war that lasts that long. I could barely live through the last six months, let alone thirty years.'

'As terrible as the Thirty Years' War was, it was very different from what we are facing now. It wasn't what's known as total war.'

'Dedushka, is the war with Germans…' She stammered. 'Total war?'

Grandfather nodded. 'Just like the Great War before it, this is indeed total war.'

'It won't last thirty years? How can it?'

'I doubt humanity could sustain thirty years of conflict on such a massive scale.'

'That's good to know.' Natasha smiled sadly. 'Soon it will all be over, and our lives will go back to normal.' She took her grandfather's hand. She couldn't believe how small it was. 'I love you, Dedushka.'

'I love you too, granddaughter,' he said. Natasha held him close and, making sure he didn't notice, made a sign of cross over him. *Please God, protect my dear grandfather until I can see him again.*

In the corridor, Nikolai was already waiting to walk her to the spot where the truck would pick her up. She glanced at her reflection in the mirror. She thought she looked ridiculous in the oversized coat her mother had borrowed from one of her friends the day before. It didn't matter. She needed to be warm.

They were running late. She pulled Nikolai by the sleeve. 'Come on, let's go.'

'Wait, I can't find my gloves.'

Her brother was stalling. She had never seen him look so sad. She put her arms around him. 'I love you, Nikolai,' she whispered.

Lisa poked her head around the corner, looked first at Natasha, then at Nikolai, chuckled and said, 'Where are you two off to? And why are you dressed like a polar bear?'

Natasha hid her backpack behind her back, hoping Lisa wouldn't notice.

'Nowhere,' said Nikolai, opening the door and prodding a reluctant Natasha who was desperate to hug her sister goodbye. More than anything she longed to confide in Lisa, but it was impossible. With a start, she realised her relationship with Mark was the first real secret she had ever kept from her sister. Hiding from Lisa that she was leaving, possibly for good, possibly to never see her again, made Natasha feel sick to her stomach and uncomfortable, as if a large fishbone was stuck in her throat.

Natasha's legs turned to jelly and she lost her footing on the stairs. Leaning on Nikolai's arm, she walked down. 'Don't worry,' he said. 'I'll look after you.'

'When did you become so grown up?'

'June 1941.'

221

Most of the roads were unusable because of the sheer amount of snow that had piled up in the last few weeks. There was only one road at the back of their building that was still kept in working condition by the Germans, and that was where Mark was meeting her. A couple of German officers wandered past, warm woolly kerchiefs under their helmets, multiple scarfs wrapped around their necks. They fell through the snow and swore quietly in German. If she wasn't so nervous, Natasha would have laughed at the sight of them.

She expected to see Mark's truck waiting for her, but the street was deserted. Suddenly Natasha felt a dark sense of foreboding. She remembered waiting for Mark on the day she had lost her best friend, just like she was waiting for him now. She remembered the feeling of acute heartbreak and despair.

There was no one outside but their mother. She embraced Natasha, handing her a small bag. 'I packed two boiled potatoes and some bread. You can have a snack in the car. There are some warm clothes here, too.' Mother sobbed, hiding her face from the wind.

'Mama, please don't cry. It's too cold to cry.' But Natasha herself was crying.

Mother looked so small in the yellow light of a street lamp, so frail and afraid, her eyes so dull. Could Natasha kiss her cheek and turn her back on her, get into the truck, look back for a second and wave goodbye? Could she do all that and break her mother's heart?

'I'm glad I don't have to worry about you anymore. You'll be safe, fed, looked after,' murmured Mother.

Natasha remembered Mark's words. *Your mother would put you on that truck herself if she had to*, Mark had said to her. Only now, seeing the determination in her mother's eyes, did she fully believe him.

Mother said, 'I know letters don't get through but write anyway. Anything could happen. After all, we did see a Soviet plane.'

'I love you, Mama. Please, look after yourself. Say goodbye to Lisa and the others for me.'

They waited in silence. Wet snow seeped through Natasha's boots. Cold wind seeped under her clothes. Layers and layers she wore, and still it wasn't enough to stave off the winter. It wasn't a Ukrainian winter anymore. By some inexplicable twist of fate, what they had in January 1942 was a brutal Siberian winter, the likes of which she had never experienced before. Shivering, Natasha rubbed her bare hands together. Mother took off her gloves. 'Take them. You'll need them on the road.'

'Thank you, Mama,' whispered Natasha, kissing her mother. Before she put the gloves on, she touched the photographs in her pocket. For a moment she wished she had a picture of Mark but then she almost laughed at herself. *I will see him in a minute*, she thought, *I don't need a photograph*. 'Mark asked me to marry him last night and I said yes.' Natasha realised Mother was about to meet Mark for the very first time. Nervously she paced.

Mother pulled her close. 'I'm so happy for you. It's wonderful news. You know, when Vasili asked me to marry him, I was already three months' pregnant with Stanislav. I was only seventeen. My father broke my mother's favourite vase when he found out, he was so angry. He didn't stop shouting for a week.'

'Dedushka was shouting? I don't believe you.' Natasha had never heard her kind, quiet grandfather raise his voice.

'He was frantic. But I was so in love, I didn't care. I said I would leave with Vasili and live on the streets if I had to, as long as I was with him.'

'Mama, I had no idea.' It was hard to imagine her proper, restrained parents being young and in love.

'It was your babushka, God rest her soul, who talked some sense into my father. "No grandchild of mine is going to be born on the streets," she said.'

'Oh Mama, I'll miss you all so much.'

223

'We'll miss you, too. But it's not farewell. We'll see each other soon.'

Natasha stared into the distance until her eyes watered. Far distance, middle distance, and still no sign of him. 'He should have been here by now,' she muttered. Cars drove by, their headlights blinding, but none of them stopped. 'What time is it?'

Nikolai glanced at his wrist and said, 'It is now ten past five.' Seeing their bemused faces, he added, 'What? I took Yuri's watch. I'm sure he won't mind.'

Ten past five. Natasha's heart sank. Mark was over an hour late.

Mother's cold fingers squeezed Natasha's hand. 'Don't worry, dear. Anything could've happened.'

'That's what I'm afraid of.'

'Anything,' repeated Mother. 'The truck could've broken down. Not surprising in this weather. The trip could've been delayed.'

Nikolai took his gloves off and rubbed his nose, which had turned red from the wind. 'We should get back. It's past the curfew.'

Natasha refused to move. 'You go. I'll wait. If he comes, I'll run upstairs and get you.'

'Mark knows where we live. I'm sure we'll hear from him tonight or tomorrow,' said Mother. 'No point staying here in the cold.'

But Natasha was adamant. Mark had told her to wait outside, and that was exactly what she was going to do. The three of them stood and paced and talked in bright voices, trying to cheer each other up. The road remained empty. Mother hopped on the spot, trying to warm up. Natasha said, 'Mama, you must be freezing without your gloves. Please, go home. I'll walk to the barracks and see if I can find out anything. I won't be long.'

Mother looked as if she was about to argue but then she saw Natasha's distressed but resolute face. 'We'll go to the barracks together,' she said.

Gingerly they walked down the icy slope. Natasha could almost make out the drab door of the building that served as barracks to the Hungarian regiment when she felt the treacherous ground slip from under her feet. Letting go of Nikolai's arm, she collapsed, hurting her knee. The snow, the street lights, the naked trees, everything span and twirled in front of her. As if through a mist she heard her mother's bewildered voice. And as if through a mist she felt her brother's strong hands shaking her.

*

Natasha woke up late the next day to find her mother touching her forehead. Cautiously she opened her eyes. She felt groggy. First thing she said was, 'Any news?' Once again shutting her eyes, she recited a prayer in her head.

Mother placed a tray on the bed next to Natasha. 'Here, have something to eat.' On the tray, Natasha saw a slice of bread and a cup of tea. 'Claudia from downstairs let me have a spoonful of butter. She insisted. Said you carried a note to a prison camp for her once. Where an old lady managed to get real butter, I have no idea.'

Natasha ate listlessly. She wasn't hungry.

'Are you feeling any better?' asked Mother.

Taking two sips of tea, licking the butter off the bread, taking one bite and putting what was left back on the tray, Natasha said, 'I must go to the barracks.'

'Wait, finish your food first. You need to eat.'

'I'm feeling a bit queasy, actually. I can't eat this, it tastes like cardboard.' Natasha held her breath, waiting for the wave of nausea to pass.

Instantly Mother looked concerned. 'Is everything okay?'

'I'm fine, Mama. Don't worry.'

'Did you say, queasy?'

'Just a little bit.'

225

'How long have you felt like that?'

'A while. Not too long. A few days, maybe.' There was realisation on her mother's face, then fear. Natasha added, 'I'm sure it's nothing. Not enough food, that's all.' Mother was watching her in silence. 'What?' asked Natasha. 'Why are you looking at me like that?'

'Could you be... you know?'

'What?'

'Pregnant.' Mother mouthed the word soundlessly, looking around, making sure there was no one else in the room.

Natasha thought of the few times in the last week when she had been sick at work. She remembered feeling too nauseous to eat, every once in a while having to sit down to catch her breath. What if she was pregnant? What would Mark say? He wanted a child so much. He would be so happy. But so were Masha and her husband when she was expecting their youngest. All Natasha could think of as she lay in bed contemplating her uncertain future was Masha's helpless tears in their kitchen on Tarasovskaya as she mourned her baby's death. Natasha lowered her head. She couldn't be pregnant right now. 'I don't think so, Mama,' she said. 'I don't think so at all.'

When Mother left, Natasha forced herself out of bed. Where she found the strength to put her coat on, to put her hat on, to tie a scarf around her neck, to make her way down the stairs and into the bitter cold, she didn't know. Her legs quivering, her heart quivering, she walked to Mark's barracks through the nearly empty streets of Podol. The intense temperatures of the last few days had subsided. It was only minus fifteen. The Siberian winter was gone. The Ukrainian winter remained.

The door to Mark's barracks was firmly shut. Natasha removed her gloves and pulled the handle, noticing that her hands were shaking. When the door wouldn't budge, she slipped on the ice and fell. Swallowing her tears, she dusted herself off. Snow clung to her coat, and she could feel slush in her boots. None of it mattered. She used both her hands to pull at the door as hard as she could.

The door gave way.

Natasha didn't have the courage to walk in. As she stood in the doorway to Mark's barracks, she wished she had brought Nikolai with her. She listened for a sound, a sign of life. All was quiet. A few weeks ago, when it was still warm enough to go for walks, she had met Mark right here, on this spot. He gave her an orange. To this day she had no idea where he found an orange in the occupied Ukrainian capital but it appeared in his hands as if by magic, making her smile. That was what he'd always done. He had made her smile.

She had to go in. She needed to know what had happened to him.

Slowly, she strolled through what looked like a large dining hall, finally finding herself in a room with a couple dozen beds. The room was empty. There were no personal belongings, no indication that a regiment of young men had lived here only a day ago.

She wandered from bed to bed, wishing she knew which one was Mark's. She felt strangely excited at being in the room where he had spent the last few months, where he'd slept and read and joked and breathed. It made her feel closer to him. After she completed a full circle around the room, Natasha leaned on the wall, wondering what to do next. It was obvious that the Hungarian garrison was gone, probably back to Hungary. There was no trace of Mark.

She was about to leave when out of the corner of her eye she noticed something under one of the beds. She crossed the room to have a better look. It was a rucksack and it looked familiar. It couldn't be…

Even before she heaved it from under the bed, she knew it was Mark's.

Slowly she unclenched her frozen fingers and opened the rucksack. It was full to the brim with Mark's things. There were maps, papers, pens, and, to her delight, a letter to his mother. She had never seen his handwriting before. It was neat, round and a little childish. The letter wasn't finished and only consisted of a couple of lines — a greeting to his family and a couple of sentences about the weather. Natasha kissed the words that were written by his hand, folded the letter and hid it in her pocket.

At the very bottom of Mark's backpack, there was a jumper and a pair of socks. Natasha hugged the jumper close, hoping to catch a trace of Mark's scent. Underneath, she found the Dumas book she had given Mark on the day the first snow fell in Kiev. She was about to put the book back in the rucksack when she noticed a piece of paper hidden between the pages. It was covered in small writing that was difficult to decipher. The writing was unmistakably Russian. Just as Natasha suspected, it was a letter from Mark's mother. Eagerly she read every word. And when she finished reading, she rose to her feet and rushed to the dining hall, where she threw up in the sink. Then she returned to the room and read the letter for the second time. 'I'm counting the days until your return,' wrote Mark's mother in her neat, grown-up handwriting. 'And I'm not the only one. All Julia talks about is your wedding. Everything is ready. She even bought a dress at the local shop. Wait until you see it, she will look stunning in it. All we need is the date of your arrival, so we can let people know.'

Everything went dark. Natasha could no longer see the beds, the room, the broken window. Her legs couldn't support her. They were no longer made of flesh and blood but of melting snow. With her eyes shut, she sat on the floor. She didn't know how long she remained there, her face dry, her heart hurting. She had never felt more alone. If only Mark was here. He would know what to say to make everything alright. He would explain everything, and it would all make sense again. Her life would make sense again.

Or was she just lying to herself, like Mark had been lying to her all this time?

But through her doubts and through her fears, something was bothering her – Mark never went anywhere without his rucksack. If he returned to Hungary without her, if he deserted her in the Soviet Union so he could marry the unknown Julia who he had never even mentioned, why did he leave all his personal belongings here, in the abandoned barracks, under his old bed?

Natasha couldn't remember how she made it back home. Once there, she collapsed on her bed and didn't get up.

*

Natasha drifted in and out of consciousness. When she finally opened her eyes, it took a few seconds for the events of the previous day to come back to her. Instantly, she regretted waking up. If only she could sleep for a week, a month, a year, the war would be over and this thing she was feeling, this excruciating pain inside her would be over, too. The Dumas book and Mark's letter to his mother were in bed next to her. She hid the letter under her pillow and thought of Mark. She desperately needed to lay her eyes on him once more. She needed to see him because she couldn't bear this crushing agony alone.

Her chest was burning. She coughed.

Her lips were dry. All she could see out the window was snow falling in a wall of luminous white. She reached for the glass of water on her bedside table and took a couple of hasty sips. Muffled voices reached her from the living room. She had to make an effort to hear them.

'Is she alright?' demanded Lisa.

Her mother replied, 'I hope so. I couldn't find a doctor to take a look at her.'

'She's coughing a lot. She's always in and out of the house without so much as a scarf. She was bound to catch something.'

Lisa sounded worried. Natasha felt a momentary wave of affection for her sister. Lisa continued, 'Is she going to die? I don't want Natasha to die.'

'She's not going to die.'

'Mama, it's all my fault,' Lisa sobbed.

The voices quietened. Why was it Lisa's fault?

Natasha slept.

Next time she woke up, it was already dark. Someone was arguing in the kitchen. This time she couldn't hear what was being said. Three distinct words reached her, however: Mark, Gestapo and arrest. Shouting was followed by the sound of a slammed door, then all was quiet again.

A little bit later, Nikolai came to see her. 'How are you feeling?' he asked.

She thought about it. Her head was heavy as if filled with lead. Her stomach hurt. Without answering his question, she said, 'Nikolai, have you seen Lisa?'

'She went out a couple of hours ago. Why?'

'Tell her to come and see me as soon as she's back.'

Mother came in with a cup of tea and a piece of beetroot. There was no bread and no butter. The sight of food made Natasha sick. She pushed the plate away but took a sip of the tea. It was hot and burned her mouth.

When Nikolai left, she asked, 'Mama, where is Lisa?'

'Eat something,' said Mother. 'You haven't eaten for two days.'

The room was cold but Natasha was sweating. She sat up and took off her jumper. 'Where is Lisa?' she repeated. Her eyes followed Mother as she flitted around the room, opening the curtains and straightening the pillows.

'She went to stay with one of her friends for a while.'

'What did Lisa do?'

'Nothing, dear. Get some rest.'

'Mama, I heard you. In the kitchen yesterday, what did she say?' As hard as she tried, Natasha couldn't catch her mother's eye. She continued, 'She said something about the Gestapo. Did she tell them about Mark? Is that what happened? Please stop moving and talk to me.' Natasha watched as the last remnants of colour left her mother's already pale face. 'She did, didn't she? What did she tell them?' she whispered.

'I don't know what she's told them. She wouldn't say. All I know is that he was arrested.'

The room swayed in front of Natasha. She couldn't think straight. What could Lisa possibly tell the Gestapo to have Mark arrested? She didn't know he was the one responsible for the murder in the park. Or did she?

'How could she, Mama? How could she?' Natasha's voice was barely a whisper.

Mother sat next to Natasha. 'I know what she did was wrong but I'm sure she had your best interests at heart.'

'My best interests?'

'She didn't want you to make a mistake. And she thought going to Hungary was a mistake. She was trying to do the right thing. She misjudged the situation, that's all.'

'Misjudged the situation? She has no idea – she wouldn't know the right thing if it slapped her in the face.' Natasha rose on the bed and then let herself fall again. She had no energy for confrontations. 'Mama, please, tell me it's not true. Tell me he left without me, tell me he went back to Hungary. Tell me he no longer loves me. I don't care, as long as he's safe.'

Softly Mother stroked her head, whispering, 'Shh, shh.'

'I can't bear the thought of him dying. Not now. Not when he was so close to safety.'

'We don't know what happened, dear. He could still be alive. He might've been arrested and at this very moment he's thinking about you and trying to figure out a way to come back to you.'

Natasha tried to imagine her Mark's face. His alive, smiling face. She couldn't. No longer able to control herself, she shook and sobbed. 'It's my fault. If he'd never met me, he would have

231

been in Hungary by now. He would have been alive.' She was convulsing in Mother's arms.

'It's not your fault, darling. He loves you very much and he knew the risk he was taking. Don't blame yourself. It is not your fault.'

'You're right. It's not my fault. It's Lisa's. Don't let her anywhere near me. If I ever see her again, I'll kill her.' She shook. 'Mama, I wish I was with him when it happened. I wish we were captured in the truck together. I can't bear the thought of him alone and afraid. I wish I was there with him. I would rather it was me dead and not him.'

'Please, don't say that. Whatever happened, he knew how much you love him.' Mother held Natasha tightly, refusing to let go. 'Please, have something to eat. You need your strength.'

'Don't you see, Mama? Nothing matters anymore. Nothing at all.'

Natasha could no longer stand the pity on her mother's face. She closed her eyes and pretended to sleep. When Mother left, Natasha prayed for the oblivion of the last couple of days but sleep wouldn't come.

She'd thought the day her grandmother died was the most painful day of her life. Yet, even then, in her grief and despair, she still had hope. She believed in so many things. She believed the Red Army would return and defeat the Germans. She believed the war would be over, as suddenly and unexpectedly as it had begun. She believed that one day she would be happy with the man she loved. Now, as she watched the fabric of her life split open, she knew that her faith was forever gone.

Blinded by tears, she tried to remember the last time she saw Mark. Was there any indication, was there a sign that it was the end? Did it feel different, more intense, somehow final? She groaned in pain. The last time she saw him, in their last moments together, as he held her in his arms, he had told her how much he loved her and although she'd wanted to, she didn't have the strength to say it back. She didn't have the courage to open her eyes and look into his loving face. Now, as she clasped her sheets and struggled not to scream, she wished with all her heart that the last time she and Mark had been together, she had told him how much she loved him. She wanted to go back in time and force her mouth open, force her eyes open so that his face would be forever etched in her mind.

Natasha could no longer breathe. She was suffocating. She stumbled outside, down the stairs and onto the freezing street. It was deserted. The cold instantly numbed her bare skin. She fell on the snow. There were no tears left. Instead, she wailed like a wounded animal. She clenched her stomach and screamed until her voice was hoarse and she could scream no more. As if in a frenzy, she repeated his name. 'I love you, Mark,' she whispered. 'I love you so much. Come back! Please, come back.'

She was the city of Kiev, ravaged by fires, decimated by mortars, broken by war. It was as if an explosion had raged through her torn and twisted heart, leaving nothing in its place but an empty shell.

An elderly neighbour tried to help her up, but Natasha struggled against him like she was possessed. Finally, the old man left her alone and went to fetch Mother and Nikolai. Together they dragged Natasha upstairs. From her bed, she could hear their voices, careful whispers that reached her through the haze of her grief.

Finally, she slept.

*

It was quiet in the cafeteria but for the ticking of the clock, but for Natasha's heavy heartbeat. 'Mark, remember when we walked in the park together for the first time?' she asked, her eyes twinkling in the dark.

'How could I ever forget?'

'I wanted to kiss you so much that day. It was all I could think about.'

'Why didn't you?'

She imagined them in the park together. Imagined them on a bench next to each other, their legs touching, their hands touching. 'I was too shy.'

'Why were you shy?' He clasped her in his arms and she groaned.

'I was shy because I couldn't believe that someone like you could be interested in someone like me.'

He looked transfixed by her. 'Well, believe it, because you are all I can think about.'

'Do you know when I first knew I loved you?'

'Tell me.'

'The day Olga was taken away. You were the only person I wanted to be with on that terrible day.'

'That's when I knew I would do anything for you. I wanted to move mountains for you, dry rivers for you just to see you smile.'

She kissed his face, kissed his hair, light butterfly kisses that tickled and soothed.

'I will never forget the autumn day when I first met you,' he whispered.

Kissing his lips, she said, 'I will never forget the day when I found my true love.'

Part II - The Everlasting Hope

Chapter 14 – Rays of Sunshine

September – October 1942

On the day Natasha became a mother, there was a storm in Kiev. After two weeks of the autumn sun shining summer bright (Indian summer, Mother called it), thunder bellowed and rain pounded. Natasha didn't notice any of it. She was blessedly, peacefully asleep, her arms around her swollen belly, her legs up on a cushion. Being almost nine months' pregnant, sleep was the only thing she could do effortlessly and well.

As if through a haze she heard her brother's voice. Reluctantly she opened her eyes and saw Nikolai perched on the couch next to her. In his hands he held a pair of knitting needles and a ball of yarn, still attached to a half-finished creation she had been working on before she fell asleep. 'What is this supposed to be? A hat?' he asked, waving it in front of Natasha's unfocused eyes.

With great difficulty she sat up. 'A sock, silly.' She reached out to wrestle the yarn from her brother, but he evaded her, moving to the opposite side of the couch with a grin and a chuckle. She could tell he was taunting her and considered going after him but the effort! If she got any bigger, she might need a forklift to help her up.

For a second or two Nikolai scrutinised the sock she'd spent the last two nights slaving over. Finally, he said, 'It's a bit big.'

'That's alright,' she replied defensively. 'The baby will grow into it.'

'A baby elephant would have to grow into it. Love the colour, though. What is it, washed-out pink?'

'That was all I could get at the market,' said Natasha.

'Does it mean I'm having a niece?'

'Of course you are. What did you think?'

'I was hoping for a nephew.'

Natasha sat up and stretched. 'Well, you were hoping wrong. It's a girl.'

'How do you know?'

'I can feel it.'

'Boys are much more fun. You can teach him how to play football. Take him to play hockey in winter. Do you know any girls who play football?'

Olga played football, thought Natasha. She played football better than any boy. But she couldn't say that to her smiling, teasing, exasperating brother.

Nikolai pinched her. 'Thought so. Boys are so much better than girls.'

Not looking up, Natasha said, 'According to Mama, all baby boys do is pee in your face and cry. Girls are so much more refined.'

Nikolai scrunched up his face in mock distress. 'Did I really do that? I must apologise to Mama for my unrefined behaviour.'

'Come here, you unrefined one. Why don't you help me make some socks?'

Red-faced and laughing, Nikolai said, 'Me, knit? Are you serious?' And he rushed off in the direction of the kitchen.

Natasha could follow him to get something to eat, to find a book to read, to talk to her mother. Or she could go back to sleep, and by the time she woke up, it would be evening and another day would have gone by. As time went by, she found it harder and harder to go about her daily tasks. Natasha was so slow, it took her twice as long to get dressed, to cook what little food they had, to make it across the road to pick up their ration of unpalatable bread. She hoped it was the pregnancy but suspected it was more than that. She was as thin as a rail, and only her round stomach protruded. Despite her family's best efforts, she wasn't getting enough food.

And yet, she was one of the lucky ones.

Almost a year after the Nazis had entered Ukraine, no one could even begin to estimate with any degree of accuracy the exact number of dead and dying in Kiev. On every corner, on every street there were children, men and women of all ages, but mostly the elderly, their hands outstretched, their mouths entreating, their faces red with embarrassment. In their new wartime lives they were reduced to begging, and yet their hardships hadn't erased from their memories their old, happier lives. Lives in which they were respected teachers, doctors or factory workers. Their need didn't make their predicament any easier or less humiliating. There were more people begging than those who could give them anything, if only a tiny morsel. Nazis, arrogant, haughty, disdainful, arm in arm with beautiful Ukrainian women, stepped out of the 'Germans Only' restaurants, contented after a hearty meal, and sauntered past the poor and the destitute, without a glance and without a thought. They didn't notice them like they didn't notice the cars that whizzed by or the trees that were turning gold. Soviet people, on the other hand, noticed everything and lowered their heads, lowered their gaze in shame because they had nothing to give. Because they, too, were only one step away from walking the streets with their hands outstretched.

Often there would be a knock outside, and Natasha would open the door to a withered, exhausted, wounded man, aged beyond his years, who was returning from one of the prison camps. He wouldn't even have to say anything, she saw it in his eyes. The hunger, the pain, the desperation, she saw it all. She would sigh and lower her head in shame because she had nothing to give. And through it all, she thought of her father. She thought of her brother and prayed that, wherever they were, someone would give them a piece of bread that they needed to survive.

She thought of Mark.

More Hungarian troops had been sent to Ukraine in the early summer of 1942. The first time Natasha had seen a soldier in a familiar brown uniform, her heart had stood still and she had paused in the middle of the street, mouth open, hands shaking. She'd dashed across the road as fast as her condition allowed, hoping to catch up with the tall figure. She didn't breathe once in all the time it took her to reach him, to grab him by the arm, to peer into his face. It wasn't Mark. The shock was so severe, she sank onto the pavement and sobbed. Seeing a crying pregnant girl on the ground in front of him, the soldier didn't know what to do. He helped Natasha to her feet and walked her home, saying something in a language she didn't understand.

The second time she had seen a group of Hungarian soldiers, she knew Mark wouldn't be among them. Still, she'd run after them, to look at them, to hear them talk, to ask questions. Although they spoke no Russian, she repeated Mark's name and the name of his regiment, hoping for a reaction, for a recognition. But she got nothing. Not only did they not know what happened to the regiment, from their confused faces she could tell that they had never even heard of it, having just arrived in Ukraine. Soon she stopped asking and only followed them with her sad, anguished eyes.

And through it all, transportation to Germany hung over their heads like the sword of Damocles. No one was safe. Women mutilated themselves to avoid being taken but it was in vain. The Nazis didn't care. Meagre possessions on their backs, the condemned boarded trains that were to carry them to their unknown destinies, trains with slogans that read: 'Ukraine gives her best sons and daughters to wonderful Germany in gratitude for the liberation from the clutches of the Bolsheviks.' Who came up with this propaganda? wondered Natasha. Whoever it was, they were unlikely to ever ride on one of these trains.

The Nazis seized children as young as twelve. Boys and girls were wrestled from their mothers' arms on the street and snatched in the middle of the night from their beds as their families screamed for mercy. Train after train of crying children was sent across Europe to German factories to replace workers who were then free to kill the children's fathers on the Eastern Front. Sobs filled the rail stations, the streets, the city, all of Ukraine as mothers said goodbye to their little ones never to see them again, while passers-by watched with pity and fear. On every face Natasha read the same question: am I next?

There was a quiet knock on the front door. Natasha moved her body slightly so that she could see the corridor. Even this small movement took most of her energy. She breathed heavily, watching as Yuri opened the door to his friend Gregory, and the two of them disappeared in the kitchen, closing the door behind them.

Natasha got comfortable, preparing for another nap. But Gregory didn't stay long. Before she had a chance to close her eyes, he was gone, and Yuri appeared in the living room, carrying a large pile of documents.

'What are those?' asked Natasha.

'They are the passports of all those who were killed at Kirillovskaya Hospital this week,' replied Yuri, placing the documents on the table.

'All these people were killed at the hospital?' Natasha shuddered, hugging her stomach. There were at least two dozen passports on the table. 'What are you doing with their documents?'

'We use them to smuggle Jewish people out of Ukraine.'

'There are Jewish people still left in Kiev?'

'Some. Not many.'

There were dark circles under his eyes and streaks of grey in his hair. Natasha touched his hand. 'Yuri, please, be careful. I keep hearing horrible stories about what happens to the partisans who are caught.'

Without looking up, Yuri sifted through the documents. Natasha peered over his shoulder. She couldn't believe how young some of the people killed at Kirillovskaya had been, how open their smiles, how full of hope. After a minute of silence he said, 'I know what we do is risky. But it's worth it.' He looked at her and his eyes grew warm. 'Don't worry. You know why most partisans get caught? Because they're denounced by the same people they're trying to help. Nine people out of ten will sell you for a piece of bread. The trick is not to confide in anyone.'

'But you confided in us. In me and Nikolai.' *And in Lisa*, she wanted to say but didn't. She tried not to think about her sister. She hadn't seen her since the day in January when Mark had disappeared. Mother did a brilliant job of keeping the two of them apart.

'You're different. You, Natasha, are one in a million.'

One after another, he placed the documents in a small bag. Soon, there was only one passport left. He opened it and gasped. There was something in his eyes that unnerved Natasha. She reached for the passport and looked at the photo page. A pleasant middle-aged woman looked at her from the photograph. Irina Alexeevna Korovina, Natasha read. Although the picture was black and white, she could almost swear that the woman's hair was fair and her eyes were green just like Yuri's, so strong was the family resemblance.

Outside, the wind was wailing. Inside, there was silence.

'Is that… your mother?' Natasha stammered.

Yuri's head was in his hands. He wasn't looking at the passport, nor was he looking at Natasha. 'I thought… I hoped she had evacuated,' he muttered.

Natasha heaved herself up and sat next to Yuri, pulling him close. 'I'm sorry about your mother,' she whispered. 'She's so beautiful.' She glanced at the date of birth. Yuri's mother was barely forty-five. She must have had him when she was very young.

'She is... was. I remember the day I left for the front. I've never seen her cry so much. But even in the prison camp, even when I saw all my comrades die, I was hoping I would live to see her again.'

'I'm so sorry.' What could she say, what could she do to make him feel better?

'She always dreamt of a big family but all she had was me. She wanted grandchildren. She hoped I would have a family of my own soon but then the war had started.' He raised his hurting eyes to her. 'Natasha, I think we should get married. The baby needs a father and you know how I feel about you.'

Natasha's face went white.

When she didn't reply, he said, 'I'm sorry, I didn't mean to spring it on you. I've been thinking about it for a while now—'

She clasped her stomach. 'It's not that, it's...' She felt a sharp pain in her abdomen.

'What is it? Are you okay?'

She gripped his hand tighter. A tremor ran through her body. 'I think the baby's coming—'

She let go of his hand and grabbed the table. Holding her breath, she prayed for the contraction to pass.

'What can I get you? What can I do?' cried Yuri.

His face was a mask of panic. Natasha would have laughed if she had the strength. All she managed was a grimace and a groan. 'Get Mama,' she whispered. 'She's at work.'

Natasha rubbed her stomach, watching Yuri as he ran out the door. She had often imagined this moment and every time she'd thought about it, she'd been afraid. But now, when it was finally time, she didn't feel scared. Nervous, yes, expectant and confused, yes, but not scared.

She was about to meet her little one. Mark's little one.

Another contraction came and went. Her eyes squeezed tight, Natasha attempted to count from a hundred to zero, to recite world capitals in alphabetical order, anything to keep her mind off what was happening. But the numbers clashed and stumbled upon each other in her head, nor could she recall any cities that started with A, B or C.

She called for Nikolai. He sat holding her hand until their overexcited mother rushed into the room, her face as red as her daughter's was white. Yuri was close behind. Mother looked as if she had run all the way from the library where she had been working since her school closed down in June. She brought an agitated old lady with her. At first Natasha didn't know who this lady was but when she looked closer, she recognised Claudia, their neighbour from the first floor.

For someone who relied on a walking stick, Claudia moved with surprising speed and agility. 'The boys have to go,' she said firmly, pointing at Nikolai and Yuri with a crooked finger. For once, Nikolai didn't argue. He and Yuri left the room, closing the door behind them. Claudia patted Natasha's stomach. 'Don't worry, dear. I've been a midwife for fifty-five years.' She placed a shrivelled hand on Natasha's abdomen. 'Why, aren't you huge! I don't think I've ever seen anyone as big as you.'

'Are you feeling alright?' Mother wanted to know.

'Wonderful,' mumbled Natasha, groaning and bending over as another contraction gripped her.

In her no-nonsense voice, Claudia interrupted. 'Come, you must lie down.' Mother helped her into bed with Claudia trailing one step behind. 'How long between the contractions?' she demanded. Natasha told her. Claudia said, 'Still a long way to go. Might as well relax and have a cup of tea.'

Natasha widened her eyes in panic, but the old lady was no longer looking at her. Mother rushed to the kitchen and returned with a cup of tea and a German biscuit – a thin slice of beetroot dried in the oven. Through the painful mist of another contraction, Natasha tried to focus on Claudia's high-pitched voice. 'For the first time in my life I'm glad I'm old. They won't send me to Germany. They have no use for me.' She sighed, made a clucking noise with her lips and pointed a shaking finger at Natasha.

'Aren't you a bit young to have a baby? What are you, fifteen?'

Natasha knew that with her hair in braids and her face without a trace of make-up she looked about twelve. 'Twenty,' she whispered.

'Mind you, I had my first child when I was barely seventeen. Didn't do me any harm. You aren't married though, are you, dear?'

The old woman's curious disapproval was the last thing Natasha needed. She shrugged and turned to the wall.

'I helped deliver four babies last month. The first three were stillborn.'

Natasha's heart skipped a beat. She tried to remember the last time she had felt her baby kick and couldn't. Mother glared at Claudia, who continued, oblivious to their discomfort. 'The last one was alive, though.'

Natasha breathed a sigh of relief.

'Barely survived a week. Died from malnutrition. Adults are dying wherever you turn, what do you expect from a newborn baby? It was a little boy. His mother was devastated. Threw herself in the Dnieper. Poor woman, she already lost two sons and a daughter. The baby was all she had in the world, heaven help her.' The old woman shook her fist, whether at heaven or at the Nazis, Natasha couldn't tell.

Natasha wanted the labour to start, a lightning bolt to strike, anything but having to listen to another one of Claudia's stories. She rubbed her watermelon of a stomach. 'Not long now,' she whispered to the baby.

Another contraction took her by surprise, and this time the pain was so severe, she almost fainted. All went dark and she could no longer hear Claudia. She moaned, desperately waving her hands. The old lady couldn't have moved any slower if she wanted to. Natasha watched her through half-closed eyes as she put her cup down, rose to her feet, picked up her walking stick and shuffled towards Natasha. She took forever to examine her and then said, 'That was quick. I didn't even finish my tea. This baby is desperate to come out.' She turned to Mother. 'We'll need some sheets, some boiled water.'

Mother left the room, pulling the door behind her, and Natasha heard her shouting for Yuri and Nikolai to help with the kettle.

Natasha bit her lip until it bled, trying to stop herself from screaming. She didn't want the men in the other room to hear. It wouldn't do for her grandfather to worry. But she couldn't help it, she cried out. She thought she couldn't take the pain any longer, not for another minute. But it was just beginning. Hour melted into hour, and Natasha lost all track of time. Soon it was dark outside.

'Push,' demanded Claudia. 'You're almost there. I can see the head. Push harder.'

Natasha wanted to but couldn't. She clenched her mother's hand so hard, she heard her gasp.

Finally, after what seemed like an age, the midwife said, 'It's a boy.' A *boy*. Natasha forced her eyes open. Claudia continued, 'He's alive. Can't believe how big he is. And he has dark hair. How wonderful.'

Just like his father, thought Natasha.

She strained her broken body, forcing herself to sit up. She desperately wanted to see her son. It was quiet. Why wasn't he crying? She wanted to ask if he was alright but her lips wouldn't move. Then suddenly a piercing shriek filled the room, and Natasha burst into tears. She heard Mother's cooing. Claudia mumbled, 'New life. How astonishing. But what a bad time you chose to come into this world, what an evil time.'

Natasha reached for her baby, wanting to hold him, when yet

another contraction made her cry out. Claudia handed the boy to Mother and inspected Natasha. 'Looks like you're about to have another baby,' she concluded. Her tone was impassive, as if she was asking Natasha to pass her some salt at the dinner table.

'I'm having twins?'

'I'm afraid you are. You poor girl. Who has twins? Never in my life have I seen anything like this. How will you feed them? Wartime twins, what a misfortune.'

Through her tears Natasha smiled. She was having two of Mark's babies instead of one. It wasn't a misfortune, it was a miracle.

The second delivery went much quicker than the first. An hour later the old lady placed two tiny bundles in Natasha's arms. She looked in amazement at the two tiny faces, kissing them one after another, first the little boy and then the girl. One of each, just like Mark had wanted. She bent her head and inhaled their scent. Warmth was emanating from them.

Natasha closed her eyes and thought of Mark standing in front of her, placing his arms firmly around her hips and lifting her high as if trying to throw her in the air so he could catch her. Afraid that it was exactly what he was about to do, she squealed, 'Put me down. I'm too heavy.'

'You weigh nothing,' he said, grinning.

'Put me down right now, you're making me dizzy.' He made her beg and then lowered her onto the ground and covered her mouth with kisses.

When Natasha opened her eyes, Mark's children were in front of her, their little eyes shut, their little lips moving.

Mother opened the door. Natasha could hear agitated voices outside. She could see Nikolai's pale face peering through the doorway. She closed her eyes and slept. When she awoke, Claudia was gone. Only Mother remained in the room. Mother, Natasha and two tiny bundles in her arms. It was too dark and she couldn't see them. She wanted to see them.

'What's the date today?' she whispered.

'The seventh,' replied Mother.

7th September. Almost a year since she had met Mark. Almost a year since Grandmother had died.

'What will you name them?'

'Larisa, after our babushka.' She kissed her daughter's tiny button of a nose. 'Mama, why are you crying?'

'I wish Babushka has lived to see this. Her great-grandchildren.'

'And I'll name the boy Costa. After Mark's father Constantine.'

Visitors soon filed into her room. Nikolai first, closely followed by Grandfather. Yuri sat on her bed for a while, holding her hand, and Mikhail came in to congratulate her. But all she wanted was to be alone with her babies. Despite the war, despite the hunger, despite the Germans still in her city, Natasha could swear that at that precise moment there was no one in the whole world who was more blessed than she was. At that precise moment, no one and nothing else existed, except for her and the two tiny new lives she was holding.

*

Natasha had spent the first few weeks of her babies' lives as if in a daze. With no sleep and two needy infants glued to her, she couldn't have coped if it wasn't for her family. Mother spoon-fed Natasha while she breastfed around the clock. Nikolai read to her and the babies. Yuri brought a guitar and sang solemn war songs to her and the babies. Grandfather kept her updated with news from the front, although she would have preferred it if he hadn't. Absorbing herself in her babies, she could pretend, for a moment, that the war wasn't even happening.

'Why are they feeding so much?' Natasha said one morning after a night of sitting up with the babies, kissing them, inhaling their infant scent and not sleeping. 'Is it normal?'

'At this rate they'll grow into those socks you've been making before you even know it,' said Nikolai.

'Completely normal,' said Mother. 'They do it for comfort. They just want to be close to you.'

'Will it ever get easier?'

'Of course it will. When they start school,' Mother joked.

But it did get easier. Suddenly, a few weeks later, the babies stopped crying every time she put them down. They started sleeping not just in her arms but in the cots Yuri had built for them. And Natasha could breathe again.

Even in her most desperate moments, she was besieged by an all-consuming love of such magnitude, it was like a volcano exploded inside her every time she saw her babies' little faces. She was a mother, and it felt magical. She was utterly, irrevocably under her little ones' spell. As unfamiliar as this feeling was, she had been prepared for it, like she was prepared for the sleepless nights and the dirty bottoms. After all, everyone always talked about it. What she wasn't prepared for was the debilitating fear that gripped her when the babies were born. She thought she had known fear before, having lived in occupied Kiev for a year. And yet, that feeling was a seedling in comparison to what raged inside her at the thought of something happening to her children. The *what ifs* inside her head drove her to distraction. *What if there's not enough food for them? What if I don't have enough milk? What if they get sick? What if they get taken away from me? What if I will get taken away from them? What if someone tries to hurt them?* And worse — *What if I lose them? How will I survive losing them?* She wouldn't survive losing them; she knew that for a fact. If she lost them, she'd lose her sanity, just like Masha, whose distorted and mournful face haunted her day and night, while the voices inside her head whispered-whispered-whispered as she clasped the babies to her chest in a protective embrace. Natasha was a lioness trapped in a small cage, ready to pounce and maul anyone who threatened her son and daughter.

And so she never left her babies' side, not for a moment. It was as if an invisible umbilical cord still attached her to her son and daughter. She wasn't the only one. Grandfather hardly had time for his books because all he wanted to do was be near his great-grandchildren. Nikolai's face would crease in wonder whenever he saw his niece or nephew. Yuri would play the guitar to Natasha and the babies, thoughtfully, mutely, with a sad smile on his face. Mother rushed to Natasha's bed as soon as she walked through the door, her shoes on, her coat on, and didn't put the twins down until it was time to make dinner. She would cry whenever she saw her grandchildren.

'Mama, why are you crying? Shouldn't you be happy?'

'I *am* happy.'

Larisa and Constantine were continuously held, rocked, cuddled, kissed. *It's lucky we have two*, thought Natasha. One baby wouldn't be enough for this family.

*

It was a quiet October afternoon, and Mother had just returned from the library. The little boy was cradled in her arms. Natasha reached for her son. 'Mama, go and get changed. You still have your coat on. Give me Costa.'

Mother was swaying the boy, rocking him, kissing him, her eyes swimming in happy tears.

Natasha said, 'He needs food. He's a growing boy.' The desire to hold her baby was like a physical pain and she twitched impatiently. 'He's hungry.' As if on cue, Costa broke out crying. His shrieks woke Larisa, whose voice joined his.

'What's all this commotion?' Nikolai wanted to know. As soon as he saw two wriggling infants, he chuckled. 'Can I hold them?'

'Not yet,' said Natasha.

'When can I hold them? You've been saying not yet for the last month. They were born a month ago and I barely know what they look like.' He was trying hard to look upset and failing. The smile was wide on his face.

250

He pinched her lightly and she reached out to pinch him back but in one stride he was behind the bed, too fast for her. She would have pursued him if a screaming child wasn't balanced on her hip.

'Alright, hold them but be careful.'

'Not both at the same time,' said Mother.

Nikolai took his nephew in his arms, swinging him back and forth, up and down in a rapid motion. 'You're doing it too fast,' said Natasha. 'It will just make him cry more.'

'Support his head,' said Mother.

'Don't turn him upside down,' demanded Natasha. 'No, not like that.'

As if by a miracle, Costa stopped screaming.

'You were saying?' Nikolai laughed. Mother, Natasha and Grandfather watched him in wonder. 'Hello,' Nikolai chanted to the baby. 'Do you like football?' Two tiny round eyes were staring up at him and a tiny mouth was open as if in a question mark. Nikolai looked close to crying, just like Mother. *What is it with my family?* thought Natasha. *They always have tears in their eyes.* 'That's right, you don't know what football is. But in a year or two you will. I'll teach you and Larisa,' he murmured.

'In a year or two?' Natasha laughed. 'Can I have my son back? He needs food, not football.'

Nikolai leaned close to the boy, inhaled, kissed him goodbye, crooned. 'You are a sweet boy, a beautiful boy. Look at these tiny feet, these tiny hands, this tiny nose.'

Mother said, sniffling, 'Tiny everything but so perfect.'

As soon as Costa left Nikolai's arms, he emitted a low wail.

Nikolai picked up Larisa and she fell quiet, watching him curiously. 'How about you? Do you like football?'

'Girls don't play football,' said Mother. 'She'll be knitting and cooking with her grandmother.'

'Well, that's just not fair, is it?' Nikolai made a funny face and tickled Larisa. 'No, it's not. It's much more fun to play football with your brother and uncle.'

'Where were you two hours ago when they were screaming the house down? How did you get them to be quiet?' asked Natasha.

'I'll tell you for a German biscuit.'

'He's a natural,' said Grandfather, watching the two little faces that were now peaceful and content. His eyes were misty, his gaze unfocused. He turned to Natasha. 'I remember like yesterday the day you were born. They look just like you when you were little.'

Natasha didn't argue with her grandfather, even though she knew that her children didn't look like her at all. They were the spitting image of Mark.

Was there a life before the twins? She could hardly remember it. Her babies' needs enveloped her and she no longer felt alone. When she opened her eyes and looked at them, their tiny faces brought her comfort. And she needed comfort because, when she closed her eyes, all she saw, all she could think of was Mark.

Night after restless night, she felt for him in the dark, imagining his face, wondering where he was. And as the twins slept by her side, she folded and unfolded the cursed letter that had sown doubt and suspicion in her heart. What if at that very moment, while Natasha was cradling his babies and whispering his name, Mark was with Julia, in his beloved Hungary, married and content? What if he never even gave a second thought to her? Had she just been a passing fancy to him, a conquest to amuse him during his time in the Soviet Union? She saw Mark's adoring face as he asked her to marry him, on what had turned out to be their last day together. Was it all a lie? Was he planning to leave her behind all along, to return to Hungary and marry someone else? And if he was, why ask her to come with him at all? Why not just slip away one day, without a word, without a goodbye? *He loves me*, she whispered to herself. *He loves me*. While another voice in her head, the voice she was doing her level best to ignore, repeated,

But isn't that exactly what happened? He slipped away one day, without a word, without a goodbye.

No, it wasn't her Mark. The man she loved more than anything in the world, who she loved since the moment he had rescued her that night in the park, wasn't capable of such deception. She wished she had never come across the letter. She didn't want her beautiful memories of Mark to be tarnished by doubt and suspicion. But if he hadn't returned to Hungary with the other soldiers, that only meant one thing. He had been arrested and possibly killed. As Natasha placed her trembling hands on the twins' chests and felt for their heartbeats, she prayed that Mark had abandoned her for someone else because the other possibility – that he had died because of her – was too terrible to contemplate.

Chapter 15 – The Utmost Chaos

November – December 1942

As the twins lay sound asleep in her lap, Natasha watched the first snow outside, while next to her, Yuri and Nikolai were playing the Russian Fool.

'Natasha, help. Your brother is clearing me out. I almost lost all my money,' said Yuri. Nikolai rubbed his hands together, looking smug.

'What do you want me to do about it?' asked Natasha.

'Come here and win it back.'

Nikolai chuckled.

Natasha frowned. 'Why? Because I'm so lucky in cards? Anyway, I don't see the point of this game. I'd rather play chess.' As soon as she said that, a needle of pain pricked her heart and she looked away, hoping Yuri and her brother wouldn't notice her tears. Remembering Mark's face as he leaned across the chessboard, touching her cheek and saying, 'You win, again! One more game?'

'Chess is too complicated,' said Yuri. 'Cards are much more fun.'

'Maybe next time. The babies keep waking.' Natasha cradled her little ones and sang, '*And with my heart I rush forth to a dark tiny orchard – to Ukraine.*' When she closed her eyes, she was no longer in their Podol apartment but walking through Shevchenko Park arm in arm with a soldier in Hungarian uniform.

'Taras Shevchenko? Is it appropriate singing material for little babies? No wonder they can't sleep,' said Yuri.

Blinking her thoughts away, Natasha said. 'It's not that. Every time Larisa settles, Costa starts crying, waking her up. And the other way around. It's a vicious circle.'

'Let's play,' said Nikolai. 'Enough distractions. There's money to be won.'

'To be lost, you mean?' said Natasha.

For a few moments nothing was heard but shuffling of cards and exasperated breaths. And then Nikolai exclaimed, 'You lose.'

'You have no one to blame but yourself,' Natasha said to Yuri. 'Haven't you ever read Owen Feltham? Do you know what he said about playing for money?'

'Who is Owen Feltham and what did he say?'

'The famous English writer said that by gambling we lose our time and treasure, two things most precious to the life of man.'

'He was right. Where did the time go? I have to run. Gregory is waiting for me.' Yuri stood up, handed all his coins to Nikolai and left.

A minute later, there was a knock on the door. 'What did he forget?' muttered Natasha.

She opened the door, expecting to see Yuri. In the hall, in a threadbare red coat that Natasha had never seen before, thinner than she remembered, stood Lisa.

So shocked was Natasha by this sudden apparition, she slammed the door in Lisa's face, leaning against it. Lisa knocked again. 'Natasha, please, open up, I need to talk to you.' She knocked harder.

Natasha walked back to the living room and shut the door to block out Lisa's entreaties. Unfortunately, either the door was too thin or her sister's voice was too loud because she could still hear Lisa for another twenty minutes.

As Lisa knocked and shouted, Natasha could sense Nikolai's gaze on her. He didn't say a word but watched her as if waiting for something. Did he expect her to open the door to Lisa and let her in? Did he want an explanation? Natasha turned away from her brother and towards the front door that was shaking under Lisa's vigour.

Finally, Nikolai asked, 'What happened between you and Lisa? Everyone behaves like she's done something terrible. But what?'

Natasha sighed. 'I wish I knew exactly.'

'You think it's her, don't you? You think she's the reason why Mark never arrived that day.'

Hearing the words out loud was a thousand times more difficult than hearing them in her head. Before Mark's disappearance, Natasha had genuinely believed that Lisa had forgiven her. They had always been so close, and Natasha had never meant to hurt Lisa. But if what Mother had told Natasha was correct, and Lisa did go to the Gestapo and denounce Mark, then she had deliberately done something to destroy Natasha, to smash her heart into a million tiny shards. How was it possible? Who was capable of such an abysmal betrayal? Not the sister Natasha had known and loved.

As if reading her mind, Nikolai said, 'Why would she do something like this? It's Lisa we are talking about. I know she's selfish, but she's not cruel.'

'I suppose she thought I deserved it.' Was that what it was: an eye for an eye? Natasha had lied to Lisa, and by doing so allowed Alexei to be taken away and killed. So Lisa took Natasha's love away from her and sent him to a certain death. Lisa's heart was broken, so she felt she had every right to break Natasha's heart in return. Natasha wondered if it had made Lisa feel better. Did Mark's arrest, if he had indeed been arrested, make Lisa's heart any less broken? It certainly didn't bring Alexei back. Or was Mother right? Did Lisa denounce Mark because in her warped mind she thought she was doing Natasha a favour, stopping her from making a mistake?

Nikolai said, 'You can't shut her out forever. She's still our sister. I feel like I'm caught in the middle. I don't want to take sides. I miss her.'

'I know you do, Nikolai. I'm sorry.' This was what the two of them had done, she realised. Caught up in their heartbreak and their hatred, Lisa and Natasha had created a rift that was breaking their family apart. And those closest to them were paying for it, as if the war and the Nazis were not enough.

*

November turned into December, and dry autumn leaves gave way to the first winter snow. Lisa hadn't come back. Natasha's daily routine enveloped her: feeding, washing, rocking, singing, day after day, night after night, a never-ending circle that left no space for feeling, no space for thoughts other than those of her babies. Soon she forgot all about Lisa until one cold day in the second week of December when it was just her and Grandfather at home with the babies. There was a sharp knock, and when Natasha opened the door, she found herself face to face with Claudia. Since the twins were born, their neighbour stopped by regularly. She seemed even more stooped and frail than before. But her no-nonsense voice hadn't changed. 'Quick, tell your mother to come and see me. I need her help.'

'Mama's at the library,' said Natasha. 'She spends all her time there now. More and more people come to read the books. She feels needed.'

Claudia waved her hands as if swatting off a fly. She didn't care about the library. 'That's a shame. I need help urgently.'

'Can I help instead?'

'I want her to mend some clothes for me. I'd do it myself but my hands shake.' She raised her hands as if to prove her point.

Natasha wanted to ask what was so urgent about mending a few old garments but she didn't want to upset someone who was old enough to be her great-grandmother. 'Maybe I could do it?'

Claudia didn't reply. She spotted the two infants who were sound asleep after their feeding. All urgency seemingly forgotten, she crossed the corridor in three long strides and lowered her head until it was level with Costa's, muttering disjointed sentences under her breath. The boy didn't stir. Natasha noticed that about her babies. When they wanted to, they could sleep through cannon and mortar.

'Look at these two little angels! Still alive and doing so well.' Claudia sounded pleased, if a little surprised.

'Angels? You should have heard them ten minutes ago.'

'Really? I didn't hear a thing. And I'm only downstairs from you.'

Natasha wanted to point out that if an explosion went off in Claudia's kitchen, she wouldn't have heard. Instead, she said, 'Come, Claudia Ivanovna, I'll help you with your clothes.'

Claudia looked as if Natasha had offered to perform complex heart surgery. 'Do you know how?'

'Of course I do. I'm good with my hands. Look at the socks I knit for my little ones.'

Claudia contemplated Costa and Larisa's tiny feet. 'You call those socks? They look like furry beetroots.'

'But they're warm and that's all that matters.'

Having asked her grandfather to keep an eye on the children, Natasha followed the neighbour downstairs. It was the first time she had left her babies since they were born. She felt lost, as if without a child attached to her hip she no longer knew how to move. She tried to spend as little time as possible in Claudia's small but unexpectedly clean apartment but unfortunately, once the old lady got hold of Natasha, she had no intention of letting her go. There was plenty of work to be done, plenty of little tasks around the house that she was too weak to do herself. Three hours, a pile of mended clothes and four polished windows later, the exhausted Natasha stumbled back home.

In the apartment, Mikhail's war songs were playing loudly on the gramophone. Grandfather was asleep, a newspaper in his lap, his glasses perched precariously on the tip of his nose. The instant Natasha walked in, she knew something wasn't right. The door to her bedroom was closed. And she could almost swear she had left it open. Did Grandfather close it? But why would he, if the babies were asleep inside and Natasha had asked him to keep an eye on them? She felt the small hairs at the back of her neck stir in fear.

Taking a deep breath, she pushed the door with her shoulder. Someone was in the room. By the worn-out red coat, by the shape of the back, Natasha knew instantly who it was. Her sister looked as shocked at being caught as Natasha was at finding her there. In her arms Lisa held Larisa. A small bag was dangling from Lisa's hand.

Natasha sprang towards Lisa and wrestled Larisa from her sister's arms so violently that both Lisa and Larisa cried out. Natasha didn't know where she found the strength. She clutched her crying daughter tightly with one hand, while with the other pushed her sister until she lost her balance and almost fell.

Natasha couldn't speak and Lisa wouldn't speak. They stood gaping at each other, panting, overwrought. When Natasha recovered her voice, she said, 'What do you think you're doing? Where were you taking her?'

Shrieks filled the room. The twins were red in the face, kicking with their little legs, lashing out with their fists. Natasha rocked her daughter, glaring at Lisa.

'Nowhere,' said Lisa. Her lower lip trembled, her hands fiddled with her hair. She didn't look at Natasha.

'Lisa, I saw you. What did you think you were doing with her?'

Natasha shouted. She looked around, expecting Grandfather to come in and enquire what all the commotion was about. But either he was still asleep in his chair or Mikhail's music was loud enough to drown their voices. It was just her, Lisa and the shrieking babies in the room.

'I was just picking her up. Don't I have a right to hold my niece? Just wanted to see her face. Look, she has my nose.'

'Stop lying.' Natasha put the wriggling Larisa on the bed and pulled at the small bag in Lisa's hands until it fell on the floor, spilling baby clothes all over the carpet. 'Oh my God, Lisa. What are you doing?'

'I'm not doing anything.'

'Were you trying to take my daughter?' Natasha went to push Lisa again but at the last moment changed her mind and paused with her arms outstretched in front of her sister.

'Of course not. Why would I do that?' said Lisa. Natasha didn't know how she was able to control her anger. Her hands shook from the effort. And her sister knew it. Shuffling from foot to foot, she mumbled, 'I was just borrowing her for an hour or two.'

'An hour or two? You have enough clothes here to last her a month.' Natasha could barely get the words out. 'Are you insane? What were you going to do with her? She needs to be fed constantly. What were you thinking?'

'I tried to talk to you. Tried to ask you nicely.'

'Ask what nicely?' Natasha wondered when Lisa was leaving. Why was she here, in Natasha's house, in the room where she lived with her babies?

'I came to see you but you refused to listen. What was I supposed to do?'

'I don't know, Lisa. What do you want from us?'

Lisa reached for her bag. She tipped it upside down and knelt on the floor, rummaging through the clothes and finally resurfacing with a crumpled piece of paper. Without a word she handed it to her sister. Reluctantly Natasha attempted to decipher the writing. Either the letters were blurry or her eyes couldn't focus. Was it in German or Ukrainian? She couldn't tell. 'What is it?'

'Read it.'

Natasha wiped her tears away. The words were no longer fuzzy. It was an order for a Lisa Smirnova to come to Nekrasovskaya Street for compulsory mobilisation to Germany. Failure to do so was punishable by death. The paper was dated three weeks ago.

'They're looking for me, Natasha. I can't hide forever. Sooner or later they're going to find me. And then I'll be on the next train to wonderful and prosperous Germany.' Lisa's face twisted as she quoted from the propaganda poster. 'Well, I'm not going. Whatever it takes, I'm going to fight it.'

Natasha watched her sister in silence.

'I can't go to Germany, you know I can't. I'll die there,' said Lisa.

'What do you want from us?'

'Mother told me you haven't registered your babies yet.'

'I haven't had a chance. What does it have to do with you? What does it have to do with Germany?'

'Isn't it obvious? They don't send women with small children to Germany. You have two babies. It could save both of us.'

Natasha blinked. 'Are you out of your mind? You want to register my little girl as your daughter?'

'I would do anything to avoid going to Germany.'

'You're unbelievable. Simply unbelievable. Just when I thought you couldn't sink any lower.'

'Please, Natasha. I'm begging you. I can't go to Germany, I just can't. I'm too young to die.' Lisa's body convulsed.

'Mark was too young to die,' Natasha whispered. Lisa didn't seem to hear.

'Please, sister. Look at me. Can't you see? I'm on my knees. Please, if not for me, do it for our Mama. I'm still your sister.'

'How convenient. You're my sister when it suits you.' When

Lisa didn't reply, Natasha hissed, 'Don't you understand? You betrayed me and the man I love.'

'No, you don't understand. I saved you. I saved you from making the biggest mistake.'

'How can you be so blind? You're blinded by your selfishness.'

'And you were blinded by your love. What were you thinking? To cross Europe in a truck, to go through a hundred German patrols, to turn your back on your family, to risk your life and for what? For him?' Lisa laughed in Natasha's face but her eyes remained cold.

'No one asked you to fix my life for me.'

'You had no future together. You thought you did but you were delusional. And for that delusion, you were ready to sacrifice everything. You were going to another country, Natasha, and leaving us behind. Mama, Dedushka, Nikolai, me. A fine daughter you are, abandoning your mother. You were leaving for good, possibly never to see us again, and you didn't even say goodbye.'

Lisa's voice was barely audible over Costa and Larisa's crying. But still audible.

'Don't make excuses, Lisa. Nothing you say can justify what you've done. No matter how much you twist what happened to make it look like it was my fault. You took my heart and broke it into a million fragments. Out of spite and jealousy you killed the only man I have ever loved. Not so brave now, are you, Lisa? Where are your friends from the Gestapo when you're faced with deportation? What, your honourable act doesn't buy you a safe pass? What did you get for denouncing Mark? A piece of stale bread? A handful of chestnuts? You went to the Nazis and betrayed us, didn't you? How can you live with yourself?'

'If you believe that, then you don't know me at all. Isn't it obvious? What if he had his way with you and left you in the Soviet Union while he returned home to his family? To his safe, happy Hungarian life.'

If Natasha had the strength, she would have slapped her sister. But she didn't have the strength. She didn't know what to believe, didn't know what was true and what was false. She wished she could trust her sister's words. But trusting Lisa was like treading through the deepest swamp in the dark of night. At any step, at any moment, when you least expected it, the treacherous earth could swallow you up. 'You are a liar,' she cried.

'I'm not the liar. You are. You built your whole life on lies. How many times did you grit your teeth and lie to your family? To me, to Mama and Papa? To Grandmother on her deathbed? Because of you and your half-truths, Alexei is dead.'

Natasha recoiled from Lisa as if she'd been slapped.

Lisa continued, her voice cracking, 'You were lying to me from day one, protecting the person responsible for the murder in the park. Protecting Mark. What, you thought I didn't know? I heard you, Natasha! You were bragging about it to Mama and Nikolai, like it was something to be proud of. Like Alexei didn't matter. You could have saved his life but chose not to. You did what you had to do, and then you refused to go to the park with me to see his dead body. I tried to forgive you, Natasha. I tried to understand and go on as before. But it was impossible. Remember what you said to me on New Year's Eve? Too much between us is broken.'

There was so much to say, and yet, no words left. The room was too small for the two of them. There wasn't enough oxygen for the heartbreak, the exasperation. All the bridges were in flames, all the ships.

'You'd better be careful,' said Lisa. 'Don't leave your babies alone for a minute. I wouldn't want anything to happen to them.'

Natasha stood up, her legs shaking. 'What are you saying?'

Lisa smirked. 'I saw something terrible today. A young girl, your age, hid some butter she bought at the market in her baby's clothes. A German officer searched her, then searched the baby, found the butter and got so angry, he threw the child on the ground. The little boy, three months old, just like your Costa, didn't even make a sound. He died instantly. When the mother attacked the officer, he shot her.'

'Is that a warning or a threat?' Natasha felt her whole body shake. The lioness inside her stirred. The room swayed in front of her as if she was on a hot air balloon. Her fear was blinding her. She could no longer look at Lisa. Too many of her own feelings were mirrored in her sister's humourless smile. 'Lisa, I want you to leave. I want you to never come back here again. If you come near my babies, you won't have to wait till Germany. I'll kill you myself, here, in our house, in front of our family.'

She held her babies close, facing the wall and not turning around until she heard the bedroom door close. Lisa shut it quietly, careful not to slam, but to Natasha it still sounded as if a high explosive went off in the room. She stared at the door for a long time, rocking Constantine and Larisa's twisting bodies.

*

It was dark and all the noises subsided. There were no cars zooming past, no trams screeching their way through Podol, no intoxicated shouts. Natasha lay very still, measuring her heavy heartbeat on her babies' tiny ones. Relaxed in her arms, they seemed so blissful, so serene. She felt herself drifting off. She was happiest at such moments, halfway between sleep and wakefulness, when she was as tranquil as the two little human beings beside her. She blinked and forced her eyes open, willing sleep away. To hold them close, to feel their small bodies heave with every breath, to know that they were all hers, what happiness. She didn't want to miss anything, not a smile, not a breath, not for a second.

She didn't hear her mother come in but she felt the bed move and could sense her perched next to her. She stretched her left arm and touched her mother's face.

'Long day at the library?' The sleepiness, the drowsiness, the tranquillity were gone. She sat up.

'Not too long. Tiring. We moved all the remaining furniture today. There are tables to sit at again and chairs, aisles of them. Just like before.' They spoke in hushed voices, not to disturb the twins. 'Guess who came to help me with the furniture today?'

'Who?'

'Your sister.'

'I don't have a sister.'

Mother shifted on the bed, and Larisa babbled in her sleep. Natasha could almost feel her mother's upset eyes watching her in the dark. 'Don't ever say that. Of course you have a sister. One who was very helpful today.'

'Lisa volunteered to do actual work? I find that hard to believe.'

'Don't be flippant. It was just me at the library. I needed help.'

'What happened to Katerina?'

Mother shrugged. 'She's gone. Her grandson died and now her daughter.'

'Her daughter? Didn't she just come back from Germany?'

'Yes, just in time to see her son buried. She came back with pneumonia but died of a broken heart.'

Natasha didn't reply. She couldn't. Placing her hand on Costa's chest, she counted seconds by the thumps of his rhythmic heart.

'Now you understand? You see what mobilisation to Germany does to people? To families?'

Natasha stared into darkness. She didn't want to see, didn't want to understand.

'Lisa needs your help,' said Mother.

'She betrayed me, Mama. If she needs help, she'll have to look elsewhere.'

'She's still family. You love her still. Don't do something now you might regret later.'

'That's why I'm doing nothing. And I don't love her, I hate her. It's the opposite of love.'

'The opposite of love is not hate. It's indifference.'

'Love is a funny thing, Mama. Even when you think it's unconditional, it rarely is.'

'It is when you're a parent.'

'Mama, no. I won't help Lisa.' Natasha hid her head under her pillow, shutting her mother out, shutting the world out, longing for the serenity of only ten minutes ago.

It was quiet but for the cars outside, but for her mother's screaming stare.

'Mama, she destroyed me. If she killed me with her own two hands, if she suffocated me with a pillow while I was sleeping, it would have been more humane.'

Mother's voice was hoarse. It sounded out of place, as if it couldn't possibly belong to the frail person on the bed. 'I know what she did was wrong…'

'Wrong? Is that what it was?'

'I haven't forgiven her yet, either.'

'Really? Then why do you always take her side?'

'Natasha, I'm begging you. You don't have to forget, you don't even have to forgive. Just be the good-hearted person you are.'

'She ruined my life, Mama. My life, the life of someone I love and the lives of two innocent babies who don't have a father. Because of her.'

'Why can't you be the bigger person? Why nurture all this hatred inside you? In Germany she will die. Your sister will die.'

'My sister…' Something was wrong with her. She couldn't speak. She breathed in, out, counted down from ten to one. 'She'll be getting what she deserves.'

Mother sat up straight. Her long piano-playing fingers toyed with the blanket, the tea tray, the sleeves of her jumper. When she spoke, her voice was no longer trembling. 'I didn't sleep at all last night. All I could think of was you and Lisa. When you were babies like Costa and Larisa, when you were five, when you were ten. Always fighting but making up every time. Memories are all I have.'

'You have your grandchildren. Your children. Me, Nikolai…' Natasha couldn't say Lisa's name.

'You know what Lisa said when Nikolai was born and we brought him home from the hospital, all wrapped up and only his pink face visible?'

Natasha wasn't sure she wanted to know. 'What did she say?'

'She said, I hope it's a girl. We don't need another boy.'

'That sounds like her.'

'And when we unwrapped him and she found out that he was indeed a boy, she sighed and said, never mind, I already have a sister. Someone who can be my friend for life.'

That didn't sound like Lisa at all, thought Natasha.

'Even at four, she knew that being sisters was forever.'

Natasha dug her nails into the soft skin of her forearm. It didn't hurt enough. 'What a shame she forgot it at eighteen.'

'What if your Papa comes back tomorrow only to find Lisa gone? What will you tell him if he asks what happened to his youngest daughter? Will you look him in the eye and say, I had the power to save her and didn't?' Mother's eyes were two empty tea cups, staring, weeping, blinking. 'Please, Natasha. I already said goodbye to Stanislav. Don't make me say goodbye to another child.'

Natasha's resolve weakened faced with the sight of her mother's heartbreak, with the thought of her father's heartbreak. She didn't have the strength to break her parents' hearts.

Mother continued, 'You're a mother now. You know that loving your children is like breathing. You never stop, not until you die. If your children are in danger, no matter what mistakes they've made, you'd give your life for theirs. You'd move heaven and earth to save them. And that's what I'm trying to do. I'm trying to move heaven and earth to save my child.'

Natasha could feel heaven and earth move.

The loudspeaker briefly came to life outside their icy window, breaking the eerie silence with a festive tune. '*O Tannenbaum, O Tannenbaum!*' Natasha put her hands over her ears, her breathing heavy. She thought of her sister, who read *War and Peace* with Natasha, even though she had no interest in Tolstoy. Who played chess with her, even though chess gave her a headache. Who spent time with Olga, whom she was jealous of, just to be closer to her sister.

'If you help her, you never have to see her or talk to her again. But please, save your only sister's life. It won't cost you anything. It's just words from you,' begged Mother.

Wasn't it just words from Lisa when she went to the Gestapo and shattered *her* only sister's life? Natasha wanted to ask. She didn't. There was no fight left in her. 'If I help her, if I let her take Larisa and register her as her own, I won't be doing it for my sister. I'll be doing it for your daughter, for my father's daughter. I'll only be doing it because of you, Mama. I want Lisa to know that. I want her to know that the day she knocked on the Gestapo's door was the day she lost me as her sister forever.'

Mother's fingers were no longer fidgeting. She was very still and only her lips moved in the dark. 'Thank you,' she whispered, barely audible. It wasn't a whisper, it was a sigh.

*

Natasha asked Nikolai to look after the twins. She didn't have to ask twice. His eyes lit up at the thought of having them all to himself. Before she left, she begged him not to fall asleep, not to let the children out of his sight, to watch them as carefully as she watched them. Over and over she instructed until he had enough and said, 'If I was old like Grandfather, you could worry. When was the last time I fell asleep in the middle of the day?' Natasha kissed first her little daughter and then her son, her heart pumping trepidation through her blood.

She met her mother outside the library, and together they walked six blocks to the building where Lisa had been staying. It was the first time Natasha had stepped outside after having her babies. Despite her mother's supplications, despite lectures about fresh air and sunshine, Natasha had never taken them out of the apartment. It was too cold, she would say. *When we have a warm day, I'll take them for a walk.* But they had many warm days in November, many more than last year, and yet she refused to leave the apartment. Maybe when the first snow comes, I will take them outside, she would say. But the snow fell, melted and fell again, finally settling, and still she wouldn't go. Adamantly she remained in her bedroom day after day, week after week, hiding behind Grandfather's stooped frame, behind Mother's fragile shoulders, behind Nikolai's perpetual optimism and Yuri's quiet devotion. And now, as she made her slow way through the snow, a terrible image haunted her. It was the image of a young mother, screaming as her baby was wrestled away from her, as he was dashed on the frozen ground, mute, petrified and unable to cry, while crowds of curious onlookers watched in silence and did nothing to stop it.

The icy air was like daggers on her skin. She inhaled like a prisoner released after a long confinement. The autumn with its golden leaves and subtle sunlight was long gone. The leaves were on the ground, covered with snow. It was piled up high, blocking the roads, obstructing the doors, making it hard to walk. It wasn't the white, virginal snow that Natasha loved. It was slush and mud under her feet.

The harsh northern wind was doing all in its power to knock Natasha and her mother off their feet. It was strong enough to bend trees but sounded pitiful, like a wounded animal. It threw dry leaves and wet snow in their faces. Natasha and her mother clung to each other, stepping gingerly on treacherous ice, struggling not to lose their balance.

Lisa lived on the fifth floor of a drab Soviet building that had

269

been damaged by a bomb at the start of the war. The first thing they noticed, even before they glimpsed the insides of the apartment, was the stench. 'What is that smell?' muttered Natasha. It smelt like unwashed bodies and cigarette smoke. 'Are you sure this is the right place?' She couldn't imagine her tidy and fastidious sister living somewhere like this.

Mother nodded and knocked. A second later, the door opened. The smell intensified. Natasha took a step back. A long-haired, sullen-faced youth stood in the doorway, his gaze unfocused. He was short and his shoulders were hunched, which made him look even shorter, almost like a child. A child with the eyes of an old man.

'We're looking for Lisa,' said Mother. 'Lisa Smirnova.'

The youth waved in a vague direction and walked off on unsteady legs.

'So she is here,' said Natasha. There was such relief on Mother's face, Natasha turned around and kissed her. 'Don't worry, Mama. We'll find her.'

'I bet they are in no hurry to send him to Germany. Did you see the state of him?' whispered Mother, pointing at the young man.

'Not so loud, Mama,' whispered Natasha.

They followed the youth inside. There were four teenagers in the room, two of them sleeping, one of them their acquaintance from the corridor, none of them Lisa.

They approached a girl with greasy blonde hair and inquired about Lisa.

'Lisa Smirnova? Are you her mother? You look just like her. But older,' said the girl.

Mother nodded. 'I *am* her mother.'

'And I'm her sister,' said Natasha.

'Her sister! I didn't realise she had one.'

'So where is she?' Mother stretched her neck out, trying to spot Lisa.

270

The girl gazed from Mother to Natasha, as if she had something to tell them but didn't know where to begin. 'You mean you haven't heard yet? You don't know?' Her eyes glistened.

'Know what?'

'They came for her last night. She's been sent to Germany.'

Natasha felt her mother's body soften, as if her legs had lost the ability to support her the instant the words left the girl's lips. Natasha held Mother up with all the strength she had. She didn't have much. She led her to a chair.

'She's halfway across Europe by now,' added the girl.

'Were you a friend of hers?' asked Natasha, holding Mother's limp hand in hers.

'We were friendly. She used to tell me things.'

'What kind of things?'

The girl's thin, bony shoulders shrugged. 'Personal things.'

'But she never told you she had a sister?' Another shrug from the girl. 'Did she leave a message for us? Say anything before she left? Maybe a note?'

'I don't think so,' said the girl and, sensing Natasha's disappointment, added, 'It all happened very quickly.'

'Why didn't they take you? Why are you still here?' asked Mother.

'I'm married to him.' The girl pointed towards the youth with stooped shoulders. Natasha widened her eyes. The two of them were the least likely couple she had ever seen. The girl added, 'They aren't taking married people. Not yet.'

Natasha guided her crying mother through the snow, through the ice. Slowly, silently they walked. Natasha turned away from her mother and towards the alien streets, the passing German uniforms, white flags with black swastikas.

A day! They had missed her by a day. Natasha wished she could turn back the clock, wished she could scream to her past self to see through her pride and her heartache to the sister she had once loved so much. Had she listened to her mother, Lisa

271

would have been safe now. She wouldn't be weighing on Natasha's conscience, the way so many other things weighed on her conscience. For eighteen years, Lisa had been Natasha's confidant and her dearest friend. So close in age, they were like twins, their lives and souls intertwined. Did this dark shadow of suspicion the war had cast between them outweigh a happy childhood of shared confidences and adventures, of shared *everything*? One thing Natasha knew for certain. Germany would break Lisa's spirit. It would destroy her, physically and emotionally.

*

On the last day of December, Natasha took her two babies and walked to the registry office, where she got her passport stamped with their names. She couldn't put it off any longer. Larisa and Costa wriggled and chuckled in her arms at the sight of the sun, at the feel of snow on their beaming faces.

Just like the year before, they didn't celebrate New Year's Eve. 'Next year,' said Yuri. 'Next year we'll celebrate. Smolensk is about to break the blockade.'

There was not a star in the sky, not a light outside. There was no sister to share made-up secrets with. Natasha was alone when Yuri's watch announced the arrival of 1943. She stared into darkness and thought of this day a year ago when she was still with Mark, when she was already pregnant but didn't know it. When she was blissfully unaware of so many things. She repeated under her breath her favourite line from *The Count of Monte Cristo*: 'Until the day when God shall design to reveal the future to man, all human wisdom is summed up in these two words – wait and hope.'

Like a lullaby, the song of her broken heart.

Chapter 16 – Tentative Promises

March 1943

One beautiful spring morning when winter was finally over and summer was about to begin, Natasha curled up in bed with the first edition of Tolstoy's *War and Peace* – her sister's present to her at the start of the war – and read aloud to her son and daughter, only occasionally pausing to look out the window.

Nikolai's voice interrupted her, making her jump. She hadn't noticed him come in. '*War and Peace*? Really? You do realise they're only six months old?'

'They love it. Just look at their faces.' The twins giggled, reaching for the book and attempting to pull at the pages.

'They would love it just as much if you were reading from the Communist Manifesto.'

'They enjoy the sound of my voice.'

She wished they lived in a world where she could dress her babies in sweet outfits, put them in a pram and walk with them to a book stall at the Besarabsky Market, where they could choose a bright picture book that they could chew, marvel at and read with their mother. Instead, they lived in a world where she couldn't leave the apartment with her babies for fear of what might happen to them.

A quick glance out the window showed her the street was empty. 'Any news?' she asked. Yuri hadn't come home the night before and the Smirnovs were worried.

Nikolai shook his head. 'We were supposed to write leaflets yesterday. I waited half the night for him. He didn't show up.' Seeing Natasha's face fall, Nikolai added, 'Don't worry, he was probably delayed somewhere.'

'Where? Doing what?'

'He is a partisan, after all. And it's not like we have a working telephone.'

Nikolai was right. The telephone on Ilinskaya had been ominously silent for a year and a half now. 'Grandfather says the streets of Kiev are more dangerous than ever,' Natasha said. 'Yesterday morning the Nazis shot someone right in front of him.'

'In broad daylight?'

She nodded. 'They shoot first, ask questions later.'

Nikolai, the perpetual optimist, replied, 'They are getting twitchy. Not doing so well at the front, are they?'

At the end of February, Yuri had heard on the radio that Kharkov, Voroshilovgrad and Krasnodar had been recaptured by the Soviets. The family rejoiced, only to find out a few weeks later that Kharkov was once again occupied by the Germans. And yet, the Soviets were advancing. Their progress was slower than the Smirnovs would have liked, but there was no denying it, as much as the German-controlled newspaper tried to. Natasha knew that the situation was worsening for Hitler because more and more wounded German soldiers were arriving from the Stalingrad front. Hospitals were full to the brim, and the Nazis did regular rounds of the apartments, collecting blankets and sheets for the wounded.

The family waited all day for Yuri to return. Every time there was a noise outside, Natasha would run to the door. But invariably the voices quietened down and the noises passed. When she finally went to bed at midnight, she didn't fall asleep until four in the morning and even then she dreamt she was wide awake, waiting for the front door to open, waiting for Yuri's heavy footsteps. In the morning, she rushed to the living room, hoping to see Yuri's sleeping body on the couch.

There was no sign of him.

After breakfast of some barley and two eggs divided among five people, Natasha and Nikolai sat opposite each other at the kitchen table. Her usually carefree brother was silent and grim. Finally, he said, 'Gregory.'

'What about him?'

'He might know what happened to Yuri.'

If Yuri had disappeared on one of his partisan missions, Gregory would be the one to ask. 'If only we knew where he lived.'

'Somewhere in Lavra. Yuri took me there once or twice. I think I could find it.'

'How will you get there?' asked Natasha. Lavra was a few kilometres south of Podol, and trams were no longer running.

'Don't worry. Unlike you, I can walk fast,' he said.

Natasha waited impatiently for her brother to return. She cleared the dishes, chewed a stale piece of bread and attempted to knit, all without taking her eyes off the kitchen window. Her hands shook badly and she missed stitch after stitch, undoing the rows she had just knit, trying again, missing another stitch. Finally, she had to give up. She didn't want to ruin the scarf. She returned to the bedroom, where Mother was looking after Costa and Larisa. A thick blanket covered the window, blocking out the sun. It was shady and dark in the room. The twins were sleeping and so, it seemed, was Mother. Natasha marvelled at the size of her children. Despite her mother's lamentations that they were too small for their age, in six months they had almost doubled their birth weight. Their eyes were a shade darker, their faces a touch chubbier. Even if Mother was right and the children did lack in size, they more than made up for it in energy. They were like magnets drawing everyone to Natasha's room, waving, smiling, blabbering, touching and tasting everything within their reach.

Natasha perched on the bed, trying not to disturb them. The bed squeaked. Mother stirred. 'Natasha, is that you?'

'Sorry, Mama. I didn't mean to wake you.'

'I wasn't sleeping.'

'Did you see yesterday's papers? Was there anything about the partisans?' asked Natasha, holding her breath in trepidation. The Nazis liked to make an example out of partisans they captured. Natasha never read the terrible stories of torture and death inflicted on them. She couldn't. Unfortunately for the Germans, their atrocities didn't seem to deter the partisans. If anything, they inspired them.

'Not about the partisans. But there was something about the Italian soldiers.'

Relieved, Natasha said, 'What about them?'

'A number of them were shot. In Babi Yar, of all places.'

'How terrible,' whispered Natasha.

'Serves them right, fighting for the Germans.'

'They're no longer fighting. Isn't that why they were shot?'

'The way I see it, they got what they deserved.' Mother reached for Natasha in the dark, taking her hand. 'Don't worry, darling, I'm sure Yuri is fine. You know how he is. Always off on one secret partisan mission after another.'

'But what if he never comes back? What if he has been sent to Germany too?' Natasha nestled into Mother's arms. It felt comforting, just like it did when she was a child. 'I wish I'd married him, Mama. I should have said yes when he asked me. He would have been safe now.'

'Yuri asked you to marry him? He would make a wonderful husband. He's loyal, honest, reliable. What more could you possibly want? He's a good man, Natasha.'

'I know. He would make a great husband. Just not for me.'

'You could do a lot worse.'

How could Natasha explain to her mother that when Yuri's hand brushed hers in the kitchen, she felt nothing? That when he smiled at her, it didn't make her heart sing? How could she explain this to her well-meaning but practical mother and expect her to understand? 'I always believed that I would only ever marry once. That I would marry for love. And I don't love Yuri, Mama.'

'Sometimes it's better to be loved than to love. Safer.'

'That's easy for you to say. You married Papa whom you adored.'

'At times I wish I loved him less. Things would be so much easier.'

'You can't settle for a safe option just because you're afraid of getting hurt.'

Mother squeezed her cheek. 'When did you become so wise?'

'It might be easier but it's not what I wanted for myself. Can you imagine anything worse than living with a man you don't love?'

'Living with a man who doesn't love you?' Mother paused as Costa stirred, mumbled in his sleep and fell quiet again. 'With time you can grow to love somebody.'

'I don't think so, Mama. You either feel it or you don't. And I don't love Yuri.'

'Gratitude often turns to love. So does friendship. Besides, children need a father. They need someone to take care of them. You need someone to take care of you.'

Larisa stirred and muttered in her sleep. Absentmindedly Natasha stroked the palm of her hand that was just visible from under the cover. 'I can't stop thinking about Mark. And you know what the worst thing is?' she said, shivering.

'What?'

'That I can no longer remember his face.'

Mother held her tighter. 'Oh Natasha.'

'I loved him so much. I still love him. But when I close my

277

eyes, I can't see his face. I want to. I lie awake at night trying to force myself to remember. But I can't. I remember other things, though. I remember his laughter. The way he pronounced my name. His smile.' She strained to see her son in the dark and couldn't. 'But his face, no.'

Natasha felt her mother's soft hands patting her back. Mother said, 'You have all these happy memories of him. Memories that no one can take away.'

'What good are memories when all I want is to see him again?'

'These memories will stay with you for the rest of your life, just like my memories of your father will stay with me for the rest of my life. We're the lucky ones. Some people never have that.'

'I don't want to forget, Mama. I don't want to go through the rest of my life not remembering.' Tears rolled down her cheeks. 'You think he's still alive? That he's out there somewhere?'

'Oh Natasha.'

Natasha contemplated telling her mother about the letter she had found at the bottom of Mark's rucksack. But putting her doubts into words would only make them real. Deciding against it, she wrapped the blanket around herself, hiding inside it. 'I wish I'd helped Yuri when I had the chance.'

They heard shouts outside. And then, a few seconds later, all was quiet again.

'It's Lisa's birthday tomorrow,' said Mother. Her voice was even.

'It's not your fault Lisa was taken, Mama. You know that, don't you?' *It's mine*, she wanted to add but couldn't.

'I should have never let her leave. For months she lived in that awful place…'

'She was the one who left. She was the one who refused to set foot in this house.'

'She left because of me. Because of all the horrible things I said.'

'She deserved to hear those horrible things.'

Would the guilt ever go away? The guilt over Alexei and over Lisa, and now over Yuri, too. She could have helped so many people but chose to do nothing. Now they were gone, and she was responsible. 'He'll be back,' Natasha whispered, reaching for Costa, who opened his eyes and looked unblinking at his mother. 'He'll be back.' It might be too late to help the others, but she could still help Yuri. As she held her son and rocked him back to sleep, Natasha made a promise to herself. If Yuri came back, she would marry him, to save him from the Germans and to save herself from her remorse.

*

Nikolai returned, grim, red-faced, dejected. There was no sign of Yuri at Gregory's apartment. Nor could he ask Gregory if he knew anything because there was no sign of Gregory either. Every day Natasha stared at the nearly empty street, her hope dwindling, until finally, four days after Yuri's disappearance, she abandoned her post by the window. Nikolai no longer mentioned Yuri. Mother no longer startled every time there was a noise outside. Grandfather stopped trying to convince everyone that Yuri was fine and instead sat in his favourite armchair, sheltered behind a newspaper. Outwardly calm, Mikhail smoked one cigarette after another. He had a few packs stowed away for a rainy day. Natasha was surprised that he managed to hold onto them for as long as he had.

It was on the day Natasha stopped watching the road and Mikhail was reduced to his last cigarette that there was a soft knock outside. Natasha followed her mother to the corridor, her heart beating fast. She didn't want to get her hopes up. It couldn't possibly be Yuri. *It's not him, it's not him, it's not him*, she repeated to herself.

But it was him.

He saw her through the doorway and his lips curled upwards,

stopping short of a grin. She sprang forward and held him tight. He smelt as if he hadn't washed in days. His clothes were torn and muddy, his face was bruised but his eyes still held their familiar twinkle.

He leaned on Natasha's arm as they walked to the kitchen.

'I told you he'd be back,' said Nikolai. 'And you didn't believe me. I'm so glad you're alright.' He hugged Yuri, who didn't look well at all.

When they reached the kitchen, Yuri fell into a chair. For a minute he looked as if he had fallen asleep, but as soon as Mother brought in some food, he sat up straight.

Mother said, 'I was able to get an onion at the market today. Made some stew for dinner.'

'Smells great,' said Yuri.

'Help yourself, have as much as you want.'

Yuri didn't wait to be asked twice. He pushed his bowl close and for a minute nothing was heard but the sound of his spoon. He devoured the stew as if he hadn't seen food in days.

Nikolai watched Yuri eagerly. Finally, he couldn't contain himself any longer. 'What happened to you? Where have you been?'

Mother said, 'You can't imagine how worried we were. We didn't know if we would ever see you again.'

Yuri was taking his time to chew a small piece of German bread. After it was gone, he picked every crumb off the table and only afterwards replied, 'When they first grabbed me, I was certain they were about to put me on one of the trains headed for Germany. But instead they marched a group of us to Kreshchatyk and forced us at gunpoint to dig trenches and build barricades.'

'The Germans are entrenching?' asked Grandfather sharply, looking up from his newspaper.

Yuri nodded. 'For four days we dug. Twenty hours a day without a break, without food. There were forty of us when we started. After four days only twelve of us remained.'

So relieved was Natasha to see him again, she squeezed his hands. He flinched. 'What is it? What's wrong?' she asked. He showed her his bleeding calluses.

'It's a miracle they let you go,' said Nikolai.

While Mother cleaned Yuri's hands and applied bandages, Grandfather said, 'The Red Army must be close. I have a feeling the Germans won't hold Kharkov for long. It could be liberated at any moment.' He started pacing around the small kitchen with excitement. '*We* could be liberated at any moment.' His hands trembled.

'Thank you, Zoya Alexeevna. That feels much better,' said Yuri. He turned to Grandfather. 'And I helped build the trenches that would stop the Red Army from entering Kiev.' He buried his face in his bandaged hands as if he was ashamed.

'You had no choice. They forced you,' said Natasha.

'It's not your fault,' said Mother, nodding.

'That's right, young man,' said Grandfather. 'Besides, what good did the trenches do us in September 1941? Did they stop the Germans? What makes you think they will stop our soldiers now?'

Yuri's shoulders relaxed but he didn't reply. Suddenly he looked exhausted. 'Come,' said Natasha, pulling him by the arm. 'Let me help you to bed. You need rest.' In silence they walked to the living room. Without removing his clothes, Yuri collapsed on the sofa. Within seconds, he was asleep.

*

A week after Yuri's ordeal, a man came to see him. With his mop of black hair, his matted beard and a scar across his face, he looked as if he belonged in Stevenson's *Treasure Island*. So striking was the man's appearance, Natasha realised she was staring right at him with her mouth open. She watched the two men disappear into the kitchen. When he left an hour later, Yuri returned to the

281

living room. Natasha waited for him to say something. When he didn't speak, she asked, 'Did he bring any news?'

'Yes. Gregory was sent to Germany.'

Natasha put her knitting down. She knew Gregory was like a brother to Yuri. 'Why would they take him? He works for the Germans. Officially, anyway.'

'He was discovered. There was a Nazi officer who knew some Russian. He noticed some discrepancies in Gregory's translations.'

'I'm so sorry, Yuri,' whispered Natasha. 'Gregory saved many lives. He's a good man.'

'The best.' Yuri rose to his feet. He paced the length of the room without looking at Natasha. 'No one is safe in Kiev. Absolutely no one.'

'At least he's still alive. That's something, isn't it? And you never know, he might come back.'

'Do you know anyone who returned from Germany?'

'When the war is over, he'll come back,' said Natasha. 'Other people, too. Stanislav, Papa.' She patted his hand. 'And Lisa,' she added softly.

He remained quiet, staring out the window at the German patrol making its way down the street. Natasha knew it was now or never. She had to ask. The moment might never come again. She might never find her courage. She whispered, 'Remember back in September you said we should get married?' She wasn't sure if Yuri heard her. She hardly heard herself. She couldn't lift her eyes. She looked at the table, at the floor, at the buttons on his shirt. When he didn't answer, she muttered, 'Just before I had Costa and Larisa, you said…'

'I remember.'

'Do you still… want to? If you don't, I'll never mention it again. But I've been thinking and… I think we should do it.'

She expected a smile, expected the sadness on his face to melt. Instead, he watched her in silence.

'Of course, if you don't want to, I understand,' she stammered.

'It's all I've ever wanted, you know that. But I don't want you to rush into something you're not ready for.'

'I am,' she said. The words felt strange on her tongue. 'Ready, I mean.'

'It's a bit of a surprise.'

'You can say no if you want to. I won't get upset, I promise.' Suddenly she wanted him to say no. If he did, she wouldn't have to go through with it. If she asked and he said no, her conscience would be clear.

'I didn't say it wasn't a *pleasant* surprise.' There it was, the smile she was waiting for. His eyes sparkled. 'We can do it tomorrow. I know someone at the registry office.' He looked at her for a second, then pulled her close. Afraid that he was about to kiss her, she stepped back and was instantly concerned he would notice her reluctance. She didn't want to upset him. He enveloped her in a hug and she found herself smothered into his shoulder. He smelt clean, of soap, cigarettes and something else, something she couldn't quite place. It wasn't unpleasant, just unfamiliar. Suddenly she could no longer breathe. She wanted the hug to be over, wanted to go back to her room where she could be alone with her babies. She leant back, resisting his embrace. And in a moment, he released her.

In bed that night, Natasha whispered Mark's name as she stared into darkness, contemplating marrying someone else, contemplating a life without ever seeing the one person she couldn't live without.

'*You are the one I want to spend my life with. You are the one I want to marry,*' *Mark said to Natasha one cold January afternoon. The last afternoon they had ever spent together.* '*When we are married, you'll be forever mine.*'

'*I'm yours now,*' *she said, touching the stubble on his chin.* '*Forever.*'

*

When Natasha woke up the next morning, it was pitch black outside. She stayed in bed until the sun was up at six and then, bleary-eyed, stumbled to the bathroom to wash. She was surprised to find everyone else in the household awake. Everyone, that was, except Yuri, who was an excellent sleeper, and Mikhail, because not even a wedding could faze him. Although she hadn't told anyone about their plans, they all seemed to know. When Yuri finally appeared in the kitchen two hours later, smiling and rubbing his eyes, Nikolai put his arm around him and said, 'Finally you'll be a part of our family.'

'He's been a part of our family from day one.' Mother pulled Yuri into a hug. 'And now it's going to be official.'

'Tell us everything. How did you propose? What did my sister say?' Nikolai danced on the spot.

'She proposed to me,' said Yuri, grinning.

'I can't believe it!' exclaimed Nikolai, staring at Natasha, his eyes like two round saucers.

'In some cultures it's considered good luck for a woman to ask a man for his hand in marriage,' said Grandfather.

'What cultures are those?' muttered Nikolai.

'Natasha knew a good thing when she saw it. No point beating around the bush,' said Mother. She was unusually chipper, flittering around the kitchen, preparing stew out of the few potatoes she'd managed to procure at the market. 'It's not the five-course meal your father and I had on our wedding day,' she said to Natasha. 'But we'll have plenty of stew to celebrate with.'

Natasha wanted to ask how one could celebrate with stew, but didn't.

'I didn't sleep for weeks waiting for your father to propose,' said Mother. 'Much better to do the asking. Then you know when it's going to happen.'

'But you don't know what he's going to say. What if Yuri had said no?' demanded Nikolai.

Natasha shrugged. 'Then he would have said no.'

'You knew I would never say no,' said Yuri, winking.

Suddenly Natasha wanted to scream. She closed her eyes and counted to ten. When that didn't help, she got up and without saying a word walked back to her room.

As soon as she closed the bedroom door behind her, wanting nothing more than to pull the cover over her head and hide, there was a soft knock and the door opened. Natasha looked up to find her grandfather smiling down at her. Even though it was early, he was already dressed in his best suit, which used to fit perfectly but was now loose around his shoulders and waist. His face looked gaunt but his eyes sparkled. He sat next to Natasha. 'Big day for you today,' he said.

Natasha sighed.

'I remember the day I married your grandmother. She was so happy. Couldn't stop crying, either.' He touched Natasha's damp cheek. 'She was barely sixteen.'

'Younger than me,' whispered Natasha.

'I wish she could see you today. She would have been so proud.'

'I miss her, Dedushka.'

'We all do. Not a day goes by when I don't wish I could talk to her, look at her, hold her. We think we have all the time in the world with someone and then suddenly, before we know it, they're gone.'

'I know what you mean. There's so much I want to say to Papa, to Olga, to Babushka, to...' She paused. 'But it's too late. I keep expecting to turn around and see her.'

'I still talk to her sometimes.'

Natasha took her grandfather's hand. 'Dedushka, do you think I'm making a mistake?'

'Do you love him?'

She wanted to tell her grandfather that she loved Yuri like a friend, like an older brother. That she would never love him like a husband. But she didn't know how to say any of it. Uncertainly she nodded.

'Then you're doing the right thing. There is no point waiting until the war is over. Life's too short, Natasha. We must live every day as if it's our last. Now more than ever.'

Natasha could hear excited voices coming from the kitchen. When she spoke, her own voice was barely audible. 'But what if I don't know what the right thing to do is?'

'Listen to your heart. Does it tell you to marry Yuri? Then you should marry him.'

Her heart was telling her to do everything in her power to protect those close to her. Then why did it feel like she was about to step on a tightrope between two tallest buildings in Kiev? 'When you married Babushka, how did you know it was the right thing to do?'

'When you meet the one, you just know. It feels right. All your doubts disappear.'

In the dim light, Grandfather put his arm around Natasha's shoulders. 'I'm very happy for you and Yuri. He loves you very much. He'll do everything in his power to make you happy. Now, look at this.' Grandfather showed her a small velvet-covered box. 'Babushka would have wanted me to give you this.'

Natasha opened the box. 'Babushka's wedding ring.' She gasped. Her hand shook so badly, she almost dropped the ring. 'Thank you, Dedushka. Thank you so much.' Her eyes bathed in tears, she held him close.

'Your babushka loved this ring. She always said she would give it to you or Lisa when one of you got married.'

'It should have been Lisa. She should have been the one who married first.' Natasha thought of Lisa's beaming face on the day Alexei had asked her to marry him. She thought of her sister's body rocked by sobs as Alexei had been dragged away by the Gestapo. 'Things should have been different.' She looked at the ring, turned it this way and that, tried it on. 'It's beautiful. It was Babushka's most cherished possession. Look, it fits.'

'It looks lovely on you. I remember as if it was yesterday placing this ring on your babushka's finger. May it bring you all the happiness you deserve. God bless you always.'

After Grandfather left, Natasha got dressed in front of a large mirror, while her babies attempted to play with their reflections. For once their antics didn't make her smile. She wore her mother's green dress with brown stripes, the dress Father bought for Mother's birthday on Kreshchatyk many years ago. He bought it one sweltering summer afternoon in a big department store that had now been reduced to ash. The dress was two sizes too big for Natasha before the war and now it hung around her like a tent. Even with a belt around her waist, the dress looked out of place.

When Yuri saw her in the dress, he whispered, 'You look beautiful.' Natasha lowered her gaze, muttered a 'thank you' and put her coat on. Just like the dress, the coat was borrowed and didn't fit.

Mikhail had volunteered to look after the babies, while Natasha, Yuri, Nikolai, Grandfather and Mother buckled their belts and left the apartment. The registry office was only two short blocks away. Yuri pointed at the drab building that was missing most of the glass in its windows. 'It was an old kindergarten. Before the war, I mean. That's a good sign, don't you think?' But Natasha couldn't return his smile. She knew how desperately he wanted children. She didn't have the strength to point out that the room registering marriages was next to the room registering deaths. The queue in that room spilled out the door and all the way down the corridor.

She felt her knees weaken.

They walked in, Natasha at the rear. She dawdled at the entrance until Mother motioned for her to join them. The room registering marriages was dark. With its heavy curtains that didn't admit much light, it looked anything but festive. There was a threadbare red carpet on the floor and no furniture other than a large table and a chair that contained a stern-looking woman in her forties.

287

On the wall there was a large portrait of Hitler. Natasha saw it out of the corner of her eye and turned quickly away.

When she was a child dreaming of her wedding day, she had imagined herself wearing a white dress surrounded by friends and family, with Olga and Lisa by her side, looking into the smiling face of the man she loved. In her fantasy, there was definitely no Hitler sneering from a faded wooden frame.

As if sensing Natasha's doubt, Yuri took her hand. She looked at him and pressed his fingers gently. But when she closed her eyes, it wasn't Yuri's face that she saw.

As soon as they walked in, the official rose to her feet, indicating the spot in front of the table where they were to stand. Natasha and Yuri advanced, leaving Mother, Nikolai and Grandfather a few steps behind. For a few seconds there was silence and then the woman spoke. Her voice, her face, her whole demeanour seemed out of place here, as if they belonged somewhere else, perhaps in the room next door.

'Entering into this marriage are…' The woman stumbled and consulted a piece of paper in front of her, then read out their names.

The official droned on about the importance of marriage and the role of family but Natasha didn't listen. She was too busy thinking of the first time she had walked through Shevchenko Park with Mark. She couldn't remember what they talked about, nor what she was wearing. What she did remember, however, was the way her heart skipped every time she looked into his face and the way his eyes lit up whenever he saw her. Mother was right. Not the war, nor her own doubts could take away the memories of those hours with him in the golden autumn park, on the burnt-out winter streets as they clung to each other in the desperation of their first love.

Suddenly there was silence in the room. The official was no longer talking. When Natasha opened her eyes, she was surprised to find everybody staring at her. 'Are you ready to accept the sacred duty of a wife?' she repeated, narrowing her eyes at Natasha.

Natasha nodded. Clearly that wasn't good enough because the official was still watching her. 'Yes,' Natasha managed in the tiniest of whispers.

The official turned to Yuri. 'Are you ready to accept the sacred duty of a husband?'

'I am,' said Yuri and although his voice shook, it was loud.

When, according to the Russian tradition, Yuri placed Babushka's ring on the ring finger of her right hand, Natasha squeezed her eyes shut, struggling not to cry. She noticed that Yuri, too, had tears on his face. The difference was that he was smiling.

'You may now kiss,' she said. Yuri kissed Natasha lightly, as if sensing her reluctance. It was the first time she had felt his lips on hers, the first time she had felt any man's lips other than Mark's. She was surprised at how profoundly unnatural it seemed.

They were then invited to sign the documents. Mother and Grandfather acted as their witnesses. Yuri was the first to sign. When it was Natasha's turn, the illegible scribble her shaking hand managed to produce looked nothing like her handwriting. Finally, the registrar put her own signature next to theirs and stamped their passports.

'From now on and forever you are husband and wife.' The words reached Natasha as if through a fog.

The ceremony was over in less than ten minutes. Before Natasha knew it, they were exiting the building and passing the queue of people registering deaths – the queue which, far from diminishing, had now increased to twice its original size.

As soon as they stepped outside, Mother, who had been subdued inside the building, exclaimed, 'Congratulations!' Her eyes sparkled. She held Yuri for a fraction of a second and then held Natasha, not letting go until Grandfather demanded his turn. Grandfather passed Natasha to the excited Nikolai and proceeded to hug Yuri.

Natasha couldn't look at the overjoyed faces around her. She watched the clouds that were gathering overhead and the dark specs in the distance that rapidly grew in size until they finally transformed into German aircrafts. She counted them. There were three, four, five, six dots in the darkened sky.

At home, Natasha sat at the table with her eyes closed, while everyone around her chattered, ate and drank tea. Mother couldn't stop hugging Yuri. Nikolai couldn't stop talking. Mikhail couldn't stop smiling. Even the twins seemed to sense that something out of the ordinary was happening and babbled happily. Only Natasha hadn't touched her bowl of stew.

'More tea, anyone? I still have a couple of German biscuits hidden away for a rainy day,' said Mother.

'I don't think today qualifies,' replied Yuri, laughing. 'Despite everything, this is the happiest day of my life.'

Mother said with a wink, 'A rainy day or a special occasion.' She looked at Yuri with wonder. 'Just look at him. How tall he is, how handsome. Look at his beautiful green eyes, his beautiful blond hair.' Yuri's face went red and he gazed at the floor. Mother added, 'This is a good sign. Marfa predicted this.'

Natasha faintly remembered the day when the two of them had walked to the outskirts of Kiev in search of answers.

'Marfa knew this would happen. Like she knew Stanislav is alive,' said Mother.

After the stew and the German biscuits were gone, Grandfather and Mikhail retired to the living room to resume their game of chess. Mother finished her tea. 'Time to go back to the library,' she said. 'Come on, Nikolai, let's go.'

'Why do I have to go? I don't work at the library. I haven't finished eating yet.'

Mother pulled him by the arm. 'Come on. Give the newlyweds some privacy.'

When they were alone together, Yuri said, 'What a day.'

Natasha nodded. She didn't feel like talking.

Yuri continued, 'Could you believe the face of that registrar? I've never seen anyone so glum.'

'Don't we all look a bit glum these days?' she said.

'But not today! I can't stop smiling today.'

'I've noticed.' Nervously she clasped her hands.

'Why don't you have a cup of tea? You haven't eaten anything since we got back.'

'Maybe later. I think I need sleep, not food.'

'Didn't sleep much last night?' When she shook her head, he said, 'Neither did I.' He finished his tea and put his cup away. 'I know this is not exactly what you wanted.' She looked up at him in surprise. He continued, 'Every girl dreams of a big wedding. When the war is over, we'll do it all again. We'll have a big celebration. We can even get married in a church.'

'A church?' She was surprised.

'I believe that marriage should be blessed by God. What do you think?'

'I've never even been to church.'

'Never? My mama used to drag me every Sunday. There was a church in the nearby village. But we don't have to do it if you aren't comfortable with it.'

'We'll do whatever you want.'

Not taking his eyes off her, he asked, 'So tell me, why did you change your mind?'

'What do you mean?'

'Why did you change your mind about marrying me?'

What could Natasha say to that? Could she tell him the truth? Could she tell him that she had lost so many people she loved, she couldn't stand losing him, too? That she couldn't live with herself knowing that she had it in her power to keep him safe but chose not to? Could she tell him all that and risk hurting his feelings? 'We are friends, aren't we? And you love Costa and Larisa so much.' She stumbled over her words. She didn't want to upset him but she didn't want to lie to him, either. He didn't deserve her lies. He deserved better. 'I thought… if we got married, they wouldn't send you to Germany. And I couldn't bear it if they sent you to Germany. I couldn't bear it if anything happened to you.'

He let go of her hand. Even though she was facing away from him, she could sense his disappointment. It was a physical presence in the kitchen, like a dark cloud over their heads. It wasn't what he wanted to hear and she knew it. But she also knew that what he wanted to hear was the one thing she couldn't tell him.

After a long silence, he said, 'It might gain us some time. They're taking single men first. When they run out of single men, they'll take those with families.'

'Maybe the Red Army will be back before then.'

'Yes, maybe.' He stood up, pulled out a cigarette and opened the kitchen window. 'This is the second time you've saved my life, Natasha. I'll never forget that.'

That night, Natasha turned to the wall, next to her babies, next to her mother, next to Lisa's empty bed. Mother shook her in the dark and whispered, 'Natasha, what are you doing? It's your wedding night. Shouldn't you be next door with your husband?'

Natasha didn't reply. She closed her eyes and pretended to sleep.

How could she be with Yuri, when her heart and soul were Mark's? How could she let Yuri touch her? Being with someone else meant admitting that Mark was never coming back. If she went next door to Yuri, she would be betraying Mark and betraying herself, and she couldn't do that. Even though Yuri was her husband, she would always belong to another man.

Chapter 17 – A World Aflutter

April – September 1943

Even though she was now a married woman, Natasha had never felt more alone. Her family adored Yuri and expected Natasha to feel the same. Sensing something wasn't quite right, Nikolai, Grandfather and even Mikhail watched Natasha and Yuri's every move.

In April, Yuri and a group of other partisans blew up a rail bridge, disrupting one of the most important communication routes for the Germans and stopping a train transporting Ukrainian workers to German factories. Two hundred souls, mostly women and children, escaped before the German authorities realised what had happened. The family celebrated the news at dinner. Grandfather and Mikhail slapped Yuri on the shoulder, while Nikolai questioned him incessantly, eager to hear every little detail about the operation. After dinner, when Yuri was alone with Natasha, he held her gently, pressing his lips to hers. When she didn't return his kiss, he didn't pressure her further, nor did he show his disappointment.

In May, when the total mobilisation of fit and able workers to Germany was announced, Yuri helped Nikolai register for farm work. Nikolai came home every night exhausted, but the job meant he was exempt from transportation to Germany. He was safe, for now. Mother cried and hugged Yuri. 'Thank God for your husband, Natasha,' she repeated. 'We are so lucky to have him. *You* are so lucky to have him.'

On the night of 8th May, the family was woken by explosions. Petrified, they rushed to the window to watch the commotion outside that was reminiscent of the beginning of the war. Scared and confused, they questioned one another, wondering what was going on. And then they saw the Soviet planes, not just one but a dozen of them.

'Why are they bombing us?' cried Natasha.

'Not us, silly. They are here to liberate us,' said Yuri, putting his arm around her.

As bombs whistled and mortars roared in retaliation, deafening in their fury, Natasha cried on Yuri's shoulder. Were they tears of fear or of happiness? She couldn't tell. A blast blew out the glass in the living-room window; Kiev was once more engulfed in fire and it was no longer dark. This time the fires were destined to force the oppressors from their streets forever. They were no longer fires of despair but those of hope. Hope that grew stronger with every Soviet plane, every bomb, every explosion. Eerie shadows danced on the walls, and Natasha could see the flames reflected in Yuri's face. Sensing her gaze on him, he pressed her close and his fingers traced the bare skin under her blouse. As if scalded by boiling water, she moved away from him.

When she looked up at him, she saw something in his face close off against her.

The Soviet planes were back again the next night and the night after, but Yuri no longer put his arm around Natasha to comfort her. They were once again two strangers living under the same roof, polite in front of others, not acknowledging each other in private.

Through June, July and August there was only one thought that occupied everyone: where was the Red Army? Was it on its way to liberate them, to bring them relief, to restore order and dignity to their existence, to wipe away the shadows of occupation? And if so, how long would it take? And through it all, Natasha busied herself with her children to the exclusion of everything and everybody else. She withdrew from Yuri, from her family, from herself.

At the end of July, the newspaper finally printed something to lift their spirits. The Fascist party in Italy had been disbanded. Mussolini had been arrested. Italy was no longer at war.

Shortly, more good news followed.

Orel was liberated.

Poltava was liberated.

Kharkov was liberated.

It was no longer wishful thinking but a fact. The Nazis were retreating. Naturally, the German-controlled newspaper didn't call it a retreat. It called it a strategic withdrawal. And yet, everybody saw it for what it really was. There was no longer any need to read between the lines. When Natasha told her family about Kharkov, Mother exclaimed, 'I can't believe it! I just can't believe it. Tell me one more time. I want to hear it again!'

'It's true, Mama. Kharkov is Soviet. Kiev could be next!'

'Not long now,' said Grandfather, his eyes raised to the ceiling as if in prayer.

Finally, in the middle of September, a miracle happened.

Natasha was knitting in her room, her two babies fast asleep next to her, when she heard agitated voices. She hurried to the kitchen to find her exhilarated mother pointing at something out the window. All Mother managed when she saw Natasha was an excited: 'Look!' Seeing the bewildered expression on Mother's face, Natasha, Nikolai, Grandfather, Mikhail and Yuri hurried to join her. Outside, a large procession was making its way past their building. Wide-eyed, the family looked on as truck after truck drove past, loaded with cannon and mortar, paintings and furniture, books and food. They saw German cars, German motorcycles, and German soldiers, all in a hurry, all leaving.

'Where did they find a truckful of skis?' asked Mother, pointing at one of the vehicles.

'I guess they won't be spending winter here, then,' joked Nikolai.

'Are they... leaving?' whispered Natasha. The thought seemed preposterous, so deeply entrenched in her mind was the idea of the German presence on the streets of Kiev. And yet, here they were, right in front of her in the timid September sun, marching away from the city. She fought a sudden impulse to shout in excitement and jump up and down on the spot.

'I never thought I'd live to see the day,' said Grandfather, taking his glasses off, wiping them and replacing them on the tip of his nose. He stared at the procession downstairs, shaking his head.

Mother waved her fist at a German truck that was fast disappearing around the corner. 'Look how much they've stolen. All those paintings, they're from the gallery. All those carpets and furniture.'

'I bet they robbed every apartment in Kiev,' said Natasha.

'To make the most of their stay in Ukraine, they're taking as much as they can carry,' said Nikolai. 'Isn't it ironic? It's the 19th of September. Exactly two years since the Germans have entered Kiev.'

They fell quiet, gazing at the endless procession outside. It wasn't just the anniversary of the occupation for Natasha. Tomorrow was the anniversary of her first meeting with Mark. She realised she had lived longer without Mark, longing for him and aching for him, than she had lived with him. Then why was the memory of him as fresh in her heart as ever? Whoever said time healed everything had clearly never been in love.

'I hope with all my heart it's the last anniversary we see,' said Grandfather.

'Two years of these animals in our city. Who would have thought?' Mother opened the window. The din of traffic filled the kitchen. 'That's right, keep walking, get out of here. Good riddance!' she shouted.

Several soldiers looked up. The Smirnovs drew back. Thankfully, the Nazis didn't stop.

They spent all day, and the day after that, and the one after, watching the retreating Germans. Truck after truck, tank after tank, motorcycle unit after motorcycle unit; the hated Nazis were leaving the Ukrainian capital. For days they marched and still there was no end to them. Nikolai elbowed Natasha to get her attention. 'Did you know there were so many of them in Kiev?'

After two years of wreaking havoc and destruction, they were finally leaving. But despite the columns of men and vehicles, despite horns blaring and the officers shouting as if pursued, it didn't feel real. Natasha tried to remember strolling through the streets of Kiev and not feeling afraid, and not feeling hunted. But all she could think of was the hunger, the bleak exhaustion, and her own helplessness. And yet, there was no mistaking it. They *were* withdrawing. When she had thought of this moment at the start of the occupation, she had imagined nothing but tears of joy and elation. Then why did she feel so empty inside? As she watched the dust kicked up by the hated boots as they walked away from her, her joy was tainted with sadness. Even if they were liberated tomorrow, it wouldn't bring Natasha's loved ones back. It wouldn't bring Mark back.

*

Babi Yar was in flames, an oppressing, terrifying sight. Villages behind the Dnieper were burning. The outskirts of Kiev were burning. Natasha sat at the kitchen window, attempting to knit but unable to take her eyes off the fires, when she heard a distinctive sound of a plane. When it appeared, her heart leaped for joy at the sight of red stars on its fuselage. It was unusual for a Soviet plane to appear in the middle of the day when it was easy for the German mortars to hit it. And yet, there it was in bright daylight, making its way through the autumn sky. Natasha wanted to run outside and salute the Soviet pilot, welcoming him to Kiev, but from past experience she knew that the plane was here to bomb the city.

Nervously she waited for the familiar whistling sound that preceded an explosion. But no bombs came. Instead, the plane released what looked like tiny white snowflakes that slowly drifted downwards. As the plane disappeared in the direction of the river, Natasha realised that they were not snowflakes but sheets of paper.

Placing her knitting on the table, Natasha shouted to Mother to look after the children and rushed outside. She didn't pause to put her shoes or jacket on. Barefoot, in nothing but a thin blouse, she almost ran the two blocks to the place where she thought the pieces of paper had landed, barely noticing the cold pavement that was scraping her feet until they bled or the rain that instantly soaked her clothes. As she reached the riverbank, she saw dozens of leaflets blowing in the wind. Her hands shaking, she picked one up. 'People of Kiev,' it said in Russian. 'We are here to liberate you from the Nazis. Under no circumstances leave the city. Soon Kiev will be ours. Until then, stay where you are and wait.'

Natasha stood in the rain, again and again reading the leaflet that promised a Soviet victory. Her hair was wet, and water was running down her face, but she didn't care. When she saw the words from the Soviet government — the first communication they had received from the outside world since the German occupation — she felt something she hadn't felt in a long time. She felt hope.

Placing the precious piece of paper in her pocket, she bent down to collect the other leaflets. They all carried the same message. Dozens of people were rushing towards her. Handing the leaflets out to everyone she met along the way, she hurried home.

The family was gathered in the living room. After everybody read the message, Mother took the leaflet, straightened it and wiped the mud from it as best she could. From the look on her face Natasha was expecting her to kiss the piece of paper. Finally, Mother folded it and hid it in her apron.

Grandfather said, 'The Soviets must be very close. The Nazis have left Kanev.'

'How far is Kanev, Dedushka?' asked Nikolai.

'A hundred and thirty kilometres,' replied Grandfather, pointing south-east.

'A hundred and thirty kilometres,' repeated Natasha. 'Our army could be here in only a few hours.'

'Not quite as quickly as that.' Grandfather smiled. 'The majority of the Germans are still here. It could take weeks, if not months. We should be prepared.'

Despite her grandfather's words, Natasha spent the rest of the day hoping to catch a glimpse of the Red Army as it entered Kiev. But all she saw from her spot by the kitchen window were endless Nazi convoys leaving her city.

*

A few days later, Natasha awoke to a familiar but almost forgotten smell. She opened her eyes and sat up in bed. For a few seconds she remained still, wondering if she was dreaming. Then she jumped out of bed, checked to make sure the babies were still sleeping and rushed to the kitchen. 'Mama, you're making blinis!' she exclaimed. 'Where did you get the flour? The oil?'

Her mother was by the stove, stirring, mixing, pouring. 'Yuri brought some home this morning,' she said. 'That man is made of gold, pure gold.' She smiled and pointed at the apple she was grating. 'Not just blinis, Natasha! Apple blinis.'

'Apple blinis, how wonderful!'

'And you have Yuri to thank for that,' Mother reminded her.

Natasha watched as Mother flipped a blini and two minutes later placed it on a plate, filling its golden insides with a spoonful of grated apple. Natasha brought her face close to the plate and inhaled. She could almost picture her grandmother's smile as she made blinis for Natasha, Stanislav, Lisa and Nikolai when they were little. Grandmother would make them first thing in the morning, so the children could wake up to the delightful treat. Just like today. 'Can I try some?' She shook a little, looking at the stack of blinis and not quite believing her eyes.

'Help yourself,' said Mother.

Natasha broke off a tiny bit and chewed slowly. 'Incredible,' she whispered, savouring the taste in her mouth. 'Just like Babushka used to make.'

'It's her recipe,' said Mother, smiling.

In under a minute, Natasha had finished the whole blini and was looking at the frying pan for more. The next one was just beginning to brown. When it was ready, Mother didn't put it on the plate but placed it straight into Natasha's eager hands.

Through a mouthful of blini, Natasha said, 'Once, when I was about twelve, Babushka tried to teach me, Lisa and Nikolai how to make them.'

'And? How did they turn out?'

'Terrible! What a mess we made. Nikolai started throwing batter at Lisa, and she chased him around the kitchen with a fork.'

Mother laughed. 'Why doesn't that surprise me?'

'Babushka never offered to teach us again. But she never stopped making them.'

Nikolai entered the kitchen, his eyes wide at the sight of blinis. Natasha could understand his amazement. She was amazed himself. It still felt like a beautiful dream. It was as if they'd woken up that morning not in Nazi-occupied Kiev but in the city of their childhood. Thank God for Yuri, thought Natasha.

Nikolai grabbed the blini from Natasha's hands and, before she had a chance to complain, shoved it in his mouth. He closed his eyes happily, golden flecks of batter on his lips. 'Bliss,' he said with his mouth full.

'Hey, that was mine!' Natasha cried.

Nikolai swallowed and said, 'I saw Larisa take her first step just now.'

'Larisa is awake?' cried Natasha, rushing to check on her babies. She returned a minute later and narrowed her eyes at Nikolai, who was now sat at the table, a blini in one hand, a slice of apple in the other. There was an expression of pure veneration on his face. Natasha thought any minute he would cover his blini in kisses. 'They are both asleep. Was that just a ploy to get rid of me and eat all the blinis?'

'Did you hear her, Mother? Did you hear her accuse her loving brother of such terrible things?'

Nikolai slid off his chair and crept closer to the pan. His timing was perfect: the next blini was almost ready. Mother, however, shook her head and rapped his knuckles with the spatula. 'No more snacking,' she said, 'and I mean both of you! We're going to eat at the table together like civilised people.'

'Civilised people don't hit each other with spatulas,' Nikolai protested, but obediently stepped back from the pan.

Nikolai and Natasha washed their hands and sat back at the table, impatiently glancing at the pile of apple blinis that was accumulating on the plate next to Mother. Finally, Mother turned the stove off and called everybody for breakfast. Just as they were about to eat, however, they heard angry German voices outside. Natasha's fork froze on the way to her mouth. The

Smirnovs looked at one another. 'What's happening?' whispered Nikolai.

His words were followed by a loud knock.

When a shaking Natasha opened the door, she breathed a sigh of relief. Instead of the Nazi officers she expected to see, it was one of their neighbours, an elderly man who had a small apartment on the first floor. He looked unkempt, as if he had just gotten out of bed. His hair was untidy, his shirt undone. 'Good morning, Petr Alexeevich,' said Natasha. 'Would you like to join us for breakfast? Mama made blinis.'

She expected to see astonishment and excitement on the neighbour's face, but he didn't seem to hear her. Without returning her greeting or answering her question, he exclaimed, his hands twitching, 'We have to leave. We were ordered to evacuate.'

'Petr Alexeevich, what are you talking about? Evacuate?'

'The Germans were here.'

'Yes, we heard the voices. What did they want?'

'We're now inside the restricted zone. If we don't move in two days, they'll kill us.'

'Restricted zone?' asked Natasha, blinking fast.

'Podol, Frunze, Kreshchatyk and Priorka. These areas are being evacuated for the protection of Kiev.'

'Is the Red Army here already?' asked Nikolai, suddenly appearing behind Natasha. He ran back to the kitchen, shouting, 'Mama, the Red Army is here.'

Natasha heard her mother gasp. She looked at the neighbour. 'Where are we supposed to go?' But Petr was already halfway up the stairs, eager to share his news with the others.

In the kitchen, Mother asked Natasha, 'Is it true? The Red Army, are they here?'

Natasha glared at Nikolai. 'No, Mama,' she said. 'I don't think so. But we have to leave.'

By midday, it was official. There were notices in the newspaper and on every building, ordering the occupants of the newly

302

established restricted zone to vacate their homes within two days. Engulfed in fire, the city was a sorry sight. The displaced and the desolate wandered in every direction, their worldly possessions on their backs. Lost, scared and exhausted, they had nowhere to go. Just like the Smirnovs.

The family sat around the table, looking at one another. After a long silence, Mother said, 'What are we going to do?'

Yuri replied, 'We have two days. I suggest we sit tight and not do anything until the last moment.'

Grandfather nodded. 'The Red Army might be here by then.'

Two days later, most of their neighbours had left and the Nazi patrols began. There was no putting it off any further. The Smirnovs didn't want to leave anything for the Germans, so they waited until it was dark and dug a hole in the garden big enough to fit their blankets, their clothes, and their kitchen utensils. Natasha kissed the picture of her brother before wrapping it up and placing it in the ground. She contemplated Mark's kerosene lamp and her favourite books. 'Can we take these?' she asked. 'We'll need the lamp.'

'No,' said Yuri. 'We need to be ready at a moment's notice. Belongings will only slow us down.'

Reluctantly Natasha buried the lamp and the books. All but Mark's copy of *The Count of Monte Cristo*. When Yuri wasn't looking, she placed it in her backpack.

After they filled the hole with soil and concealed all traces of their hiding place with grass and autumn leaves, they returned to the kitchen. Mother packed some potatoes she had boiled earlier, two dozen chestnuts, a few apples, and some bread. The blinis were gone. Natasha wondered if they had been nothing but a dream that had been interrupted by the dreadful news from the Nazis.

'We have enough food for a couple of days,' said Mother.

'And then what?' asked Natasha.

No one replied.

303

The German patrol marched in just before midnight and ordered everybody out of the building and onto the street. When the patrol moved on to the next apartment, Mikhail muttered, 'They can't force me out of my own house. I'm not going anywhere. I've lived here all my life and this is where I'm going to die.'

Grandfather said, 'Don't be foolish, Mikhail. The Red Army will break through soon, and then we can return.'

'Exactly. They'll be back soon. And I'll wait for them right here. It's late. The Nazis won't be back tonight. You should all stay here with me. The children need rest, and so do we. In the morning we can decide what to do.'

Natasha was tempted. To stay in their apartment, to sleep in their beds and to have what little food they had at their kitchen table. It was almost worth risking her life for. But not her children's lives. Not her mother's life. Not her grandfather's life. Not Nikolai's life.

Reluctantly they left after hugging Mikhail goodbye. Mother cried, clutching their small bag of food. Grandfather and Nikolai carried the clothes. Yuri and Natasha carried the twins. For a few minutes they stood on the corner, not knowing where to turn, and then joined the procession of people like them, people without homes and without hope, who were moving west.

When they were finally outside the restricted area, Natasha said, 'What's the point in going any further? We have nowhere to go. We might as well stay here.' She pointed at dozens of unfortunates who were doing exactly that.

The others agreed, not because they thought sleeping on the street was such a good idea but because they were out of options. They found a spot on the ground that was reasonably clean. Mother placed a towel where the ground was soft with fallen leaves, and they sat down. It was cold. Natasha's head felt heavy, as if filled with brick and scraps of metal, and sleep evaded her.

304

She leaned on Mother's shoulder. Mother didn't stir. 'Mama, are you awake?'

'Yes, dear.'

'Do you know a prayer?'

Mother shook her head.

'Didn't Babushka teach you?'

'A long time ago, when I was a child. Just close your eyes and pray. Pray in your own words. Ask God to protect us, to give us strength.'

'Do you think our soldiers are close?'

Mother's hand felt cold in Natasha's. 'They must be,' she said. 'Why would the Germans be in such a frenzy otherwise?'

'What do you think is going to happen to us?'

'I don't know. Ask your dedushka.'

Grandfather appeared to be asleep, his head resting against the wall. His face looked pale in the dark. Natasha couldn't close her eyes, couldn't stop staring into the darkness, not for the dull ache inside her head, not for her weary eyelids, not for anything. She watched the shadows whirl past them, listened to children cry. A woman was screaming because she had lost her son in the commotion. Natasha's gaze followed the woman, and she clutched Costa close to her chest. She tried to think of a prayer, of words that would give her strength. 'Wait and hope,' she whispered feverishly. 'Wait and hope.' She prayed silently and waited for the morning to dawn. She knew everything would seem less hopeless as soon as the sun was up.

Yuri was sitting on the grass a few steps away from them, smoking a cigarette. Natasha passed Costa to Mother and walked over to him. 'I remember you telling me about your mother's house. Where was that?'

'South from here, in Solomenka.'

'Could we go there? How far is it?'

'Not too far. Ten kilometres. Maybe twelve.'

'Who lives there now?'

'It was empty the last time I saw it,' he said. 'But that was a while ago.'

'Let's go there tomorrow. We can't possibly spend another night on the street.'

Yuri remained silent long enough to finish his cigarette and light another one. Then he said, 'It's been very hard for me, you know. You and me. Seeing you every day…'

She couldn't look at the outline of his pale face in the dark. She blinked and turned away. 'I know. I'm sorry.' What more could she say? She bit her lips.

'Knowing I'm like a brother to you, knowing I could never love anyone the way I love you… I just don't know what to do.'

'I wish things were different.'

'They could be. If only you gave us a chance.' When she didn't reply, he continued, 'When we got married, I thought everything would change. For a minute in that registry office, I hoped it was for real. I hoped we could be happy. It was the happiest morning of my life.'

'I'm sorry,' she repeated. The words didn't come easy. It was like learning a new language. 'I never meant to hurt you.' She didn't want to have this conversation with him.

'Don't apologise. I'm grateful to you for that moment of happiness, however brief.'

'You are my friend and I care about you. You do know that, don't you?'

'I wish it was enough. But it isn't, not for me.'

Natasha moved back to her babies. Holding them close, listening to their breathing, she fell into troubled sleep. Around seven in the morning, they woke up and Yuri walked back to Ilinskaya, returning with Mikhail, who told them he had no intention of leaving Podol, even if it was to stay at Yuri's old house in Solomenka.

'If you disobey them, they'll kill you,' said Grandfather.

But Mikhail was adamant. 'I can't leave. If Oksana and Olga

return, this is where they'll look for me. I want to be home when they come.'

For a few moments no one spoke. Mikhail stood in front of them, old beyond his years, hunched, grey and thinner than Natasha had realised. Behind him, a column of dark smoke rose from Babi Yar, coloured purple by the sun. Natasha knew that no matter what they said, they couldn't force the old man to part with the place where he saw his daughter and granddaughter alive for the last time.

*

When they finally reached Solomenka, it had just started to get dark. The house that had once belonged to Yuri's mother looked so small in the setting sun. Was it possible that after all this time it was still unoccupied?

'The boards I nailed to the door are gone,' said Yuri.

Natasha shivered at the possibility of another sleepless night under the open skies. She could hear a rumbling noise overhead. She looked up, expecting to see a plane, and realised it was only thunder. A minute later the rain poured down.

Yuri pushed the door open and it gave way. Inside, the house was as small as it looked. There were only four rooms – a bedroom, a living room, a tiny kitchen and an even tinier bathroom. In the kitchen they found a candle and lit it, looking around.

'Where are the floorboards?' exclaimed Nikolai.

'Everything has been stripped,' said Mother. 'There is nothing left but the walls.' She was right. Someone had taken all the personal belongings, the clothes, the books, the cookware. Only a rickety table remained.

They gathered in the living room, the largest room in the house. Natasha patted Yuri on the arm and said, 'Never mind the floorboards. We'll sleep on the ground. Better than sleeping outside.'

Mother mumbled something and sat on the floor. Yuri bolted the heavy wooden door. It didn't make much difference because the windows lacked most of the glass but it made everyone feel a little bit safer.

'Eat something,' said Mother, placing some boiled potatoes on the newspaper next to them.

'I don't know about you but I'm too tired to eat,' muttered Natasha.

'Speak for yourself,' said Nikolai, biting into a cold potato. 'Tastes amazing, Mama. Can I have one more?'

Mother pushed the bag of food in his direction.

With his mouth full, Nikolai said, 'Tomorrow, as soon as the sun comes up, Yuri and I will go back to Ilinskaya to get Mikhail.'

'Go into the restricted zone? Are you out of your mind?' cried Mother, glaring at Nikolai.

'Don't worry, Zoya Alexeevna. I'll go. Nikolai can stay,' said Yuri.

Nikolai protested, 'I'm coming with you. It should still be safe tomorrow.'

'Over my dead body,' said Mother.

'Nikolai, if both you and Yuri go, who will protect us from the Germans?' asked Natasha, attempting a wink. Her eyelids were so heavy, she could barely manage a grimace.

While Mother and Nikolai argued, Natasha hugged the twins and fought against sleep. She didn't fight for long. Soon her family's voices faded away. When she awoke a few hours later, it was completely dark. It was impossible to tell what time it was. It felt like the middle of the night. For a few seconds she felt disoriented, as if she was in a strange and unfamiliar place she'd never visited before. And then she remembered. She *was* in a strange and unfamiliar place. Once again, they had been forced out of their home. For now they had a place to stay but how long before the Nazis barged in once more and ordered them to leave or, worse, rounded them up and took them away?

In the light of the fires that were blazing in the far distance, Natasha could see her babies' sleeping faces. She brushed her lips against their hair and kissed their foreheads, then made her way to the window to watch the fires. She was surprised there were still buildings left in Kiev to burn, after all this time. It broke her heart to see her beautiful city destroyed in front of her eyes. What she needed was something to take her mind off her bleak thoughts. In her bag, she found the copy of *The Count of Monte Cristo* she had given Mark all those months ago. As she sat by the window and touched the snow-stained cover, she could see Mark's smiling face as he read to her, could hear his voice break as he told her to wait and hope. Mark was gone, but Natasha was still here, without him.

She opened the book, and inside found the letter Mark's mother had written. Instantly she regretted picking it up, but it was too late. Her fingers, stiff from the cold, reached for the letter. She read it under a burning candle and cried softly, careful not to disturb her family. Her face in her hands, she cried for all her hopes and the twins' future. Was Olga right? Had she been a fool for trusting Mark? She remembered her friend's words. If Mark had wanted to fight the Nazis, he would have. But he didn't. It was true that he didn't choose to enlist on Hitler's side, but he went along with it. He didn't oppose it. The question weighing heavily on her heart was this: if Mark could betray his principles so easily, could he also betray her? Could he say he loved her one day, and turn away from her the next? Could he promise her everything, knowing he could give her nothing?

What was she even thinking? Here, right in front of her, was Yuri, always there for her, through sunshine and rain, through loss and hunger, taking care of her, feeding her, helping her, ready to take her with someone else's children, ready to love her – and them – unconditionally. Here was a man who was prepared to risk his life for her and expected nothing in return, who did risk his life every day to oppose the Nazis and help those in need. Yuri might as well have been invisible because Natasha was blind and didn't see him. All she saw was ghosts, all she longed for was the past.

Was Mother right? Could she learn to love Yuri?

For the first time in her life, Natasha could see clearly. Yes, her heart belonged to Mark. And maybe it always would. But there was someone else who deserved her love, and if it was at all possible, she would do her best to love him with everything she had.

A faint strip of light escaped through the door that separated the two rooms. Her heart beating fast, Natasha walked a few steps and pushed the door open.

On the floor she saw Yuri. He didn't look up, didn't even notice she was there. He seemed lost in thought, staring at a candle that had almost burnt out. Closing the door behind her, Natasha approached him, touching his shoulder. 'Yuri?' she whispered. He shuddered. She added, 'Sorry, I didn't mean to startle you.' She sat next to him. 'What are you doing here all by yourself?'

'This is the first time I've seen this house since the war had started. I was right here in this room when we heard the announcement on the radio.'

'Is this where you grew up?'

Another nod from Yuri. 'War was the last thing on my mind that day. And then, suddenly, there it was. When it's all over, I'm going back to university. I'm going to make something of my life.'

'What did you study?'

'Medicine,' he said.

'You were studying to be a doctor?' When he nodded, she added, 'I can't imagine my life after the war. I can't imagine waking up in the morning and not feeling afraid.' She was afraid now, in this strange house, with German patrols outside their window. She was afraid her family wouldn't make it. That the war would be over and they wouldn't be there to see it. She watched the twirling shadows on the wall until the candle blinked one last time and went out, startling her. 'I'm sorry about your mother,' she said finally, touching his cheek.

'So am I. I'm sorry she died alone. I'm sorry she died not knowing I was still alive.'

A wind blew through the broken window, and Natasha shivered. Now that September was coming to an end, the days were chilly and the nights bitter cold. There was an icy feel to the air, and the wind carried with it a warning that winter wasn't far off.

Dawn coloured the sky orange, and she could see Yuri's silhouette clearly in the eerie light. He looked so sad, his shoulders hunched over, his head hung low, she wanted to put her arms around him, wanted some warmth and comfort, for him and for herself. She moved closer until her hand was touching his. Taking his hand, she kissed it. He blinked in amazement. Her fingers, her lips touched his cheeks. He sighed and whispered her name.

For a long time they kissed.

His body enveloped hers and his hands caressed the bare skin of her back. She felt his need for her, his body close, and suddenly she was not as sad, a little less lonely. Under her fingers he felt so strong. He unbuttoned her nightgown and kissed the base of her neck and the top of her breasts. His hands stroked her back, moving lower. It happened so quickly, she thought it was a dream. It couldn't be happening.

It couldn't be her, touching another man, kissing another man.

The floor was cold. He took off his jacket and placed it next to her, whispering, 'Here, this will be more comfortable.' This simple gesture conjured memories that were almost forgotten, of another night, another dark room. The broken pieces inside her stirred and stabbed. When he removed his shirt and turned towards her, she could no longer kiss him. When he took her in his arms, she cried, trembling. She tried to push him away but was too weak. 'Please, stop,' she whispered, almost choking. 'I can't do this. I'm so sorry.'

Yuri let go of her. He didn't argue, didn't question her, didn't protest. They sat in silence, not looking at each other. Finally, he asked, 'What's wrong?'

'I can't. I'm sorry.'

'Was it me? Did I do something? One minute you were here and then I lost you.'

She shook her head, reaching for her nightgown. He turned away while she dressed. Outside their window, the world gradually woke. Voices filled the room, and dark shadows moved past. She followed them with her eyes, grateful to have something to look at other than his anguished face.

After a moment of silence, he said, 'Tell me about him. The twins' father. You still love him, don't you?'

The last thing she expected was for Yuri to bring up Mark. 'What makes you think that?'

'Because if your heart was free, we wouldn't be sitting here right now. You would be mine.'

Her heart throbbed. 'I do still love him.' She turned away from him, back to the window, back to the moving shadows.

'Tell me about him,' he repeated, his face grim.

'His name is Mark.' She stopped. 'Was Mark.' Suddenly she couldn't continue.

'I knew that. Nikolai told me.'

'Oh, that Nikolai. His tongue is longer than the Dnieper. I'll have to have a serious talk with him.'

'Don't be upset with him. I kept asking until he told me. How did you and Mark meet?'

'Do you really want to know?'

'I need to know.'

'He saved my life. He helped Babushka and I when a Nazi officer confronted us in the park.' She was trusting Yuri with her life by revealing her secret. She knew he would never betray her.

Little by little, she told him everything. She told him about the hours she spent with Mark on the streets of Kiev and their endless evenings in the cafeteria, about Hungary and the plans they had made together. When she cried, Yuri held her, and when she paused, he waited patiently for her to continue. In the end, she reached in her pocket and showed him the letter Mark's mother had written to Mark. 'I don't know what happened to him. I don't know what to think.'

Yuri read the few lines she pointed out to him. Afterwards, he said, 'Natasha, I can't imagine anyone loving you and forgetting you so easily. I am sure that whatever happened, he loved you till the end. If he died, he died loving you.'

'Do you really think so?'

'I know so.'

This conversation must have been so difficult for him and yet, not a muscle on his face moved. 'Thank you for being so kind,' she whispered.

For a second he looked embarrassed. Then his face grew serious. 'There's a return address on the envelope. When the occupation is over, why don't you write to Mark's mother and ask her what happened to him? If anything happened to Mark his parents would have been notified.'

He took her hand and added, 'Either way, you need to know. You can't go through the rest of your life not knowing. You need to find out what happened, so you can move on.'

'You are right,' she managed in the smallest of whispers. 'I'll write to Mark's mother. As soon as the occupation is over.'

Yuri pulled Natasha closer and his lips touched her forehead. 'As to you and me, I'm not giving up. I'll wait as long as it takes. One day you will realise how much I love you and notice me. When that day comes, I'm planning to be around.'

Relaxing into his arms, Natasha cried silently. She wished she could feel for Yuri what he felt for her, but it was impossible. Her heart belonged irrevocably to Mark. He had saved her life, and

313

she was his, forever. No one else could breach her defences, not even Yuri with his kindness and his patience.

*

In the morning, the family woke to find two strangers asleep in the garden. They were sprawled on the damp grass, while hundreds of evacuees ambled past, glancing into the windows to see if there was a place for them.

'Who are they, Mama?' Natasha asked. 'Do you think they'll leave soon?'

'Doesn't look like they have anywhere to go. Should we invite them in?'

Natasha looked around the cramped house. 'We don't have much space.'

'No, we don't. But we can't let them stay outside.'

Natasha invited the couple in and they introduced themselves as Anatoly and Alina. They were barely through the door and out of their jackets when they told the Smirnovs that they had arrived from Priorka late the night before, after the Nazis had taken their cattle and burnt their house down. 'Could we possibly stay with you until tomorrow?' Anatoly begged. In his eyes, Natasha saw the familiar anxiety and desperation. 'We can sleep in the garden if we have to. Better than sleeping on the street.'

'Of course you can,' said Mother, inviting them in for breakfast. The Smirnovs still had some potatoes and half a dozen chestnuts. Their guests had some bread and cheese. There was a stove in the house but no cutlery or plates or pans, so they sat on the floor in a circle, eating their food cold.

Alina thanked Mother with tears in her eyes. 'God bless you and your family,' she repeated. 'We didn't know what to do, where to turn. All our belongings burnt, all our money and our documents.'

'How did it happen?' asked Mother.

'The Nazis set fire to our house when they realised we didn't have anything of value. What are we going to do?'

'Wait for the Red Army to return, Comrade. When they are back, you won't have to worry about a thing,' said Grandfather.

'You clearly haven't heard what's been happening in Kharkov,' said Alina, widening her eyes.

Mother said, 'More potatoes, anyone?'

'I'll have a potato,' said Nikolai.

'Have it on a piece of bread. Natasha, you want some?'

'Mama, wait. What is happening in Kharkov?' asked Natasha.

'The arrests, the executions, the reprisals.' Alina shook.

Suddenly Natasha was no longer hungry. 'Reprisals?' she whispered.

'The Bolsheviks are punishing everyone they suspect of collaborating with the German regime,' said Alina, shuddering.

'Stop talking, woman,' barked Anatoly. 'We aren't collaborators. We have nothing to fear.'

'How will you prove that without our passports?'

'The Bolsheviks are no Nazis. They can tell the good people from the bad.'

'Tell that to those who were shot in Kharkov.'

'Shot?' exclaimed Natasha.

'By the NKVD,' replied Alina. 'From what I've heard, many of them were innocent people just like us. Their only crime was trying to survive under the German regime. Taking jobs in German establishments. Digging trenches under the German guns.'

Natasha glanced at Yuri. The piece of bread she was holding in her hand trembled.

'Haven't we been through enough?' cried Mother. Natasha turned away from Mother and away from Alina. Facing the wall, she chewed her bread listlessly. She didn't want to hear any more rumours. What she needed desperately to get through her day was her faith in the Red Army and the

Bolsheviks. She needed to believe that they were coming to protect them, not prosecute them. Without that faith, what did she have left?

'Those who were shot deserved it,' said Anatoly. 'And anyway, before we worry about the Soviets, we need to survive the Germans. The Red Army isn't here yet.'

'But it will be here, right?' exclaimed Nikolai eagerly.

Anatoly shrugged. 'Eventually. They're waiting for the ice to form on the Dnieper before they make their final attack.'

'That could take months,' mumbled Grandfather.

Natasha shivered. 'Months, Dedushka? We can't live like this for months.'

'Yes, and by the time they come, who will be left to welcome them? The Germans are taking all the men. Young, old, they are taking them all,' said Alina.

'Taking them where?' asked Mother, glancing at Grandfather and Nikolai.

'West somewhere. We managed to escape two round-ups yesterday.' Alina clasped her hands together as if in prayer. 'Thank God.'

'What do they want with all the men?' asked Natasha.

When Alina didn't reply, Grandfather said, 'To dig trenches, no doubt, and to throw in front of the Soviet tanks.'

'I'd rather die than help the Nazis against our soldiers,' stated Nikolai, waving his hands about and almost hitting Natasha in the face with a piece of potato.

Mother paled.

Lowering her voice, Alina murmured, 'Is there a hiding place here? Somewhere we could hide the men?'

Mother said, 'I doubt it. This place is too small. It's nothing but bare walls.'

'We have to find somewhere,' wailed Alina, clinging to Anatoly. 'I've lost so many people I love. I couldn't bear losing my husband. It would kill me, absolutely kill me.'

Mother's face darkened. Natasha knew she was thinking of her own husband.

'There's a cellar underneath this room,' said Yuri. He tapped a stone and pulled a hidden handle. A tiny entrance appeared. It was as if the cellar was built for this very purpose, to hide them from the Nazi patrol. A small ladder led downstairs. Yuri, Grandfather, Nikolai, Anatoly and Alina climbed down.

Natasha peered down the ladder, putting her foot in front of inquisitive Costa to stop him from falling in.

Just as Natasha was about to join them, there was a knock on the door. 'Quick, Mama, let's hide,' she exclaimed.

Another knock followed.

'If we hide, they'll break the door down. What if they have dogs? Someone has to stay up here and distract them.' Mother leant close to Larisa, who whimpered in her arms.' They don't care about us. They are after the men.'

Natasha closed the opening to the cellar, while Mother unlocked the front door to three officers in Gestapo uniforms. The Germans barged in, demanding to know if there were any men in the house. Natasha shook her head. 'No men here, only women.'

'Then you won't mind if we look around.' With a start Natasha realised that not only did the officer speak perfect Russian, but he was Russian. What a traitor, she thought, as the three of them pushed past her and proceeded to search the house. Not even glancing in the women's direction, they walked from one empty room to the other. Natasha shuddered when they stepped over the trap door but it was so well camouflaged, the officers didn't suspect a thing.

The house was small and the search didn't last long. A few minutes later the officers left without a word. Natasha realised she had been holding her breath the whole time. Only when the Nazis disappeared around the corner was she able to breathe freely.

'That was lucky,' she whispered.

'I hope they'll leave us alone now. The twins are asleep. It's almost lunch time,' said Mother, disappearing into the kitchen.

And then they heard another knock. Natasha clenched her fists in fear. What did they want now? Wasn't one search enough? Her hands shaking, she opened the door.

In the doorway stood Mark.

Chapter 18 – Against All Odds

September 1943

As if in a fog, Natasha watched Mark standing in the doorway. For a long time neither of them spoke. She blinked – once, twice. She closed her eyes. She had been dreaming of seeing his face for so long, she didn't trust that what she saw in front of her was real. And then he said her name, so quietly, she could barely hear him. It wasn't a whisper, it was a sigh, filled with pain, with longing. He was the only person she knew who pronounced her name that way, drawing every syllable as if in a caress.

She opened her eyes.

Mark's face was very close. She could see his lips, his eyes, his beard. Beard! She looked at him in silence. If she raised her hand, she would be able to touch him. She raised her hand, choking on her tears.

'Natasha, who is it?' Mother called from the kitchen.

Natasha couldn't reply. She stepped into Mark's arms. He held her tight, his face in her hair, his breathing heavy. His body was shaking just like hers.

'Natasha, don't cry. Please don't cry,' he repeated, stroking her hair. He kissed her lips; soft, tender kisses barely touching her.

'Mark,' she whispered. To be able to say his name out loud after all this time, not just to herself but to him, what happiness! She looked into his face, looked into his eyes and pressed her body close to his. As close as she could. 'Is it really you? Please tell me I'm not imagining this.'

'It's really me.' He pulled her up, his arms encircling her, his eyes bright.

'Oh my God,' she whispered. 'Oh God.' Her throat was suddenly dry. He was much thinner than she remembered, his face barely recognisable under the beard. But the smile was unmistakably his, the twinkle in his eye all too familiar. The same smile, the same twinkle she saw in Costa and Larisa every day.

She touched his face and cried. She kissed his callused hands and cried. He whispered, 'God, Natasha. Look at you. Finding you here, alive. I can't believe it. You have no idea—'

'I can't believe it either.' Her head on his chest, she listened for his heart. It was beating fast. 'I can't believe you're here. Where did you come from? How did you find us?'

So engrossed were they in each other, they didn't notice Mother only a few steps away. 'You must be Mark,' she said.

Natasha moved away from him. Not too far. She was still holding his hand. 'It *is* Mark, Mama. Can you believe it?'

'And you must be Zoya Alexeevna.' Mark stretched his hand out for Mother to shake. 'It's a pleasure to finally meet you.'

Mother motioned him inside and closed the door behind him. 'Come in, come in.' She turned to Natasha and tutted. 'What are you thinking, standing in the doorway with patrols everywhere? Are you hungry, Mark?'

'I am a little hungry.'

'What can I get you? We have some potatoes. Would you like some?' Natasha let go of his hand and made a move towards the kitchen.

'Wait, not now. Let me look at you first.' He reached for her and suddenly she felt light-headed, almost faint.

Mother said, 'Well, don't just stand there. Natasha, why don't you show the man in?'

Natasha led Mark to the kitchen, with Mother following close.

'How did you find us?' asked Natasha.

'I stayed at Mikhail's last night. He told me where you were.'

'Is Mikhail alright?' asked Mother.

'He's fine. Told me to give you all his love.'

'Oh, thank God. We were so worried. Why don't you unpack? Your rucksack looks heavy,' said Mother, taking his bag from him. 'What do you have in there? Bricks?'

'Maps, mostly,' he said. His eyes were on Natasha, who was watching him, unable to speak.

Mother nodded and said, 'Well, I'd better go and tell the men to stay in the cellar until it's dark. It's not safe for them here.' A moment later she was gone.

Mark took Natasha in his arms again. 'Come here,' he whispered. 'Look at you. You're so beautiful. More beautiful even than I remembered,' said Mark.

Mother returned, carrying some bread and boiled potatoes on a piece of old newspaper.

'I'm sorry we don't have any plates,' said Natasha. She laughed. Suddenly she felt so happy.

Mother placed the food on the floor. 'It's not much but better than nothing. Would you like to wash? We can fetch water from the pump.'

'Thank you, Zoya Alexeevna. Show me the pump and I'll bring the water,' said Mark.

She looked at Mark. 'Do you know what's happening at the front? Where is the Red Army now?'

'They are at the outskirts of Kiev, waiting to liberate us.'

'I hope they don't wait too long,' said Mother. Finally noticing Natasha's frantic face, she added, 'I'm going, I'm going. I'll go check on the tw—' She caught Natasha's eye just in time and stopped abruptly. Nodding to Mark, she left the kitchen, closing the door behind her.

Instantly Natasha moved closer. 'You're so unshaven. I've never seen you like this, with a beard.' She stroked it gently. It felt soft.

'You like it?'

'I do.' She touched his cheek. 'Mark, I never thought I would ever see you again,' she murmured.

'Neither did I. I never thought I would make it back to Kiev.'

She sat up to better see his face. 'What happened to you? Tell me everything.' It was quiet in the kitchen. She could hear the birds outside.

'On the day we were supposed to leave for Hungary, I was arrested.'

'Lisa,' she muttered with loathing.

'You sister? What about her?'

'She betrayed you to the Gestapo.'

'Lisa did that? But why?'

Natasha lowered her gaze, staring at the mud of their bare floors. She didn't want Mark to see in her eyes what she still couldn't fully admit to herself. As much as she tried, she couldn't forgive her sister. 'She thought going to Hungary would be a mistake. She didn't want me to leave our whole family behind. Maybe she thought by punishing me she would make herself feel better. She was selfish and vindictive, and you paid for it.'

'Did you say, was? Natasha, where is Lisa now?'

'They transported her to Germany a year ago. We haven't heard from her since. I wish she was still here. I don't know why. I don't know if I want to make up with her or kill her, but I want her here either way.'

'She's your only sister. You love her.'

She wanted to tell Mark that despite everything that happened, she still missed Lisa. Sometimes, in the middle of the night, when

322

she was too afraid to sleep, she would close her eyes and think of her sister. She thought of the seven-year-old Lisa riding a bicycle next to Natasha, of the ten-year-old Lisa playing with their dog Mishka in Taras Shevchenko Park, climbing trees and skating on the frozen lake.

She didn't have to say any of it. He knew. 'Don't worry. People come back from Germany all the time. She will, too.'

'I hope so, for Mama's sake. I tried to help Lisa but I made it clear to her that she'll never be a part of my life again.'

'Don't say that. I'm sure she regrets what she's done. She's been through a lot, just like the rest of us. This war has changed all of us.'

Natasha knew he was right. She could barely remember herself before the war. But right now she could barely remember herself a month ago, a week ago. All she could see was his breathtaking face.

'What about you? What has happened since I left? Where are your brother and grandfather?'

Natasha shivered in Mark's arms. She didn't want to answer his questions. She didn't want to tell him about Yuri. She wanted to pretend for a little while longer that it was just the two of them, just like before.

'Oh, they're in the cellar hiding. The German patrols...'

'I see. Why aren't you hiding too?'

'The Nazis don't care about the women. They're after the men.' Although the door to the kitchen was firmly shut, Natasha lowered her voice. 'Wait. You haven't told me anything yet. Why did they arrest you?'

'They knew about my plan to take you out of the city. They arrested me on the day we were supposed to leave Kiev. I was interrogated. I denied everything of course, and they had no proof, but, as you know, the accusation is all that matters.'

'You must have been so afraid.' She entwined his fingers with hers, kissing them.

'I was frantic. We were so close to freedom. I had no safe way to get in touch with you. I imagined you waiting in the cold for hours, thinking I had abandoned you.'

'I did wait for you in the cold for hours,' she said sadly. 'I didn't know what to think.'

'That's what I was afraid of. I wrote to you. Every day for months.'

'Your letters wouldn't have reached us.'

'I know. That's why I've never sent them.'

Natasha thought of his disappearance, of long miserable days that turned into long miserable months. 'The first week after you were gone was the hardest. I didn't know if you were dead or alive.' *I didn't know if I was dead or alive, either,* she thought.

'I'm so sorry, Natasha. Do you hear me? I'm sorry.'

'There was nothing you could have done. Where are these letters now? I'd like to read them.'

'I lost them near Stalingrad. Our military truck blew up. Fortunately, I wasn't on it at the time. Others weren't so lucky.'

'Stalingrad?'

'Three days after I was arrested, the Gestapo put me on the train bound for the front. Me and two hundred other unfortunates. Stalingrad was… What can I say? It was hell on earth.'

After a moment of silence, she whispered, 'Oh my God, Mark.' She remembered what her grandfather had said about Stalingrad. She believed the word he had used was a massacre. From what she'd read in the newspaper and judging by the number of wounded German soldiers who had arrived from the front, she knew her grandfather was right. She touched Mark's hand as if to make sure that it was truly him next to her. That he was real and alive.

Mark continued, 'The Germans issued our unit with an obsolete howitzer and corroded shells. We were in a snow-bound village ten kilometres from the Don, with the Red Army across the river. Our rifles were useless. It didn't matter. None of us wanted to fight the Soviets anyway.'

'So what did you do?'

'We were talking of surrendering, changing sides, fighting the Nazis. But all I wanted was to get back to you.'

He fell silent. The colour had left his cheeks and his face looked grim. He was no longer looking at Natasha. And Natasha desperately wanted him to look at her. Touching his face, she asked, 'What happened next?'

'Soon we stopped receiving news from the headquarters. Our radio was mute for over a week. A couple of days later, we found out that our headquarters had been destroyed. We were surrounded by the Soviets.'

'Oh my God, Mark,' she whispered, horrified. 'How did you cope?'

'Everywhere around us there were dead horses, tanks buried up to their turrets in snowdrifts, soldiers dead and frozen. After a couple of weeks I joined a column of men walking west. I was determined to get back to you. But I didn't get very far before I was captured.'

'By the Soviets?' In all her days of not knowing what had happened to him, she had never come close to imagining what he was describing now.

'I was given a choice. A hard labour camp in Siberia or to join one of the Soviet penal battalions and fight the Nazis.'

She watched him with adoration. 'So you joined the penal battalion?'

'Gladly.'

She kissed his hand, placing it on her heart.

He continued, 'Finally I could live with a clear conscience. But it didn't last. As you can imagine, Stalin used us as cannon fodder for the Germans. Our battalion was destroyed within a few weeks. I was one of the few who survived.'

Natasha crossed herself and whispered, 'God was protecting you.' Tears were running down her face onto his bare arms.

'I had to survive. I had no choice. I had to see you again.' He smiled and she tried to smile back but couldn't. He continued, 'I had no money, no documents, no maps. But I slowly made my way back to Kiev.'

'How did you get back?'

He was staring past her face into the darkness, his eyes unfocused. Her heart racing, she waited impatiently for him to tell her the rest. He shuddered and said, 'It's taken me over eight months to return. Through it all, only one thing kept me going. Kept me alive. You.' He pressed his lips to her quivering fingers. 'Sometimes in the middle of the night I would lie in the snow, freezing cold and unable to sleep, look up at the stars and think of you. I'd think of you looking at the same stars, waiting for me.'

'I did wait for you. Every day. I can't fathom everything you had to go through to come back to me.'

'How could I not come back? Can't you see? Nothing could keep me away.'

'I love you, Mark.' Finally saying it out loud made her chest hurt a little less. 'You are my life. And you don't know the half of it.' She smiled, anticipating Mark's reaction when he found out about the twins.

'Why are you smiling?'

'I'll show you in a minute. Can you wait here?' Kissing his bewildered eyes, she got up and, unstable on her feet, walked to the living room. 'Mama, where are the children?'

Together Mother and Natasha carried Costa and Larisa to meet their father. Mark's eyes widened. Natasha couldn't help it, she laughed. He reached for Costa. The boy babbled happily, grabbing Mark's fingers and trying to bite them. 'Are they yours?' he asked.

She waited for Mother to leave the kitchen. 'There's something I need to tell you.' She took a deep breath, wondering what to say. How to say it. How to explain how things had been. How to explain Yuri. She needed to be the one to tell him. If only she could find the right words.

She was about to speak when they heard loud voices. The men were returning from their hiding place in the cellar. Grandfather was the first to walk in. 'Natasha, talk some sense into your husband. He completely cleared me out. I have no money left.'

Mark stood up.

'I guess I'm lucky in cards.' Yuri followed Grandfather into the kitchen, grinning from ear to ear.

Nikolai peered in and said, 'That's why I don't play anymore. I'd rather be lucky in love.' Seeing Mark, he fell quiet.

Natasha couldn't bear the look on Mark's face. She muttered, 'I was just about to explain—'

'No need to explain. I'm glad you are well and…' he hesitated. 'And happy. I'm very pleased for you. I was worried about you and your family, and I'm relieved to see that you are doing fine.' He sounded so calm, so collected. His coldness was like a sharp razor blade on Natasha's heart. Even if she knew it was an act. His pale face and trembling hands gave him away. 'Anyway, I have to go. I wish you all the best. Tell your mother I said thank you for everything and goodbye.' And just like that, he walked out of the kitchen. Natasha heard the front door close softly.

'Mark, wait,' cried Natasha. But it was too late. He couldn't have possibly heard her.

After a moment of tense silence, Grandfather asked, 'Who was that?'

Natasha didn't reply.

Nikolai said, 'That was Mark.'

Natasha wasn't looking at Yuri but even she noticed the sudden change. It was as if something had shattered inside him.

Pushing her brother out of the way, she ran after Mark.

*

Natasha paused on the busy street, hoping to see Mark in the crowd of lost, ghost-like figures. The cold September air numbed her bare skin. It would have been completely dark if it wasn't for the fires raging on the outskirts of Kiev. Natasha could almost sense the inferno closing in on them. She could smell the putrid smoke. Pushing her way through women and children, she looked for him. She glanced into every garden, every side street, every alley. She shouted his name, not caring if it attracted the attention of the Germans strolling on the opposite side of the road.

As hard as she tried, she couldn't find him.

What if he never came back? Or worse, what if a Nazi patrol took him away? To have him return, only to lose him again – Natasha couldn't take it. To dream of him for two years, through hunger and desperation, and finally to see him again but only for a moment. But he came back for her! Nothing had stopped him, not the distance, nor the Soviets, nor the Germans. He had overcome it all to be with her. And now that she knew he was alive, now that she knew he loved her, she would overcome everything to be with him.

Natasha walked faster.

After two hours of frantic searching, when her throat was sore and her feet frozen, she thought she heard someone call her name. She turned around eagerly, hoping it was Mark.

It wasn't.

'Natasha, wait,' cried Yuri.

She slowed down but didn't stop.

'You need to come home.'

'I can't. Not yet.'

He grabbed her by the arm. 'It's late. And dangerous.'

'I know. Which is exactly why I need to find him.'

Yuri shook his head. 'He could be anywhere right now. If he doesn't want to be found, I doubt you'll find him. There's no point.'

No point? What was he talking about? She squared her shoulders. 'I'm not going anywhere without him.'

Yuri tightened his grip around her wrist. 'Come home this

instant. Haven't you seen the Germans walking up and down the street looking for their next victim? Do you want it to be you?'

'What are you, my mother?' Natasha tried to free herself but couldn't. He was too strong.

'No, I'm not. I wish I could say that I'm your husband but you made it clear that...' He didn't finish his sentence but his disapproving eyes spoke volumes.

The air felt stifling, almost suffocating. Natasha didn't know what to say.

Yuri muttered, 'Sometimes I wish I'd never met you.'

She recoiled from him. He let go of her arm. 'I'm sorry,' she said. Dozens of Soviets walked past, as if in a rush to get away from something. Eagerly she peered into every face but none of them was Mark.

'Don't be. I can't say I'm surprised. To still hold any illusions about our marriage after all these months, I would have to be stupid or blind. I was blinded by my feelings for you for a very long time. I kept hoping...' He shook his head. 'How stupid of me, how naïve.'

They stood in silence, while the passers-by hurried fearfully past.

When he finally spoke, his voice was steady. 'You can stay out here on the street if you like but I'm not leaving your side.'

'I'll be fine on my own.'

'If anything happens to you, I'll never forgive myself.'

'Go home, Yuri. I'll be back soon.'

A plane roared overhead as Yuri pulled her in the direction of the house. 'Your Mama's worried sick. You can look for him tomorrow.' His face twisted when he said that. Sad and discouraged, she followed Yuri.

Home, in the room where she had been so happy what seemed like moments ago, she found Mark's rucksack. For a long time she sat on the floor, clutching it, watching the candle.

'Eat something,' said Mother.

Natasha shook her head.

'At least he's still alive. That's something, isn't it?' When Natasha didn't reply, Mother added, 'Don't worry. He'll be back in the morning.'

'What makes you think that?'

Mother pointed at the rucksack. 'His things are still here.'

'What was all that about?' asked Nikolai, appearing in the doorway.

Natasha turned away from him. The last thing she wanted was to talk.

'Leave your sister alone,' said Mother. 'She needs rest.' To Natasha, she said, 'Try to get some sleep.'

That was easier said than done. Natasha closed her eyes but sleep wouldn't come. She only moved when Costa and Larisa's voices rose in a unified scream for attention. Like a ghost that moved in a slow motion, she picked them up and fed them, rocking them. Finally, the babies fell asleep. When morning dawned, Natasha was still on the floor, holding Mark's rucksack, staring into space.

*

With her eyes firmly shut, Natasha listened as the family awoke, had breakfast, and discussed the German retreat. She listened to the men as they descended to the cellar. Her eyelids were heavy. She needed food and sleep. But sleep most of all.

Mother walked into the room. 'Look who I found,' she said.

Natasha raised her eyes. Mark stood in front of her. All thoughts of sleep forgotten, she leapt up. 'Where have you been?'

'I'll leave you two to talk,' said Mother. 'I'll be in the kitchen if you need me, feeding the twins.'

When the door closed behind her, Mark said, 'Can I have my things, please?' He sounded so cold, Natasha shivered.

'Is that why you came back?'

'I won't get very far without my maps.'

Her heart beat faster. 'Where are you going?'

He didn't reply. For a very long time they were silent. She took his hand in hers. He didn't pull back. 'Please, don't go. We need to talk.'

'What's there to talk about?'

'Please, Mark. You don't have to go just yet, do you? Have you eaten anything since yesterday? Where did you spend the night?'

She wanted to touch his face but didn't dare. His eyes were like two daggers keeping her at a distance. Two sharp, furious daggers. 'You want to talk, then let's talk.' He moved away from her. 'Why don't you start by telling me about your marriage?'

'Please, Mark. Don't be angry.'

'You said you waited for me.'

'And I did. I waited for you...'

He interrupted. 'How long? Two months? Six? How long did it take?'

'It's not what you think.'

'I come back to find you married to someone else. What do you expect me to think?' He raised his head and looked straight at her. Natasha felt so small under his glare, she felt her whole body shudder. 'You should have told me.'

'I tried. I was just about to.'

'It should have been the first thing that came out of your mouth. I'm so glad you're alive, you should have said, and by the way, I'm married now. I have a family now. It would have been easier coming from you.' He shook his head, turning not just his face but his whole body away from her. 'No, that's a lie. It wouldn't have been easier. But it would have been fair.'

'You have no idea what it's been like here.'

'You're right. I only know what it's been like there, when all I could do was pray that the next shell wouldn't hit me, so I could come back to you.'

She clasped her fists, trying to stop herself from crying. She

331

wouldn't cry, not now. Not while he watched her as if he didn't know her. As if she was a stranger.

'You should have told me,' he repeated.

'Please, don't do that,' she whispered.

'Do what?'

'Make me feel like I've done something wrong. I only did what I had to survive.'

'I can see you did your very best.'

'You're judging me?' Her voice cracked. It was too loud for the small room, too loud for the two of them. 'Who are you to judge me? I did nothing wrong. Not once have I lied to you. Unlike you.' She whispered the last two words.

'What are you talking about?'

'Your letter. Rather, your mother's letter.' She closed her eyes and took a deep breath. Where was her courage when she needed it the most? 'Who is Julia?'

At the mention of Julia his face changed, his incomprehension morphing into slow realisation. It wasn't what she wanted to see. He reached for her and she turned away. 'You said you told your mother about us. You lied. You said you wanted to marry me. And all that time you were engaged to someone else.' She reached into her pocket. Crumpling the letter in her fist, she threw it in his face. 'Here, take it. I've been carrying it with me long enough. Almost two years. How dare you say I didn't wait for you?' If she had the energy, she would have pushed him. She was horrified at herself. There was nothing scarier than her own anger at the man she loved more than life itself.

He unfolded the letter. By the look on his face she knew he recognised it. She waited.

When he spoke, his voice was calm. 'A week after I met you, I wrote to my mother and told her about you. I don't know if she ever received my letters.'

'Oh,' whispered Natasha. She couldn't think of anything else to say. Her anger was gone and suddenly all she wanted to do

332

was cry. 'I can't believe we're fighting. I can't believe you're back and we're fighting.' She trembled.

'I know.' He made a move to take her hand, then changed his mind and simply moved closer. 'Are you cold?' he asked. She shook her head. 'Look at you. You're shivering. Here, wear this.' He took off his jumper, draping it around her.

'Thank you. But now you're cold.'

'I survived the Stalingrad winter. Kiev in September is nothing.' He smiled. She smiled tentatively back. 'Julia and I grew up together. She's like a sister to me. Our families always assumed we would get married. Julia and I just went along with it.'

'And are you going to?'

'Going to what? Marry her? After everything that has happened? What do you think?'

'I don't know, Mark. I don't know what to think. Does Julia still think you're getting married? She's bought a dress.' The accusatory tone crept back into her voice and at that particular moment, Natasha didn't like herself very much. She didn't like herself for feeling like this, for doubting him. For not being able to hide her doubt.

'I wrote to Julia and told her I couldn't marry her. A week after I met you.'

She looked up into his face, no longer crying.

'I knew for a long time that marrying Julia was a big mistake. Neither of us is in love with the other. I was just waiting for the right moment to tell her.'

'Poor Julia. She must have been devastated.'

'She'll be fine. I'm sure she feels the same way.'

Natasha put her arms around him, pulling him close. 'And here I was, thinking you'd left me in Kiev so you could go back to Hungary and marry your Julia.'

'My God, Natasha. How could I marry anyone but you? I love you so much. What are you even thinking?'

'How was I supposed to know that?'

333

'Didn't I tell you often enough?'

'Yes but…' Even in his jumper, she shivered. 'When you didn't come for me that day, I was so scared. The next day I went to your barracks. That's where I found the letter. I don't even remember how I made it back home. I didn't get up for weeks.' Tears ran down her cheeks. 'Everyone thought I was dying. For a while so did I.'

'I'm so sorry. You didn't deserve any of this.' He held her and she clung to him, sobbing, struggling for breath. When she finally fell quiet, he asked, 'Is that why you married him? Because you thought I'd chosen someone else over you?'

'Of course not.'

'Do you love him? If you do, I'll understand. I won't get in your way. All I want is for you to be happy.'

'You know I don't love him. You know I only love you.' There was doubt in his eyes. Doubt and fear and sadness. *He's as bad at hiding his feelings as I am*, she thought. 'I love him as a friend, a brother, nothing more. Like I love Nikolai. Like you love your Julia. You don't know what it's been like in Kiev. Mass transportations to Germany started, just like you warned me. Nobody was safe. But they weren't taking married men. Not at first.'

'And that's why you married him?'

She nodded. 'To protect him.'

Relief on his face was instant. 'That sounds just like you. You have a heart of gold. That's why I love you. That and your beautiful lips.' He kissed her lips. 'Your beautiful eyes.' He kissed her eyes. He kissed her and kissed her, not letting go. 'When did you get married?' he asked at last.

'About six months ago.'

'Only six months? And the children? They look just like you, especially the girl. Beautiful like you.'

'No, they look like you. Both of them look just like you,' she whispered.

She watched him closely. Everything she was hoping to see

334

was in his face. Everything and more. Incomprehension at first, then disbelief, and finally, realisation and wonder. 'You mean…'

'Yes.'

'They are…'

'Yes.'

'My God, Natasha,' he whispered. He was crying and not even trying to hide it.

Natasha kissed his eyes and whispered, 'They have your eyes.' Kissed his mouth. 'And your mouth.' Kissed his damp cheek. 'Your cheeks.' Finally, she tweaked his ear and added, 'And they are stubborn, just like you.'

'I can't believe it. It's the last thing I expected. I just can't believe it. What did you call them?'

'I called the girl Larisa.'

'After your grandmother. And the boy?'

'Constantine, after your father.'

'Just like I wanted,' he whispered.

'Just like *we* wanted.' She stroked his fingers.

'So what are we going to do now?' whispered Mark. Natasha could swear that he held his breath, waiting for her to reply.

'About what?'

'You and me. Your husband.'

Did he have to ask? Wasn't it obvious? She peered into his face. 'Mark, there hasn't been a day, not a minute in the last two years when I didn't miss you. You really think I could be with anyone else?' She swallowed. 'You're still the only man I've ever been with.'

'I don't believe it.'

'You don't trust me?'

'I just can't believe how lucky I am. To be loved by someone like you.'

She kissed the palm of his hand and pressed it to her heart. 'Yuri is a good man. He loves me very much.'

'I don't blame him.'

335

'But I haven't been with him, Mark. I couldn't. There were times when I wished I could. When I wished I didn't love you so much. It would have made things easier.'

She climbed into his lap just like she had done a lifetime ago. But just as she was about to kiss him, Nikolai burst into the room. In his left hand he held a piece of bread. In his right hand was a book. Natasha slid off Mark's knee as Nikolai came to an abrupt stop and muttered, 'Sorry, I didn't know anyone was in here. I was going to read my book.' He watched them curiously.

'Mark, remember Nikolai?' asked Natasha.

Mark nodded and said, 'I remember. We met once before.'

'Outside our building on Tarasovskaya,' said Nikolai.

'Why aren't you in the cellar with Dedushka and Yuri?' asked Natasha.

Nikolai shrugged. 'It's too dark to read in the cellar.' She must have looked concerned because Nikolai added, 'Don't worry. Nothing is going to happen to me.'

'Where did you get that book? What is it?'

Nikolai held it up. It was Dostoyevsky's *Crime and Punishment*. 'Our next-door neighbour has quite a library. He told me I could borrow anything I wanted.' Nikolai turned to Mark. 'So are you here to stay?'

Natasha held her breath.

Mark said, 'I might stay for a little while.' And smiled. She pressed his hand gently.

'And Stalingrad, what was it like?' asked Nikolai. But then he saw the expression on Natasha's face and muttered, not waiting for Mark's reply, 'Well, it's good to see you. I'll be in the kitchen.'

And then it was just the two of them in the room once more. Their arms around each other, their eyes closed. She relaxed into his body, breathing faintly. They sat like that for a while, and then he said, 'I am a little hungry. I haven't eaten anything since yesterday.'

Instantly she jumped up. 'Oh God, I'm so sorry. How selfish of me. Here I am, talking about myself, not feeding you.'

Slowly they walked to the kitchen. There was something peculiar in the way he moved, as if every step was a struggle. 'You are limping,' said Natasha. 'Are you hurt?'

He shrugged. 'It's not a big deal. Just an old wound. I'll be good as new soon.'

'You can hardly walk.'

'I walked a thousand kilometres to be with you. You think I can't make it to the kitchen?' He lifted her then and carried her struggling, giggling, squealing body through the doorway, as if they were a married couple on the night of their wedding.

Chapter 19 – Waiting for a Miracle

October 1943

The days that followed were a happy blur of talking, playing with their children together, Mark's arms around Natasha when they were alone, his leg touching hers under the kitchen table when they were not. When she begged him to join the men in their hiding place, he refused. 'I didn't come all this way to hide in the cellar,' he said. Soon she stopped asking.

One day Yuri brought home a small kerosene stove. Mother asked her new friends next door for some cutlery and plates. It was the chestnut season and there were apples in their garden. In the cellar they found a supply of carrots and potatoes that Yuri's mother had prepared for the winter. The vegetables were old but who were they to complain?

Alina and Anatoly had moved on, but every night, strangers appeared in the garden, where they would sleep on the cold grass only to move on the next morning in their elusive search of a safe place to stay. At first, Natasha made an effort to welcome the newcomers to the house, to talk to them, to ask their names. But soon it became hard to keep track of everyone.

Every once in a while she would look up and see Yuri's cold

eyes as he watched her and Mark together. Sometimes her glance would meet his and there would be so much hurt in his face that she would turn quickly away – back to Mark and his adoring smile and his welcoming arms. Fortunately for Natasha, Yuri was hardly ever home, so busy was he with the partisans.

Just like Natasha knew he would, Mark fell utterly and hopelessly under the twins' spell. He would hold them breathlessly, hugging, tickling, rocking, making up for lost time. When they did something he found amusing, he would shower them with kisses. When they slept, they slept in his arms. When they played, they played by his feet. Natasha would spend hours watching Mark with their children. At times she would pinch herself to make sure she wasn't dreaming.

Despite the constant threat of German patrol and nightly bombings, Natasha couldn't have been happier.

One evening in early October, she was resting against the wall, Mark's arms around her. The twins were asleep next to them, Mother and Grandfather were by the window and Nikolai was reading. She didn't know where Yuri was.

'Nikolai, how long have you been reading that book?' asked Natasha teasingly.

'I finished it days ago. Now I'm re-reading it.'

'Stop reading in the dark. You'll ruin your eyesight,' said Mother, not taking her eyes off the fires in the distance. Nikolai made a funny face but Mother didn't notice. There was fear on her face and tears in her eyes.

'Why don't you read something new?' asked Natasha.

'But what if something new is not as interesting? Then I'd be wasting my time. This way I know it's going to be good. I can't lose.'

Outside, orange streaks illuminated the ruins of once-beautiful buildings. 'What did they do to our city?' muttered Mother, turning away from the window. 'Our Kiev.'

'Don't worry, Zoya Alexeevna,' said Mark. 'There is no way they can win this war now. They stand alone against all of Europe.'

'That means a lot coming from someone who once fought on Hitler's side.'

'Mama!' exclaimed Natasha, looking at her with reproach.

'It's okay,' said Mark, pressing her hand gently. 'I did fight on Hitler's side, Zoya Alexeevna. But not through choice.'

'Leave the young man alone, Zoya,' said Grandfather. 'From what I've heard, he gave the Nazis a hard time at Stalingrad.'

'We learnt our lesson, Zoya Alexeevna,' said Mark. 'Learnt it the hard way. Most Hungarians vowed they would risk execution before fighting for Germany again. All we ever wanted was to go home. Bardossy and his supporters are seen as criminals for dragging the nation into this war. Hungarian units mutinied. Many soldiers deserted, especially after Babi Yar. Sometimes I wish I had deserted then, too.'

'What a waste this war is,' said Mother.

They were interrupted by the sound of planes overhead. Engines rumbling like distant thunder, they flew steadily over the sleeping city, unleashing havoc and destruction. The twins awoke, crying. Mark cradled both of them, one in each arm, and rocked them until they fell quiet again. It was a beautiful night and the stars were bright but the sky rained bombs, which produced a shrill whistling sound that appeared to get closer and closer each time. Natasha couldn't shake the feeling that the next bomb would find them. The only surviving glass in one of the windows rattled.

'Time to go to the cellar,' said Mark, handing the children to Mother and Natasha. He was already up, opening the trap door, helping everyone down. Natasha paused at the top of the ladder. 'Are you not coming too?' she asked him. Knowing he would never allow her to stay above ground during the bombing, she tried to make herself look stern and failed. 'I'm not going anywhere without you.'

'Down you go,' he said. Seeing her face, he added, 'I'm not

afraid of a little shelling. Besides, someone needs to stand guard and make sure the Nazis don't search the house. Now go.'

He was right and she knew it. Reluctantly she climbed down, sinking to the floor next to her mother, brother and grandfather, straining to hear what was happening upstairs. All was silent but for the muffled rumble of the cannonade and her own stifled sobs. Mother looked at her harshly. 'Stop that. You're upsetting the children.'

Natasha wiped her face with the back of her hand. 'I couldn't bear if anything happened to him. Not now when I just got him back.'

In the light of a candle, Natasha could see her grandfather's face. Why was he looking at her like that? What was it in his eyes? It almost looked like disappointment. 'Dedushka, what's wrong?' she whispered.

For a few seconds Grandfather didn't speak. Natasha braced herself. Her grandfather was the most righteous person she knew. She had a feeling that whatever he was about to say, she wasn't going to like it. 'I must be getting old because I don't understand,' he muttered finally. 'Marriage is a sacred institution. Your babushka and I were married for fifty years…'

Ah, thought Natasha. She knew it was coming, and now here it was. There was no escaping it, nowhere to hide in the crowded cellar. 'I feel awful about Yuri, I really do.' It was true. She did feel awful. 'But what you and Babushka had, that was different. I married Yuri to keep him safe. I love him like a brother.' She rubbed her finger where her grandmother's ring had once been. The ring she no longer wore but kept in the inside pocket of her jacket. She whispered, 'I'm sorry, Dedushka.' The last thing she wanted was to upset her grandfather.

'I might be old but I'm not blind. I can tell when someone is hurting. And Yuri is hurting. You might have married out of necessity, but he married for love.'

*

The next morning, when Natasha was still groggy and barely awake, the family heard clomping boots march up to their front door. There came a loud hammering and then the boots marched away. When Natasha fearfully looked outside, she found a leaflet nailed to the door.

'Eviction!' Mother cried, 'Not again!'

'Not eviction,' said grandfather, reading the leaflet. 'They want us at the railway station by tomorrow. They want to transport us.'

'I can't run anymore,' said Natasha. Under the table, Mark's fingers found her thigh, pressing gently. 'The last time we received an order like that, the Nazis...' She couldn't continue.

'What's going to happen to us?' cried Mother. 'What about the children?'

Mark said, 'Don't worry, Zoya Alexeevna. The Germans are too busy to worry about us. They simply don't have the time, with the Red Army so close.'

'Before they break through, the Nazis will kill us all.'

Mark said, 'Rumour has it the Red Army is in Darniza. We need to sit tight until they arrive. If the patrol comes, we can hide in the cellar.'

After a quick breakfast, Nikolai took the children to the cellar and everyone else went outside to look for chestnuts. Mark and Natasha were left alone together.

'When you were gone, I wished I had a photo of you. Anything to remind me of your face,' said Natasha.

'I had this,' said Mark. He reached into his pocket and a moment later there was a photograph in his hands. Natasha recognised it as one of the pictures Mark had taken of her in Shevchenko Park. She looked so cheerful and carefree, it was as if there were no Germans on the streets of Kiev, no war, no hunger. It was as if there was nothing but the two of them, young and in love.

'I remember that day. It seems like a lifetime ago. Oh, Mark.

What are we going to do? How are we going to keep you safe? If the Germans find out we are hiding you, they'll kill you.'

'They won't find out. Not unless someone tells them,' said Mark. 'Don't worry. The Nazis are too busy saving their own skin. We just have to hold on until the Red Army gets here.'

'But what do you think will happen once the Bolsheviks are back? They have been shooting anyone suspected of collaborating with the Germans. Innocent people, most of them. What do you think they'll do to you?'

Mark watched her thoughtfully. At last, he said, 'Forget about me for a second. What about all of you? What will the Bolsheviks do to you if they find out you are hiding me?'

Natasha took his hand. 'I know what you're about to say. Don't say it. Don't even think it. You're not going anywhere. Not without me.'

'But if I'm putting you all at risk—'

'No one but our family knows about you. No one will say a word.' She squeezed her eyes shut. She didn't want Mark to see fear in her eyes. She wanted him to believe her even if she didn't believe herself. After all, the NKVD had a way of unearthing even the most well-hidden secrets. How long would it take them to find out about Mark?

When Natasha opened her eyes, Yuri was watching them through the doorway, and Natasha froze in fear. Hadn't he once told her that anyone could sell you out for a piece of bread? No one could be trusted, absolutely no one, Yuri had said to her. And here he was, with his broken heart in his eyes, looking at Mark and Natasha as they held each other at the kitchen table. Did he hear their conversation? What if he mentioned Mark to someone? *No*, Natasha said to herself, *he would never do that*. Everything she knew about Yuri told her she could trust him. But once, a long time ago, she had thought she could trust Lisa, too. If her own sister could betray her, anyone could.

And then she remembered the conversation they had had on their first night in this house. Yuri knew about Mark. He knew Mark was responsible for the murder of the officer at the start of the occupation.

Chapter 20 – The Battle of Kiev

October – November 1943

One evening in the last week of October, Mark and Natasha stayed in the kitchen, talking late into the night about the latest news that had reached them. There was fighting all the way from Chernigov to the outskirts of Kiev, Zaporozhye had been evacuated, the so-called enemy, meaning the Red Army, had crossed to the right bank of the Dnieper. It was after midnight when they heard the front door open. A minute later, Yuri appeared. Closing the door to the kitchen behind him, he said, 'I need to talk to you both.'

He didn't sit down next to them, nor did he come any closer. He looked exhausted and thin, skeletal almost. He smiled sadly, then reached into his pocket. 'I wanted to give you this.' He took out a small parcel wrapped in newspaper and handed it to Mark. 'What is it?' Natasha asked as Mark unwrapped it.

'It's a passport,' said Mark, his eyes widening.

'I wanted you to have it. It's one of the documents Gregory was hiding in his apartment.'

'Is that where you've been? At Gregory's? Any news of him?' asked Natasha.

Yuri shook his head. 'A group of Germans are staying there. I had to wait two days before I could get in.'

There was a photograph of a smiling young man on the front page. 'Dmitri Antonov,' Natasha read the name aloud. Judging by the date of birth, he had just turned twenty-four. 'Why are you giving us this?'

'Who does Dmitri remind you of?'

She brought the candle close, peering at the black-and-white picture. 'If it wasn't for the long hair, it would look almost like—' She glanced at Mark.

'Exactly,' concluded Yuri.

Suddenly Natasha understood. 'You mean…' she whispered.

Yuri turned to Mark. 'You'll need a passport when the Red Army comes back.'

'Thank you,' said Mark, rising to his feet and shaking Yuri's hand. 'It means so much.'

'You won't need to hide if you have valid documents,' said Yuri.

'And I'll be able to join the Red Army when they return. I can fight the Nazis. The war is far from over.'

'You did this for us? For Mark and I?'

Yuri nodded. 'Dmitri Antonov was a partisan. I knew him well. His whole family was wiped out by the Germans. No one is left to contradict Mark if he decides to use this passport.'

Natasha watched Yuri in silence. She wanted to thank him, wanted to say something, anything. If only she could get her voice back.

Yuri continued, 'We couldn't save Dmitri but maybe his passport will save Mark.'

'I can't believe you would do this for us.'

'You saved my life. I'll never forget that,' he said and his voice trembled. 'The Red Army is about to enter Kiev. We don't have long to wait.'

Yuri turned and left the kitchen but Natasha caught up to him in the corridor. 'Thank you so much. I can't believe it. I thought you hated me, hated us.'

'Of course I don't hate you.'

'The day Mark came back, you said you wished you'd never met me.'

'Forget what I said. I was upset and didn't mean it. Without you who knows where I'd be. But I have to leave. I can't stay in this house. I hope you understand.'

She wanted to touch his hand but couldn't. It was as if an invisible wall separated Yuri from Natasha. She nodded. 'I understand. Where will you go?'

'I'll stay with a friend for a while. If you ever need me, here is the address.' He handed her a piece of paper. 'Come and find me. We can sort everything out. The divorce…'

Natasha's throat was dry. 'So what are you going to do?'

He shrugged. 'Fight the Nazis. Then find a nice girl.' A sad smile, a sad glance between them. 'Settle down. Have a family.'

After he left, Natasha sat in the kitchen in silence until the candle burnt out, thinking about Mark leaving her again to join the Red Army and thinking about Yuri, who was one of those rare people in whom love and kindness were stronger than anger and jealousy.

*

It was the first day of November and the family were huddled together in the kitchen. There was no food, no candles left, no other hope but one – that the Red Army would reach them before it was too late. Nikolai was at his usual observation post by the window. Suddenly he cried, 'Something is happening. They are blocking our road.'

'They are what?' whispered Natasha, joining Nikolai. A dozen Germans armed with machine guns were knocking on the doors of every house on the street. Only a few more houses separated them from the Smirnovs. It wouldn't take them long to reach them.

They heard gunshots and voices. Angry German shouts followed by desperate pleas in Russian. Mark ordered everyone to go down to the cellar. Just as Natasha reached the bottom of the ladder there was another knock on the door and more shouts. Natasha looked up. Nikolai was the only one left to go down. 'Nikolai, hurry,' she cried and her voice broke. Then she heard a terrible blow, followed by the sound of smashing wood. Loud voices filled the house. The trap door leading to the cellar shut with a loud bang. 'Nikolai!' Natasha whispered and she would have rushed back up if Mark hadn't kept hold of her, urging her to be quiet.

Mother struggled against Grandfather, who was holding her tight, whispering, 'There's nothing we can do. Nothing we can do.'

Through the ceiling, they could hear harsh German shouts, then a softer voice – Nikolai's. It sounded firm and steady. Natasha felt pride for her little brother. Nikolai didn't sound afraid. *He's being so brave*, she thought.

And then, a gunshot sounded. It was loud, even through the layer of wood and stone. Natasha felt a shudder run through Mark's body, felt her own body convulse in fear. Mother whimpered softly like an animal in pain. Another shot followed, and they heard loud footsteps that gradually faded away. Suddenly, there was silence.

Cautiously she opened the trap door. All was quiet. The house seemed deserted. She could smell the gunfire, putrid, disturbing. She climbed outside, followed by the others.

The trembling light of burning Kiev lit the room, and Natasha saw her little brother. He was on the floor, motionless. She whispered his name. As if through a wall she heard her mother's screams. And then, a few seconds later, they stopped. Out of the corner of her eye Natasha saw Mother unconscious on the floor.

Nikolai's body was sprawled across the front door, as if guarding the entrance. Natasha wanted to run to him but couldn't. Instead, she walked slowly, almost reluctantly. When she reached him, she slipped. She didn't know how she found the strength to get up but when she did, her knees, her arms, her hands felt damp. She looked down and saw that she was covered in blood. She cried out in terror and rushed to Nikolai, shaking him, calling his name, listening for his breath, searching for his pulse and not finding it. He wasn't breathing. His heart was still.

'Why didn't he come down to the cellar? If only he came with us...'

'He didn't have time. He couldn't do it without betraying our hiding place,' Grandfather said, his face bathed in tears.

Mark pulled Natasha close. 'He saved our lives,' he said.

Natasha blinked and forced herself to look. Through her tears she looked at Nikolai's face, at his stiff arms, his wide-open eyes.

Without a word, the Smirnovs held each other and cried. The night passed without any of them noticing and suddenly it was light again. How they spent the next day, Natasha couldn't remember. Finally, when evening fell and they could no longer hear German voices, when the streets seemed to fall into a guarded, uneasy sleep, they carried Nikolai's body outside and buried him in the garden. Mother was inconsolable and unable to speak. Grandfather tried to say something but his voice cracked and he broke down. Overhead, a Soviet plane flew past, and was it Natasha's imagination or was its engine softer than usual, as if the plane, too, was mourning Nikolai?

*

Every morning, when Natasha opened her eyes, she expected to hear Nikolai's laughter. Everywhere she turned, she expected to

349

see his cheeky grin. But what she saw instead was his book abandoned on the kitchen table and his jumper draped over a chair.
And her heart would explode in agony.

As the Smirnovs grieved, mortars roared and planes rumbled.
The deafening noise never stopped, not at night, not during the
day, not for anything. When night came, Natasha was too scared
to sleep. She didn't want to admit it even to herself but she was
afraid that the minute she closed her eyes, something terrible
would happen. She closed her eyes in the cellar and when she
opened them, her brother was gone. And so she lay wide awake,
watching the fires, thinking about her brother.

One night, around midnight, Natasha thought she saw shadows
outside. She sat up quietly, careful not to disturb Mark. Warily
she made her way to the window and peered out. The shadows
were gone. She could no longer see anything but the blazing
streets. Nothing but fires, nothing but explosions. She was about
to return when subdued voices reached her. She held her breath.
Someone was murmuring outside their window, measured whispers in hushed tones. By the soft, melodious sounds she knew
that the words were Russian. She waited. A minute later she
noticed three silhouettes disappear around the corner.

And even though she could hardly see them, Natasha could
swear they were dressed in uniform.

*

The next morning, something felt different. It took Natasha a
few moments to realise what it was and when she did, she jumped
to her feet and ran to the kitchen. It was quiet! The noise of the
past few days was gone. No more mortars, no more cannon, no
more planes, no more explosions. The streets were deserted.

'No sign of the fighting, Mama,' she said.

Mother didn't reply, her eyes closed.

Grandfather said, 'No sign of the Red Army, either.'

'I heard something last night. Someone was whispering under our windows.'

'Well, that's hardly unusual,' said Grandfather.

'They wore uniforms, Dedushka. And spoke Russian. Or maybe I imagined it. Maybe it was just wishful thinking.'

But it wasn't wishful thinking.

Around noon the streets filled with people. Everyone congregated around a group of men in uniform and when these men approached, Natasha saw that their uniforms were light green and their caps were adorned with red stars.

'Our army!' she cried, pointing out the window. 'Our soldiers!'

'Are you sure?' exclaimed Mark.

Natasha was speechless and so, it seemed, was everybody else. They watched the soldiers for a moment, then rushed outside. Only Mother remained in the house, her eyes staring, Nikolai's pillow clasped in her arms.

Outside, there was chaos. But it was happy chaos. Natasha could hardly believe her eyes. Red Army trucks drove past. Tanks, mortars and katyushas followed. Soldiers smiled and waved at Natasha, at Grandfather, at Mark. The Kievans approached the soldiers, hugging and thanking them with tears in their eyes. They talked loudly, all at once. They interrupted one another. The streets that for the past few weeks had been petrified into uneasy silence were now deafening. Natasha stopped the soldiers, hugged and kissed them. 'Do you know my brother?' she asked every single one. 'Have you seen him?' In her hand was a picture of Stanislav.

'Don't worry, Comrade,' the soldiers replied, laughing. 'Your brother is liberating someone from the Germans as we speak. He has a job to do. When that job's done, he'll come back.'

Only when they returned home did Natasha realise that she'd run outside in just one shoe. She invited the soldiers in, to have lunch, to talk, to wash. Because the family had nothing left, it was the soldiers who shared their food with the Smirnovs. Their usually quiet kitchen filled with loud voices and laughter. It filled with the smells of a lifetime ago – fried meat, potatoes, eggs. White bread was on the table, the likes of which the Smirnovs hadn't tasted in years. The soldiers reached for the twins, picking them up, holding them close, kissing them, talking of their own children back home. Grandfather hugged them all and repeated, 'Is it over? Is it all over?' The soldiers smiled and without saying a word tucked into their meat and their bread and their potatoes.

*

After the soldiers had left and Natasha had cleared the dishes, the family decided to return to Podol. At first Mother refused to be separated from the place where her younger son was buried. She cried and clung to the damp soil as if tearing herself away would break her heart all over again.

'Come on, Mama,' said Natasha. 'We have to go home. What if Papa comes back?'

That was enough to convince her mother. Sniffling, she followed them through the streets of Kiev. When they saw the house on Ilinskaya where they had spent most of the occupation, their hearts sank. The building had been completely destroyed by fire. Mother made a move to climb the burnt-out stairs, to search what was left of their apartment, but Natasha stopped her. It was too dangerous. The building could crumble and collapse at any moment. Mother cried, clinging to Natasha and not taking her eyes off the place they had called home for two years. 'What about Mikhail?' she asked. It took all of Natasha's strength to lead her away.

To Natasha's surprise, their building on Tarasovskaya was still standing. Slowly they walked up eight flights of familiar stairs. Mother tried to open the door but couldn't. Mark took the key from her shaking hand and unlocked it. Inside, there was no furniture, no books, no personal belongings apart from an old mattress that had been forgotten on the living-room floor. As Natasha walked from one room of her childhood home to the other, she whispered a quiet prayer of gratitude. She never thought she would see the place where she grew up again and now, as she stood at the entrance to the bedroom she had once shared with her sister, for the first time since June 1941 she felt safe. It was more than coming home. It was like finding an old friend you thought you had lost forever.

Mother cried, 'Look at the state of this place. Where is our furniture? Our china? Our photographs? They took everything.'

'Not everything, Mama.' Natasha pointed at her parents' wedding photograph on the wall. Through the war, through the occupation, through Germans in their apartment, it had survived. 'Don't be upset, Mama. We are home.'

'I just thought… I was expecting to see…' Mother fell quiet. Her eyes were on the photograph.

'Oh, Mama,' whispered Natasha. 'Papa will come back. Now that the Germans are gone, he'll come back.' She rocked her mother gently, all the while struggling not to cry. *I have cried so much already*, she thought. *I cried when the war started and when Grandmother died and when Olga and Alexei were taken away from us. I cried when Papa was arrested and when Mark disappeared and when Lisa betrayed me. I cried for each and every one of them, and for Nikolai. But I'm not going to cry now when we are finally home. Not now when we are safe.*

They had a feast for dinner, thanks to the generosity of the Soviet soldiers. White bread and eggs and milk and even some chocolate. *How Nikolai would enjoy this*, thought Natasha, chewing her food. It was while they were finishing the last bits of chocolate that Zina and Timofei Kuzenko knocked on their door. Accompanied by Mother's tears and exclamations, they made their way to the kitchen. The Kuzenkos had spent most of the occupation north of Kiev in Kurenevka. Thin and grey-haired, Zina talked and talked. Mother held Zina and sobbed, telling her all about Father, Lisa and Nikolai. Timofei didn't talk and didn't cry. He was grimmer than ever.

Even though it was long past midnight, Zina and Timofei didn't look like they were ever going to leave. Nor did Mother look like she wanted them to. But Natasha was tired. She said her goodbyes and got ready for bed. Mark and Natasha had a room to themselves. The twins were asleep in Mother's bedroom. For the first time since Mark's return, Mark and Natasha could be alone together.

Mark was already waiting for her. 'I've been thinking about this moment for two years. To touch you again, kiss you again,' he whispered. 'You can't imagine what it means.'

'I can,' she said, touching and kissing him back. 'I know.'

She let him undress her. One after another, he removed the straps off her shoulders. The nightie fell to the floor, leaving her completely naked in front of him. He traced her lips with his fingers, then kissed her deeply. She moaned softly, self-consciously, looking around, checking that the door was firmly shut.

'Don't worry. No one can hear us,' he said. It took him under five seconds to undress. 'Military training,' he explained, sinking to the floor and pulling her to him. *He's not shy being naked around me*, she thought. *And I don't blame him. How beautiful he is.*

Her body, never touched by another man, was his. Her heart was his, too – a heart that had never loved another man. And he knew it.

They couldn't wait another moment. They had no patience for preludes, no time to waste. They had already waited too long. She wanted to close her eyes but couldn't. 'I love you,' she whispered.

As they held each other in the dark and as he repeated how much he loved her, she thought of the first time she had seen him. The first time they'd kissed. The first time they'd made love. She thought of all their firsts as he clasped her in his arms, tighter and tighter, more and more desperate. She was light-headed, short of breath, falling into an unknown abyss and yet knowing that she was not going to die. This feeling of happiness, not touched by doubt, was so extraordinary, so overwhelming and so unfamiliar that she trembled in his arms.

And then she realised. Today was a first, too. Today was the first time they could be together and not be afraid.

*

It was raining heavily and the bedroom was dark. Serene and undisturbed, Natasha slept like she hadn't slept in years. Now that Kiev was free, now that the Nazis were gone, she could finally sleep without fear.

When she awoke, it was long past noon. It took a few seconds to remember where she was. Her heart beating fast, she touched the wall of her bedroom, stroking the tattered wallpaper, the wallpaper of her childhood.

Her heart skipped when she saw the empty bookshelves that still remained in the far corner of the room. She could almost see her brother Nikolai as he had smiled wickedly and whispered, 'I hid it,' while her frantic sister had searched these bookshelves for her missing diary.

The doorbell rang. Natasha hoped that whoever it was would go away, so she could go back to sleep. But the bell was insistent. She sat up.

Reluctantly she got up, stretched and walked down their long corridor. Yawning, she opened the door. The man standing outside had his back to her, as if he was about to walk away. He wore a Red Army uniform. His hair was long and unkempt.

But the curve of his neck, the back of his head was instantly familiar.

The man turned around and suddenly she was being lifted, squeezed, held and kissed. It was perfect timing because her knees had buckled under her. 'Stanislav,' she whispered. And louder, 'Stanislav.' Laughing, messing up his hair, she repeated his name again and again as if she couldn't believe that her older brother was home.

Her arms around his neck, she held him as tight as she could. 'Careful, you're going to strangle me.' Stanislav laughed, twirling her around like he used to when she was a child.

'Oh God,' was all Natasha could manage. Stanislav was thin, there were dark circles under his eyes but he looked at Natasha as if he never wanted to take his eyes off her again.

'Look at you,' she whispered. 'So unshaven. You look like a pirate.' She didn't think he could hear her over the noise of her beating heart. 'Stanislav,' she murmured. 'It's you. It's really you.'

'It is, it is,' he exclaimed, twirling, kissing, laughing. 'It's been so long, I'm surprised you recognised me.'

When he let go of her, she kissed his cheek and ran to the kitchen, shouting, 'Mama, Dedushka, you won't believe who's here.'

Mother was holding a plate in her hands. Natasha knew that the plate was Mother's favourite. Hidden away in the furthest corner of their cupboard, it had miraculously survived the occupation. When Stanislav strolled through the kitchen door, tall, handsome and smiling, the plate fell to the floor and broke into a dozen little shreds. Mother didn't even notice. She rushed to her son, knocking into him, holding him close. Grandfather leapt up, embracing his grandson. For a few minutes nothing was heard but sobs, unconnected words, and broken sentences.

When the crying subsided, Stanislav looked around the kitchen and spotted Costa and Larisa. 'And who are these little people?'

As Mother clung to Stanislav, not letting go for a second, as if afraid he'd disappear the minute she stopped touching him, Natasha introduced the twins. There was delight on Stanislav's face at suddenly finding himself an uncle to not just one but two adorable children. Stanislav picked up the twins, who squealed in delight at having another grown-up to croon over them and spoil them.

When Mark walked in, more introductions followed. Not straying far from Stanislav's side, Mother laid the table, inviting everyone for lunch.

'How I missed your stew, Mama,' said Stanislav. He couldn't stop looking at each of them in turn.

Natasha put her arm around her brother. She couldn't believe she was seeing him alive. 'Tell us everything. Where have you been?'

'On the outskirts of Kiev. It felt like it went on forever,' said Stanislav. 'We haven't been able to enter the city. Until now.'

'My son is a hero. Wait till I tell everyone.' Mother dabbed her eyes with her kerchief. 'All this time you were so close and we didn't even know.'

'Yes, all this time I was just across the Dnieper, coming to liberate you. General Vatutin planned to free Kiev on the 7th of November, the anniversary of the October Revolution. And we did it, a day early.'

'I can't believe it,' cried Mother. 'I just can't believe you're back home safely.'

'Not for long, Mama. The war is far from over. My job is not done until Hitler is out of the Soviet Union for good.' He swallowed a spoonful of stew and asked, 'Where is everyone else?'

There was a moment of silence and then Mother said, tears streaming down her face, 'Nikolai and Babushka didn't make it. They are gone. And we don't know what happened to Lisa and Papa.'

Stanislav's face crumbled. In his eyes Natasha could see his heartbreak. He hugged Mother, and together they cried.

An hour later, Natasha found her mother in the doorway of Stanislav's bedroom. Tears were running down her face. She watched her sleeping son with such tenderness, such love, such anxiety, Natasha felt close to tears herself. 'Mama, are you okay?' she whispered.

Mother sighed. 'He's still here. And I thought it was a dream.'

*

The rain had stopped and the timid autumn sun peeked through the cloud. Mark and Natasha strolled through the streets, smiling at passers-by, who smiled happily back. Finally, for the first time in over two years, their city belonged to them once more. As she made her way through Kiev, holding Mark's hand and every now and then pausing to look into his face, Natasha couldn't believe that their victory was real.

Kreshchatyk, the most famous cobbled street in all of Ukraine, was unrecognisable: it was in ruins and most of it had been destroyed during the occupation. But Kiev was free again. Free to live, to breathe, to rebuild, until it was more beautiful than ever. Everywhere Natasha looked, the streets were awash with red flags. Kievans made flags from every type of material at their disposal. Some of them were just red towels or red bed sheets or even an occasional red shirt hastily draped over someone's balcony, while others were real Soviet flags, with the hammer and sickle and a golden star. Natasha's heart beat faster, lighter at the sight of the Soviet triumph on the streets of her city. She vowed to make a flag of her own as soon as they returned.

They turned onto Institutskaya Street. Although there were fewer people there, the crowds were no less ecstatic. Russian songs were heard and Russian shouts. They paused outside a building that was completely demolished by fire. Her eyes twinkling, Natasha turned to Mark. 'Remember this place?'

'Our first barracks. How could I forget?'

'No, silly.' She shook her head and laughed, shoving him. 'This is where you kissed me for the first time.'

'Oh, is it?' Grinning, Mark kissed her deeply until her knees felt weak. If it wasn't for his arms holding her, she would have lost her balance and fallen. The emotion, the joy, the relief, it was all too much.

When he let go of her, she said wistfully, 'I wish they were all here to see this day.'

His arms tightened around her. 'The Soviets are liberating prison camps as we speak. Your Papa could return any moment.'

Natasha hoped Mark was right. With all her heart she hoped that her father would be able to see his city liberated from the Nazis.

Holding her hand firmly, Mark asked. 'Remember our last night together in the cafeteria?' His eyes grew serious.

She blinked. 'Of course I do.'

'You made me a promise that night.'

Shyly she looked up at him. 'What promise was that?'

His eyes sparkled. 'You promised to marry me.' He pulled her close. 'So what do you say? Will you marry me?'

She nodded mutely. She wanted to say yes, wanted to shout yes from the top of the tallest building in Kiev but couldn't find the strength for even the tiniest of whispers. As they held each other in the midst of happiness and celebrations and laughter, surrounded by red Soviet flags, with not a swastika in sight, not a single German plane and not a Nazi officer, Natasha cried tears of sorrow and tears of happiness – for everyone she had lost and everything she had been given.

Epilogue

December 1945

It was New Year's Eve, and Kiev looked like a fairy-tale kingdom hidden away by snow, with festive lights on every street corner and a giant tree on Mikhailovskaya Square, its snow-capped branches reaching for the sky. Instead of Christmas carols in German, the loudspeakers played Soviet war songs, even though there would be no place for war in the New Year, no place for fear, loss or heartbreak, because 1946 was going to be the year of peace.

The Smirnovs had a beautiful tree of their own at home. It stood tall and proud, almost touching the ceiling, filling the house with the smell of fresh pine, of childhood and laughter, of dreams and happiness. The twins wanted to decorate it all by themselves, and so the bottom of the tree was heavy with baubles and tinsel, while the rest of it remained bare but for the red star that Mark had placed at the top. Mother had told Costa and Larisa there would be many presents waiting for them under the tree on 1st January, delivered by Grandpa Frost, a magical character who lived in the Arctic and travelled through chimneys. The twins took turns hiding under the green canopy, determined to catch the mysterious Grandpa Frost as he brought their presents.

Natasha was cleaning frantically, mopping the floor, dusting the table, arranging flowers in vases, the usual last-minute preparations that preceded a celebration. And it was going to be a true celebration this year. Zina and Timofei were coming with their cousin. Mikhail was already there, discussing Napoleon's Peninsular campaign with Grandfather, who opened his best wine for the occasion. Stanislav was bringing a girl he'd met at the factory where he was working after the war. And Lisa was bringing her new husband.

Outside, Mark was teaching the twins how to make a snowman, and their excited voices reached Natasha from the park. Earlier they had snuck into the kitchen and, when her back was turned, taken a carrot that was meant for the salad. If she looked out the window, she could see the carrot adorning the snowman's face.

The twins bounced through the door, followed by Mark. 'Mama, Mama, we did it all by ourselves. Papa didn't help us.'

'You did what, little ones?' Natasha kneeled and opened her arms. When they ran to her, she showered them with kisses.

'We built a snowman. His name is Frost. Larisa named him. Do you think Grandpa Frost will like that and bring us more presents?' Costa extricated himself from his mother's embrace and danced on the spot excitedly. Her son and daughter were bundled up nice and warm, so cute in their winter coats, with only their eyes and noses visible from under the scarf. They looked like little snowmen themselves.

'Of course he will. And why didn't Papa help you?' She smiled at Mark, and he smiled back.

'We didn't want him to.' The children spotted Mother in the corridor and ran to her, shouting, 'Babushka, we did it! We built snowman.'

Natasha turned to Mark. 'Don't you know how to make a snowman?' she teased.

'Of course not. It's not like we have snow in Hungary.'

'Stop teasing me. I can never tell if you are joking or if you are serious.'

Mark crossed the room and took her in his arms. He walked with a slight limp – a reminder of his time at Stalingrad. There was a large scar on his right hand – a souvenir from his days in the Red Army. 'Do you need any help? I can mop the floor.'

'Do you know how?'

'*That* I know.' His eyes twinkled at the memory of a different time, a different life. 'Let me finish here. Your sister came in with us. She brought meat for the pelmeni. She might need your help in the kitchen.'

'Might?' Natasha laughed, kissing him. Lisa in the kitchen was akin to a natural disaster.

Long gone were the days when all they had for dinner was potato peel. Although still not readily available, with patience most food could be found in stores or at the market. For the last two days, Mother had been busy making Napoleon cake. It was their pre-war tradition to have the cake for New Year's. It had been so long, Natasha had almost forgotten what it tasted like. And now the cake sat proudly on the living-room table, waiting for midnight, while the family eyed it with longing.

It had always been Nikolai's favourite cake. Her little brother would get up at dawn with Mother, pretending he wanted to help, just so he could lick the bowl and eat the trimmings. Natasha couldn't look at the cake without thinking of Nikolai, without seeing his mischievous smile as he woke her far too early, a bowl of cream in his hands. Would she ever be free of the shadows? Underneath the happiness, there was a darkness that never let her go. Every smile was touched with sadness, every embrace with a loved one brought tears. The war might be over but inside her it still raged. It had seeped into her soul and become a part of her, and Natasha knew that for as long as she lived, she wouldn't be free from it. None of them would.

In the kitchen, Lisa was rolling out the dough for pelmeni. Natasha hugged her sister hello, washed her hands and put her apron on.

'Wait till you hear the secret I have for you this year,' said Lisa, a satisfied grin on her face, like a cat on a sunny deck.

The war had turned Lisa's beautiful red hair grey. At twenty-two, Lisa dyed her hair religiously. It was her little secret that she was determined to keep from everyone. But just like Natasha, Lisa had her own shadows, and they were harder to hide than the grey streaks in her hair. The shadows were apparent in her face when she talked, in her eyes when she tried to smile, even in the way she moved, no longer with the self-confident stride of someone who wanted the whole world to watch her.

'Another one of your made-up secrets?' asked Natasha, salting the mince and inhaling the oniony smell.

'Laugh all you want but it's the best secret yet.'

'Better than Zina kissing a stranger on the stairs?'

'Oh, much better.'

'I have a secret for you too.'

'I bet it's not as good as mine. How about the loser has to cook for the winner for a week?'

'But you can't cook.'

'That's okay. I'm not going to lose,' said Lisa, winking.

'You go first,' said Natasha. Lisa seemed to hesitate. Suddenly she looked nervous. Natasha said, 'Let me guess. You found a job?'

'No, silly. I don't need to work, I'm married now.'

'Of course you are. What was I thinking?'

'Keep guessing.'

'You are taking a cooking class.' Natasha winked at her sister and pointed at the pelmeni Lisa was carelessly pasting together. Different shapes and sizes, they looked like they had been made by a child.

'I know how to cook better than some.' Lisa glared at her sister, whose pelmeni were perfect like soldiers on parade.

'I don't know then, Lisa. What is it?'

'Do you give up?'

'Just tell me.'

Lisa dusted the flour off her hands and smoothed the apron she was wearing over her best dress. 'Do I look any different to you?'

'You are as beautiful as ever.'

'Do I look heavier? More filled out?'

'No, of course not.' Natasha appraised her sister. Her stomach was flat, her hips narrow. Why would Lisa, who had always been obsessed with her weight, ask Natasha if she looked heavier and seem so excited about it? It didn't make sense unless... 'Oh my God, Lisa! Are you—'

'Yes!'

'Pregnant?'

'Yes!'

'That's fantastic!' Natasha jumped up and down on the spot, finally pulling Lisa to her and kissing her on the cheek. 'How far along?'

'Not far. I just found out.'

'Have you told Dmitry?'

'Not yet. I wanted to tell you first.'

'Your sister before your husband?'

'My sister before anyone.' Lisa's cheeks were flushed, her eyes twinkled. 'I'm so excited, Natasha! After everything we've been through, it's a new beginning for our family.'

'I'm going to be an auntie. It's the best secret ever! I can't believe I'm saying this but you win.'

'Wait, you haven't told me yours yet.'

Natasha reached into her pocket. 'We received this in the morning.'

Lisa opened the letter with a frown, as if expecting bad news.

But as she read, her eyes grew wide. 'Papa is coming home?' she whispered.

'He is,' Natasha said. 'He's coming home.' Natasha held Lisa in her arms as they cried – happy tears, tears of hope and relief. She knew that her sister was right. It was a new beginning for their family. A beginning to the rest of their lives that would forever be touched by war, but not broken. Never broken.

Acknowledgements

I would like to thank my family for always being there for me. Thank you to my mum for her wisdom and kindness, to my husband for his love and support, and to my beautiful little boy for filling every day with joy, laughter and cuddles.

Thank you to my talented friend and writing buddy Mark Farley for being the first person to read this book and for holding my hand every step of the way, encouraging, helping and advising.

Thank you to my amazing editor Cara Chimirri, whose vision and ideas have made this story the best it could possibly be. Thank you to Hannah Smith for noticing my manuscript and getting me on board, and to the HarperCollins design team for my beautiful cover. And thank you to everyone at HQ Digital for making my dream come true.

I am especially grateful to my favourite history teacher at the University of Southern Queensland, Catherine Dewhirst, who told me many years ago that I should be a writer. I wrote my first short story the next day and have never looked back.

And finally, thank you to everyone who has read and reviewed the previous edition of this book, especially Tina Gohar for her wonderful feedback that inspired me to write more.

Dear Readers,

Thank you for choosing this book. I hope you have enjoyed reading it as much as I have enjoyed writing it.

The story of Natasha and her family is very close to my heart. Like most Russians, I grew up hearing about the war from my grandparents. These stories are in our blood, like our love for Pushkin and our penchant for drinking tea with every meal. My grandparents were too young to fight in the war but old enough to remember the hunger and the fear for everyone they loved, especially their fathers, far away at the Eastern front and inching their way towards Berlin.

Despite the order to hold Kiev (or Kyiv, as it's known in post-Soviet era) at all costs, on 19th September 1941, three months after Hitler had attacked the Soviet Union, the Nazis entered the city. Although many people had evacuated or joined the army, 400,000 still lived in Kiev when Hitler's Army Group Centre marched through the streets. The occupation would last 778 days. It was a time of terror, hunger and persecution for the local population. Historians estimate that between 100,000 and 150,000 people perished in the tragedy of Babi Yar. Another 100,000 were forced to Germany for work. Most of them never came home. When the Soviet Army finally liberated Kiev in November 1943, only 180,000 people remained in the city.

Having lived in Kiev for three years as a child and fallen in love with its cobbled streets and golden domes, I knew that was where I wanted to base my story. One of the first short stories I ever wrote was about a couple in love, trapped on opposite sides of the most brutal conflict the world had ever known. It was inspired by an article I came across many years ago, about a famous Soviet actress who had survived the war thanks to the kindness of a German soldier, who twice a day for the duration of the occupation fed the local children. When the short story was published in a magazine, people reached out to me, asking questions. They wanted to know how long the occupation of Ukraine had lasted and what life had been like for the ordinary Soviets. I realised there was more to the story than I first thought, and two years later it became a novel.

While researching the period of occupation, I have read dozens of memoirs and diaries of the survivors. Two of them have made a great impression on me. One was the hauntingly beautiful and disturbing diary of Irina Horoshunova, whose family had been shot by the Nazis for their connection to the partisans. Irina worked as a librarian and wrote her diary throughout the occupation, describing her daily life, hopes and fears. Another diary was that of Alexandra Sharandachenko, who worked as a school-teacher and, later, a registrar in Kiev. These women were incredibly brave to detail the horrors of the occupation under the Nazis' noses. Had their diaries been discovered, they would have been arrested and most likely shot.

I'm always happy to hear from my readers and would love to know what you thought about the book. Please consider leaving a short review on Amazon or any other platform, and feel free to get in touch or subscribe to my newsletter at http://www.lanakortchik.com.

Thank you for reading!

Thank you so much for taking the time to read this book – we hope you enjoyed it! If you did, we'd be so appreciative if you left a review.

Here at HQ Digital we are dedicated to publishing fiction that will keep you turning the pages into the early hours. We publish a variety of genres, from heartwarming romance, to thrilling crime and sweeping historical fiction.

To find out more about our books, enter competitions and discover exclusive content, please join our community of readers by following us at:

🐦 *@HQDigitalUK*

𝐟 *facebook.com/HQDigitalUK*

Are you a budding writer? We're also looking for authors to join the HQ Digital family! Please submit your manuscript to:

HQDigital@harpercollins.co.uk.

Hope to hear from you soon!

ONE PLACE. MANY STORIES

If you enjoyed *The Story of Us*, then why not try another sweeping historical novel from HQ Digital?

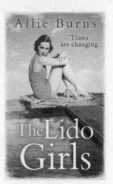

If you enjoyed *The Night Off*... then why not try another engaging historical novel from HQ Digital?